THE·LIFE·AND ADVENTURES OF LYLE·CLEMENS

Also By John Rechy:

Novels:
City of Night
Numbers
This Day's Death
The Vampires
The Fourth Angel
Rushes
Bodies and Souls
Marilyn's Daughter
The Miraculous Day of Amalia Gómez
Our Lady of Babylon
The Coming of the Night

Non-Fiction:
The Sexual Outlaw: A Documentary

Plays:
Rushes
Tigers Wild
Momma As She Became—But Not As She Was *(one-act)*

THE·LIFE·AND ADVENTURES OF LYLE·CLEMENS

A·NOVEL

By·JOHN·RECHY

GROVE·PRESS
NEW·YORK

Author's Note: This novel is a work of fiction. Any resemblance to actual persons living or
dead is purely coincidental. While some of the characters bear the names of famous people,
the portrayal of them in this novel is entirely fictitious.

Published simultaneously in Canada
Printed in the United States of America

FIRST EDITION

Library of Congress Cataloging-in-Publication Data
Rechy, John.
The life and adventures of Lyle Clemens : a novel / John Rechy.
p. cm.
ISBN 0-8021-1746-5
1. Motion picture industry—Fiction.   2. Los Angeles (Calif.)—Fiction.   3. Las Vegas
(Nev.)—Fiction.   4. Fundamentalism—Fiction.   5. Young men—Fiction.
6. Gambling—Fiction.   7. Texas—Fiction.   I. Title.
PS3568.E28L54 2003
813'.54—dc21   2003049070

Grove Press
841 Broadway
New York, NY 10003

03 04 05 06 07   10 9 8 7 6 5 4 3 2 1

I thank Michael Earl Snyder for his invaluable creative observations, suggestions, and encouragement, from the inception of this novel as an idea to its completion as a novel. I also thank Georges and Anne Borchardt for years of friendship.

For the Memory of my Mother, Guadalupe Flores Rechy,
and for the Memory of Michael's mother, Juan Marie Snyder

CONTENTS

BOOK ONE

TEXAS

*In which Lyle Clemens is born to Sylvia Love, and Fate sets
out on its wayward course.*

CHAPTER ONE

CHAPTER TWO

CHAPTER THREE

CHAPTER FOUR

CHAPTER FIVE

CHAPTER SIX

CHAPTER SEVEN

CHAPTER EIGHT

CHAPTER NINE

BOOK TWO

HOLLYWOOD, THE LORD'S HEADQUARTERS IN ANAHEIM, AND AN UNEXPECTED DETOUR

In which disparate lives wait to entangle Lyle's.

CHAPTER TEN

CHAPTER ELEVEN

CHAPTER TWELVE

CHAPTER THIRTEEN

CHAPTER FOURTEEN

BOOK THREE

LOS ANGELES

In which Lyle Clemens finds himself in the City of Angels.

CHAPTER FIFTEEN

CHAPTER NINETEEN

CHAPTER TWENTY

CHAPTER TWENTY-ONE

CHAPTER TWENTY-TWO

CHAPTER TWENTY-THREE

It is well remarked by one (and perhaps by more) that misfortunes do not come single.

—Henry Fielding,
The History of Tom Jones

THE·LIFE·AND ADVENTURES of LYLE·CLEMENS

BOOK

I

Texas

*In which Lyle Clemens is born to Sylvia Love,
and Fate sets out on its wayward course.*

CHAPTER ONE

1

*Lyle Clemens is delivered, alive; how he came to be born. The horror
at the Miss Rio Escondido Beauty Pageant recalled briefly.*

When Lyle Clemens was born, in Rio Escondido,
Texas, in 1984, his mother quickly covered his
rosy nakedness just before she fainted, either
from the rigors of the birth or from her first impression of the child. Sylvia Love was surprised
that he was alive, thinking he'd died inside her. That's what Clarita,
her trusted Mexican friend and self-appointed midwife, had told her
after having listened for any stirrings within Sylvia's belly. So when
Clarita pulled out the bawling child, and snipped the binding cord,
she shoved him back at Sylvia in bewilderment that her powers of divination had failed again. Sylvia Love blinked in double surprise. Not

only was the child alive and yelling lustily, but—she would swear she
saw this during the fluttering of her eyes—he was big, brawly, and
aroused—"just like his goddamn father, and no doubt he's his," she
managed to say aloud. That, and a fleeting memory of her disastrous
experience as a contestant in the Miss Alamito County Beauty Pageant
earlier that year, caused her to toss a sheet over the child who would
grow up to become the Mystery Cowboy who appeared naked along
Hollywood Boulevard.

2

A view of Rio Escondido, where it all began.

The City of Rio Escondido—which means "hidden river" in Spanish—
was not unlike other smallish cities that sprout within the environs of
larger ones in Texas, cities that stay in a limbo of time at least ten years
behind all others. The city boasted a population of "nearly 20,000,"—
a figure that did not include the seasonal migrants who worked and
lived in the fertile fields outside the City. The permanent population
was made up of mostly middle-class white people, middle to lower-
class Mexican-Americans, some much better off, and a few rich white
families with farms or ranches in what was referred to as the "Valley,"
its denizens called cowboys, whether they rode a horse or not, and most
did not.

Oleander shrubs, white, pink, red, with sparkling green leaves, added
to the prettiness of the City with its tidy neighborhoods and small shop-
ping center that outlined an old plaza—no building taller than three
stories. No one was sure whether the hidden river—the Rio Grande—
had ever really run here, but in the Valley a strait of luxuriant green
trees dotted seasonally with flowers indicated where it might have
flowed.

There was a main library, a City Hall that was once a jail, four movie
theaters, three grammar schools, one high school, two Catholic churches
and four Protestant ones, and a Billy the Kid Museum that housed
Western artifacts, including a hat that Bonnie had worn (with a band
of artificial daisies Clyde had woven onto it), and a Texas history book
open to a page with umber spatters—the blood of a former sheriff shot
while he sat reading the Bible.

"Ain't no discrimination in Ree-oh Escon-dee-doe," the cheerful, rotund Mayor Gonzales was fond of saying at Chamber of Commerce meetings. That always got approving applause. Mayor Gonzales had inexplicably developed a Texas drawl; but to show his pride in his Latino roots, he sported a full, brushy black mustache that evoked Mexican rebels of the past.

A grand hotel, aptly named the Texas Grand Hotel, continued to assert a stubborn pride in its Spanish terra cotta architecture and its ornate dining room. Bonnie and Clyde stayed there one night—"before their bloodiest raid." So did Judy Garland and Clark Gable—"separately"—on their way to the mineral springs in the nearby City of Mineral Wells. The hotel remained almost guestless now, new travelers choosing to stay in one of several motels that border the main highway with sizzling electric signs.

During two occasions, the Texas Grand sprang to full life—when its chandeliered dining room was taken over for "big weddings" and when its rooms were occupied by evangelical preachers here for the twice-a-year Gathering of Souls, a loud, quivery orgy of sermons and healings held at the local Pentecostal Hall and later televised through a mega-network of stations headquartered at the Lord's Headquarters in Anaheim, California.

3

*A move back in time, before Lyle's birth. Eulah Love prepares
to speak in tongues, and a golden voice arouses hope.*

Lyle Clemens's journey to become the Mystery Cowboy who appeared naked on Hollywood Boulevard might be said to have begun years before his birth, perhaps during a certain time of the year when Eulah Love, Sylvia's mother, prepared to speak in tongues at the Gathering of Souls. An isolated unhappy woman with no friends, often glowering at her daughter as if she did not recognize her but was nevertheless angry at her, Eulah left her small house only to attend religious meetings, and when otherwise necessary. As if to underscore her drab existence, dry vines drooped over her house—a cluster of feeble green here and there struggling out—only in summer—in contrast to the tidiness of other houses nearby.

Why her mother was so hostile to her was a mystery to Sylvia from as far back as she could remember. Even an ordinary child's question would arouse her ire.

"Why did you name me Sylvia?"

"Because it's a name."

"Why is our last name Love?"

"Ha!" Eulah laughed without mirth.

Eulah's revival meetings terrified Sylvia and had made her wonder, at a very early age, what kind of God would inspire such frightening shrieks and trembling. At the height of the frenzy in the Pentecostal Hall (Eulah dragged her there, clasping her arm fiercely), she would find refuge under the rows of seats. When someone spotted her, she would tremble and moan, pretending she had been "slain in the spirit" that was, somewhere in the hall, seizing her mother and so many others and causing them to shake, mumble, and quake. That was something else that baffled Sylvia about God; if her mother was the saintly woman she claimed to be—and that's what they all said at the Hall, that she was a servant of God—how the hell could she be so goddamn mean?

There was one time when Sylvia came out of hiding in the Hall. A beautiful voice emerged out of the cacophony of crashing "hallelujahs" and "amens," a voice so commanding that the shrieking of the incensed congregation began to fade, then faded, forced back, driven away by the power of that single voice.

On the stage, Sister Matilda of the Golden Voice, a hefty black woman in a flowing white gown and wearing a brilliant crown atop her glistening black hair, was singing before a choir of trilling "little angels" in puffy cassocks. Her eyes were closed, her hands reached up toward Heaven. They did not grasp like those of the others here who seemed to Sylvia to be wanting to tear down something; no, her hands seemed to be encouraging, greeting, welcoming a benign connection. And she sang in a thrilling voice that roamed through sorrow—deep, mournful—delivered sorrow to hope, stayed there lingering, and then released hope to joy. The voice rose, finally jubilant, in amazement at such a possibility:

> *Amazing grace, how sweet the sound*
> *That saved a wretch like me,*

I once was lost, but now I'm found,
Was blind but now I see. . . .

As Sylvia listened to the wondrous voice, she clasped in her mind words
and phrases that addressed her: "lost . . . now found . . . my fears relieved . . . hope . . . a life of joy and peace."

She held her breath. The song offered hope!

After the meeting (and she hid again because the chorus had retreated
to allow on stage a man who moved like a mad puppet, strutting back
and forth across the stage, then taking mincy steps backward as he
howled, "Woe-*uh!*"), the words of the song the black woman had sung
stayed in Sylvia's mind. Long before she knew they had, she had memorized them. The hope that the song—and the golden voice itself—conveyed allowed her to conceive of escaping the miserable life her mother
was assuring for her.

4

Sylvia's aspirations for a happy life. A way out.

She would *not* live in misery!

What had saved her, so far, from being the strange, twitchy, retiring
girl her mother was determined to make her was that she was pretty,
very pretty—eventually, she was sure, she'd be beautiful—and she had
spirit, and determination, even before she recognized the fact.

At almost eighteen, she was so lovely that, often, looking at herself
in the mirror—her hands propping her splendid breasts—she would
whirl around with the sheer joy of being herself. Her dark auburn hair
had golden streaks where the sun had kissed it, and she had almond-
shaped, amber-flecked green eyes that Eulah insisted were "ordinary
brown." During summer, her velvety complexion deepened, darker than
it really was, and her full red lips had a sensual tilt even when she wasn't
smiling.

And her body!

It was slender where it should be slender, and full, quite full, where
it should be full. She walked with a slight swing that showed it all off.

All she needed to be free was to separate herself from Eulah and her
denouncements of the flesh. How?

She was pretty enough, now, to be Miss Rio Escondido!

Then Miss Alamito County!

After that, Miss Texas!

And then! And then . . .

. . . her freedom!

She easily pictured herself walking along the magical extension of stage (was it really sprinkled with silver sequins, or did she only remember it that way from the images she had seen on the small television kept secretly in her room?), holding her bouquet of roses, the crown firmly on her head—not tilted—and *she* would not be crying—why, if she was happy?

Her mind spun with the possibilities life would extend to her away from the miseries of her mother. Before the mirror, she lowered the top of her blouse, off her shoulders, deeper down. She hugged her gorgeous curves, the bare flesh of her lovely shoulders.

"Posing like a harlot in the mirror! Woman of sin!" It was Eulah, out of her usual religious trance and in Sylvia's room, (which she regularly invaded, often cornering the girl, demanding she confess "all sinful thoughts of the flesh" before Sylvia knew exactly what that meant). Now Eulah held her Bible before her like a black brick she might throw. "Woe on those who violate the sanctity of their flesh! Woe to those who sully it with lewd displays!"

Sylvia pulled the top of her blouse up.

Eulah was on her, flailing at her with her free hand, thrusting out with her Bible, forcing Sylvia back, back. "'I shall strike out in fury at your sins!' saith the righteous Lord."

As Sylvia recoiled from her mother, Eulah Love yanked her Bible back, as if her daughter might snatch it away from her. She shouted: *"Wanke y-hune epistrog! Mastek!"*

"What?" But Sylvia knew her mother had lapsed into tongues, her eyes wobbling in their sockets. Now she would return to her room to prepare for her performance at the Gathering of Souls.

When Eulah left, Sylvia drew her blouse back down, even lower. She would not allow Eulah to smirch her flesh! When she won the beauty contest, and, even before that, when she appeared in her bathing suit, the applause and admiration that would greet her would be like collected blessings thrust against Eulah's prohibitions.

She faced herself haughtily in the mirror—though she must not appear haughty when the title was announced and her bright future began, as bright and unblemished as the crown she would wear.

5

Possible intrusions on the way to the pageant.

There were negative considerations to take into account as the time for the preliminary pageants neared. Sometimes she suspected she was part Mexican. In her religious frenzies, Eulah had once blurted out "damnation on that Mexican who lured me." Was he her father? Sylvia wondered, studying her own tan-hued skin—Eulah always looked pale. If so, was he responsible for her mother's anger at her? She would welcome being part Mexican because she had heard someone at school claim "mixed blood," and that had seemed very dramatic to her, passionate blood whirling inside her. Or was her father really the "righteous man" Eulah claimed had been "murdered by those heathens, those ungrateful Vietnamese"? Sylvia remembered no man, not even a picture of one, during her early years. Still, if she *was* part Mexican and it was known, that might compromise her chances among still-bigoted judges at the Pageant.

The fact that she might be pregnant wouldn't help, either.

6

Further back in time. The "sexy Chicano" introduces Sylvia to the Catholic church and its glamorous saints.

Sylvia had met Armando in high school when her dream of winning the beauty title was beginning to bud. Everyone—especially giggly girls—agreed that he was the handsomest boy—*and* a "rebel." Athletic-looking with wiry muscles, he nevertheless disdained school sports, "because I'm not a team kind of guy, ya know?" He did, though, like to toss a basketball around by himself in an outdoor court when girls sat in the bleachers. Shirtless, he would whip about, bounce the ball steadily—tap, tap, tap!—and then, in a sudden leap, pitch it expertly through the rim—*swoosh!*—leaving his arm up, holding the pose for seconds after the ball was tossed, glancing at the girls and then spreading his lips in a smile that revealed his white teeth, which, uncannily, always caught a glint of sun.

Adding to his romantic reputation was the fact that he insisted on calling himself "Chicano" and addressed other Latino boys as "*vatos locos,*" a phrase young men in large cities were using to acknowledge "wild gang brothers." But there were no gangs in Rio Escondido, not even in Alamito County, and, really, he was not particularly "wild." He held a job as a mail boy in a legal office. He owned a car, not last year's nor the year before's, but not bad. His father was a family doctor and his mother had joined the PTA years ago—but, he claimed, proudly, some of his distant relatives still worked "in the sweaty migrant fields."

"You know why I'm going to ask you out?" he asked Sylvia as she left the school grounds one day and he was leaning against his car, one leg crooked on its fender.

"Why?" Others, several, had asked her out, but she had not considered them "matured" enough for her, and, too—perhaps more importantly—she was afraid of Eulah's certain intervention if they came to pick her up. The fact that Armando was known as a rebel, the way she secretly saw herself, impressed her.

"Because"—he did not remove his foot from his fender—"you're the prettiest girl, and I'm—" Instead of finishing, he flashed a dazzling smile.

She waited.

"—and I'm—?" This time it was a question that required an answer. He waited longer.

What did he want her to say? Sylvia shook her head.

"—and I'm the handsomest guy, a handsome *vato loco,*" he finished, a hint of annoyance at her earlier befuddlement tempering his smile.

"Oh."

On their first outing, their last year of high school—she met him at a street corner, safe from Eulah—Armando took her to the Catholic Church of Our Mother of Perpetual Concern. At the door, he offered her his red-print bandanna to cover her head in the old tradition: "Women have to do this, men don't." Inside, he spattered holy water on his forehead and bowed reverentially in silent prayer.

Sylvia fell instantly in love with the paintings and statues surrounding her. Look at the bright colorful costumes and the thick makeup on the faces of the women! Despite the heavy clothing, it was clear they had curvaceous bodies. Glamorous enough to be—to be—in a beauty pageant! A tinge of rivalry made her add an extra swing to her hips as she moved to join Armando, slightly ahead of her and advancing toward the altar. So quiet here—they were the only ones in the church—so different from the rambunctious revival meetings, all screeches and distorted faces, that she was forced to attend with Eulah.

At the altar, Armando knelt in emphatic meditation, his head bowed almost to his chest. When she saw the almost-naked, muscular Christ before them, Sylvia uttered a gasp of admiration. That was when Armando, who had stood up so quickly she hadn't been aware of it, put his hand about her shoulders and let it slip to her waist. "This is how we stand when we get married," he whispered right into her ear.

After they left the church, Sylvia was still feeling reverential. She kept the red handkerchief as a band about her hair. She was still wearing it when, a short time later, in the remote thickly treed area that Armando drove his old car to, he kissed her, kisses that turned wet and that she found disgusting and then exciting—no, disgusting—no, exciting! When he touched her breasts, she tensed, and then allowed a pleasant sensation that soon became frightening.

"I have to go home right away!" she said firmly.

He tried a few more kisses. For a moment they made her tingle, but apprehension was crowding out the excitement and she did not respond.

He hummed confidently as he drove her back to within three blocks of her house.

Sylvia walked bravely past Eulah's glowering stare. She had taken a long step away from her mother.

7

Can virginity be lost twice? A welcome confusion of memories.

Throughout her life, in moments of confusion, Sylvia's thoughts and memories would spring into her mind seemingly unconnected to anything present. This would occur when thoughts of the debacle at the Miss Alamito Beauty Pageant, and of the first Lyle Clemens's perpetual arousal, would cause her to cover her newborn's nakedness. So it was that a memory of Eulah encouraged her to lose her virginity to Armando.

He took her back to the Church of Our Mother of Perpetual Concern. Again, she was bedazzled by the glamorous statues, especially one who seemes very aware of her beauty, the way she held her hands to her breasts, the way she tilted her head, just so, the way she had attired herself.

"That's our Holy Mother," Armando introduced, "the Mother of Jesus, and *that* is our Jesus." He pointed to the sinewy almost naked body on the cross, next to the beautiful woman. As Sylvia stared in awe from one to the other—Jesus, then Mary, Jesus, Jesus, Jesus—she felt Armando's hand traveling down her back, onto her buttocks. He gave them a firm squeeze before she moved away.

"Do you know what we call nuns?" he asked her in an intimate whisper, his lips tickling her ear, or had his tongue dabbed them?

"Those women who wear wingy hats and black dresses?" She had seen some when they visited the city. Very strange.

"Yes. We call them the brides of Christ," he told her. "Of him." He pointed to the almost-nude figure.

"The brides of—?" She looked up at the body at the head of the altar. "His *wives?*"

"Yes."

"He is *so* handsome," Sylvia sighed. "Just look at those ridges on his stomach."

"Feel mine."

Until he placed her hand on his own abdominals, Sylvia hadn't realized that Armando had raised his shirt to allow her to touch his bare, tensed stomach. "Girls don't have these," he informed her, "but they have *these*," and his fingers cupped her breasts. She didn't push his hand away because she felt enraptured by the awesome atmosphere of the Catholic church, and her feelings had bunched into one that was exciting.

He drove her to the same spot they had gone to their first time out, off the main road, onto a dirt road, among clusters of trees and the sweet scents of orange blossoms.

He jumped out of the car, nodding at her to follow.

"Maybe this is where the hidden river ran," he said to her. "Isn't it romantic?"

It was, the thought of being out there, alone, where a river had once meandered, leaving smatterings of wild flowers and then disappearing. Oh, yes, that was romantic—and so were Armando's hot tonguing kisses, so exciting. Were they? She tested, pushing back with her own tongue. She withdrew it. She wasn't sure what she felt. She leaned back. His hand explored between her legs. She thought of closing them tight—yes!—but didn't. She would allow this for only a few more moments. Longer? When he opened his pants and pointed his erect thing at her, she felt frightened and was about to pull away. Then it was that fragments of Eulah's warnings against sins of the flesh raided her mind.

"Yea, ole Satan makes it feel good—so goood," Eulah quivered and moaned in Sylvia's mind. *"Lust! Wicked pleasures! Seduced flesh! Lust, flesh, pleasures, flesh, pleasure, pleasure . . . makes it feel so goood—so goooood—so damned gooooooood!"*

"How did it feel to lose your virginity to a Chicano *vato* like me?" Armando asked her afterwards, buckling his pants, giving his belt a flip of the tip.

She didn't tell him that, yes, it felt good, especially because of Eulah's words echoing encouragement. Nor did she tell him that she was considering becoming a Catholic as a result of their visits to the colorful church. Not a nun, no. Their drab garments would spook her. She could easily become, though, a devotee of the gorgeous virgin and the almost-naked man.

"Well?" he waited proudly for her answer.

"What?" She had forgotten what he had asked, so delirious had she become at the prospect of her newfound devotion, another step away from Eulah.

"I said, How did it feel to lose your virginity to a Chicano *vato loco* like me?" He frowned at her forgetfulness.

She remained silent, hoping that she was blushing, although she knew she wasn't.

Another afternoon, among the same green cluster, it all felt even better to Sylvia Love when she lost her virginity again (again goaded by Eulah's feverish warnings). That's how Armando made her feel when, afterwards, as he shined the buckle of his belt with his spit-moistened handkerchief and gave the tip of his belt an extra flip before looping it, when he asked her, again, "How did it feel to lose your virginity to a Chicano *vato loco*?"

Her sassy spirit sparked. She heard herself answer him. "Wonderful. Did it feel wonderful for you, too—to lose *your* virginity to a white girl?"

He sulked all the way back to the city, where he dropped her off in the business section—farther than before. On her way home, Sylvia wondered what Armando's reaction would have been if she had told him that she might be part Mexican herself.

When she passed Eulah and her Bible that had become an appendage, Sylvia allowed herself to pause triumphantly smiling near the woman who would soon have no power over her at all. None.

She remained friendly enough with Armando, talking at school, even flirting for others to see, but that was all. Soon, she saw him in his car with one of the blonde girls who had once called out to him, "Hey, sexy Chicano." He coughed and coughed to call attention to the fact.

She didn't have to pretend she didn't care. She was too young—and he was too silly—to carry on seriously with anyone. Besides, her goal of winning the beauty title occupied her increasingly. She began to walk as if she was carrying a book on her head.

8

How Sylvia Love became Miss Rio Escondido. The full
horror at the Miss Alamito Beauty Pageant.

It was by default that Sylvia became Miss Rio Escondido. No one else competed. She was sure the reason was that all the other girls, both the white ones and the Mexican Americans, knew she would triumph, handsdown, and so they had decided it was wiser not even to compete.

Another factor for the default might lie in the fact that in Rio Escondido, there were many Baptists, Catholics, and, of course, the Pentecostals—and they all variously denounced "sins of the flesh," although it seemed to Sylvia that no one did so more passionately than her mother.

Mayor Gonzales, his face redder than usual, honored Sylvia with the beauty title during lunch in the best coffee shop in the City, The Lone Star Café. She didn't mind being given the great title without fanfare—at this stage, anyway—because news of it might jolt Eulah out of her religious trance. The Mayor was proud to be seen with such a pretty girl, lowering his voice to whisper ordinary matters so that others in the café might suspect him of speaking intimacies. What he was telling her was that the City of Rio Escondido would proudly support all necessary expenses involved in her travel to the City of Lariat, Texas, where all contestants from the sprawling Alamito County would gather. He was so sure of the generous procedure—and no need for her to mention it to anyone else—no one—that he took money out of his wallet and presented it to her. She rewarded him with a spectacular smile and a kiss on the cheek.

"A kiss!" he exclaimed loudly for everyone to note. "This beautiful girl gave me a kiss!" After Sylvia left, he retained his hand on the exact place where she had kissed him, storing it.

When Sylvia missed her period, she decided that telling Armando, at least now, might complicate matters. Nothing would show before the crucial crowning.

The day before she would leave Rio Escondido to participate in the Miss Alamito County, she went early to the Catholic church. Her head covered with her own scarf this time, she knelt before her favorite statue, the most beautiful, the most alluring, the one who might, herself, be a candidate for the title of Miss America, the Most Holy Virgin Mother Mary, the mother of the sensational, almost-naked man on the cross.

"If I win Miss America"—she saw no reason to pray for the lesser title coming up—"I'll place my crown at your feet," she promised. She made a sign across her chest, the way Armando had. She rose—and then knelt hastily again and added, "And please don't let me be pregnant."

For years, Eulah had hounded Sylvia about attending "youth camp retreats." That's where she told her mother, who managed an approving nod without breaking her trance, that she would be going for the next few days.

Other contestants gathered for the Miss Alamito County Beauty Pageant at Lariat were atwitter with excitement when Sylvia joined them at the dusty motel where they stayed. She didn't like the bouncy girls—not a single other Mexican American among them. All of them seemed to resemble each other, with stiff hairdos, most often blonde, and bright teeth, curvy bodies, permanent smiles, and real or pretended Texas drawls. Sylvia decided she would be more sophisticated than the others—friendly, yes, but aloof. "Just who do you think you are?" one of the giggly girls asked her. "I think I am Sylvia Love," she answered, and truly felt that she was finally herself, now that she was so far away, in so many ways, from Eulah Love. At last!

One particular contestant, Miss Canutillo, annoyed her because she told all the girls that *they* were the prettiest and should win, probably because she had given up on the title herself and was hoping to be named Miss Congeniality. Still, there was much excitement in sitting around the motel pool and being ogled and snap shot by the local newspaper. There was the further excitement of being groomed, fitted, told how to walk—all this by an effeminate man and a masculine woman.

"Walk as if you're carrying a book on your head," the man instructed. "I already do," Sylvia informed.

"The *good* Book, the Bible—that's what *I* imagine I'm carrying on *my* head," Miss Canutillo offered, "and the Lord will be our guide, God bless."

Responding to a chill at the memory of Eulah in her vine-choked house thinking her daughter was at revival retreat camp, Sylvia Love did not even try to muffle a groan at Miss Canutillo's sticky declamation, a loud groan which was rewarded with a throaty hoot from the masculine woman and a secret—to one side of his hip—thumbs-up from the man, and a puckered frown from Miss Canutillo.

"What will you do for your talent performance?" a severely serious older man wearing a red bow tie and writing on a pad asked Sylvia as she and the others stood on a small high-school stage.

"Talent?"

"Yes. Exactly like for the Miss America Contest," the man emphasized the importance of this phase, huffily. "Do you dance, act, sing? What?"

"I sing," Sylvia said.

"What are you waiting for?"

> *Amazing grace, how sweet the sound*
> *That saved a wretch like me . . .*

It was her own voice! Her voice was singing the song the black woman had sung long ago, the song she had rehearsed so often in her mind.

> *I once was lost, but now I'm found,*
> *Was blind but now I see. . . .*

In a sweet, lovely voice she sang the words, slowly, giving them her own meaning, making it her own song, tinged the words at first with the sadness of her past, and then with the hope of her future. The girls fluttering about her paused to listen.

"Good!" the stern man said.

The night of the pageant arrived, an appropriately starry Texas night when even the seasonal Texas wind was hushed in awe of the proceedings.

Then it was as if time had whipped itself up, existed only in flurries for Sylvia Love. During one of those flurries she was walking in her luminous white gown along the small stage—alone, all eyes on her!— nervous and praying that she wouldn't perspire before the judges: two stern men and one smiling (at her? Sylvia wondered)—and one woman, all out of shape, seated in the front row of the full auditorium.

Another flurry! The interview! Miss Canutillo had just answered what she would ask for if she had three wishes: "That everyone heed the Lord's word . . . To serve the Lord with my body and soul . . . To spread the Lord's word." Sylvia longed to elbow her when she walked past her as if she was hoping for a halo instead of a crown.

"And you, Miss Love, what would be your three wishes?"

"That there be no meanness in the world," Sylvia answered without an intervening pause. She thought, But before that, I wish Eulah would stay out of my life!

"And?"

She didn't have to think; she said: "That no one would ever be mean to anyone."

"And your third wish?"

Sylvia straightened up proudly and said, "That all meanness would vanish from the world"—and to herself she added: that Eulah would shut up and not push me around with her damn hideous Bible and that I'll be free of her forever!

Another flurry—the talent phase. Although, the day before, she had managed to sing the wondrous song, she was certain that, this time, the borrowed words would stop flowing, turn into gasps, stick in her throat. She would have to spit them out. She closed her eyes and evoked the black woman who had sung the song that distant time, remembered how she had looked up, how she had held her hands, out, up. She did the same. Her voice became firmer, stronger, and soon she didn't have to rely on the memory; the words of the song, propelled by hope, were coming from her, only her.

> *Amazing grace, how sweet the sound*
> *That saved a wretch like me. . . .*

As she sang the words she cherished most—"my fears relieved . . . hope . . . a life of joy and peace," her voice gained strength, and rose, firm, serene.

Applause! More than anyone else had received.

Another flurry—and she was waiting in the wings in her bathing suit, white so that her skin glowed golden.

"Miss Rio Escondido, Sylvia Love!" announced a slick dark-haired man. Feeling a series of trembles of ecstasy as she heard her name called out for the most important phase—yes, yes, yes, this was real, the beginning of a new life—Sylvia Love made her way past the twenty or so other contestants, including Miss Canutillo, who whispered, "Oh, *you're* the prettiest, Miss El Rio, that's why *you're* going to win."

Sylvia had taken only a few steps onto the stage when she heard a commotion behind her. She didn't turn to look. That would compromise her walk before the panel of judges—had she heard a murmur of admiration when she appeared on the stage? She did not turn to look back even when she heard a terrifying voice screech:

"I command you in the Lord's name to let me through!"

Sylvia had to glance back then, to make sure she was wrong, that the voice did not belong to—

Eulah Love.

Eulah was scuffling offstage with the attendants, and with some of the heftier beauty contestants, who had joined spiritedly in trying to subdue the raging woman.

Walk faster? Run? Sylvia considered her dour choices. She stopped, frozen.

Wresting herself free of hands grabbing her, Eulah rushed onstage with her black Bible in one hand and an ominous white bundle in the other. "Woe to allow your body to be exposed!" she screamed at Sylvia. "Shame, shame, shame, shame on you, and shame on your exposed body, shame! This is my curse on you! Unhappiness will follow you, forever, for your sins!" Unfurled, the bundle she carried became a sheet, and she flung it over Sylvia, covering her.

Gasps from the audience, then scattered muffled bursts of laughter.

Trying to throw off the sheet, Sylvia shouted at the raging woman, "Get away from me, you awful woman!"

Titters and giggles erupted into more laughter, loud laughter, growing laughter.

Sylvia managed to thrust off the sheet, but it wrapped about her feet. When she attempted to resume her graceful walk—head up, shoulders squared, one foot before the other, not straight ahead—she stumbled, fell, heard new waves of uncontrolled laughter. She rose and tumbled down again, rose, and fell again, the sheet clinging to her feet, wrapping about her legs. Then she heard, like a knife slashing, the gleeful shriek of Miss Canutillo: "Hallelujah! The haughty bitch is *out*!"

Sylvia ran offstage doing what she had sworn she would never do at a beauty pageant. She cried.

9

The beginning of the aftermath.

How Eulah found out about the pageant, and how she managed to reach the site of the competition in time to do what she did, would remain a mystery to Sylvia, as would her mother.

Soon after, as she stood in front of the mirror admiring her gorgeous body, the memory of Eulah's ranting made her turn away abruptly, and she pulled up her blouse to cover her breasts. No! She forced back her defiance and pride. She lowered her blouse, and she faced her reflection, boldly. So much for Eulah Love's silly curse!

CHAPTER TWO

1

*A return to the time of Lyle's birth. A prediction
altered into a new prophecy.*

Sylvia Love fell into a deep sleep and woke startled—today?
yesterday? tomorrow?—having forgotten that she had
given birth. Scrutinizing the bundle beside her, she discovered what it was—her baby, a boy, now nuzzling too
cozily against her breasts.

Clarita, who had remained in the room with her beautiful young
friend, still pondered how she could possibly have gone wrong in her
prediction that the child was dead inside the womb. After all, she, a
proud, sturdy middle-aged Mexican woman with one cloudy eye that
underscored her spiritual powers—"my deer eye," she called the smoky
eye—had done everything right. With a rosary wound around two fingers, she had tapped three times about the young woman's swollen belly,

placed her ear against the swelling—all while saying two Hail Marys and one Our Father, in Spanish. The result—silence—led to her pronouncement: "Be thankful, my beautiful friend, that this child died in your womb, because he was about to start weeping when I listened, and when a child weeps inside his mother"—the Mexican midwife had made a sign of the cross—"that means he will have a troubled life!"

Now, with the strange bundle of pink flesh beside her and the little mouth seeking her nipple, Sylvia ventured: "Does his being born alive after all mean he'll have a happy life?"

"Yes!" Clarita adjusted her prediction further. "He'll have a happy life because he overcame the stillness I heard in your womb. He's going to grow up to be *un doctor famoso.*" She pondered further. "A specialist." She peered over the child. "He'll be *muy guapo*—very handsome"—she closed her eyes, to allow a full vision—"a very handsome heart specialist." Satisfied with her clarification, she sat near Sylvia in the comfortable chair she had lugged in from her own room, and she fell into one of her instant dozes.

Sylvia had winced at Clarita's last words—"a very handsome heart specialist"—which struck at her own heart and loosed memories of Lyle Clemens the First, a handsome heartbreaker. Her thoughts couldn't linger on that memory, even if she had wanted them to because she was startled, not by Clarita's sudden jerking awake—that was also familiar—but by her sudden words.

"I suppose—" Clarita's eyes shot open after a severe nod of her head. Staring at Sylvia as if for the first time, she said, her voice throbbing with lament, "I suppose I didn't rush you quick enough to the hills!" She shook her head, shedding a lingering daze, and she added, *"Ay, Dios mío.* Damned if I wasn't back there again."

Sylvia Love was too weary now too ask what the hell Clarita meant, but she would later, especially since the older woman had said those very words when they had first met, a few months ago, months filled with unusual events.

2

How Sylvia met Clarita. Clarita's duel with Eulah Love.

After the Miss Rio Escondido debacle, Sylvia prepared to move out of her mother's house. Her silent rage grew with the conviction that she would have gone all the way to the Miss America Pageant—and would have won the title. The glamorous Holy Mother Mary had proven to be a partial ally, since her period had resumed, informing her that she was not pregnant; and news of the debacle did not reach Rio Escondido, thanks to the influential Mayor Gonzales, who owned the City's only newspaper.

"Where are you going?" Eulah Love had just become aware that Sylvia was taking out the last of her possessions from the sadly vined house.

"Away from you."

"Why?"

Her mother seemed so genuinely baffled that Sylvia did not even answer. Soon, deeper into her concentration for her approaching speech in tongues at the nearing Gathering of Souls, Eulah Love would simply assume her daughter was still there.

Sylvia found an attractive apartment in the center of the City. She had easily gotten a job at the perfume counter of the only department store there, the Fashion Store, a two-story building with variegated counters. She did not return to school; but, thanks to Mayor Gonzales, she had a diploma—he gave it to her in the same coffee shop, same table, during which he had awarded her the title of Miss Rio Escondido. "A diploma says you're smart, and you are smart and very pretty," he told her, and received another kiss, which he warmed for long seconds with his hand on his cheek.

Leaving work one afternoon, she encountered a Mexican woman who was arriving with another Mexican woman, both custodians at the store. The older of the two women, with blue-tinted white hair in careful waves, halted when she saw Sylvia. She closed her eyes and struck her forehead with a clenched fist. About to reel, she said, "*Dios mío!* I must take you immediately to the hills to hide you from the rapists!"

Sylvia ran away from her. The last thing she needed was another lunatic in her life. Catching up with her, one of the salesgirls informed her that the woman was Clarita, who had made quite a reputation for herself among the salesladies by conducting "private *consultas,*" during which—this was her specialty—she prophesied good news even when they sounded bad at first. "I sure could use her," Sylvia said dourly, with no intention of ever speaking to the strange woman who, she remembered noticing, had one strange eye as if mist had settled into it.

Soon after, Sylvia was again leaving the store with the other young woman, a plain young woman, always out of breath and thrilled by her association with Sylvia, who retained her aloofness from other girls she was sure disliked her because of her looks. The plain young woman had just mentioned that tonight the "big beauty pageant" was being televised. "I just love watching it because the girls are so silly and untalented, unlike you, Sylvia; I bet you could win if you entered."

"I did enter and I would have won," Sylvia heard herself say. "Except that—" The harsh memory stopped her words. "I withdrew."

Before Sylvia's friend could react in wonderment, the woman with the strange eye was there as if she had materialized. Insinuating herself into the conversation as if Sylvia's words had been directed at her—she said. "I've seen those others on television, string beans, flat women. But just look at *your* breasts!" She cupped her hands under her own ample bosom, heaving it up.

Sylvia Love was won over. She smiled at Clarita, but she stopped smiling when the older woman banged her forehead again, closed her eyes, and repeated, somewhat, what she had said on first encountering her, "To the hills! Pancho Villa is coming!"

Sylvia's apartment became increasingly pretty. She bought flouncy drapes, a white sofa, and she filled the place with real-looking artificial flowers.

"I'm here for a visit—"

Sylvia had answered an insistent knock at the door. There stood Clarita. Startled, Sylvia invited her in, leaving the door open in case she was here for some brief message or other. But she stayed, sitting down comfortably on the one chair. "—and to tell you that are a very special person," the older woman continued, as if she had received that message on highest authority—she had closed her eyes and pressed her hands to her temples for intense concentration. "Thank you," Sylvia said, genuinely delighted.

There was such immediate closeness between them that Sylvia told the older woman about the debacle at the Miss Alamito Pageant; she was astonished and pleased to see that Clarita understood fully, presenting, as evidence of that fact, copious tears. "Oh, the sadness of it, the sadness," she wept, sobs that Sylvia soothed.

"Woe! Scarlet woman! Woman of shame!" Eulah had shoved her way in. "Repent!" With her Bible, she rushed at Sylvia.

Clarita stepped in front of her, pushing her back. Eulah pushed back. The two women froze before each other, as if to test whose cold stare would vanquish whose.

"Stand aside, harborer of wanton women, whoever you are!" Eulah shouted at Clarita.

Out of the large bag she carried with her for such emergencies, Clarita brought out a dried palm leaf—"blessed by the priest," she intoned—and lighting it with matches that were part of her magical arsenal, she waved it in front of Eulah Love—"to banish your emanations, ranting woman!"

Eulah coughed and battled the smoke with her hands.

"This *demonio* can't stand the smell of holy palm!" Clarita said triumphantly.

"I am here to warn you, Sylvia Love, that I will drag you if necessary to the Gathering of Souls to be cleansed of your naked sin!" Eulah promised—and swept out, ranting and coughing.

"She'll take you to those crazy *protestantes* over my dead body," Clarita swore, deftly smothering the smoking palm between her cupped hands.

That increased Sylvia's affection for the Mexican woman, who became a frequent visitor.

Before long, Clarita would come over on Sundays to make a "special Mexican meal" for Sylvia, who bought and paid for the ingredients. Clarita would then hold court, informing Sylvia about "mysterious matters" that only she was privy to, generalized prophecies ("the world will endure"), and more specific ones that didn't hold up—she was always wrong about the weather. Often she made pronouncements that Sylvia did not understand. Perhaps that was so because Clarita might have been translating them from Spanish, although she was justifiably proud of her proficiency with the "foreign language," having taken many courses to further herself. Still, she often mixed the two, adding to the mysterious quality of her pronouncements.

"Life," she said with a sigh, "is a series of circles, never enclosed. *Así es el mundo.*"

3

*Still back in time, Lyle Clemens the First enters,
resurrecting smothered hope.*

Sylvia Love sat in a booth at the Lone Star Café where she often stopped for breakfast before going to work. She stared morosely at a bunch of waxy artificial flowers on the table, realizing that the ones she had bought yesterday would eventually look like these, worn, tired. She heard words coming from the television screen behind her, near the cashier.

"—exactly how it felt when you heard your name called."

"Egg-stat-tic! Of course, Ah couldn't believe it. All the othuh girls were prettier, and Ah—"

No! It couldn't be. Sylvia tried not to turn around to look. But she already had, she was already looking at the television screen, where—

An older woman, all bright teeth, her hair a blonde hornet's nest, sat on a sofa as if she was in her own living room. Facing her, her back momentarily to the camera was—

"Miss Canutillo!" Sylvia screamed aloud.

"Of course, you're too modest, Miss America," the older woman on television said. "But, after all, the judges determined that you were the one to bear the crown and glory of Miss America!"

"Yes, and Ah thank Jeezus for that, just as Ah did that night," Miss Canutillo said. Her lips were etched into a smile that might as easily be a grimace.

No question about it. That creature on the screen was the woman who had gone around telling everyone else they should win because they were prettier, the one who had shouted "Hallelujah" when she had stumbled on the lunatic's sheet, the one who—

"—because you see, Barbara," the drawly voice continued, "Ah know it wahn't me—I—who won. It was the Lord workin' through muh body."

"He had a lot of curves to work with," said Barbara.

CRASH!

The cashier ducked, people at the counter ducked.

Sylvia had sent a pepper shaker hurtling toward the screen, barely missing the television.

"Ah, hon, you don't haveta do any such thing—"

Sylvia whirled about to tell whoever had dared interfere with her to leave her alone, get the hell away from her, go to—

My God! She faced the handsomest man she had ever seen. He was tall, wearing a tailored suit, polished cowboy boots, and a cowboy hat, which he removed and, bowing, swept before her in an arc. He had dark brown hair whose natural shine tempted the Texas sunlight. His eyes were—she'd assert this later—blue!

"—don't haveta do any such thing," the man had resumed, smiling, "—cause you're so much prettier'n her. I bet you'da won if you'da been there. Hon, you're about the prettiest girl I've ever seen, ever."

That was Lyle Clemens the First—of course, he wouldn't become "the First" until "the Second" was born—and he was already coaxing her to sit back down with him as if it had been his booth all along and he was inviting *her* to join him. He made no attempt to hide the fact that he was eyeing her breasts, leaning to one side to get a better view. No, Sylvia thought, he wasn't looking at her breasts, he was making love to them with his eyes.

"Now, Sylvia, hon," the manager was there, a round red-faced man—his face redder now—I know the strain your odd mamma puts you through, but throwing a shaker at—"

"Sir," Lyle Clemens the First said, "this beautiful young lady is just spirited, that's all. This should cover any damage she may have created—and it doesn't look like much, does it?" He shook the manager's hand. The manager closed his own hand over the bill Lyle had put there.

"No damage, no," he said.

"I know I'm prettier than that bitch," Sylvia mused.

Lyle Clemens the First laughed at her easy acceptance of his compliment. He leaned closer. It was now as if he was breathing on her breasts, might be about to kiss them, right here, now! She must have been blushing, because she *felt* red.

4

The passion of Lyle Clemens the First and Sylvia Love.

This is lustful! That's what Sylvia thought happily, savoring the word her mother often tossed at her during her recurring incursions.

Lyle Clemens the First confirmed all the warnings her mother had plagued her with. Lust consumed, it made you its captive, you had no time to think about matters of the Lord, it made sinfulness attractive—lustful, lustful, lustful!

All true!

Especially since, it seemed to Sylvia, Lyle Clemens was always aroused, always ready to do it—with his boots on.

He kept a pair of new boots—there was never a smudge on the bed—to be worn only when he was "ready." He'd take off his "walkin' boots," then all his clothes, and then he'd put on the "love boots"—each time—explaining to Sylvia with the broadest smile ever that, "Ya cain't be a cowboy without your boots, and a cowboy makes the best kinda love." When he was through, he would remove them and replace them carefully in their box—TONY LAMA, the box proclaimed.

The way he made love! He would begin tenderly, nuzzling up to her, moistening her ear, then kissing her. His hands were everywhere on her body at once. And! He made love—made *love*!—to her breasts, hugging them at first with his large hands, his fingers cupping them, squeezing just slightly, and he would be talking to them, *talking to her breasts*! "You're the prettiest damn things God ever made, I swear, look how y'all perk up and turn deep pink like you're blushin'. I jest wonder—jest wonder—what would y'all taste like? Ummmm, ummm. Sweeter'n honey in a honeycomb." He would kiss them with his mouth closed—kiss them loudly between "ummm-ummms"—many times, over and over, and then his lips would part, right on her nipples, and he would warm them with his mouth, and his tongue would dab, swirl about them, and he would be whispering, "You're even more beautiful now, you gorgeous goddamn tits."

He made his words sound like a song. "What is *this*? A pink rosebud? I think maybe I'll open your petals, you pretty thing you. There, ah, yeah, sure, moist with dew, sweet thing, little dabs of honey. Ummmm, ummm—"

Right about then, he would begin speaking out what he was doing, would be doing. "Now I'm gonna touch this beautiful little sweetheart between her legs, touch you, sweet thing, with my fingers, I'm gonna part you just a little, like a flower. Dewy flower." The rough words he sometimes uttered never sounded nasty, always only like love words: "Now I'm gonna fuck you, my pretty sweetheart, gonna put my big cock into your beautiful quiverin' snatch, darlin', darlin' fuckin' sweetyheart, loveya, love *yah*! Oh, shit, oh, fuck, oh, *Jee-zuss Christ!*"

When he was coming, it was as if that was all there was in the world, for him, and for her. Her body would match his every thrust. Just before he came, he'd shout, "I love ya, *sweet*heart," and push all the way in at "sweet" and stay there pulsing inside her for an eternity. Eulah Love was right! Lust sure could rule your senses. But Eulah was wrong, wrong, wrong about her life being unhappy.

After sex, and having taken off his sex-boots, Lyle would instantly fall asleep with a smile on his face, his body naked, so naked that, at times, blushing and cherishing the warmth on her face, Sylvia would close her eyes, then open them to relish the spectacle, including the sight of his still somewhat aroused cock. The only other one she had ever seen was Armando's, and either Armando's was small—although he'd displayed it as if no one else had one—or Lyle's was very large. She suspected that both conclusions were correct.

Once, when she was sure Lyle was asleep, she bent down and touched his cock with one finger. It jumped up. He woke with a wide smile— and off they went.

Sometimes, after they made love and he fell asleep, she would cover herself entirely with a sheet, telling herself she was cold. Once, Lyle woke and saw her doing that. Lazily, he attempted to lower the sheet, to make love to her breasts. She grasped it tightly. "What the hell?" Lyle said.

5

The courtship of Sylvia Love.

Of course she was in love.

Lyle was *so* good to her, never arrived without a present, earrings, a necklace, a gorgeous dress from Dallas, exactly her size. Always, he brought flowers. Sometimes he waited until after they had sex to present her with gifts. At first that bothered her, because it seemed he meant to reward her. But soon she dismissed that as yet another of his endearing quirks, like the boots.

And this: She woke one morning to the strains of a guitar—a guitar she'd never seen before, new, bought for this occasion only, she knew, and he sang notes, only notes really; and there he sat on the floor, naked, with his cowboy hat on, his long legs crossed before him and his boots on—just sat there like that, smiling and singing to her—words, only words, the same words, repeated—"love . . . sweet . . . beautiful Sylvia, my Sylvia . . . my sweet love." Then they had sex—again!—and she knew that happiness would never end.

She mentioned aloud one day that she was worried that her friend Clarita had not been by, had walked past her at the grocery store, something she had managed to ignore because Clarita was given to intense moods, during which, she said, her visions came. But as the days passed without a word from her, she worried.

"Just sulkin' probably, cause she thinks Ah'm gonna take her friend from her. But Ah'm not," Lyle soothed her, with words and with kisses. "I'd never do anything that would hurt my Sylvia."

He lived in Dallas—but he could live anywhere, he had that kind of business—"cowboy business, prize horses"—he told Sylvia. He flew back and forth, driving a rented car—always new, always fancy, a different one each time—the few miles from the airport nearest Rio Escondido. He came and went—going away only on cowboy business.

6

A warning is adjusted.

"Beware of men with black hair and blue eyes," Clarita told Sylvia sternly as she was leaving the department store and Clarita was going to work with the other custodian.

"Clarita! Where have you been? You've been avoiding me. Now come out of the shadows as if you don't know me!"

Clarita had seen Sylvia with "the Cowboy," the first time when she had been going to drop by for a visit. She had dashed away. Another time, she saw him leaving at an hour that signaled only one thing: Sylvia was having an affair. She pondered the matter deeply, over herbal tea. She had a signal of complications. A bird with a slash of red flew before her. Now she could tell Sylvia what she had withheld.

"Clarita, stop it, you're acting stranger than usual standing in the shadows to talk to me."

Clarita removed herself from the shadows. "I said, beware of a—"

"I heard you." Sylvia was so relieved to see her that she didn't walk away from the annoying warning. "Besides, Lyle's hair isn't black, it's brown."

"The color of smothered coals," Clarita adjusted.

Sylvia linked her arm through the older woman's, walking her back to the store. "He makes me very happy, Clarita." She had inferred that

Lyle had been right, that Clarita was nurturing some apprehension that he would come between their close friendship. "I want you to meet him, I've told him about you, he already likes you. Look." This was inspiration. She took one of the jangly bracelets he had bought her—"just trinkets in place of the real things that're comin'," he told her—and she held it out to Clarita. "He bought you this."

Clarita studied the bracelet. Pretty, and not inexpensive either. She accepted the gift.

Without even banging her forehead to indicate a sudden vision, Clarita said to Sylvia, "A man in your life is going to make you happy— a man with brown hair and blue eyes."

Sylvia smiled. Yes, Clarita was right, Lyle would make her very happy.

7

The deepening prospect of happiness.

"Goddamn, Ah love ya, sweet little hon. You gotta be my wife or I'll just die, ya hear?" he said, lying in bed next to her, his love boots in their box—for now.

If she had loved him before, it was nothing compared to how she loved him now. Of course she would marry him.

"In a Catholic church?"

"Wherever you want, sweetheart."

"Where will we live?" She thought of Clarita, having to leave her if he'd want to take her away. She'd take her with her! That settled that.

Lyle left to make necessary arrangements before their marriage—"and to buy-ya some thangs, muh sweet, sweet little girl."

Sylvia Love did not need to employ Clarita's psychic powers to know that, from now, her life would be happier than—well, just as happy as— if she won the Miss America title, although she would still, sometimes, touch her head as if the glittery crown would miraculously be there.

8

Eulah Love invades again.

"Sin! Woe unto sinners! They shall be plunged into hell to howl for eternity in blazing fire." Eulah Love had burst in and was standing rigidly like a scarecrow—that gaunt now—with her black Bible brandished before her.

It was past noon, Sunday, and Sylvia was still in bed. Lyle would be returning later that night, had called to tell her he was "tied up on business for justa while longer, hon."

"The Lord has ordered me to do today what I have long promised Him since the licentious exposure of your sacred body!" Eulah Love pulled her daughter forcefully out of bed. Sylvia was still groggy and bewildered. For a frail woman, the lunatic had a lot of strength. "The Lord has ordered that I take you to the prayer meeting to be purged."

"Let me go, you lunatic!" Sylvia was now fully awake. "I don't want to go to your fuckin' prayer meeting." She had stored some of Lyle's words for the proper time, like now.

"If you don't come with me, I'll stand outside and shout." She yowled: "*Strummmmm-pet! Woman of Babylonnnnnn!* Whore who exposed her sacred body for all to covet, whore who shamed herself and her flesh!"

Sylvia could hear the family in the apartment next to hers responding to the noise. She knew her crazy mother would carry out her promise. What if Lyle turned up now? She lived in fear that she would attempt to burst in while he was there. She had planned to pretend not to know "the crazy woman" if that happened, and then to push her out.

It seemed much easier to pretend to be going with her, then dash away, Sylvia determined. Too, she thought vaguely, there might be another purpose she might discover for *wanting* to be there. She put on a full sweater, which Eulah yanked even higher over her breasts as they walked out.

9

Eulah's dramatic speech in tongues as she's slain in the spirit.

At the Pentecostal Hall, the Gathering of Souls was riding a high tide of frenzy.

People from all around Alamito County and beyond crowded the cavernous hall for this mighty affair. Television cameras glowered from every direction. On the stage, a choir of men and women in red and black smocks sang gospel. The stage resembled a living room in a tacky motel suite—or a gaudy rectory—replete with puffed couches, crouched tables, a tawdry chandelier that seemed about to melt under glaring lights. Behind all this, high up, a painting of a rosy-cheeked Christ in splendid vestments, hands out, loomed over all.

In the center of the stage stood a woman with big breasts and a huge blond wig, almost a foot high. Her eyes, closed now, were laden with mascara so that they looked like dark holes carved into her white-powdered face, a stark, glossy red mouth its only other intrusion. She wore a cotton-candy yellow dress, with coils of ruffles, a dress a child might have been forced to wear to a birthday party. She held a large gleaming-gold Bible to her bosom so that it pushed her breasts into more aggressive prominence.

Beside her, a man with prematurely gray hair—even his skin looked gray—clutched his own Bible to his sunken chest. He had the slithery looks of a failed gigolo, long sideburns, a tiny mustache, darty eyes.

"Roll up your sleeves and let's grapple with the old Devil and cast him out!" the man shouted to the cameras.

"Hallelujah," the woman echoed. Giant tears exploded from her eyes, streaking her cheeks black.

"Do I hear an Amen?" the man goaded the audience.

"Amen!" men and women, grasping at the air, answered.

"Amen!" Eulah Love announced her entrance into the Hall with Sylvia. "I'm here to purge a grave evil! Stand aside!" She clasped Sylvia's hand.

"Well, I told you she'd be here," said a heavy woman with a trembling chin to a silent mousy man next to her. "Well, you know, she speaks in tongues once a year. Well, she's *inspiring.*"

"Come and be cleansed!" the gray man exhorted.

"Shed your burden of woes," the blond-wigged woman said in a childish voice, tiny, almost petulant.

A line of men and women, young, old, children—standing, crouching, bending, limping, marching, running, hobbling, stumbling—instantly formed, hands in the air, fingers weaving invisible pleadings. They cried, they sighed, they wailed and tears flowed, they moaned, they groaned, they pled and tears flowed, they mumbled, they stumbled, they screamed and tears flowed, they screeched, they beseeched, they implored and tears flowed.

Where was the woman who had sung so beautifully, those many years ago? Sylvia wondered, longing to hear again the voice that might have calmed this frightening pit of men and women writhing in what seemed to be ecstatic pain. She searched for her. She was not here.

On the stage, four burly men gathered around the two evangelists. A balloon of a woman in paisley print trembled before them. "Endless pain, can't walk, can't even crawl, can't move!" she wailed.

The gray man babbled words, planted one hand on the woman's forehead, and shouted, "I banish Satan, I banish pain, you are slain in the spirit of the Lord." The woman attempted to fall; her weight would not shift. Two men behind her pulled her back, and two before her forced her down until she managed to lie quaking on the floor.

"You are cured!" the gray man called.

The woman tried to get onto her feet and fell back several times. The men lifted her, ushering her across the stage with difficulty while she screamed, "I can walk without pain," as she hobbled, lurching about the stage.

"Let's hear it for the Lord!" the man screamed.

The congregation praised God.

Cameras pursued the cured.

With Sylvia no longer resisting, Eulah worked her way to the crest of the crowds. Those who recognized her from previous revivals alerted others. A circle formed about the two. A camera swooped to gawk. Eulah trembled, her hands clasped nothing, her words tumbled out, sounds jumping on each other. Alerted, the gray preacher and the blonde woman cleared their way into the circle, locating themselves squarely before the cameras. "Speak the Lord's Word, Sister Eulah!" the man demanded.

"I am here with this scarlet woman, my own blood, to proclaim, before the world that she—" Eulah began.

To speak it all again, to curse her again, to humiliate her even more publicly!—that is why she had dragged her here, Sylvia knew, enraged. But it might all turn around. Now!

"Speak out for the angels on earth to heed!" the blonde woman's tiny voice squeaked at Eulah.

"—to proclaim before the world that she—"

Sylvia blocked Eulah's further words. "Yes, mamma, speak! Tell them what a goddamned vicious and cruel woman you really are!" she

screamed at the old woman, her words pitched into the frenzied cacophony of groans, moans, shouts.

Eulah fell back, clutching her chest, her hands grasping Sylvia's,
pulling her down to kneel next to her on the floor. She gasped: "You
lived to kill me! *My curse on you and your vile flesh forever!*" Then she
moaned: "Brggg—ugghhh—crsss—"

"Sister Eulah's speaking in holy tongues!" the tinny voice of the blond
evangelist announced.

"Grggg unhhhhh—"

"Sister Eulah talks with the tongue of the Lord!" the gray man intoned.

"She is slain in the spirit!" the blond woman's squeaky voice
proclaimed.

"Ughrrrrrr . . ."

An old man crouched over Eulah. "She ain't slain, she's dead, choked
on her tongue."

The gray man, the blond-wigged woman, and the camera fled from
the dead woman.

Sylvia laughed so hard she doubled over on the floor until her laughter
became sobs, not of sorrow—no, no; they were sobs of anger that Eulah
had bested her again, had lived to curse her one more time, to blame
her for her death. Looking down at the finally calmed face of the dead
woman, Sylvia Love saw something that astonished her: Eulah Love must
once have been very pretty!

Not wanting to see more, Sylvia ran out of the Hall.

10

Who is Sylvia's father?

At the funeral, Lyle Clemens the First stood next to her with a sad face,
a brand-new cowboy hat pressed against his chest. "Bought it just to
honor your dear dead mamma," he said. Clarita had refused to come,
fearing evil vapors.

Sylvia was astonished to see that the few people who turned up were
those she had never seen before, sad older faces. Had her mother once
had another life? Who was that good-looking dark-skinned man, so
sad? He might have been Mexican, she wasn't sure. He was staring at

her intently. In the next moment he turned away and left the funeral site.

Her father? She would have followed him to ask, demand, but, just then, she saw a tall, fair-haired man she had not seen before either. He was holding a hand over his heart and bowing before the lowered coffin. He, also, turned to face her. Was *he* her father? He dashed away. Had that pretty woman she had glimpsed in repose once had romantic yearnings? Sylvia did not welcome that question.

"Good riddance," Sylvia said later to Clarita.

"Shhh—don't speak about the dead, not yet. Her spirit has hardly had a chance to go to"—Clarita pondered—"wherever it's going. The dead do retain some power, you know, especially the wicked ones, and especially soon after they've died, when their souls are still turning to smoke. *Ay!*"

11

A white rose is presented.

Sylvia was not entirely sure that she was pregnant, but she wanted to share the possibility with the man she was about to marry—and she would test his reaction. So she told him she was sure she was pregnant.

"Oh, hon, do ya know how happy ya make me?" Lyle spun her about in her apartment. As if remembering that she must be treated more carefully, he put her down gently. They had not yet made love, although she could tell by the bulge in his pants that he was ready. He touched her stomach gently. He had brought her one rose bud, white, not yet open, its petals huddled together, in a beautiful small crystal vase.

He did love her. How could she doubt it? His reaction had confirmed it, if it had needed confirmation—and it had not.

They made love, wonderful love, better each time.

The next day the bud opened and became the largest rose Sylvia had ever seen. She would constantly go to it and kiss it as she waited for Lyle.

He did not come back that day. Nor did he return the day after that, nor the week after.

Sylvia kept the rose until its edges turned brown, ashy. She crumbled it and put it in an envelope.

A letter arrived, postmarked Houston. She read the few words on a piece of plain paper exactly as he would have spoken them:

"Ah love ya, sweetheart. Don't ever doubt it. Love ya with all muh heart. Your Lyle." He had enclosed five new hundred-dollar bills.

"So you'd get an abortion, that's why the *desgraciado* left you that money, I see it in a vision." Clarita declared. She observed everything as if it were a revelation known only to her. "Be glad you're rid of him, he would have broken your heart."

"He already has," Sylvia said. Would she be able to abort his child?

12

A figure from the past is summoned.

"Hello, sexy Chicano," Sylvia smiled at Armando as he left the place where he was now a senior clerk. She had waited outside the building for him, knowing the approximate time when he would be leaving. She wore one of her sexiest dresses, coral, so perfectly fitted to her that it made love to her body when she moved.

"Sylvia! Wow!" Armando linked his finger under his belt in satisfaction that she was waiting for him, and with such admiring words! The times they had run into each other before, they had waved, nodded. He opened an extra button on his shirt; a few dark hairs peeped out.

"I've missed you," Sylvia said.

"Oh, me, too. Oh, yeah, me, too!"

"Let's do it again, sexy Chicano—the same place, just like before?"

"Oh, God, yes!" he was ready.

He raced with her in his new car to the same spot where they had first had sex, and they did it again. It was dusk and the lush greenery along what might have been the site of the hidden river had darkened, the pale sky auguring a Texas windstorm.

When they returned to the City, Sylvia asked him to drop her off where he had earlier times.

"Sure. Goddit! Everything just like before. Next time, I'll rent a room at the Starlight Motel, we'll spend the whole day and night fucking. Would you like that, gorgeous?"

She stepped out of the car. "I never want to see you again," she told him. She didn't look back to see his reaction.

13

Sylvia's motives. Clarita struggles with an ethical consideration.

Now she would not know who had made her pregnant—if she was; and, if so, it would be easier to lose the child if she could tell herself it was not Lyle's.

When she was sure that she *was* pregnant, she explained to Clarita: "I'm not ready to be a mother, but the thought of having a baby pulled out of me frightens me; I would keep thinking he was already alive." And Lyle's, she didn't say.

That's when Clarita bent over Sylvia's stomach and tapped it several times.

Was she trying to make the inevitable easier for her friend, or was she convinced that her prognostication was accurate? Clarita would often ponder that later. Who knows? What is certain is that she said the child was already dead. "You can go ahead and do what you have to do."

"You can tell, this far ahead that it's dead?"

"Revelatory visions are timeless. *La vida pasa así.*"

Sylvia touched her stomach. Had the shame Eulah had denounced— her wantonness—led her to all this?

14

A vine is resurrected in the house of curses.

Now that she needed more room, Sylvia moved back into the house she had once occupied with Eulah, and had now inherited by default. Ferociously, she watered the vine that had withered over the small house once full of Eulah's anger. She listened, no whisper remained. Soon, she saw clear hints of the vine's resurrection, splotches of green struggling out of the gray tangles. By mutual invitation, Clarita moved in with her, assigning herself the role of housekeeper, cook, nurse, and, eventually, mother.

Lulled by all her confusions about the birth, taking sips of bourbon to allow her to cope with them, Sylvia postponed the constantly planned abortion, time after time—*was the child Lyle the First's, oh, was he?*— until it was too late and Lyle Clemens the Second was born.

CHAPTER THREE

1

A return to Sylvia's bedside.
A pending question is asked.

After a deep, long sleep during which Clarita kept watch, Sylvia Love woke to another ambush of surprise at seeing the child lying next to her. She touched him tenderly, and then edged him away, just slightly. The words Clarita had spoken, before her deep sleep, popped into her mind as if they had just been spoken. "Clara!"—that's what she called her when she wanted to assert firmness. "Tell me what the hell you mean about not taking me to the hills in time when the rapists were coming. Tell me now!" she said with accrued irritation.

The demand wasn't necessary. Clarita was ready, on this eventful day, to roam through the past and its effect on the present. With a weary sigh and a grave sign of the cross, she told her long-withheld story. "It began, as many stories do, in Chihuahua," she gave universality to her personal epic.

2

A pullback in time; Clarita's flight to the hills of Chihuahua;
the ravages of Pancho Villa; and an apparition
by the Holy Virgin Guadalupe.

Clarita—*Doña* Clarita as she was then called, although she was a young woman of fifteen herself and that designation is usually reserved for older, very dignified women—was given the task of herding her three pretty nieces, ages fifteen, sixteen, and seventeen, into the hills near Chihuahua City when word reached their father, a wiry tangle of a man, that Pancho Villa was on one of his rampages raiding villages and abducting and raping the prettiest girls. He had been a good man, Pancho Villa, a man of the people; he had opposed the dictator Porfirio Diaz. But like others who wander away from *Jesucristo,* Our Lord and Savior, he had, himself, become a tyrant. "He's coming!" said a worker on the *rancho,* "and he has that look in his eyes."

"Route the girls, Clarita!" Doña Lupita, Clarita's sister and the mother of the pretty girls, ordered. Lupita was a beautiful woman who might have aroused Villa's lust herself except that he preferred young girls.

"Clara!" Lupita's husband, father of the girls, summoned Clarita. "Take them to the hills, and then come right back so Villa won't suspect anything." The three pretty girls fluttered about, excited and terrified.

That day, Clarita's back ached, and so she released the withheld question, "Why me? Why shouldn't *I* run up to the hills and stay hidden from danger?"

"*Ay,* Clarita," Doña Lupita said, not meanly, "Pancho Villa would never bother with you, my dear."

"No one would look at you twice," the husband said. "Even if his men caught you, you'd be safe."

It was during that sulking incursion into the hills that the Blessed

Mother granted Clarita spiritual powers. Having safely hidden the three pretty girls—who giggled during the ordeal—she was on her way down the dusty hills when she stumbled on a rock and hit her head. She saw bursts of bright light, then only solid darkness. When she opened her eyes again, the light gathered into one brilliant flash within which stood the Holy Virgin Guadalupe.

"How pretty you are, my dear," the Holy Mother said and touched her on the throbbing lump.

Clarita knew that not only was she being granted magical powers—after all, the Holy Virgin had touched her!—but she had become pretty, uniquely so because after the harsh fall she developed a misty eye—her "deer's eye." She was so secure in her feeling about the transformation brought about by the Holy Mother that she was not affected when she returned to the rancho and Lupita's husband said, "What are you talking about? You look exactly as you did before, you're as plain as ever."

She understood a grudge—and so what he said did not faze her. Even if somewhat moderately, Lupita did graciously acknowledge the fact. "Well, there is something different about you, Clarita, my dear sister. Your eye is smudged."

The next time the cry came up that Villa was raiding the village for the prettiest girls, Clarita was the first to take off and not come back to the *rancho* until it was entirely safe.

Years later—after the turbulence of the Mexican revolution when from day to day you didn't know who was the enemy and who was not and the family fled to the border town of Juarez, Mexico, with trunkloads of money that was now worthless and they were penniless, the loaded suitcases kept for a time that would never come, when the money would again have value—the currency having collapsed—years later, several years later, when the family had crossed the border into the United States without even knowing they had—they had just kept fleeing—years later, when they had settled in the city of El Paso, in Texas, years later, years of sorrow—loss, deaths—and joy—marriages, children born—years later when the Depression struck the new country, years after that, and to survive poverty, Clarita, by then a grown woman, opened a small establishment which she called, in English, the Such Is Life Café. Soon after, she was arrested for bootlegging.

3

*A pause in Clarita's recollections. An unwelcome
question occurs to Sylvia Love.*

Sylvia had succeeded in listening attentively, so tired, hoping she
wouldn't doze off during the tearful saga, glad she had been able to say,
at the crucial point in Clarita's story, "But of course you're pretty,
Clarita," although she wasn't—or, well, she was in her own way. As if
to signal his next action, the newborn child drew attention to himself
by making a series of gurgly sounds. With powerful kicks, he threw off
the sheet covering his body and smiled at Sylvia.

"He wants your breast," Clarita said, standing over the bed, her misty
eye clouded further by the warmth of tears. "Here," she coaxed Sylvia
to bare her breasts to feed her son.

When Sylvia felt the little mouth attached to her flesh, she welcomed
a tingling sensation. She had felt the same when Lyle Clemens the First
made love to her breasts! She tried to urge the child away, but his little
mouth insisted. When she surrendered the nipple to him, she thought
she heard him purring. Lord, he was a strapping child, with a shock of
already-brown unruly hair, just like Lyle the First's, and his eyes—his
eyes? Difficult to tell. What if they were brown, like Armando's? What
if Lyle really was the son of—? Impossible!

Nudging the child closer to his mother—Clarita continued her saga,
warning that she might jump a bit ahead, because: "The journey back
is wearying and time darkens like a bird in flight."

4

An injustice at the Such Is Life Café.

The Such Is Life Café—a phrase Clarita had borrowed from a Jeannette
MacDonald movie she cherished, the singer being her second favorite star, the Mexican siren Maria Felix her first—was located on a
corner not far from railroad tracks. The unit, in which she also lived,
consisted of the restaurant, her quarters, and a room she rented out—
to her everlasting regret, because how could she know—*how?*—that
the woman who took the rented room was making *alcohol contrabando?*

A highly intelligent woman, Clarita was aware of the skepticism that development might arouse in some, about the brewing of alcohol occurring without her locating the smell. The woman, Concha, was canny; she explained the smell came simply from the fact that she was developing arthritis and constantly rubbed her joints with alcohol. Who would question a sick woman tending to her illness? Besides, despite the miraculous granting of powers by the Holy Mother Guadalupe in the hills of Chihuahua, Clarita's powers of divination had not yet been refined.

Having gotten wind of a possible raid, Concha fled, leaving her implicating implements behind. When the Liquor Commissioners arrived, there it all was, the bootlegged alcohol in tin cans. That was very serious, especially in Texas—trains riding through had to close their bars as they crossed the State.

"*Ay, qué injusticia!*" Clarita cried. "What have I done, tell me? Who has ever been hurt by a small sniff of a drink? My customers need something to get them through hard times—"

5

An adjustment of memories.

"—and those were *very* hard times. People needed a *traguito* to get them through, and I provided it—" Clarita's memory had run away beyond her control. When she heard an echo of her words, and saw Sylvia's reaction of surprise, she shrugged, "*Son cosas de la vida.* Matters of life. So it was me, yes, and I was making some very good liquor. So what? (Of course, I intended to tell you all this.) I went to jail for a year," she confessed flatly. "But I came out with refined powers, and a determination to educate myself. I have a diploma, you know, from night school," she said proudly. "Still, that arrest, *ay!*—that's why I work as a cleaning woman instead of teaching," she rued.

"What an unfair arrest," Sylvia managed to console her friend, although her body ached, an ache soothed by the mouth still nibbling at her breast too delightedly.

"So long ago," Clarita extended her lamentation, "and I still remember it so well, remember the raids of Pancho Villa, the hills, back in 1920. What a memory I have."

Sylvia frowned, baffled by the story she was now concentrating on to lessen the pangs in her body. If all that had occurred so far back, then how old would she be, her friend? Impossible. She ventured cautiously, "Clarita, that would make you almost eighty years old."

"What?" Clarita was aghast. "It would not! It's true all records of birth were lost, but eighty years old? Of course not!" Trying to hide what she was doing, she gathered her fingers on her lap and figured. She laughed. "I can understand your being baffled. You thought that had happened to *me*, didn't you?"

"That's what you said."

"Haven't you ever heard a story told so vividly that you absorb it? Especially when it's told to you by your mother?"

"I hardly ever spoke to my mother."

"*La loca*? I don't blame you. . . . The flight into the hills happened to my *mother;* she told it to me. It's become so real—"

Nothing surprised Sylvia for long about Clarita. "Did *any* of that happen to you, really to you?"

Clarita's voice was firm. "The part that happened to me was the miracle. And the bootlegging."

Sylvia had no problem believing the part about the bootlegging.

6

The present moves on. Lyle the Second grows up quickly and speaks an unwelcome word.

Clarita—although she had never married—taught Sylvia how to care for the child, insisted she not run away from him when the new presence overwhelmed her. Lyle Clemens the Second still baffled Sylvia at times when she looked at him—and at times she was frightened, not of him, but of the thought that she was a mother and he was her son.

At times, she sat—it seemed—for hours watching what she had created, at times giggling at the thought. After all, she was hardly nineteen. Other times, looking at her child, she felt an icy fear, the reason for which eluded her.

She began saying this to Lyle, while tickling him fondly: "Do you think I'm pretty?"

Lyle the Second would giggle, nodding his head—or so Sylvia would swear to Clarita when she returned with that day's groceries for some special enchiladas she was concocting, with sour cream, for dinner.

"Mujer," Clarita would shake her head. "He's too young to notice such things."

"Oh, I'm not sure," Sylvia Love said.

The child took steps, walked, ran—and he learned to say something that sounded very much like, "Yes, yes!" every time Sylvia asked him the familiar question: "Do you think I'm pretty?"

"Yes!" He threw his arms about her and kissed her neck.

"You're surprised I'm so young, aren't you?"

"Yes!" Lyle answered.

She held him at arm's length before her, marveling at how handsome he already was.

"Mamma—"

"What did you call me—?"

"Mamma—"

She sat him back down on the floor where he had been playing. "What?" She shook her head.

"Mamma—"

Sylvia Love stood abruptly. "No!"

"Mamma—"

"I said, no. Don't call me that. My name is Sylvia, call me Sylvia."

"Mamma—"

"I said, no!" Sylvia tapped him lightly on his hands, one and then the other. He must have heard the word from Clarita. She tested another word, only in her mind. Son. She did not speak it aloud.

She saw the child's hurt look. She hugged him. Then she hummed the song that had been powerful enough to draw her out of hiding at the Pentecostal Hall, the song she had sung at the Miss Alamito County Pageant, her favorite song. She sang it now to her son, but the joy of the song kept stumbling on still-open wounds and hurt bled into its joy.

"Amazing grace, how sweet the sound. . . ."

Lyle listened attentively each time she sang her song, so sweetly, so tenderly, a sad note now and then. Eventually he could conjure up the regal figure of the black woman she told him about, who had sung the song, the woman with a golden crown and a golden voice.

More time flew. Lyle was seven. In the boy's walk, Sylvia avoided detecting the beginning of his father's swagger. Impossible! Too soon. This had become apparent: Lyle's complexion was darker than hers—a light-brown tinge, and his eyes were brown, not blue like Lyle the First's. So what? The growing child was becoming a replica of Lyle the First. Sylvia dismissed any silly doubts about Armando.

As she stared at the child, she wondered what she would do when Lyle the Second grew up to look exactly like the man she had loved. To put an end to her silly conjectures—about what, about what!—she took a sip of her private bourbon, before the early-evening hour she had set for herself now that she had discovered its soothing qualities.

Clarita affirmed her early prophecy. "You're going to become a heart specialist, little Lyle, just like in my vision."

"A heartbreaker," Sylvia said. Bitterness seeped into her voice.

7

A disturbing question.

"Who is my father, Sylvia?" Lyle had begun asking that question to himself sometime ago, but he had not spoken it—not wanting to offend his mother, who winced every time he began, "Who is my—?" He verbalized it only now, when he was eight and bolder every day.

"You don't have one." Sylvia had rehearsed her answer, and so it came easily. Why should he know about his father? *She* had never needed one.

"At school everyone has a father," Lyle said.

"I doubt it," Sylvia said.

"Who is my father?" Having spoken the question, Lyle was not thwarted by the dark look that crept over his mother's face.

"A son of a bitch," she said, and closed her lips tightly, but opened them only to add, "A *goddamned* son of a bitch."

"What did the goddamned son of a bitch look like?"

"You're the spittin' image of him." Except for his coloring. Except for . . . his cruelty?

Lyle rested his head on her chest. "Did he ever see me?"

"Doesn't know if you were born."

Lyle closed his eyes, to shut away any vision of a father.

Clarita had been listening, wondering where all this would lead. She pretended to have just walked into the room. She herself had come to detest Lyle the First for how deeply he had hurt her Sylvia, but it was much too cruel to tell him what Sylvia was saying, words Clarita wished she could have thwarted. Looking away from Sylvia, she soothed Lyle's frown. "Your father was a very handsome cowboy, very handsome, like you," she said.

Sylvia laughed, coldly. "He sent me money, Lyle. You know what for?"

"Sylvia, no!" Clarita cautioned.

"So you wouldn't be born."

Lyle touched Sylvia's chest, because from the way she had placed her hand there, he supposed she might have a pain in her chest. "I won't be a goddamned son of a bitch like him," he told her. "I would *never* be mean to you," he added, perplexed.

"Won't you?" Sylvia asked vaguely. She kept his hand on her chest, warming her flesh with it.

8

A gift and a vow.

For his twelfth birthday, Sylvia impulsively bought Lyle a pair of cowboy boots—Tony Lama cowboy boots and a cowboy hat. Oh, and he looked handsome.

"What the hell is the matter with you, Clara? Every boy wants a pair of boots and a cowboy hat," Sylvia said when she was alone with Clarita.

That did not lighten Clarita's glower.

"Here. Let's have a small drink to cheer you up," Sylvia forced a light tone. "I happen to keep some liquor for—"

Clarita retained her sternness. "You don't have to hide your bourbon from me. I know you take a *traguito* now and then. I'll have one with you, only one, because no one should drink alone." She added, "It might even sharpen my visions."

After Sylvia had silently poured the two "short nips" from the bottle she kept in the pantry.

Clarita said, "Some day, you're going to have to tell Lyle more."

"About what?"

"Everything. Not only about the cowboy. But about your mother."

"Why?"

"So he can understand you." She had decided to approach this matter now when Sylvia would have been mellowed by her bourbon. Clarita knew how wrong she'd been when she saw Sylvia's warning expression, eyes narrowed.

"Tell him everything?" she said bitterly. "He knows as much about his goddamned son-of-a-bitch father as he needs to know. You told him he was a handsome cowboy, and I told him he was a son of a bitch. What more is there? And about Eulah? Tell him everything? About that woman, about my mother? About how she cursed me?" She was breathing harshly, even a discussion of the possibility enraging her. "Tell him about what she did to me? The humiliation, in front of all those people, laughing at me?—tell him *that*?" Never would she want to see him looking at her and know that he was imagining her during that time, imagining the echoes of degrading laughter, hearing Eulah's vilification.

She stood only one foot away from Clarita now. "Tell him all *that*? Never! Not as long as I live—and I demand that you honor that."

"I promise," Clarita said somberly.

9

About the unique nature and manifestations of intelligence.

"He jist don't wanna larn!" Mr. Bean, a despairing assistant principal, told Sylvia after she had stomped into his office in response to his written summons, brought to her by Lyle—who had smiled on presenting it, as if he had brought her a gift. The inked note was enclosed in an envelope that had been opened, with no attempt made to reglue it even cursorily.

"He's my son, and so he's bound to be smart," Sylvia said, "and he's only thirteen."

"Dammit, ma'am, I know he is smart, can't deny that, but he's inattentive—"

"For a good reason perhaps."

The assistant principal ignored that. "Do you know, ma'am, that sometimes, in the middle of a lesson, he stands up and walks out in those cowboy boots he says you bought him?—it's like he's turned invisible and someone's calling him."

"Hmmmm." Sylvia needed time to figure out what to make of that. "Where does he go?"

"To a vacant lot near the school grounds. I've looked out and seen him myself, and there he is just starin' around like he's tryin' to understand everythin'—and then starin' up at the sky like he realizes he don't. I think, ma'am, if you'll pardon me, that the young man has problems."

"Lyle has no problems, sir. What are yours?"

With that, she left.

Lyle, seeing her outside through the classroom window, walked out to join her. She welcomed him beside her. My God, when had he grown so tall, become so mature?

As they passed a music shop, Lyle paused to look at a guitar in the window, displayed alone, like something special.

A car that had been parked a short distance away drove alongside them, slowly. Sylvia stared at the driver's side. Lyle followed her look. But the sun's glare on the windshield did not allow him to see what had turned Sylvia's face livid.

She grabbed Lyle's hand and hurried him away.

10

Lyle's education is taken over by a firm authority.

That evening, when Lyle was not present, Sylvia told Clarita about the encounter with the assistant principal.

"Ha! Lyle's too smart to listen to the tripe they teach him at that Protestant school," Clarita said. She refused to correct her reference although Sylvia had told her he was not going to a "Protestant school," that she misheard "public school."

"I couldn't be more certain of it myself." Sylvia held up her sip of liquor to toast their conclusion.

"I will be his teacher," Clarita toasted back. "I have a diploma, I am a graduate."

11

Clarita upholds em-pa-thy for the down-trotten.

When they began his lessons, Clarita would frequently remind Lyle about her cherished diploma earned years ago. She had kept her grammar textbook and dictionary from that time and used it to guide Lyle. "I could have been a teacher," she often said wistfully, "but—" She would stop there, with a long sigh. Lyle suspected that something in the past had interfered with her goal. Often she would follow her sigh with a wistful: "Ah, such is life!"

She would write out his lessons in careful phrases, sauntering inconspicuously every now and again to her dictionary and casually flipping through the pages to find an exact word. If Lyle caught her—and at times he would pretend not to, at other times he would playfully let her know he'd seen her—she would claim she had been "dusting this large book." During those times, and often making her discoveries at random—or searching through until she found a word that touched her—she added impressive words to her vocabulary. "Empathy" became her favorite. She would always separate its syllables, to cherish it a bit longer. "Em-pa-thy." "You must always have em-pa-thy for the down-trotten," she said to Lyle after two visits to the dictionary, locating herself against a window so that her raised chin, in profile, would indicate the nobility of her feelings.

He knew she wanted him to ask. "What is em-pa-thy?"

"Why, everyone knows that. I'm surprised by your question," she pretended to scold. "Em-path-y is when you know what people feel when they're hurt, try to feel like them, and that's how you know why they do what they do. You understand?"

"Yes," Lyle said. "Yes, I really do." Would that allow him to know what hurt Sylvia so deeply? he wondered.

12

Lyle's extended education.

In temporary agreement that soon would become permanent, Clarita remained at home, taking care of the house while Sylvia continued to work at the perfume counter.

Clarita allotted at least one hour a day to teach Lyle about matters that were far beyond the stupid grasp of his classes at school.

He listened attentively.

About science: "Everybody knows the earth is round, but nobody knows why."

"Do you?"

"Of course."

"Why?"

"That's your first assignment. . . . In life there are always two sides, the good side and the bad side—on the bad side are the *cabrones*—"

"*Cabrones*," Lyle added a word to his vocabulary. "The sons of bitches, like my father?"

"Yes." Why should she adjust what had already been established?

She taught him about Pancho Villa, Porfirio Diaz, and about all the confusion at a place called the Alamo: "There were *cabrones* on both sides, and no one won."

"That's not what—" Lyle started.

"I know that's not what they teach you, and that's why I'm your teacher." She added sagely, "What happened is what you think happened—and what needs to happen, that's all."

Lyle nestled his head against her shoulder, enjoying the sweet scent she sprayed herself with after each day's bath.

She resumed her lessons: "Rivers always flow into the ocean because that's what they flowed out of in the first place, and everything always returns."

"Even to Rio Escondido?"

"No. That will always be hidden. Mystery should remain, it's a part of *la vida*." She hardly paused before she jumped to another lesson: "And don't ever, ever talk to strangers." She had introduced her admonition about strangers years ago, but now that Lyle was the handsomest fourteen-year-old she had ever seen, she emphasized it often.

"Why not?"

"Because."

"Oh."

13

Time passes, obscuring Clarita's warning.

"Hey, kid!"

Lyle had, again, wandered away from school, just stood up during arithmetic and walked out as if someone was calling to him. The stringy teacher's mouth flew open and stayed open, her sentence chopped right at the point where she had begun to explain that if you kept multiplying and multiplying you'd never, never reach the end and if you kept going back and back you'd never reach the beginning. A dark-haired girl—beautiful, beautiful, Lyle thought every time he saw her, which was often since he would prop his chin on his elbows and stare at her—stood up as if to leave with him—he would encourage her with a sideways nod of his head; but, by then recovered from Lyle's easy walking out, the teacher snapped her fingers as if to bring the girl out of what must have been a contagious trance. The girl sat back down, watching wistfully as Lyle disappeared.

Lyle sat in a vacant lot, where wild desert flowers grew, puffy buds that crumbled when you touched them but that survived the wind. A short building that had once stood there had been torn down to make room for something else that never went up. There remained only the props of what it would have been, blocks of concrete, wire twisting out of them like veins, boards, some cans with hardened white paint, one left there with a stiffened brush.

"Kid! Hey, kid!"

Lyle turned to see a man standing there.

The man was dark-complected, in his thirties, good-looking, not tall, with gleaming white teeth. He was dressed in casual clothes, with a jacket.

"How old are you, kid?"

"Fifteen."

The man squatted beside him, not too close. "Fifteen, huh?" He mumbled to himself, "I was hoping you were younger." He was about to sit down next to Lyle, against the unfinished wall, but, brushing the seat of his pants as if he had already sat down and regretted it, he remained squatting, looking around fretfully.

"Are you a Catholic, kid?" the man asked.

Lyle wasn't anything, although sometimes his mother took him to the pretty Catholic church, where he sat with her while she stared wistfully at the saints around her. He supposed they went there because Clarita was always insisting that he, and his mother, should become "real Catholics." Now he answered, "I'm not sure."

"You go to church?"

"Sometimes."

"You think the saints are pretty, the women saints, I mean?"

"Yeah—they look like movie stars."

"Oh, my God!" the man said, and slapped his forehead. He said abruptly, "You sure are fair under that tan, aren't you?"

"It's not a tan, that's my color."

"No." The man shook his head. "What color are your eyes?"

Lyle opened them, wide.

"Damn! You got brown eyes, I was hopin' for blue. How old you say?"

"Fifteen."

"Pretty big for a kid fifteen, huh? I got a daughter, about that age. But it's not the same—a girl, ya know? You mind standing up?"

Lyle did. Although the questions were very odd, they seemed terribly important to the man, who was so nervous about them.

"You're tall, too, already taller than me!" The man measured himself against Lyle. "Gee, kid, you're sure good-lookin'. Like me. Hmmm. . . . Your mamma—she's got brown eyes, your color?"

"No—they're green. . . . Why are ya askin' me all those questions?" Lyle took a firm posture, boots apart. He wasn't about to hear this man talking about his mother even if she didn't want him to call her that.

"Just asking," the man said, moving away hurriedly. He turned back. "Don't tell anybody about me talking to you, okay?"

14

A startling revelation.

"Armando!" Clarita said. "It was that *cabrón* Armando trying to determine if you're his son."

Laughing as he recalled the questions, Lyle had just told Clarita that a very inquisitive man had asked him a lot of odd questions. "Am I?"

Lyle wanted to catch up on what he was feeling, confusion, conflicts, sadness, exhilaration.

"Absolutely not," Clarita said. "You are the cowboy's son, and everything about you verifies that." She glanced up and down at the tall, handsome boy with dark hair and the boots he cherished. Cherished because Sylvia had first bought them for him? Very likely. Now that he replaced them himself when necessary, did he cherish them because they asserted a connection to the missing cowboy? "Everything, including—" She peered into his eyes. "—Sylvia's brown eyes."

"Sylvia has beautiful green eyes," Lyle corrected her, "with yellow dots."

Of course, and she knew it, had forgotten it, conveniently, only for that strange moment. Lyle the First had brown eyes. No, Sylvia had doted on his blue eyes. Clarita adjusted nervously, "I believe Sylvia's green eyes are tinged with brown, not yellow. *That's* where you got the color of yours." Lord, did that *cabrón* Armando have brown eyes?

CHAPTER FOUR

1

Why Lyle Clemens did not become a "geek."

y certain cruel definitions of his peers, Lyle would have been a "geek"—an outcast, the odd one, the one who didn't go out for sports, who didn't "hang out," and was considered "weird." At times he would simply start running after school and disappear, or so it seemed, in a second.

"Where'd he go?" someone might ask.

Shrugs were the only answer.

He *would* have been a "geek" except for this powerful factor: He was so handsome and sexy that girls giggled and nudged each other when he appeared, looking back at him, smiling flirtatiously; some ran away squealing as if in grave danger of succumbing to him. Their boyfriends could not easily taunt him, because of his appearance, leanly muscular, tall, agile.

He did not court popularity, did not care what anyone said about him. Still, he was "popular" in a unique way. Boys his age, the ones who were not popular and were, themselves, considered "geeks," lingered about him because they saw in him a hero, their king, someone like them who was not exposed to the harassing they were objects of. Even some of the more popular boys seemed at times to be courting his friendship, although cautiously and perhaps mainly because their girlfriends were infatuated with him and some of his aura might transfer to them—and also because he had the nerve to walk out on classes at school, the way they might want to but didn't.

Only giggles resulted now from his sudden exits as if he was invisible, always with a smile, as if someone was calling to him from the vacated field he went to in order to think and figure out life. Still, the beautiful girl who indicated intending to follow him had not done so, even though he paused next to her on the way out recently and would have bent to kiss her—the urge was so powerful it seemed to come beyond his volition. He *would* have kissed her, except that at that moment he stumbled, taking a step forward to recover, and so resuming that direction out.

Often in his field, he recalled the strange man Clarita had identified as "Armando." He had kept the matter from his mother, just as Clarita had instructed, because, she had said, "Telling her about that other son of a bitch will only make her sadder, and she's sad enough already."

Why? Why was Sylvia sadder each day? When she was drinking, she'd turn giggly for sporadic moments, as if long-withheld happiness was bubbling over, and then instantly she turned moody, angry, sullen when her moods were challenged.

"You can't understand, Lyle," she told him when she caught him staring at her during one of her dark moods. In a whisper he barely heard, she said, "Don't even hope."

Don't even hope? Had she meant that he shouldn't ever hope to understand her? Or had her sadness reached the point where she was telling him that she had stopped hoping?

Increasingly, he came to feel that it was within his capacity—if he could only know how—to change Sylvia's life, to edge it away from her sadness.

2

The unique nature of amoebas, according to Miss Stowe.

A young teacher arrived as a substitute to teach the high school students biology. Miss Stowe wore a tomato-red sweater-dress that hugged her assertive breasts and curvy hips. That made Lyle keep blinking, to focus more closely on them. She had introduced the racy subject of procreation, beginning with something called amoebas that reproduced by simply splitting apart.

"They don't have no father?" a freckled boy asked forlornly.

"Naw," said another, a burly boy who would be fat in less than a year, perhaps by next week, and whose girlfriend had earlier given him some gum, which he chewed relentlessly between words, "that's—chew— why they—chew, chew—call them bastards."

"Now—" Miss Stowe attempted to steer back to amoebas.

The burly boy forged ahead. "That makes Lyle an amoeba—"

Lyle shook his head, to brush away words that had intruded on his concentration on the substitute teacher's tight-fitting sweater—the dark-haired girl was not in that class to draw his attention. At the same time—and he could do this, easily—he had been listening attentively and learning all about amoebas.

"—'cause he doesn't have a father, either."

Lyle stood up, smiling. "I do have a father, and he's a goddamned son of a bitch."

Titters, laughter.

"Just that," said Miss Stowe, "would make a lot of children bastards, including—" She was about to point to the burly boy, but she caught herself. "Let's restore order to the class," she admonished, "so that we may—"

Not satisfied because Lyle had brushed away his insult and that his girlfriend with braces was now moonily eyeing Lyle, the burly boy pointed to a girl who was usually alone, a sad girl about to burst into tears at any moment. "She's a bastard, too, an amoeba, because she doesn't have a father, either, like Lyle."

The girl ran out of the room crying.

The bell ending the period sounded, and the students scrambled away. The burly boy lingered in the hall, chuckling at his own cleverness,

looking around to see whether any of his new fans had stayed to cheer
him on.

That was when Lyle would begin to think that his hands and his legs
had a mind of their own. In the hall, while he remained smiling, his legs
took two strides toward the burly boy. His hands grabbed him by the
shoulders and, still smiling as if he was about to introduce himself, he
shook him and shook him and shook him, and then with a shove, sent
the boy reeling against his locker. The burly boy remained there,
scrunched, shocked, looking at Lyle, who was still smiling as if they had
just become friends, except that his hands prepared to grab the boy again.

"Lyle! Don't you dare!" Miss Stowe was there.

Lyle welcomed the opportunity to be closer to her, at least to glimpse
more closely the curves the sweater was hugging.

The burly boy pretended to swagger away—"Damn!" he muttered
when he tripped and fell; he didn't bother to brush his clothes, streaked
with chalk that had fallen to the floor at one time or another and that
other students had crushed into white powder.

"I'm not going to report this," Miss Stowe said, sounding stern, "and
I think he's too humiliated to report it himself." Her lips puckered,
and she closed her eyes.

Was this happening? It sure was. Responding the way his hands had
earlier, his head bent down on its own volition and his lips moved toward her. Before he knew it, his mouth was pressed against Miss Stowe's
in a quick kiss; maybe the one he had intended sharing with the beautiful dark-haired girl had stayed there waiting.

When the kiss ended, Miss Stowe's head remained tilted as if in expectation of another kiss, which Lyle eagerly supplied.

3

A discovery in the vacant lot.

In his lot—he had begun to think of it as his own—Lyle found a guitar
someone had abandoned there. He plucked a string, a sweet twang.
When he had it adjusted at a musical shop in Rio Escondido, he would
write a song and sing it to himself, in his lot.

The man at the shop said the guitar wasn't in bad shape at all. "Won't
take much to fix it. Then you'll be able to play it again."

"I don't know how to play it," Lyle said.

"This'll help you," the man said, and sold Lyle a booklet: "Learning How to Play the Guitar on Your Own." Lyle was glad to pay with his own money—he made a big show of taking it out of his wallet to emphasize that fact, now that he had a job after school in the warehouse of a stationery store.

After he picked up the adjusted guitar—"I made the notes nicer for ya," the man said, "specialty of mine, sweet notes"—Lyle took it with him to his lot, along with the booklet he had bought. He learned easily. He began to compose his first song:

If you ain't got a father but you got a beautiful mamma—

He revised: ". . . but you got a beautiful Sylvia."

"Where did you get that?" Sylvia questioned him when he returned home with the guitar.

"I went back to that shop and bought it," Lyle told her so she wouldn't be reminded that he continued to walk out of the classroom.

4

Lyle's unique popularity is rewarded; Sylvia Love responds.
A prophetic warning from Clarita.

His odd popularity at school baffled Lyle, especially on the morning when all the upper grades were called into the school auditorium—which had the flags of Texas and the United States crisscrossed evenly on its stage—for "announcements." Today's assembly was to reveal who had been nominated for school offices. This was done by "secret ballot," individual students having gathered petitions. The principal read off the names of the nominees.

"—and Lyle Clemens."

"What?"

"You've been nominated to run for president of the school," said the principal, a fat man who had greeted the announcement of each candidate with exuberant clapping to show his impartiality.

"What?"

"I said, you've been nominated—"

Lyle looked around for some clue as to what had occurred. The very pretty dark-haired girl he often stared at lowered her head as if to show that his glances turned her bashful. Girls near her nudged her. She had radiant olive skin, eyes the color of toasted almonds.

"I don't know why, but I'm running for president of the school," Lyle told Sylvia and Clarita.

"You *must* win," Sylvia greeted the news as if it was inevitable. Her look cautioned Clarita not to interfere.

Clarita closed her eyes, courting a vision. "He'll win," she predicted. "Easily." She opened her eyes. "But watch what *you* do," she told Sylvia.

Sylvia bought poster paper, crayons, water colors, poster paints, markers, scissors. She placed all those on the dining room table that Clarita had decorated with artificial flowers. Posters were essential in Lyle's campaign, posters that couldn't be ignored.

"Perhaps the flag of Mexico and the United States, crossed?" Clarita offered.

"Ordinary," Sylvia rejected.

Lyle listened, every now and then plucking a chord on the guitar he kept in his locker at school and carried home with him. When either Clarita or Sylvia made a point he agreed with, he would pluck a lovely sound—if he disagreed, he would make a protesting twang. Now he sang:

> *If ya wanna win at somethin', you gotta care deep,*
> *and me, I tellya, I don't even know what I'm runnin' for—"*

"That's an awful song, Lyle," Sylvia protested, "but you sing it really nice."

"Perhaps a suggestion of the Holy Mother—?" Clarita offered. "Just a ghostly outline, like the one that appeared to me in the hills of Chihuahua."

Lyle made a sweet note, for Clarita and the Holy Mother.

"Well—" Sylvia remembered the glamorous woman she still went to visit at the Catholic church. "It sounds good. But I'm not sure—" She stood up, placed her hands on her hips, and moistened her lips, posing for a few moments. "His poster has to yank the attention of everyone, everyone! He *has* to win."

Clarita marveled at the fact that, for the first time in her recent memory, Sylvia was missing some of her "bracing nips."

Armed with her arsenal of supplies, she withdrew to her own room—
she had always been good at drawing—and she went about preparing
the poster from which others would be copied and that would assure
Lyle's victory.

"VOTE FOR LYLE CLEMENS!" Lyle read aloud from Sylvia's poster she
was unveiling. Almost at the same time, he gasped, "Wow!"

On the poster was a drawing of a beautiful young woman in a bathing suit.

Did Sylvia realize she had drawn herself? *Jesucristo,* keep us from
disaster! Clarita prayed.

5

The eye of the beholder.

"Those posters have to come down," Mr. Bean told Lyle, summoned to
his office.

"Why?" He had proudly had them copied, and the boys that followed
him around had put them up all over the school.

"They're dirty," the tight-lipped man managed to squeeze out of his
lips, "the drawing of this woman is disgusting!"

He couldn't finish his sentence because Lyle's fist popped him on the
side of his cheek—not on the mouth, and not hard, just enough to stand
up for Sylvia's drawing.

Mr. Bean was so humiliated he didn't report the incident.

Lyle didn't know what to tell Sylvia. He consulted Clarita.

"You punched the *cabrón?*"

"Yes."

"Good. But now we don't want to hurt Sylvia." She thought: The
last thing she needs is to imagine that she lost again. "The posters have
to come down?"

"He took them down himself," Lyle told her.

"We'll tell her—I know! We'll tell her that the figure she drew was
so beautiful that in the middle of the night the posters were stolen by
admiring boys."

"Can you blame them?" she asked Sylvia when she told her that later.

Sylvia smiled. "But Lyle—?"

"He'll win anyway, because the posters already had their impact."

Lyle didn't win, despite the best efforts of the beautiful girl's friends and the boys who saw Lyle as their hero. Lyle did nothing to support his candidacy, he didn't care at all and had never even wondered what he'd do if he won. The only thing that bothered him—other than that Sylvia's posters had been criticized—was that, on meeting the pretty girl he was sure now had been behind his nomination, she looked very sad before she managed her prettiest smile—and then she ran away to her friends, pretending to faint at whatever rush of emotion had over-come her.

By that evening, the joy of having her pictures stolen had faded, and Sylvia turned darkly moody. "We lost."

6

About love, hate, and desire, and the invisible
demarcation that separates them.

The more Sylvia Love came to hate Lyle Clemens the First, the more she realized how deeply she loved him. That confusion occurred because what she hated him most for was taking away what he had brought to her.

The feeling of being desired, appreciated—and loved. He could not have pretended any of it. There had been ample manifestations. The way he made love to every part of her had made her tingle with life. His words!—the way, he augmented their lovemaking by speaking it all aloud. His joyous laughter! A cherished, banished laughter that echoed when she woke each morning, cherished laughter that faded when she reached out next to her, and there was—

No one.

Never mind! She was proud of this: If anything, she was prettier now than ever. Certainly she could attract someone else who would love her even more. There was an army base in the outskirts of Rio Escondido, the only town available to recruits after a brief bus ride. On weekends, young soldiers roamed the streets, usually ending up at a certain popu-lar bar. Sylvia liked to walk past it, welcomed the laughter and music spilling out into the placidity of Rio Escondido. Of course she wouldn't go in. Still, she welcomed the expressions of admiration; often some soldiers came out to see her walk by. At times she allowed herself a flirtatious look back, letting her skirt whip up just a bit in her Miss America walk. Perhaps she could be attracted to one of those good-looking men. Once, she even paused to be approached—allowing one to introduce himself, and that was that.

At work, she discussed perfumes with men who wandered over to her counter at the Fashion Store with no intention of buying a perfume. She told herself she might allow something more, dinner, yes; why not? But she turned down invitations. She would even, at times, imagine herself with another man—that one handsome soldier, say, imagined herself with him, naked on white sheets—her body on display for him to anticipate, one leg over the other, yes, and his body tanned except for the line where he would have been wearing army shorts as he did his duties, and their bodies pressing—when, then, she would imagine that, beginning to succeed in considering a possibility, the memory of Lyle Clemens the First would shove everything aside as brashly as he had shoved into her life, obliterating even the fantasy of another man.

The thought of the act she had allowed with Armando recurred with a sense of desolation. There was no question in her mind—none at all, none, she told herself—that her son was Lyle the First's. Every day he became a younger version of him.

Once, she heard Lyle's laughter before she had entirely wakened, and she had thought, Lyle the First is back!

Never! She never allowed herself to expect that man to return, never, never, never. Even if he came back—She felt her heart flutter. Even then, she would reject him.

Those thoughts led her to take a few extra swallows of her liquor, alone, no longer allowing Clarita into her solitary moments.

7

A declaration of undying love.

"Where do you think *you're* going, young lady!" said the general science teacher when the pretty young woman with cascades of dark wavy hair was walking out of his class after Lyle. This was the farthest she had gone in her attempt to join him, having been halted by the arrogant teacher during several earlier attempts.

This day as Lyle moved toward his destination, the abandoned field
—after stopping to get his guitar from his locker—the pretty girl
caught up with him. He turned to face her.

He shook his head, reeling at the sight of her, so close, alone with
him. Her slightly dark-hued skin was framed by a corona of black hair
that gleamed naturally. Her body was—Lyle had to twist one leg over
the other—and almost stumbled when his boots tangled—to conceal
the fact that he might become aroused. Did his cock have a life of its
own, like his fists?

The girl lowered her eyes as if bashful, and then looking up at him
as if she had managed to overcome her shyness, she said, "My name is
Maria, and I love you with all my heart and soul, and I will love you
forever."

Then why the hell did she run away? Lyle wondered.

8

Unwelcome news, quiet plotting.

"She's a beauty, all right, and she's Mexican, like me," Clarita informed
Sylvia.

"Who are you babbling about?" Sylvia felt an immediate pang of
anger, not at Clarita but at whomever she was talking about. She had
heard the spoken words, had only pretended not to.

"A young girl, Lyle's age, *mujer.* When I went for the groceries late the
other day, I saw him walking along with her. Not really with her. He
was walking backwards, looking at her as if he didn't want to miss a
glimpse of her. She was staring up at him—she's somewhat short—as if
she couldn't believe how handsome he is—and he is, you know. *Ay!* If I
had known him when I turned beautiful after I stumbled in Chihuahua."

Sylvia turned up the television, to interrupt Clarita's news. She didn't
succeed.

"I wouldn't be surprised if, soon—"

Sylvia raised the television even more.

"Are you losing your hearing, or are you angry because someone other
than you is pretty?"

Sylvia raised the television higher, drowning further words.

Clarita knew she'd heard everything and was plotting . . . something.

9

A mysterious confrontation.

Boldly, Sylvia walked up to the soldier—he wasn't in uniform but she had seen him at the bar—who had twice driven by her house and parked at the time she usually came home from work; today he had got out of his car. He was handsome, blond, tanned, with a crooked smile.

Probably, a corporal, Clarita conjectured as she spied them through her window, keeping the curtains discreetly close so she would not be seen. Now what was Sylvia saying to him?

"I've seen you loitering around my house," Sylvia said to the soldier.

"I'm sorry if I've bothered you. It's just that," the soldier said, "I saw you once—and—the first time—I thought, wow, that woman's got it all over any Miss America!"

"What?"

"I said, you got it all over any Miss America. Another time when I was with my buddies, one of them said you even walked like Miss America. You could be!"

"Oh—" Sylvia closed her eyes, remembering. "My name's Sylvia Love Clemens."

"My name's Tristram Jones," the soldier said.

"That's a funny name."

"I know, everyone says so, but it's my name, really."

She thought he was about to salute, to verify his name.

"There's a new restaurant I heard about, I haven't been there. It's called the Lamplighter, it's supposed to be the best. They even require reservations. You think—?"

Sylvia was no longer listening. Lyle the Second was walking toward her, just as she had known he would be, at this time, coming home from his job.

"I'm sorry," Sylvia said to the soldier, "but—another time?"

"When? Soon?" He waited for her answer.

She withheld it until Lyle had almost reached them. Then she shook her head, No. Lyle approached—smiling.

Smiling! Hadn't he seen her with that good-looking soldier?

CHAPTER FIVE

1

Lyle's nature is further manifested.

"I am sorry to tell you, ma'am," Mr. Bean was pleased to have another opportunity to inform Sylvia Love of her son's transgressions, "that Lyle was seen trying to kiss a girl in the classroom."

Sylvia refused to show her anger. "Did the girl run away from him? Are his grades suffering?"

"No, ma'am, either way. He manages all those A's." He shook his head in bafflement. "And! He's announced he won't take driver's education because he likes to walk and run."

"He does," Sylvia said flatly.

Mr. Bean released the next words as if he was firing a bullets at her: "He stole from another child!"

"He did not!" Sylvia was about to walk out.

"Hold your horses. You ask him yourself, ma'am. He's outside. Send Lyle in," he called through the door to a mousy secretary, who had sniffed jealously at Sylvia, as if her sweet perfume—which she dabbed on when she left the counter at work each afternoon to disguise her midday "nip"—had displeased her.

There stood Lyle, smiling at his mother. She stood next to him, to indicate that she was unshaken by the accusation. "Lyle, this man dared to tell me that you stole—"

"I did," Lyle said.

"—from another student," Sylvia had not heard his admission.

"I did steal." Lyle touched her, to bring her attention to his words.

"No, you didn't!" Sylvia refused. She knew Lyle too well to accept that, that he had attempted to kiss a girl—probably the one Clarita had told her about—that wasn't difficult to believe; he was Lyle the First's son. She could deal with that in another way, another time.

"I did. I stole from that piggy guy who called me an amoeba once—"

"—a what?"

"—an amoeba, because they don't have fathers, and I don't either."

Sylvia held her breath. She would not reveal her sadness to this terrifying assistant principal and the mousy woman, who was also in the room, hoping things would go wrong.

"He brings lots of food, and he places it next to him during lunch, on a bench, showing it off—he gobbles most of it, but sometimes he throws some of it away, and I just walked up and took a couple of sandwiches from him—" Lyle was explaining easily.

"See?" Mr. Bean was triumphant. "He's a thief!"

The mousy secretary made an attempt at a clucking sound, which sounded more like the click-click of dentures.

"—and I gave them to that kid who brings only a piece of bread to eat, and he hides so no one will know, and I kept thinking how awful it would feel to go hungry like that. I felt a lot of em-pa-thy—"

"What!" The mousy woman was taken aback by the unexpected word.

"Em-path-y for the down-trotten," Lyle repeated, knowing Clarita would approve, "and I gave him the sandwiches."

Sylvia smiled, welcoming Lyle's act. She faced the distressed assistant principal and the mousy woman, who reeled back as if she thought Sylvia might assault her. "You see! Lyle did not steal. He did an act of goodness. *I* gave him my permission to do it when he consulted me."

Halfway to the door, she turned back, addressed the man and the woman, "I'm assuming that you will remedy the situation of the hungry boy now that you know about it so that Lyle won't have to provide another act of misunderstood kindness."

Bristling, the assistant principal reminded her: "He keeps walking out!"

Sylvia halted. "Walking out?"

Outside, she said to Lyle, "Now what the hell makes you think you can walk out just like that, and kiss whoever the hell you want, Lyle Clemens?"

Lyle didn't answer because it had seemed to him that she hadn't really expected him to.

As they proceeded home, he heard a distant but loud commotion. Sylvia did, too. She stopped, listening. A cacophony of voices—shouts, shrieks, noisy singing—was coming from—

The Pentecostal Hall.

It was again the time of the seasonal Gathering of Souls.

2

A command from beyond the grave?

What am I holding in my hand? Sylvia Love wondered, as she stared down at the harsh-black object.

When had she gotten up from her favorite chair? When had she opened the door to the closet where she had thrust everything that belonged to Eulah Love? When had she rummaged through those old boxes?—scattered on the floor where she had pushed them in and closed the door on them? When had she done all that, to find this horrifying thing in her hands, to find—

Eulah's black Bible.

Within the same daze that had sent her searching for this terrible book in her hand, she opened it, to a place Eulah had marked, with a piece of sturdy cardboard stuck between the pages. She saw highlighted words:

"And on her forehead was the name written, Whore—"

She shut the book, pushed it back with all the boxes into the closet.

When had it turned so goddamned hot?

Why was she clinging to it again, clutching Eulah's Bible and waiting for Lyle to come home from his job?

What am I doing? That sudden clarity came to her when she saw that Clarita was watching her intently and she realized she had spoken words aloud—"waiting for Lyle to come home."

She dropped the Bible.

Clarita picked it up. Was it possible that Sylvia had been preparing to go to that thing they called the Gathering of Souls—and to take Lyle with her?

Sylvia inhaled and shook her head as if in answer to Clarita's silent question, No, she would not go there.

But, Clarita thought with apprehension, the evangelists would be back again in six months.

3

On the perils of not being a geek.

Among the malicious boys who marveled at the fact that someone who otherwise would have been tortured as a "geek" could make their own girls drool over him, there was one who was lying in wait for Lyle. Spud was planning to humiliate him by knocking the shit out of him in front of everyone, and then the geek would be shoved off his pedestal. The conniving young man was nicknamed Spud because his face, his friends said, looked like one—with blemishes that never disappeared, only multiplied. Still, he was hefty, a tackle on the football team, and so he was popular.

He met up with Lyle when Lyle was doing his daily pushups in the playing field, apart from the others.

"Hey!" Spud called out. His friends gathered, including the one Lyle had shaken outside the classroom. Spud's girl was there, too, with others, several of whom had expressed the opinion that Lyle was not only "gorgeous" but cute as well. A few of the girls upheld that he was conceited, though he was not. They thought that only because that allowed them to dismiss why he might not be interested in them.

Lyle stood up, wiping with his shirt the perspiration the 250 pushups had inspired. "Hi," he greeted Spud, whom he felt sorry for because he knew it hurt him to have such a blemished face. "Whatya up to?"

"This!" Spud aimed his fist at Lyle's jaw.

Lyle fell back. Everything went pitch-black, and then he saw glittery flashing stars. He shook his head, his vision clearing. "Wow!" he said to Spud, who stood over him, inviting catcalls aimed at Lyle from his friends, including the girls who thought Lyle was conceited. "Wow, that really hurt." Lyle rubbed his jaw, shook his head. "Hey, how'dya do that?" He stood up.

Was the guy really so fuckin' dumb he was asking him how he'd managed to knock him down?—and giving him another chance to show how tough he was before the others. "Look, stupid," he said, "you hold your fist like this."

Lyle did.

"Not like that, stupid," Spud corrected, basking in the laughter he was inciting.

"Like this?" Lyle asked.

"Tighter at the thumb, dumbo, don't you know nothing?" Spud said, and demonstrated with his hand, aimed menacingly at Lyle.

"You mean like *this*?" Lyle's fist shot out at Spud's jaw. Spud toppled to the ground.

Lyle looked down at him, waited until Spud, too, had shaken away glittery stars and was rubbing his own jaw. "Thanks for the tips," Lyle said as Spud got up, saying only, "Shee-it."

"Ooooh, my God," a girl squealed, "he's so strong—and so kind—and he's *so* cute!"

Wait a minute, wait just a fuckin' second! What the fuck was going on?

That's what Tim—"ole Tim," his cohorts called him, in buddy-camaraderie—thought as he ambled onto the scene and saw his friend Spud wiping away dust from his ass where that fuckin' geek had just knocked him down. Ole Tim was a hefty wrestler who lifted weights and thought he would be Mr. America although he was flabby.

That son of a bitch Lyle was too fuckin' smart-ass for a geek—and, goddammit, he *was* a geek. But why the hell weren't the girls laughing at him? The geek was odd, right?—took some guys' lunches to give to geeky Mexicans who hung around him like he was king geek, with those boots and cowboy hat. How was it that a geek—a fuckin' *geek*—could get the best grades when he didn't listen to anyone? Smart-ass geek!—punching out Spud and shaking that other guy. Odd? Shit, he carried that guitar with him to that vacant lot and sat there serenading himself.

"I say you're a goddamned geek," ole Tim stood right in front of Lyle and shouted.

"Yeah, *geek!*" Spud's courage resurged. Shit, the geek had taken him by surprise earlier, that's all. Shit.

"Yeah?" Lyle said to ole Tim, vaguely because—look!—the beautiful dark-haired girl Maria was suddenly there with her girlfriends.

"Don't you like sports, geek?" Ole Tim touched the large REV on his jersey—Rio Escondido Varsity.

"Maybe sometimes," Lyle said. The day was warm, the warmth felt good on his skin, especially since he had opened his shirt wide over his chest. He blinked up at the sun, not wanting any interruption from this wrestler during these pleasant moments. Besides, he was aware that Maria had sidled closer to him; he'd like to bask in the warmth with her.

"Not knowing if you like sports makes you a geek," ole Tim said.

"It sure does," Spud joined in, and his pals approved.

"Geeks don't look like *him!*" A fluttery girl pointed to Lyle.

Among those who had gathered was a somewhat small Mexican boy with thick, long dark eyelashes. He followed Lyle around quietly all the time, trying to imitate him—trying to strut like him, even though he had to stand on tiptoes since Lyle towered over him. "He ain't no geek, man," the Mexican kid, Raul, said. "You're the geek 'cause you're jealous of him 'cause you're so damn ugly."

Maria giggled in approval, punching at the small boy playfully, an ally.

"What the fuck's the matter with you, squirt?" ole Tim demanded of Raul. "I'll take care of you later, creep-shit."

"The little fag called you ugly, man, you gonna let 'im get away with that?" Spud encouraged ole Tim. He looked around to recruit several team guys, including the burly guy Lyle had shaken in the hallway.

"Yeah, fag, that's what you are, a faggot, that's why you hang around the geek all the time," the red-faced wrestler said to Raul.

Raul winced and looked away, shuffling his shoes on the dirt.

Encouraged by the fact that Lyle was still smiling as if he wanted to placate this incident, ole Tim pushed on: "Maybe you're *both* faggots." He consulted his comrades. They elbowed their approval echoing him, aiming at Lyle: "Are ya?" . . . "Are ya a fag?" . . . "Hey, fag!"

"Maybe——" Lyle had not been listening. His cock had fluttered when Maria lowered her blouse and blew between her breasts, cooling herself.

"Goddamn! Are you admitting you're a fuckin' fag?" the boy Lyle had shaken crowed. "You *are* a fag."

"So?" Lyle said, surrendering to the pleasure of being aroused, especially now that Maria had tilted her head and a portion of her blouse had slipped slightly over her shoulder.

"You gonna let 'im get away with that, Lyle?——calling us both fags?" the kid Raul demanded of his hero.

"What do you want me to do?" Lyle asked him, earnestly, for his opinion. He liked the Mexican kid. Although they'd never spoken, he'd noticed him trailing him, trying to become friends, and then dashing off.

"Punch him out," Raul said.

"Okay." Lyle's fist moved forward and punched. Ole Tim reeled back, collapsing on all his weight. Three of his buddies, joined now boldly by Spud, advanced on Lyle.

"Cowards!" Maria threw herself in their path, one hand on her throat as if to still a scream of anguish. "You'll have to go past me first."

"What the hell?" Ole Tim was genuinely baffled as he turned to consult the others now standing with him.

"Yeah, what the hell?" one of his friends echoed.

Maria cried out, "Take one more step, you cowards, and I shall——I shall——" Not knowing what to threaten, she spread her hands out, extending the protected territory to include Raul.

Lyle bent down and helped the pudgy wrestler up and assisted him in rubbing the dirt off his jersey.

"You're still a fag, fag!" ole Tim shouted at him.

"Hit him again, Lyle!" Raul coaxed.

Lyle's fist did. Ole Tim reeled back again.

The four buddies stared at Lyle, then at Maria, and then at each other, puzzled. Rush Lyle?——past the bitch with her arms outstretched like that? Shove her aside? Fuck, man, this was getting too geeky. So they just said, "Shee-it," and spat on the ground.

Lyle sauntered along. He turned back, waved at Raul——who was dashing away——and he waited for Maria to catch up with him.

Shaking her head as if to shed a decision she must nevertheless make, she ran away. Again!

Why was everyone wanting to punch him out and everyone else running away from him?

4

A lesson well learned.

Clarita got to thinking: Lyle needs to be taught what a father would teach him—she had just earlier noticed a bruise on his face—but he has no father. So—

"Today, I'm going to teach you how to fight—but only to defend yourself, *only* then."

Lyle rubbed the bruise under his eye. "I already know how to fight," he said.

"Oh? Who taught you?" Clarita felt a twitch of jealousy.

"A guy named Spud." He smiled, not at the memory of Spud punching him out and being punched out but at the memory of Maria standing real close to him.

"All right. Show me!" Clarita demanded. She did not know how to go about it, but she assumed a position she had seen on a television series, her feet somewhat apart, her hands, gathered into fists, flailing about as if she was swatting flies, her large earrings bobbing.

"Clarita, stop, you look silly!" Lyle threw himself on the floor, twisting with laughter.

Clarita assumed her usual dignified demeanor, arranging her hair carefully, secure in the knowledge that Lyle was capable of learning some things on his own. She moved on to another lesson: "Now sit up and listen: Television is nothing but a telephone with pictures."

5

The call of duty.

There was a woman named Rose who had lived for several years in Rio Escondido—some said for "at least twenty years," in order to add to her age, which was forty; she was one of those whom time seems to indulge longer than it indulges others. She was, by all accounts, a very attractive woman, if not beautiful. But, oh, she was sexy, had a full, lush body that had survived as an object of desire even when fashions decreed otherwise. She had black hair—well, it wasn't quite as dark as it had been once, and so she helped its color a little—and her skin was white, creamy white. She kept it that way with Noxzema moisturizer and Olay night cream. To celebrate the endurance of her desirability, and to assert her name, she almost always wore, in season, a fresh rose in her hair. In winter, she wore a felt rose. She often laughed a rich, full-bodied laughter.

She had lived in Dallas, and God knew where else, because she was reputed to have been, and who knew whether today she still was, a "whore," according to some women in the City. That rumor was not true. But this was: At certain stages of her life, she had accepted presents, and those had included presents of money—"donations," she called them; but she had never made her favors contingent on being paid. She brought up the subject of a "donation" casually, to be picked up or not. She might say, "Those bills pile up before you've had a chance to pay last month's." She heard rumors about herself and was not upset, sometimes they pleased her if they made her sound scandalous. She lived in a small house in a neighborhood that was neither good nor bad, "at the edge of everything," she would have described it.

A man had brought her here on their way to be married somewhere, and he had left her in a motel. One place was as good as another. Besides, she liked the name of the city; it had a sense of mystery— "Hidden River"—and God knows that Rose appreciated mystery, because she was a very soulful woman who responded always to a sense of duty.

Lyle often passed her house on his way to work. What a splendid young man! she had marveled to herself, trying to gauge his age. Young people grew up so quickly, and he was already a man—look at him. She had noticed one pretty girl, especially her, going out of her way to cross his path. I wonder if she's a virgin? she thought, and concluded, Yes, of course she is.

She wondered all that wistfully, remembering the young man who had lost his virginity with her—and had taken hers, clumsily, painfully, in St. Louis, mauling her, groping himself. When he was through, he had shoved her away. He screamed when he saw that she had, naturally, bled, and accused her of having somehow done that to herself. He had demanded that she tell no one what had happened, saying he regretted it all, and that—in some mysterious way—she had hurt *him,* right here—he clutched his groin. "That's what I'll say, that you're a liar!" he shouted at her before he ran out. She had thought, I wish he'd known what he was doing so it would have felt good instead of terrible.

Now, in Rio Escondido, Rose stood at the window, waiting. This was the usual time that the fascinating young cowboy walked by. Look! There he was, on his way to his job. How to save that pretty young girl from the kind of awkwardness she herself had first experienced?—and, from what she saw in glimpses of them on the street, the threat would be occurring soon if, as she had come firmly to suspect, he, too, was a virgin.

Duty was calling her, and she would heed that call.

6

Out of the sad decline of Sylvia Love,
a question about amazing grace.

Eventually Sylvia made not even the most cursory attempts to hide her drinking from Clarita. She pushed the bottle under the cushion of the sofa only when she heard the door and knew it was Lyle. Even then, she didn't make much effort to conceal it if she had not managed entirely on the first attempt.

There were days, and they increased, when she fell into terrible dark moods. At work, she would sometimes walk away from customers who were sniffing perfumes. If it was a weekend, she might remain in her room with her bottle. She smoked so much that Clarita had to light some incense about the house to banish the odor.

Sylvia was aware that often Lyle stood outside her room, listening. She could tell his footsteps, easily. She tried to muffle her crying, but the thought that he was out there worrying about her made her sadder, and she couldn't stop her tears.

Lyle would remain outside his mother's door, listening to her sorrow. He wouldn't knock, although he longed to assuage her. He knew she was drinking, but he didn't want to let her know he knew. He would listen outside her door, trying to draw out her pain, into him.

She began appearing—he didn't notice this until it had progressed far because it occurred gradually—began appearing in increasingly staid

clothes, plain, darkening colors. Whereas, before, she had worn tight
clothes that revealed her still-formidable figure, now she wore clothes
that concealed it. It was as if she was slowly sinking into a state of
mourning. For what? About what?

"Why does she cry so much? Why is she always so sad?"

Clarita was cooking some flavorful chicken rich with red and green
peppers, one of Sylvia's favorite dishes, to lure her to eat.

"Because of my goddamned son-of-a-bitch father," Lyle said. "But
there's much more, isn't there, Clarita?"

Clarita tried to shoo his questions away by indicating that he was
interrupting her cooking. She would not break her promise to her beloved Sylvia.

"Have you noticed that sometimes she seems to be brushing something awful off her body? Why?" Lyle asked.

Clarita shook her head. She had noticed that, and dismissed it as a
nervous gesture. That was all it was.

"What's the name of the song she hums?" Lyle asked. "She used to
hum it to me. She hums it when she's alone now."

Clarita's eyes grew misty. That song meant more to Sylvia than even
she, Clarita, understood. "It's called 'Amazing Grace.'"

"What does 'amazing grace' mean?" Lyle asked.

"That's your lesson." She would consult a priest later to get an official answer. Now she needed to move away from the subject of Sylvia's
moods. She said: "I hear *you* singing in your room and playing your
guitar, so sweetly; you deserve to learn a beautiful Mexican song, It's
called 'Las Mañanitas.'" She stood very stiffly, a commanding teacher.
"The song refers to the songs King David serenaded women with.
Mexican men sing it now to pretty ladies, on their birthdays; they sing
it at dawn, at their windows. Now you sing the words while I pronounce
them."

Lyle learned to sing "Las Mañanitas" in Spanish and learned what
the words meant in English:

> *These are the morning songs that King David sang;*
> *To beautiful girls, he would sing them like this. . . .*

Humming, warmed by the romance of the song, Clarita leaned back,
becoming the pretty lady at her window.

7

What is strange?

"You're so strange sometimes, Lyle." Maria said to Lyle. She added quickly, "but I don't mind because, as you must have noticed, I'm strange, too, in a wonderful way, like you, don't you think so, Lyle?—that I'm *very* strange?"

They were walking toward Lyle's field, taking short steps there, to extend the anticipation of being together. Today, she had easily gotten up with him, to leave class—and the teacher just sighed and gave up.

To indicate how strange she was, Maria looked up at the sky—bursting with giant cumulus clouds like bolls of fresh-picked cotton. She assumed a rapt look, as is expecting a distant call that only she would be able to hear, perhaps share with Lyle, strange one to strange one—the latter possible sharing conveyed when she transferred her eyes onto him, the rapt look holding.

"Was it strange of me, Lyle, not to follow you, yesterday—or the day before—isn't time strange?—was it strange that I didn't follow you when you clearly wanted me to and I had defended your life with my sacred body against those bullies? Was it, was it?"

"Yes," Lyle knew he should agree.

"You want to know why I didn't follow you?"

"Because you're strange?" Lyle asked.

"Yes!"

He studied her, to locate their mutual strangeness. He didn't feel strange.

"Oh, I don't know," Maria pretended Lyle had asked her what she had wanted him to ask. "Why do *you* think I'm strange? Because of how I look—?" She waited for him to remark.

"You're beautiful," he said.

"I know. That's strange, isn't it? Because not everybody is beautiful—or handsome, like you. I think about that a lot, you know, it's so mysterious, isn't it?" As if overwhelmed by the mystery of things, she paused to look up, up. A bird sliced across the windy blue sky. "Oh, my God," she trilled. "A bird, at this exact moment! Imagine!—*at this very moment a bird flew across the sky!*"

"Wow!" Lyle said, although he had no idea what was strange about a bird in the sky.

They walked toward the unfinished wall where he often sat in the abandoned lot.

There, they faced each other, his guitar slung over his shoulder.

"Your body——" He couldn't find words. He outlined her form, without touching her, the curves, his hands drawing the shape of her hips, as if he was caressing them without touching her, though in his imagination he was, touching her warm flesh, his hands resting on her breasts, his mouth kissing——

"And yours——" she said. She couldn't find words. He was so handsome, so sexy, so different from anyone else, so marvelously strange, so wonderfully strange, like her! She raised her hands, to outline the length of him, while he continued to shape her with motions. When they both lowered their hands, slowly, Maria laughed, shy and bold at the same time.

Lyle imagined they *had* made love, although they hadn't touched, not yet—just shaped each other's bodies, desiring, imagining——

"Goddamn!" Lyle said in appreciation.

"Goddamn!" she echoed him.

They sat together, among the now-aging pieces of the uncompleted building. Tiny buds of flowers sprinkled the patches of brave grass. He bent over and kissed her, a long, eagerly accepted kiss.

"Will you sing to me?"

He strummed a few chords, a few more, making up a song for her, just for Maria the Strange One.

> *If you looked any more beautiful than you do*
> *—and were even stranger, then . . . then—*

"Dammit!" He plucked a dissonant note, to accentuate his frustration at not finding the exact word.

"That was beautiful," Maria said, leaning her head against his.

He held her face, and kissed her again, eagerly, and she responded just as eagerly.

"This is so romantic," she said. "Will you sing me the Amazing song?"

Sylvia's song? How did she know about that? He messed up his hair, as if that would help him decide what to do. He was crazy about this beautiful girl, God knew. But that song—

"Will you?"

"How did you know about it?"

"Clarita—you know?—isn't she marvelously strange?—I run into her now and then and she told me you were asking her about that song that your mother loves so much. She said she thought you were practicing it in secret."

He wasn't. That song belonged to Sylvia.

Maria leaned back, closed her eyes. "Sing it for me, Lyle, make it special for me."

Goddamn she was beautiful, so beautiful he had to gasp. His desire pushed against his pants, and he rubbed his legs to welcome it. Goddamn where had he gotten all this horniness? Not that he minded. . . . Oh, that flesh of hers!—light brown—and her breasts!—not large but round and full and perfect, and he longed to lean over and—

"The special song, please, Lyle." Her eyes remained closed.

Lyle sat upright. He fumbled with the guitar.

"Don't you love me?"

"I do, I do. But—"

"Lyle?"

Maria stood up. "You won't sing the special song for me?"

Lyle shook his head, No.

Maria got up, ran from him, pausing, with a smothered but loud cry, to throw up her hands toward heaven to indicate her despair at having her loving request turned down. She waited, sobbing loudly, before disappearing.

8

A definition of where love is and isn't, according to Rose.
A lesson well taught, well learned.

It's entirely possible—quite probable, perhaps certain—that Lyle inherited Lyle the First's lustiness, without having known the cowboy, or anything about him. Perhaps a gene—a sex gene, or many—flowed, or overflowed, from one to the other within Sylvia. How else to account for the fact that Lyle detected the possibility of sex almost as if it were a vapor he breathed, like the time Miss Stowe had, perhaps without even knowing it herself, invited him to kiss her. He longed to lose his virginity, longed to lose it several times, if possible—and that was possible only in his fantasies. In his daydreams, he lost it with Maria, who gave him hers.

He was ready, for sure, when, walking to work, he saw a woman he had seen before about town—and, sometimes, thrillingly, sitting on her porch—an older woman who was goddamned sexy. There she was now, standing in front of her porch, one hand on her hip, which was ample enough, and a blouse that exhibited her breasts, which were more than ample.

"Hey, cowboy!" she called.

He tilted his hat at her. "Hey yourself, ma'am. Oh, and, uh, I'm not a cowboy, I've never even been on a horse—"

Rose didn't hear his protestation. Her heart had sunk when he called her ma'am! But only for a second because when duty calls, there are always obstacles, and she knew that. "Come over here, I wanna ask you something," she said.

He welcomed this opportunity to come closer to her. He inhaled deeply because he could smell the rose in her hair, and it added to the sensuality of the moment.

It was there, all right, desire, Rose knew. In fact! She glanced down between his legs. In fact! "Got time for a cup of coffee?" What a dreadful line. But what else?

Lyle looked toward his destination, the stationery warehouse. He went there early because in the shift before him there was an old man who often had a backache. Lyle would know when it was bothering him by the way he planted his hand on his back. He would then relieve him early. Now he told himself that yesterday the man had seemed all right, and so there wasn't any reason to think that his back problem had flared up overnight. So—

"What about it, cowboy?" Why was he hesitating? Rose's smile held, despite a tinge of apprehension. Had she lost this opportunity to help the young girl he was courting?—an opportunity which, of course, would help him, too, making him worthy of her prized virginity. "Well, cowboy?"

"Ma'am, I'm not a cowboy, I've never been on a horse. Yes, I could do with a cup of coffee." He didn't like coffee, and he didn't like liquor because he associated it with sadness, Sylvia's sadness.

"Come on in." She gave a nod of her head that displayed her luxuriant hair. Her duty was progressing.

No coffee, no. Just water. He didn't ask for his favorite, iced tea with a wedge of lime, because that might take time to make, and he just knew that time should not be squandered now, not with the urgent itch he was feeling.

"You a virgin?"

"Uh . . ."

"Oh, come on, nothing wrong with that. Everyone is at one time or another. I was. Are you?"

"Yes, ma'am." He hoped he hadn't blushed; he did feel a certain warmth on his face, or was he confusing the source of the warmth? This woman, so near him, was—Wow!

"Wanna stay like that?"

"No, ma'am, but there's a girl, Maria—"

"Very pretty, too. I've seen her. She deserves you."

"Thank you." Maybe she did deserve him, but she was still sulking after the incident in the vacant lot.

"Deserves you to be experienced, not clumsy, not awkward."

He understood what she was suggesting; she had emphasized it with a smart heft of her breasts. Still, he felt he had to say, "You mean—?"

"I do for a fact, cowboy. Women's virginity—girls' virginity—that's special, they give it over only once, whereas men—" She shook her head, the rose remained within the cascade of waves.

He wondered how he could lose his virginity more than once. However that could be, it seemed promising.

"When men take a girl's precious virginity, that should be a special time for her, and if it's clumsy, it turns all wrong." She spoke from memory, and for a moment her voice quivered. Then it was husky again. "How can that be avoided?"

"I guess—"

She wasn't going to risk a wrong answer. "With experience, that's how. You don't wanna hurt that pretty girl, do you?"

"Hurt Maria? Never!"

"Then you owe it to her to lose your own before you take hers."

Lyle kept sniffing at the rose perfume on her; it seemed to come from between her breasts, wafting the air every time she breathed. He shook his head. "I'd feel . . . unfaithful." He was disappointed to have to say that, disappointed to feel it.

"Unfaithful!" Rose stood before him. "Unfaithful isn't *here*—" She placed a hand almost on his groin, held it away, pointed with a finger. "That's not where infidelity is. Unfaithful is *here*—" She touched her heart. "That's the only place where infidelity occurs, and that's the only place where love endures." It was true, she knew it. Many men had made love to her; she had loved only one. "So, cowboy?"

He nodded. What she had said made sense. In his fantasies, he sometimes did something wrong during a sex encounter, wondered where his legs would be in relation to hers when . . . The position would shift in his mind, and, sometimes, limbs would tangle. Too, there was this important consideration. His cock was about to bust right out of his pants, that's how horny he was feeling. He straightened out his legs, to conceal from her what was happening—he felt suddenly shy—but that only increased the fact of the situation.

Her hand fluttered down to touch him there. "Oh, Lord," she said. "Oh, yes, Lord," she said.

So Rose taught Lyle how to make love to a virgin, patiently, carefully, lovingly—and passionately, sighing through it all.

When the lesson—several lessons—were over, Lyle dressed, feeling exhilarated while Rose lay in bed with a robe on, the rose still miraculously in her hair, although slightly askew—there had been a lot of motion, a lot.

Lyle knew that he would be rehearsing, in his mind, all that he had learned, all this wonderful woman had taught him. He felt terrific, ready for Maria, to do justice to her now, to her virginity. He kissed Rose, the way she had taught him. Was what he felt now love? If love made you feel this great, yes! "Thank you, Rose," he said. "Thank you a lot."

"Goodbye, cowboy," Rose said, feeling sad because her duty was over.

9

Can King David's serenade withstand the passage of time?

Sylvia shook herself awake. What was that singing? It was hardly dawn. She stumbled to the window.

From her own room, Clarita looked out. How beautiful, how beautiful—on Sylvia's birthday!

Lyle was outside, under Sylvia's window, with his guitar, singing:

Estás son las mañanitas, que cantava el rey David—
A las muchachas bonitas se las cantava el así—

Lyle was serenading her! Sylvia leaned out of her window, arranging her hair to look her prettiest for—

When had she rushed away from the window? Yesterday? Today? The day before? What was that sound in her throat? What was this moisture on her face? Who sobbed so hideously? When had she reached for another sleeping pill to swallow with the bottle she kept next to her? Oh, but everything was fine now. She felt the world before her grow light. Then the lightness became an increasing heaviness that seemed to be pulling her down, down into a pit of darkness. Was she asleep? The darkness pulled lower, darker.

"Sylvia! Sylvia!"

Lyle was trying to rouse her, calling her name, and Clarita was slapping at her wrists, as if to waken her. Where was she? On the floor, yes. But why?

She had stumbled, Lyle had run to her, Clarita had joined him.

Sylvia opened her eyes, looked at Lyle. Her vision blurred, and then memory settled it.

"You came back, you son of a bitch," she slurred.

CHAPTER SIX

1

The mystery of a grain of sand.
A painful confession.

A grain of sand, raised by a whip of sudden Texas wind, made its way into Lyle's eye as he sat alone in his lot, considering life's mysteries. He blinked several times, the grain smarting. That grain of sand had probably roamed the world—perhaps the universe—for centuries, maybe once aroused by a caveman chasing or being chased by a saber-toothed tiger, and it had floated on, and been stirred up by a flood that swept it over the land and spilled into the ocean, tossing it with a million others onto a beach, where feet had trampled on it—bare feet—and it had clung, and the feet, now wearing shoes—or boots—had trudged on across continents, maybe onto a boat—or a horse—and then it was shed among other grains of dust and someone sneezed and roused it, sneezed again, and sent it on its way—Lyle shortened the journey—into his eye! Damn!

Amazed, he went on to ponder the intricacies of a tiny purple flower sprouting on . . . a *weed*!—a sputter of beauty, within which a golden stem popped out, growing there, unseen by anyone if he hadn't come along and sat at this exact place today.

If only life could be that clear! What a mistake he'd made on Sylvia's birthday, to serenade her, to try to lift her deepening moods. That had only stirred her anger in a way that added to his bafflement about her, especially since, after that, she alternately dismissed it ("I was just over-whelmed, that's all," she dismissed), or pretended not to remember the incident at all ("except that you sang so sweetly"); had her memory been so blurred by that day's liquor and pills that she actually forgot most of it? But if—

Then Raul was there, in the lot—he had walked back and forth before deciding to approach Lyle in the lot. "Hello, Lyle," he said, without facing him.

"Hi, Raul." He was glad his thoughts about Sylvia were interrupted.

"You know my name?" Raul was delirious.

"Yeah, sure," Lyle said—he liked to remember people's names. The kid—cute kid—was shy now, although he had been aggressive during the fight.

"I wanna thank you for punching out that bully the other day. He and his friends used to call me shitty names all the time, and shove me around, and that's stopped. . . . If they'da done that to you, what would you've done?" he asked gravely.

"I guess," Lyle pondered it, "I'd've told them to stop it."

"Stop it? Man, they're bullies. You wouldn't kick ass?"

"If they didn't stop it," Lyle extended, "then I think, yeah, I'd kick ass. If they hadn't stopped messing with you, I'd do the same, if you didn't."

Raul beamed. "Lyle, you're really strange."

Oh, no, not from him, too!

"What I mean is that with your looks—you are really good-looking, you know?—with your looks, shit, you could be the biggest bully in the City."

"Wouldn't want to be," Lyle said.

"What makes you strange is that you look one way and act another, like you feel for other people, like with that kid you give sandwiches to. I guess you got a lot of empathy, huh?"

Clarita's word must be spreading; she'd probably been using it a lot around town. He supposed that was what he felt; it pleased him that Clarita would approve—and you sure might consider this kid "downtrotten," with those bullies doing bad stuff on him. Lyle had a feeling about this kid, that he was stronger than he thought he was.

"Uh——" Raul was clearly uncomfortable. "You mind if I ask you a real personal question?"

Weird, Lyle thought. How did he know whether he'd mind before he heard the question? He answered, "No," to find out.

"Are you a bastard?"

"Yes," Lyle answered. "My goddamned son-of-a-bitch father just disappeared. Did yours?"

"I'm a bastard twice. I don't have a father and I don't have a mother and they're not dead. I have an aunt, who can't stand me."

That was really sad, Lyle thought, no mother, no father, a mean aunt. At least, he had a mother, who loved him, never mind that she didn't want him to call her that.

Raul sat down when Lyle moved over to make room for him on the weathered step he was sitting on.

Raul gasped, "Can I tell you a secret?"

"Oh, sure. We got a lot in common."

Raul was very serious. "You know what those guys called us—I mean, me—I mean, you know, Lyle?"

Lyle had forgotten the name they had called him and Raul. Bastards? But he didn't want to reduce the gravity of what the kid was preparing to say, and he was clearly trying to string difficult words together, not succeeding. He seemed about to speak, instead wiped his lips, finally expelled more words:

"It's true, about me. I'm——" He paused, shook his head.

"You're what?" Lyle encouraged. He suspected what the kid was about to say, and he wanted to make it easy for him.

"I think . . . Well, I know . . . Yeah, I'm gay."

Lyle looked at the kid's pained look, half expectation, half apprehension. He wondered what to say. "Yeah?"

"You don't care?"

Lyle shook his head and smiled wider.

"Really?"

"Really."

"And Lyle—"

"Yeah, Raul?"

"—a lot of times, I imagine what it would be like—please don't be mad at me, but I have to say it, because I keep rehearsing it—a lot of times I imagine what it would be like, you know, to . . . kiss you—" He shot up and braced his feet firmly, preparing to run away. He winced, as if he was already being pushed away, even hit. He managed to say, "I'm sorry, I shouldn't've said that, I—"

"Why not?"

"My God! You're not mad?"

"No."

"You understand what I told you?"

"Sure, yeah, I do."

"I mean—" Then Raul ran away.

Damn! Someone else running away from him after calling him strange and telling him how much they liked him.

After that, Raul avoided Lyle, dodging away along the hall. That saddened Lyle because he preferred that they be friends. It saddened him even more deeply that the kid no longer tried to imitate him as he walked along, that he walked as if he was trying to hide from others, but mostly himself.

2

A fierce rivalry stirs in Rio Escondido.

"You're still very beautiful, I've seen you at a distance but never this close, but that's not why I'm here. I'm here to tell you that I'm not going to give Lyle up," Maria said to a startled Sylvia Love on her porch.

"Who the hell do you think you are, yelling for me to come out?" Sylvia paled with anger at the sight of the pretty dark-haired girl before her.

"I didn't yell. I called out because nobody was answering the door when I rang and knocked, and I saw you looking out the window."

Clarita, who had been the one peering out the window, as she often did, and had recognized the girl but decided it was best not to answer her, thought aloud, "Why am I such a blabbermouth?" Earlier, alone, she had felt a chill that augured something—or someone—moving in a dangerous direction.

"Whoever you are, you move your feet because you're stepping on the vine I've spent a hell of a lot of time cultivating," Sylvia ordered the girl—thank God that today she had decided to pretty herself up. Of course she recognized the girl from Clarita's description. She had to admit she was pretty—well, somewhat pretty. Beyond her control, she felt a pang of admiration for her, so defiant, a reminder of herself, before—before so much had happened. In acknowledgment of that memory, a smile fluttered on her lips.

"I just want to be fair in all this," Maria persisted. "I know that Lyle loves you a lot—so much that he won't sing your song to me—"

"What song?"

"That Amazing song."

"Amazing Grace!" Sylvia's heart warmed. Lyle knew she cherished that song, although she had never heard him sing it. She would have hummed the melody, right now, if it wasn't that the girl was rushing on.

"—and he should love you," Maria was enunciating her words carefully. "We should all love our mothers, but they shouldn't interfere with our love lives. Why shouldn't Lyle sing me a song just because you love it?"

Clarita began a series of promises to the Holy Mother Guadalupe: "If you allow this to end without violence, I will say twelve novenas in your honor, I will light twelve candles for the souls in Purgatory."

"Who are you?" Sylvia pretended bafflement.

"My name is Maria. I love Lyle, and he loves me, and it is entirely possible that, very soon, we will become intimate, whether you like it or not—and I'll make sure he sings me your song!"

Sylvia's anger surged; it *was* her song, the song she had sung to Lyle, that he had listened to so attentively, the song that had silenced all the beauty contestants into attention when she'd sung it. How dare this girl think she could take away her song, replace her in Lyle's affection! Whatever vagrant admiration she had felt for this girl's reckless audacity vanished. "You get the fuck away from my house—now!" she demanded. It had been a long time since she had used Lyle the First's favorite word, which sometimes he said when he was making love and sometimes he said when he was angry at someone, never at her. She was glad she had reserved the angry word for this occasion.

"Consider yourself warned," Maria said, and moved away, her dignity intact.

3

A warning justified. Rose is heard from again.

There she came, Maria, probably delayed by one of the teachers who had attempted to stop her from joining Lyle in his lot, where he spent more and more time moodily practicing on his guitar and composing songs in his mind. She looked so beautiful that he knew he had to do something to express his feelings before he even talked to her. He stood up and applauded as she approached.

She laughed joyously at his greeting. She clapped back, welcoming the sight of him. She ran up to him. He grasped her by her tiny waist, raised her, and spun her about.

"Oh, I forgive you for what happened the last time we were here, I forgive you, I forgive you, because I want to make love to you, wonderful love, delicious love, memorable love, passionate love," she gasped.

"And I want to make love to you," Lyle said, still whirling her around, and grateful that she hadn't added "strange love."

She managed to release herself from his spinning, but she held both his hands close to her. She pressed her body against his, and looked up at him with eager eyes, one leg bent, the way she had seen so often on television. She understood why that happened, though, it was as if a part of her body was electrified with anticipation.

"Let's." He brushed her face with his lips, as if he was redrawing her face on her, the way he saw her, the way she was.

"We shouldn't." She cocked her head so that his lips would touch hers, just the edges.

"Why?" He kissed her on the lips, wanting to open his mouth on hers, pry hers open with his tongue. Oh, thank God for Rose. *God bless you, sweet Rose, terrific Rose.* Now he would know what to do.

"Why shouldn't we? Because we're not married, and I'm a Catholic. But, oh, oh, Lyle, how I wish to break those sacred sacraments, for you, for you, oh, oh!" She opened her mouth, greeting his tongue, which darted in and then quickly out. "But we would be committing a grave sin, my beloved," she breathed huskily.

"I'll marry you and become a Catholic." He pressed his lips on hers, keeping them open. Their tongues touched, in dabs. This felt even better than with Rose—no, it was different, not better, Rose would always occupy a special place in his heart. What was different with Rose was that she had been guiding him—well, most of the time. Now he would be on his own. He faltered, a tinge of apprehension piercing desire. He heard Rose's voice, *Not too fast, just hold your lips there, and now your tongue*—When Rose had pushed her tongue into his startled mouth, he thought he would explode, and was glad he didn't, because he pushed his back into hers right away, and thought, again, he would explode.

"I can't wait. I'm a progressive woman. You don't have to become a Catholic first. Let's make love now." Maria said.

"Here?" He didn't care who saw, because this was beautiful, and wonderful.

"No, in my house. My mother's at work, my father doesn't live with us most of the time—and so, oh, oh, Lyle, we shall sin together!"

They went to her house, attractive house, in a good neighborhood, two stories, with a garden.

Lyle followed her up the stairs.

She stood looking down at her bed. "This is so wonderfully strange!" she gasped. "Isn't it, Lyle, isn't it?"

"Yes!" he answered emphatically and quickly, to hurry other things along. He did. He lifted her, kissed her, and, responding to memories without antecedent, images of what this would be like, rehearsals elicited from yearnings, all falling into place, naturally, logically—but, no, no, no, no, that wasn't so, he was responding to Rose's guidance—he eased her back in her bed. He stood back, studying her. "My God, oh, my God," he said. He wanted to touch her, but he didn't want to move in a way that would thwart his full view of her, fully, fully, as she lay in her bed. *Delight in it all*, Rose reminded, *cherish the anticipation, look, watch, and let her see you.*

Maria cocked her head. Her black hair kissed one side of her face. She parted her lips, and she crossed her legs, as if to emphasize what she covered. One hand touched one of her breasts, and the other reached out toward him, inviting him.

He came closer. "Oh, my God, my God!"

"Oh, my God," she echoed him this time. "This is wonderful, wonderful, terrific, oh, my God."

He leaned over her and started to raise her skirt. (*Whoa, whoa, not that yet, leave it for a little later.*) He parted her blouse. He stared at what he had revealed, beautiful breasts, perfect flesh, not large like Rose's. (*Don't be disappointed if you don't see better ones than mine.*) But they were perfect. The pink nipples strained to be kissed. She slowed him with her hands. Had Rose instructed her, too? Of course not. Her fingers roamed over his shirt, pulling carefully but urgently at the buttons, letting her fingers discover his flesh.

Lyle inhaled, and touched each of her nipples with one finger, once, then both, again, with another finger—(*stay there, cowboy, and let her hands explore, let my hands explore*)—to connect the sensation, try to grasp the enormity of all this. (*There's nothing like it, cowboy, nothing.*)

She touched his chest, the light brushing of hair there.

He lowered her skirt, slowly, slowly, to enhance the expectation. (*Increase the longing, cowboy, touch here, touch there, and then you'll be touched there and here, too—just like I'm touching you, oh, my, yes.*) He was about to erupt with desire and love, burst, burst—(*What a shame that would be— too soon, too soon!*) Now his body pressed against hers, both still half-dressed. His cock assumed its own urgency, pushing out of his pants. (*Hold on, cowboy, we're just beginning.*)

"Oh," Maria said, "look at that. I always wondered what it would look like. Oh, look at that. Lyle! Is every man's *that* big?"

"I don't know," he said. It was true, he didn't. (*Lordee, cowboy boy, lordee, you've been blessed!*) At school when they took a shower after physical activities, he never joined the other young men snapping towels at each other's butts, and he hadn't thought much about it when one of them, looking down at him, said, "Jesus Christ!" So he said to Maria, "But I'm sure not every woman's body is as beautiful as yours." (*Thank you, cowboy, for saying that, my body's not as good as it was once but it's still damn good.*) Without removing his lips from her, he pulled off her skirt. He got up and placed it carefully on the carpet. He returned to her body— which was there for him, as his was there for her. (*Remember: Share and share alike, do unto others as you would have them do unto you.*) Slowly, slowly, slowly, he pulled down her panties—and stood up, to look at her, to look at this most wondrous spectacle of her, naked. (*Really something, isn't it, cowboy? God's gift, isn't it? Look here, see this? That's what it's all about, finally, getting in there—and now look there, at yours, that's what goes in it; basic as that, cowboy. Of course you know that, just wanted to emphasize for you. Excite the senses, excite anticipation. Yeah, like that. No, no, stay back a little. Yeah. Okay, okay, come ahead. Whoa, cowboy, don't ride too fast, you're gonna spoil it for yourself, and for me and her.)*

He shook his head and laughed deliriously with pleasure, laughter bubbling with longing and yearning.

"It's so wonderful," she said, "even before—"

He leaned over her. He blew his breath between her legs, arousing the delicate puff there, then touching it. (*Hey, cowboy, who taught you that? I didn't. Do it some more, and now bring your lanky body over here so I can do it back to you. That's the whole thing of it, see? You and me, me and you. For now we're the whole world.*)

"Let me, too," Maria said, and she put her hand on his cock, letting her fingers circle it, travel from its tip—it was slightly moist!—to his balls. "Oh, my God!" she said. "Oh, my God!"

He kissed her, and then his lips traveled down to her breasts. "Oh, you are beautiful," he said to them, "so soft yet firm, and your nipples are so wonderful, and, look, my hands are touching them." (*Don't know where you learned that, cowboy, but it's good, talk along, doubles the sensation. . . . Let me talk for a while, okay? Got your big rod in my hand, gonna rub it up and down.*)

"My hands are touching you, there—" Maria cupped his balls, lightly, "and, oh, oh, how strange and wonderful. Please, Lyle, do something more. I don't know what. Please, please do something more, anything!"

He stopped his movements, waiting. (*Pretend you don't know what's next, and then surprise me. Yeah! Like that!*) He straddled her carefully, parting her legs—and she parted them herself—and he put his cock at her opening, just the opening, and remained there, rubbing around, around. (*Stay there, stay here, anticipate, make it know that's where it belongs. Soon you're gonna feel my sweet honey kissing your cock, let her feel your cock sweetening her honey.*)

"That's where it belongs," Maria spoke aloud, "and it's going to go into me and pull in and pull out, and I'm so excited, and I feel the head of it right against my parting—"

"—and my cock is pushing in—"

"—gently, gently—" (*Make her feel it inch by inch, and that way you can feel it inch by inch, and, cowboy, you gotta lot of inches to make feel. . . . Gently, but gradually deeper, and then not quite as gently.*)

"There, it's in, just the head of it—" (*Not yet like that, slow, slow. Otherwise you'll ruin it. Then you won't be able to ride me like a cowboy. . . . I told you, ma'am—uh, uh—that I'm not a cowboy, never rode—uh, uh—a horse. . . . Doesn't matter-um-mmmmmm—you know how to ride-um, cowboy. Riiide! Whoa! Yippee-yah!*)

"Hold it there, please, just there, a little more, Lyle, so I can feel it— oh, my God, oh, Jesus, oh, oh—"

"Now more of it is in. It feels like nothing else in the world, it feels like—like—like nothing else in the world—" (*That's a fact, cowboy, and when you do it again, it'll feel even better, thanks to me—maybe not better, but different.*)

Thank you, oh, thank you, Rose!

"—like nothing else except when you put it in more—"

"—more, more—"

"—all the way in now, yes—" (*Now ride, ride, mount, mount, colt, stallion, go, go, up, down, up—down, down, down, deep!*) He stopped, she had winced. (*I just winced to prepare you, that might happen, pause till I signal.*) She smiled, nodding that it was all right, and he pressed again, into her.

"I'm inside you, and our naked bodies are pressed against each other, as close as they can be. No, not yet, I'll pull out and then pull in, inside you—"

"—inside me. Now kiss me, and raise yourself at the same time, and kiss me—"

"I'm pulling it out, and back in, and kissing your lips—" (*Don't need any more teachin', cowboy, you sure as hell got the gist of it!*)

"Lyle!" Again, she had turned away in pain, but now she faced him with beautiful eyes full of yearning, and—

"Maria!"

"Lyle!"

"I love you! In—in—in—!"

"I love you! More, Lyle, more, mo—"

"Ohhhhhh!"

"Oh, oh, oh!"

He burst inside her, her body contracted—once, twice, again!—their lips together.

She closed her eyes as he eased off her. He lay back. "Wait," she whispered to him. She stood and disappeared.

He sat up, waiting for her.

"I bled," she said.

"Maria! No!" He stood up, to get help, to—

She laughed. "It always happens, the first time." She eased him back down beside her.

"You're sure you don't hurt?" (*Might bleed a little—I don't, see, because I'm broken in, but, cowboy, you made me feel like a virgin again, God love you for it.*)

"I'm sure," she told him. They lay back together on the bed.

"I love you, Maria."

"I love you, Lyle. I shall always love you, until I die."

"Me, too," Lyle said, not knowing what else to add to her declaration.

4

An odd connection, and a loving acknowledgment.

Before her mother would arrive, Lyle walked down the stairs with Maria—kissing her each few steps. He saw on a table in the living room a photograph of a man.

"That's my father, most of the time he lives in another city," Maria said, following his gaze.

Lyle moved closer to the photograph. The man looked familiar. Very familiar. Who was he?

Outside, Lyle went out of his way to walk past Rose's porch. There she was, resplendent with her red rose. She smiled and waved in a way that convinced him that she knew that he had just followed her expert instructions and that in his mind he had included her.

To assert that, he blew her a spectacular kiss, which she returned, a kiss just as spectacular.

5

A startling possibility?

"He's after me, he says he's going to kill me!" the distraught girl screamed at Clarita.

It was late afternoon. Clarita had been napping, her daily siesta, but she sprang into action to save this young girl from the perils of Pancho Villa, who was again on his rampages to pluck away the pretty girls.

"Come with me, and I'll hide you in the hills!" Clarita almost toppled over the porch. Where had this odd porch come from? Where were the hills? Where was she? Oh, about to save this young girl—

"The hills? There aren't any hills in Rio Escondido, Clarita. Just hide me inside your house," said Maria.

Oh, it was that beautiful girl she had run into once or twice, and talked to, the girl who was so enamored of Lyle, the girl to whom she had told more than she wanted to, even about the song Sylvia cherished. No, she wasn't back in Chihuahua. "Who's chasing you?"

"My father! Lyle forgot his shorts, and my mother found them and told my father, and he asked me if what he suspected was true and if so with whom—and, of course, I couldn't lie. I said, 'Yes! With Lyle!'—and he said he was going to do what any decent Mexican-American father would do—kill me, Lyle, and himself. Oh, God, God, God, please help us out of this terribly strange situation!" she entreated Clarita and Heaven.

"I don't think it's that bad, is it?" Clarita had to hold on to a pole on the porch because she had not finished her siesta. She almost slipped sideways and grabbed an unpredictable vine, which dodged her grasp meanly.

It was true that Maria's father was upset. Divorced, he lived in Dallas but he came back now and then to Rio Escondido, mostly to quarrel with his wife, once pretty. She had, as usual, told him that he was a bad father, and as powerful evidence informed him about the shorts.

"I don't see anyone chasing you," Clarita said, squinting in case she had missed the pursuer. How could Lyle forget his shorts? She must make sure he always had fresh ones in his drawer. Certainly it was no surprise that he had become involved with this pretty young woman. The Holy Mother had blessed him amply; she had given him handsome looks, endowed him conspicuously, and, apparently, had given him the power to use all his blessings.

"My father's hiding, crouching in the shadows—ready to spring on me! Let me in, please, please! I *beg* you!"

Clarita couldn't remember whether Sylvia was home. If she was, this girl would be in graver danger with her than with her father, even if he was chasing her with a machete.

Too late. Maria, sobbing loudly, had pushed in. "Where's Lyle? We have to warn him."

"He's working."

Maria was despondent. She had longed for him to see her breathless, running away from anything that threatened their love, running to him, choosing danger over—

"What the hell are you doing here?" Sylvia Love stood like an executioner before the girl.

"My father!"

"I just ran into your father earlier today."

"You know him?"

"Yes."

Clarita clutched for her rosary. Where had she left it? No time to go looking for it. She'd just say her beads on her fingers. But first she had to hear what she knew she would hear:

"Yes, I know your goddamned father!"

"*Armando!*" Clarita breathed before she blacked out, first backing away slowly onto a comfortable sofa.

6

The past catches up with Sylvia Love.

"*Cabrón! Maldecido!*" Sylvia Love Clemens had riffled through her memory of Lyle the First's toughest vocabulary and had, instead, stumbled on Clarita's. "How dare you try to push yourself into my life?" She faced Armando in her living room; she was glad she had braced herself with an emboldening extra nip of her bourbon.

Armando faced her back.

When he had run in, moments earlier, Maria screamed loudly, alerting Sylvia, if her sobs hadn't already alerted her.

Clarita oversaw it all from the hallway, where she had retreated after her unnoticed faint. She had rushed to her room and found her rosary, which seemed now to be a permanent prop in her hands, didn't it?

Lyle—having received the news at the stationery warehouse that his beloved had run screaming through town to his house and that a man was chasing her—rushed there to save her. Now he stood staring at the man who had talked to him in his vacant lot—yes, it was him in the picture!—Clarita lurking in the doorway—as if anyone might miss seeing her there—Sylvia, her face white with rage—and Maria, alternating sighs and sobs until she saw him and ran to him, proclaiming, "I shall die in your arms, my beloved!"

"How dare I push myself into your life?" Armando shoved Sylvia's question back at her. "You pushed yourself into mine, remember? Now I'm here to protect my daughter"—he pointed at Maria—"*and* my son." He pointed at Lyle.

"What!"

"What!"

"What!"

"*Qué?*"

"Yes, my son. I'm his father."

"You are *not*!" Maria was emphatic. "Because that would make us brother and sister!" The full horror of it smacked at her. "Oh, God!"

"Oh, God!" Lyle echoed, and clutched his groin as if to forbid it ever again to transgress.

Sylvia grabbed Armando, shoving him toward Lyle, who backed away from both, causing Maria to grab him, because this gave her the opportunity to hug him.

"Let go of me, let go of me, woman!" Armando demanded of Sylvia. She had pushed him next to Lyle. "Stay there!" she ordered Armando.

"*Ave Maria, madre de Dios*—" Clarita prayed.

"Stand up straight, your full length, Lyle, stand up!" Sylvia said to Lyle, and shoved Armando right up to him. "He's a foot taller than you, squirt!" she pointed out the obvious to Armando.

Clarita prayed aloud now: "*Bendita tu eres*—"

"So what? You're not tall yourself," Armando shot back at Sylvia's comparison of his small stature and Lyle's much taller one. Realizing he had produced evidence he didn't want for these moments, he said, "My father was very, very tall, just like Lyle! Lyle is my son, and you know it. Look at his eyes!"

"Blue!" Sylvia said, but she knew otherwise.

"Brown," Armando upheld, "like mine."

Lyle shut his eyes tightly.

They're brown that sometimes manages to look blue, though God knows how, Clarita thought to herself, and started another decade on the rosary.

Sylvia grabbed Armando's hand and held Lyle's against it. "Brown!" she described Armando's skin.

"White!" she described Lyle's.

"Wrong!" Armando said. "Brown, like mine. Well, not as dark," he had to admit.

"That's a *tan,* you son of a bitch, fucking *cabrón!*" Sylvia used everyone's vocabulary of anger. "Besides, you never knew that my father was brown, did you, did you? I saw him at Eulah's funeral." But she had also seen another man, not brown—white—who had wept.

Lyle's skin is darker than Sylvia's, Clarita evaluated, but not as dark as Armando's. Lyle always looked as if he had a tan, and she thought in elevated moments that that was because God, through the intercession of the Holy Mother, the Sacred Virgin Guadalupe, held a special guiding light over him that tanned him.

Sylvia pointed to Armando's hair. "Dark!" She pointed to Lyle's. "Auburn."

"Brown, and almost as dark as mine," Armando said.

Sylvia groped hard at Armando's groin. "And *this?* Tiny!"

"Ow!" Armando clutched himself.

Clarita had to interrupt the new comparison because the fire she saw in Sylvia's eyes warned her that she would go right up to Lyle and pull out his—"Stop!" Clarita commanded. "You listen to me, Armando. You know there's no way that Lyle could be your son. He's the image of the tall cowboy—"

"That's right," Maria agreed, although she had never seen the tall cowboy, "and he wears boots, too, and a cowboy hat, even when it seems strange." She pushed herself closer into Lyle's body, fitting wonderfully into it. Lyle put his arm around her, holding her close, as if any moment someone might pull her away, easily forgetting the promise he had just made to his groin.

Sylvia seemed to see Lyle and Maria for the first time—close together. Her eyes narrowed, to filter the sight.

Clarita thought, Sylvia is about to do something horrible.

"You know," Sylvia said, placing one hand against her cheek to add thoughtfulness to her measured words. "You know, Armando, maybe you're right, maybe—"

"Sylvia!" Clarita had to stop her. Had she become as crazy as her mother?

Sylvia continued, "Maybe, Armando, it's possible, yes, that you are his father—"

Maria raised her face toward Lyle, and he bent down toward her, about to kiss—

"—and that would make him," Sylvia said to Armando and Maria, "yes, that would make Lyle Maria's brother."

"*Mujer*! Woman!" That's all Clarita could think to say now in protest—as Lyle and Maria eased away from each other.

CHAPTER SEVEN

1

*A confrontation, and a reminder
of what might have been.*

ow could you say such a thing?" Clarita demanded of Sylvia that night when the two were alone.

"What?" Sylvia pretended.

"That Lyle might be Armando's son."

"He might."

Clarita grasped for indignant words. She found only these: "He looks exactly like the cowboy, you've said so yourself."

"He does have brown eyes, though, like Armando—"

"*Loca!* That's what you are. Tell me! Where did Lyle get his height? Not from you—and certainly not from that *baston . . .* that squirt."

"My father"—Sylvia chose the tall man she had seen at Eulah's funeral—"was tall and handsome."

"Lyle is the cowboy's son!" Clarita asserted, and crossed her arms over her bosom, firmly, to emphasize her declaration. "You know that, too." She had begun rehearsing the entreaties she would have to make later to the Holy Mother to yank Sylvia away from this terrible charade.

"Oh, I don't know. I don't know everything—like you, Clara." Sylvia started to walk out of the room. "All I know is that he might be Armando's son. Have you forgotten?"

"No, I have not forgotten all the crazy things you did," Clarita said. "But nothing as crazy as what you're doing now. You don't fool me, Sylvia. You want to come between him and that beautiful girl—"

"Oh, do I? Do I?" Sylvia challenged Clarita with a cool look.

"—and she is beautiful," Clarita extended her accusation, "perhaps as beautiful as you when you were her age, and that too is the reason that you—"

Sylvia turned around, ferocious. "How dare you!"

Clarita could no longer withhold these words. "You have to face that you're never going to be—" She couldn't finish.

"Miss America," Sylvia whispered, so softly she seemed not to have spoken at all. She placed one hand on her hip, held the other out lightly, as if to initiate the royal walk. "I *would* have been Miss America."

Clarita relented. "Yes, I'm sure you would have been."

Sylvia smiled, accepting the words graciously; but then she thought of Eulah, and her curse, and of Lyle the First, who had left her so easily—*who had confirmed the curse of a miserable life!* "Eulah was right," she gasped, "I was sinful, and I'm being punished for it; all I was for the cowboy was flesh to lust after—that's why he could discard me like he did, the way Eulah knew." She frowned, brushing away at something she felt on her shoulders, something clinging there.

"Are you ever going to let that crazy woman leave you in peace?" Clarita wondered. "Are *you* ever going to leave *her*?"

Sylvia Love shook her head in bewilderment.

For days she stayed mostly in her room, coming out in a long robe that concealed her body; she pecked at delicious food that Clarita fixed for her, all her favorites. Clarita would try to coax her appetite by announcing her most delicious delicacies: *Tomatillas, arroz con pollo, empanadas.*

Lyle watched Sylvia as she walked by him like a ghost, touching him on the shoulder, as if to assert that she wasn't a ghost. To Lyle it seemed that way: that she was a ghost of Sylvia Love, of his mother, whom he loved and suffered for, so much, and who was becoming more and more of a mystery to him, the more he longed to understand her.

2

A secret sortie into Sylvia's past yields new questions.

Clarita knew that Sylvia kept papers—perhaps only mementoes—gifts from Lyle the First?—in a wooden box in her bedroom. Clarita was, it must be understood, not a curious woman; she respected people's privacy; she would never have thought of rummaging through that box—
Except that she needed to know!
She pulled out the box. It was not locked, and so what harm was there in looking? She opened it. There was a note from Lyle the First, when had left Sylvia. . . . Within its fold something dusty, umber—the crushed petals of a white rose?
And a newspaper account:

The Alamito Gazette

HOWLER AT MISS ALAMITO BEAUTY PAGEANT!

An enraged woman claiming to be the mother of Sylvia Love, a contestant for the Miss Alamito County Beauty Title, stole the show last night when she rushed onstage brandishing a Bible and then threw a sheet over her daughter during the bathing suit competition. According to others onstage, the contestant's mother shouted a series of curses at her daughter for exposing her body. Miss Love attempted to flee the stage but tripped on the sheet, creating a scene that could have come out of a slapstick comedy and that was greeted with howls of laughter from judges and spectators alike, a hilarious commotion that must have lasted 15 minutes, during which Miss Love continued to struggle with the sheet, stumbling over and over, causing gales of laughter each time, until she managed to leave the stage. According to one judge, Miss Love impressed the panel during the talent competition, when she "sang 'Amazing Grace' very sweetly," and when she said her first wish would be "to banish meanness from the world." According to this judge, right up to the time of the uproarious intrusion, Miss Love was the leading contender for the title that would have taken her to the Miss Texas competition and eventually might have earned her the Miss America title.

There had been more than a chance of Sylvia's winning the title. Oh, the heartbreak of it all! She had kept the vile account because it affirmed that she might have won. . . . Clarita was about to locate the newspaper clipping exactly where it had been, along with the ashes of the rose, when, through her tears, she saw what she was looking for: Lyle's birth certificate.

Footsteps. *Dios mío!* It was Sylvia, coming home early, as if she could not cope with anything other than her sorrow and her anger, and her increasing "nips." Clarita put the birth certificate in her pocket and dashed out of the room.

3

And still more mystery.

It wasn't Sylvia who was returning. It was Lyle. Ordinarily she would have known that. Lyle made a distinctive sound as he walked in, his bootsteps soft for such a tall young man. Only her fear of being caught going through her things made her believe it was Sylvia.

"Clarita! You look scared."

"No! Relieved!" Clarita said. "Because I'm going to give you evidence you need so you can go on with your sweetheart."

"My sister—" The words had come unwanted.

"She's not! Look." She shoved the birth certificate at him. That would end it. Sylvia would have had to give the cowboy's name as the father.

Lyle looked at the paper. He frowned.

"What?" Clarita grabbed it back and looked at it for the first time. She read the entry for Father: Unknown.

And Lyle's name had been entered as Lyle Love.

4

A melancholy interlude. A firm decision is made,
the risks not considered.

Lyle was sadder than he had ever been, sadder than he had ever imagined he could become, so sad that he wondered, whether, without knowing it, he had always been sad. Of course, there were intervals of joy, but only now could he compare his greater sadness with his earlier state.

If Maria was his sister—

That was it, cut it out!

She *wasn't* his sister. Still, she hadn't been at school the day after the confrontation with Armando and Sylvia when she had run out crying, "Oh, God, oh, God, oh, God! Incest!"—and so he didn't know how she would react to him, whether she had changed toward him, or would gradually.

He lay on his bed in his room, his guitar across his stomach. Try as he might not to, he felt enraged at Sylvia for announcing that he could be Armando's son, and then in a moment pity would wipe away the anger, which would surge again.

"What'll I do, Clarita?" he asked her when she came into the room to "teach him history," although her lessons had all but stopped some time back. She had come here only to talk to him.

"Sylvia, beautiful Sylvia, your mother, is a sad woman, she never recovered from the dual loss, that son-of-a-bitch cowboy leaving her and—"

"What?"

"*Ay, Dios mío.*" She had slipped.

"Tell me what you were going to say!" Lyle coaxed her silence, because she had zipped her lips shut.

"Nothing, nothing!" It would be selfish of her to relieve the pain Sylvia's secret caused her. "I was only going to say her suffering doubled, that's all, when the cowboy left her."

"*He* is my father," Lyle asserted. "Isn't he, Clarita? Maria isn't my sister. The cowboy is my father—not Armando—isn't that right, Clarita, isn't it?"

"Of course!" But, oh, oh, she thought, Sylvia's confused even me.

Unable to keep anger from his voice, Lyle said, "I'm going to talk to Sylvia, I'm going to ask her a lot of things."

Lord God! Blessed Virgin Mary, look down upon us in these moments of woe. That was all Clarita could pray for now, although there was more to contend with: The Pentecostals were back in Rio Escondido for the Gathering of Souls.

5

A passionate confrontation.

That very evening, Lyle asserted his resolve to speak to Sylvia as soon as he came home from his job. Knowing what was about to occur, Clarita fled to her room, intending to say a full rosary while that encounter occurred.

As if she had been waiting for him—she often did—Sylvia walked toward him as he entered. He had intended to talk to her when she had not been drinking, but that was impossible now. "Sylvia, there's some questions I have to ask you—"

"Don't ask me anything! Nothing. Don't ever question me!"

She turned to walk away from him.

"Sylvia! I *have* to talk to you. Why did you say that I could be Armando's son?"

She whirled around. "Because you could be!"

"You're lying, you just want to—"

"Didn't you hear me? Don't ever question me! Don't you understand what I said?"

"I don't understand you at all, Sylvia." He felt only anger now. "Nothing you do makes sense. Nothing!" He relented. "Why, Sylvia, why did you do stuff like that?"

Anger smeared her face. Her lips parted, about to shout fierce words. Then her shoulders sagged and her lips closed.

"Why, Sylvia?" Lyle pled.

"You can never understand."

"Never . . . understand?" Lyle whispered to himself.

"Never," Sylvia said. "You can never feel what I've felt. You can never understand."

6

Has Lyle the First returned?

"Am I still pretty, Lyle?" Sylvia asked her son. She stood unsteadily in the pose she would have adopted after she would have been named Miss America. Might still be? After all, she was only thirty-seven, and—

The sad wistfulness of her once-familiar question—withheld for long—swept away all the anger Lyle had gathered in the past days. "You're more than pretty, Sylvia," he said. "There's no one more beautiful than you," he added, because she seemed more desperate than usual to be assured.

Sylvia touched the smile on her face, as if to assure it was there and that he would see it. She stumbled, holding on to the staircase.

He led her to her favorite chair in the living room. "That's what the cowboy said, that I was the most beautiful woman—and then he left me."

"My goddamned son-of-a-bitch father shouldn't've done that, he was wrong to do that," Lyle said.

"How wrong was he? Tell me." Sylvia almost didn't recognize her own voice, that's how husky it had turned. Sitting on the chair Lyle had bought her when she complained that she had to sit on the bed of her apartment to watch television—and remembering that time—she closed her eyes and touched her breasts briefly, remembering, remembering, the way the cowboy who made love with his boots on used to touch them—remembering—his long, lanky body lying next to hers and—remembering—how he would throw off any covering, even when it was cool.

"My goddamned father was *real* wrong to leave you." Lyle seldom thought about the fact that the cowboy had also left *him*. He hated him for what he had done to Sylvia. For him, he was an absent presence. "I bet he regrets leaving you, regrets it every goddamn day of his goddamn life."

"Regrets? Oh, yes, tell me how much he regrets—" Her eyes still closed, Sylvia leaned back on the chair. She swallowed from the bottle on the table beside her chair, long swallows, welcoming a warming haze, a warm, dark haze. "Come over here and tell me, tell me about regret."

Lyle moved toward her, thinking she was falling asleep. He reached to take the bottle gently from her before it fell to the floor.

She grasped his hand, held it close to her, to her chest.

He looked down at her, puzzled.

"Go ahead, go ahead and tell me," she sighed and kept her eyes closed, and parted her lips to Lyle Clemens the First, who was there now within the darkness her shut eyes had converted into a warm night, who was back, full of regrets for leaving her. He stood there, in the soft darkness of her memory—Lyle the Cowboy, Lyle the First, yes, he stood there, within that blur of her vision, a blur that gradually cleared within the sealed darkness, and, yes, he stood there, oh, yes, becoming clearer, taking full form within that gentle darkness, stood there so tall and handsome, and she held his hand to her chest. "I love you, Lyle," she sighed.

Lyle was startled, not by the words—his heart clasped them eagerly— but by the knowledge that she had never spoken them before. "I love you, too—" He longed to say, "I love you, too, Mother," but must not. "I love you, too, Sylvia."

"Kiss me, Lyle," she said to the man who had finally returned after all those years of her waiting.

Lyle tried to ease his hand away, kindly, from her increasing grasp.

"Kiss me, Lyle." When he did, it would all disappear, all the cruelty of long years, the memory of a single white rose, of a brutal letter.

Lyle bent over and kissed her on the cheek, lightly.

"Lyle—" she said to the man who had left her, and had returned, the way he did often in her dreams, but she was awake now and he had come back to tell her he loved her, couldn't live without her, and he had just kissed her, the way he did, lightly before they made fervid love, and so she held his hand gently, guiding it to her breasts so that again she could feel him making love to them, could feel his mouth there, the moisture of his tongue, and then afterwards, they would—

He would—

She would—

Lyle yanked his hand away.

Sylvia opened her eyes. "Oh, my God!" she screamed.

Lyle staggered back.

"What the hell were you doing?" she shouted at him, at her son, who stood before her, where, only moments earlier, within the lucid darkness she had courted, Lyle the First had stood.

Lyle shook his head. "I wasn't doing anything, you told me to kiss you, you—"

"Goddammit, how dare you accuse me? How could you even suggest that I—?" She brushed her body urgently with her hands, as if to push away the contact that had occurred, had almost occurred. Her body shot up, flung itself against him. Her hands lashed out at him, striking him over and over. "Damn you, damn you, damn you!"

When she released him, her body collapsed on the chair.

Mother, he wanted to say, but the forbidden word would not form. "Sylvia—" he said. "I'm sorry."

7

A return to the Gathering of Souls
with Brother Bud and Sister Sis.

"You can't go there, it's a pit of horrors," Clarita told her when she realized that Sylvia was not only going to the Pentecostal Hall but that she intended to take Lyle. Clarita had thwarted this once before; could she again? The two women stood on the stairway, Clarita on the bottom landing, prepared to block Sylvia's passage.

"I have to."

"Why?"

"I have to face my sins."

"Go to confession, then; speak to a priest."

"It has to be there, at the Revival Hall. Get out of my way, Clara!"

"*Estás loca!*" Clarita retreated. She saw another woman now, a crazy driven woman. She had even dressed to look different, in a dress she had never seen before—Eulah's!—loose, dark, and she was pale, even paler without makeup. The fact that she had been drinking all day and could still speak with such determination added to Clarita's fears.

"It has to be there," Sylvia spoke now as if only to herself, "where Eulah cursed my sinfulness, before she said I killed her, cursed my sinfulness for everyone to hear!" The words echoed in her mind, strange, dark, hers. "That's where it has to be faced, for everyone to hear and know that I have sinned gravely, that I am being punished for my sins. There—and with Lyle."

8

Amid frenzy a star emerges.

Home from his job and lugging his guitar to practice on later tonight, Lyle had surrendered himself to Sylvia's demands that he must come with her. He did so, willingly, to be with her, wherever she needed to go, during this time of terror that was etched on her wracked face, emphasized by the drab clothes she wore. What had occurred, that earlier time between them, had mystified him, and he had not yet sorted out what exactly he had done, but he suspected that her urgent pleading that he come with her now had to do with that. Clarita had followed them for more than a few steps, pulling at Sylvia's sleeve, shouting that she was surrendering her soul to hell by going to "that gathering of *locos.*" Sylvia had moved along, now silent, Lyle beside her as she hurried—at times stumbling and he helped her up—down the streets of Rio Escondido toward the Pentecostal Hall.

They entered the huge hall, swarming with hundreds of souls who had come from all around, as far as El Paso, as far as Albuquerque, a contingent from Dallas, another from Georgia, all forlorn, crying even when they smiled, young and old, men and women, children, their arms held out, hands reaching, bodies swaying—and a dog was running around under the seats howling in terror to the cacophony of hallelujahs and praise-Gods.

Television cameras scoured the auditorium, electronic eyes glaring at the audience, capturing the most enraptured, the most tortured.

Against the backdrop meant to suggest a rectory but looking more like a room in a gaudy motel—a happy picture of Christ in resplendent robes pasted against a wall—a gray-haired preacher jerked about, shaking and thrusting, then walking backward in short, jerky steps, then hopping forward, ranting unintelligible words punctuated now and then with a shouted, "Do I hear an amen?"

"Amen!" Near the gray man, and dressed in frilly ruffles and wearing a huge blond wig, his wife shook and shook, her formidable breasts about to pop out of her red-ruffled blouse. Every time the gray man paused to gasp, she slapped her tambourine and interjected: "Hallelujah, praise Jee-zuss!"

Sylvia recognized the gray man and the blond-wigged woman who had hovered over her dying mother years ago. How was it possible that Sister Sis had not changed during that long interim?—no; she had changed, had camouflaged her age with even heavier makeup. Brother Bud had only grown grayer.

A chorus of black and white men and women in robes hummed over it all. Apart from them—as if purposely separating herself and wearing a much more regal robe than theirs—was an imposing, heavy black woman with a glittery gold crown.

Attempting secretly to loosen his tight corset to allow freer struts as he hip-hopped back and forth, Brother Bud waved a Bible in one hand and clutched a microphone in the other.

"Let's hear it for the Lord-*uh!*" He bumped at each *"uh!"* "Do I hear an Allelu-*jah-jah!*" He bumped twice.

"Allelujah!" "Allelujah!" "Allelujah!" the audience screamed. "Tell it to us, Brother Bud!" . . . "Tell it like the Good Book says." . . . "Cast Old Satan back into the Pit!" The congregants waved their hands to intercept the preacher's words, then clasped them to their hearts, to bury them there.

Shaking, swaying, Sylvia pitched herself into the enraged spirit of the congregation.

Lyle clenched his guitar, as if the greedy fingers about him might tear it away, fingers that seemed to be scratching at the air. He glanced at his mother, and then away from someone he had not seen before, a strange agitated woman clawing at the air like the others here, her eyes closed, lids quivering.

Brother Bud shouted, "Take sides, all you who hear the Word, for the time is at hand and those who wait shall find no salvation out of the flames of hell!"

"Praise God's harsh judgement on those who do not repent!" Sister Sis joined. The mountain on top of her head did not budge.

"Amen, amen!" . . . "Praise Jesus!" . . . "Tell it to us, Sister Sis!" screamed the congregation.

"Give and it shall be given to you," Brother Bud said, jack-hopping forward, then back. "Give as he has given to you."

"Let your gifts match your abundant love for him!" Sister Sis spoke into her own microphone. Tears streaking her cheeks sparkled with unglued glitter. Then her sobs broke into girlish giggles that she muffled by jiggling her tambourine.

Glaring at her, his heavy gray eyebrows entangled into a frown, Brother Bud intoned, "Give, give, give!"

The congregation responded, plopping bills, coins into baskets passed among them by somber attendants who looked like morticians.

"Let's hear it for the Lord!" Brother Bud accepted the largesse.

Lyle saw the black woman with the crown shake her head.

"Now come, shed your sins, give yourselves up to the Lord. Come!" Brother Bud summoned.

"Be saved, be healed! Be slain in the spirit!" Sister Sis beckoned, between sobs.

"Cleanse me!"

Who had screamed that out so violently? It was Sylvia—no, a woman Lyle tried to recognize as Sylvia Love, his mother, a woman with her hands raised tearing at something invisible that must be brought down. Lyle tried to hold her hands, coax them back down. But her body, every limb, was rigid.

From all over the hall they rose, some quickly, some slowly, some shoving away others, some hesitant, being shoved, some ambling along on crutches, others running, others pushing quivering beings on wheelchairs, all flowing in a tide of pain toward the stage, where Brother Bud, flanked by four husky guards in suits, awaited the approaching procession.

Sylvia took Lyle's hand. He surrendered it to her.

Brother Bud shoved his palm against the head of each congregant begging salvation. "Be cured!" . . . "Speak!" . . . "Walk!" "Be slain in the spirit!" Each fell back, cradled by the attendants. "I can walk!" . . . "I can see!" . . . "I can hear!" They trudged and crawled and ran, to applause and hallelujahs—and to the maddened tinkling of Sister Sis's tambourine.

Lyle marched forward with Sylvia, clutching his guitar. He would walk with her, stand with her, help her. Whatever she needed that might break the terrible sadness that drenched their house, he would try to provide. He moved, close to her, protecting her, breathing the heavy stench of alcohol that had become her perfume.

No question about it. The black woman with the crown was glowering fiercely. At him? At Sylvia?

"*Lubyah misque ilyalon!*" Brother Bud lapsed into tongues at the enormity of his miraculous cures—and more to come. "Not my cures, the Lord's," he had asserted to applause.

Lyle echoed the sounds he had just heard—"*Lubyah misque ilyalon.*" He located his guitar in front of him. "*Lubyah misque,*" he repeated, "*ilyalon—lubyah misque ilyalon. . . .*"

Sylvia surged forward, those in her path parting to let her pass.

Now she stood with Lyle before Brother Bud on the stage. Sister Sis moved in for a closer look at Lyle. She shook her tambourine and cried, "Lord, Lord, *Lord*!"—and slapped her thighs spiritedly.

Lyle felt the stare of the black woman on him. "Uh-uh," he heard her say in loud disapproval. "Uh-uh."

"Hmmmmmm, Lord, hmmmmmmm—" the chorus translated.

Sylvia looked beautiful in this light, the shadows that liquor and pain had dug into her face absorbed by the cleansing glare of light.

Sister Sis held her gaze on Lyle and made a loud smacking sound with her lips, accompanied by several jiggles of her tambourine.

"Uh-ummm." This time, Lyle was sure, the black woman's harsh disapproval was being directed at him—or Sylvia.

"Hmmmmm," the chorus sang.

Sylvia Love grabbed the microphone extended to her. "I am here to be purged of my grievous sinfulness!"

"No, Sylvia!" Lyle protested. He turned, now entreating, toward the woman with the glittery crown, as if she might help them. She only shook her head in even more emphatic disapproval.

Sylvia Love shouted: "Cleanse me!"

Before the readied palm of Brother Bud could strike her forehead, Lyle plucked an assertive chord on his guitar—stopping the motion. Another chord, another. "*Lubyah misque,*" he sang the weird words he had memorized. "*Lubyah ilyalonnnn—lubyah misque—*" He struck more chords, sweeter ones, and then—thinking of Sylvia there beside him, trying to punish herself in front of all these people, and for God-knows-what—he plucked sad notes, sadder ones, and sang, "*Lub-yah mis-que il-ya-lonnnn!*"

"The Lord's Cowboy is singing in tongues!" The excited word spread through the congregation.

CHAPTER EIGHT

1

*Eulah's curse at bay? Lyle does the
preacher-strut, guided by Rose.*

All he knew as he sang was that he had to stop Sylvia from shouting out harsh judgments on herself.

So he sang Brother Bud's tongued words, and as he sang them, they changed—"Love-ya, miss-ya, all alone"—and he plucked out a riffy rhythm that became urgent when Sylvia seemed about to resume her harsh declarations. The congregation buzzed and hollered, "Hallelujah!" and "Praise God!"—and, look, the black woman with the golden crown was clapping in rhythm to his song, encouraging him as he added words from songs he had been writing, until now mostly in his head:

Never seen the ocean,
Never touched the sky,
But if I keep a-movin'
I know that I can fly—

He was stumped for a word to rhyme. He extended the last one:

Fly-uhhhhhh, fly-uhhhhh—

Nothing more came. He strummed and sang a refrain:

Lub-yah mis-que il-ya-lonnnn!
Love ya, miss ya, all alone—

"All alone—" he stumbled, "all alone—" What next? Quick!—because Sylvia was about to start up her tirade—clasping a microphone to her mouth—before the befuddled, angered faces of Brother Bud and Sister Sis. Wait! Sister Sis was slapping her tambourine to his rhythm; a trill of giggles had stopped her sobs.

"I was trapped in a prison of lust!" Sylvia cried out, and Lyle sang louder, much louder:

Never seen the ocean,
Never touched the sky—

What had he rhymed with sky? He filled in with a few twangs of the guitar, heartened by the nodding and spirited clapping and swaying of the black woman. He hummed, repeated words, uttered sounds, echoed Brother Bud's tongued words, stretched notes, lonely notes, strong notes, assertive notes, sad ones, lots of sad ones, sorrowing ones for Sylvia, and his voice was deep, then soft, and then it resonated.

Sylvia looked at him in bewildered anger. "What the hell do you think you're—?"

The annoyed voice he recognized was back. Never mind that she was angry. Her quivering had stopped. The Sylvia he was used to was back!

He felt an assertive nudge; actually it was a shove—an elbow jabbed, hard, into his ribs. He turned to see the hefty black woman next to him.

She adjusted her crown and burst into his song with one long note, which she held, trembling, at its peak, and then she shattered it into several, which cascaded about as she added her own words to his in a golden, beautiful voice vibrating throughout the hall:

> Lord, I never seen the ocean,
> Lord, I never touched the sky,
> But I know if I keep trust in Jesus,
> I'll be able to touch His sky. . . .

It was her! Sister Matilda of the Golden Voice! The woman who years ago coaxed her out of hiding under her seat, the woman who had sung the song she had sung at the beauty pageant, the woman she had sought when Eulah had dragged her into this very hall. She was back! Sylvia stared at her in awe. Her hair had stayed dark—almost. She was heavier, but she conveyed the same remembered grandeur. Seeing the woman from the remembered past, and looking out at the writhing hands before her in the audience, Sylvia shook her head and looked out into the squirming, screaming audience, trying to locate herself.

Smiling at his mother, Lyle repeated the black woman's adjustments to his song, while she interjected, "Hmmmmm, Lord, hmmmmmmm," her dulcet sound gliding like a blue bird over his singing. Lyle felt bold, great, began another stanza:

> Moving on, I'll be able to look up, and—

Too soon for another stanza. He disguised his hesitation with notes on the guitar. Shaking her head in reproval of the notes soured by anxiety, the black woman sent her voice climbing, held it aloft over everyone in the auditorium, then let it descend, surrendering sweetly to his voice, then joining it as they moved together.

The chorus took up their rhythm, clapping, swaying: "Hmmmm-hmmmmm, uh-ummmmmmm."

Then Sister Matilda abandoned him, right there on the stage. She stood aside with her arms crossed, challenging him—testing him—to go on by himself.

Lyle started, restarted, felt himself sweating anxiously, words disappearing from his mind. Okay! He'd sing the song Clarita had taught
him, in Spanish, the song he'd serenaded Sylvia with.

> *Estás son las mañanitas,*
> *que cantava el Rey David. . . .*

Clarita wouldn't like this, but there were quite a few Hispanics in the
crowd of *protestantes.* He heard them echo:

> *A las muchachas bonitas,*
> *Se las cantava el así. . . .*

"Hallelujah!" Excitement rippled. "He's singing in tongues. . . ."
"Singin' in tongues!"

When she heard the serenader's song Lyle had sung at her window,
Sylvia leaned back, assuming the sexy pose she had first assumed that
damning morning before it had all turned chaotic; and at that moment
she thought: What the hell am I doing here with all these crazies?

Now what? Lyle wondered, feeling hot. No more words would come
to him. He strummed the guitar, pulled cords, waited for inspiration.

He began to sway his body—and then he hopped back, back, forward, forward—just like he had seen Brother Bud do earlier—but not
exactly like that; his body let go, releasing tension, converting tension
into a bounteous vigor. As he took the strutty imitated steps back and
forth, forth and back, hopscotching, his dance altered, his body swayed,
his hips gyrated and ground, thrusting forth and back, back and forth.
Where had he learned to dance like this? From whom? When?

From Rose!

"Lord, have mercy!" cried Sister Sis, her tambourine jiggling, her
flouncy ruffles fluttering like butterflies. "The spirit has groped this
boy for sure, darned if it hasn't!"

Brother Bud hopped about—with increasing difficulty—as the chorus hummed and the congregation praised the Lord. One man threw
away his crutches and leapt about.

In surprise, Lyle felt himself becoming aroused because damn if
Rose wasn't at it again. (*Do it from the hips, cowboy, yeah, yip-pee-yay!*—

and now back and forth!) He followed her instructions, arched his body and pushed forth, then back (*now out, but not entirely out, so you can come back in smooth*). He stomped up and down to calm his arousal, but, instead it grew, hardened, and he danced and twisted and lunged even more spiritedly. (*Oh, yeah, cowboy, you got it, you got the rhythm just right, now thrust, thrust, thrust but don't come yet, not yet! Who-a!*) He thrust, and almost—

The congregation screamed and spun and shook and jumped and swayed and thrust in praise of the Lord and the Lord's Cowboy.

2

The origin of the preacher-strut, according to the angels,
Sister Sis, and Brother Bud. A guarded warning from
Sister Matilda of the Golden Voice.

Still bewildered by herself—had she been in some demon's trance, encouraged by Eulah's agitated ghost?—Sylvia Love left the auditorium with as much dignity as she could muster—after Lyle's extended performance had generated a chorus of loud hallelujahs.

And applause!

Startled by the applause and the praise-God's he had received—including from both Brother Bud and Sister Sis—Lyle scouted the auditorium for a back exit. He saw one and headed for it, quick. The black woman with the crown intercepted him, linked her arm through his, and guided him firmly to a more secluded back part of the hall. White-robed angels drifted by, with halos propped on wire hangers.

"I am Sister Matilda of the Golden Voice," the woman announced, adjusting her crown to allow no possible rebuttal. "What is your name, cowboy?"

"Lyle Clemens—and I'm not a cowboy, I've never even—"

Sister Matilda of the Golden Voice wiped away irrelevancies "Where'd ya learn to sing like that?"

"On my own," Lyle said.

"In tongues?"

"Well—" He considered what to say; it wouldn't be easy to lie to this imperious woman, and probably not wise to tell her about Rose's instructions.

She didn't give him a chance to. "Huh! Taught yourself how to sing!" she sniffed. "Shoot—that's why it's all wrong."

"If it was all wrong, why the hell did everyone start singin' and dancin' and clapping like they did?" Lyle felt good enough to say—he had dissuaded Sylvia, and that had been his purpose.

"Partly because you were shakin' your hips all around," Sister Matilda said, "grindin' and shovin' like you were crazy, that's why!"

Lyle turned his flushed face away from her.

"Don't you turn blushing away from me!" she demanded. "Whatever brings righteous folks to the Lord is okay by me."

If that's what had happened, Rose had done it. "I didn't do any of that for the Lord," he said firmly. "I don't even think about things like that."

"What you say? You don't think about the Lord! Shame on you!" She shook her head vigorously; some of the glitter flew off her crown. "You couldn't've sung like that—bad as it was—without inspiration from the Lord, moving in mysterious ways. . . . You gonna deny you put lots of pain into your singing?"

He had put pain into his song; he felt it every day now.

Along came Brother Bud and Sister Sis.

Sister Matilda hurried her words. "You watch what you agree to, cowboy!"

No time for clarifying he wasn't a cowboy. They were upon them.

"Boy, I tellya you got an act and a half," said Sister Sis to Lyle, and poked him with her tambourine. She said dourly to Sister Matilda, "Now you ain't filling this boy with all kinds of imaginings and nonsense, are you?" Her glare on Sister Matilda almost cracked the makeup.

Sister Matilda crossed her arms over her bosom—so vast that her arms rested there easily. "Now what kind of imaginings would you be suspecting me of, Sister Sis?"

"Now you know you *are* prone to some powerful imaginings, Sister Matilda." Brother Bud tried to smile at her but did not succeed.

"Dear Sister Matilda, we wanna talk serious with this cowboy," Sister Sis said. "So do you mind?" She gave her head a sideways jerk to emphasize her meaning. The blond wig did not budge.

When Lyle had been on the stage with Sister Sis, she had seemed like an apparition, her features blurred by the heavy paint. Now that she stood near him, the impression increased that she was unreal. Under thick, black mascara, her eyes disappeared, lashes glued like bristles, the wig so blond and rigid it might have been frozen spun candy. Even her remarkable breasts appeared appended to her, as if flesh had been pushed up by the tight black belt she wore, her skirt flaring under it like a ruffled umbrella.

Brother Bud placed both his hands on Lyle's shoulders. "We'd like to talk some business with you, cowboy." His stare urged Sister Matilda away.

"I'm not a cowboy," Lyle started. "I've never even been on a horse."

"That so?" Brother Bud dismissed.

He was as unreal as Sister Sis—so gray he almost faded.

Sister Matilda said, "You go on now and talk with them, cowboy"— she paused—"and listen carefully to everything they tell you."

The way she spoke that exhortation, slowly, emphatically, conveyed a further meaning, confirmed by the stabbing smiles the evangelists aimed at her.

"See ya, Sister Matilda of the Golden Voice," Lyle said when the queenly presence walked away, her crown winking golden sparks.

Flanking him, the two evangelists led him along swiftly, down the corridors of the Pentecostal Hall.

A woman in an evangelical robe intercepted them. She held a small candy jar filled with jelly beans, black and orange. "Will this do for the—?" Catching sight of Lyle, she blocked further words.

"Gotta melt 'em first," a man in a ministerial robe was joining them. He halted when he saw Lyle. "Evenin', Sister Sis, evenin', Brother Bud." He and the woman retreated fast along the hallway as Brother Bud and Sister Sis menaced them with their glares.

Jelly beans? Melted? Lyle had no more time to wonder because he was soon marveling at the office Brother Bud and Sister Sis led him into.

It was large, opulent, with stuffed chairs with tassels, velvet drapes, a thick fluffy carpet that gleamed as if sequins had been woven into it. A Technicolor painting of Jesus in festive robes hung on a wall.

"That was some singing' and dancin', thrustin' and grindin' ya did for the Lord out there, cowboy," Sister Sis congratulated.

"I'm not a cowboy, ma'am, never even—"

"Don't matter!" Brother Bud insisted. "You look like one, and that's what you are."

"—and," Lyle had continued, "I didn't do that for the Lord. I did it
to stop my—"

"Don't matter why you *thought* you did it, cowboy, it's what you *did.*"
Brother Bud said. "Now you sit down and let's talk." He positioned
himself beside his wife on a sofa that devoured them within its soft puffs.
When Sister Sis smiled, only the makeup shifted, slightly. The man's
smile didn't alter his face.

Lyle remained standing.

"You've found your way to the service of Our Lord," Brother Bud
said.

"Amen," Sister Sis intoned.

Lyle shook his head, No.

"Can't resist the Lord's call," Sister Sis warned. "The Lord has
clearly sent you to help inaugurate our Write-a-Love-Letter-to-Jesus
Campaign."

"You want me to write a love letter to—?" Lyle shifted his guitar
from one shoulder to the other, because everything was suddenly heavy.
He sat down, not knowing what to do with his legs because his form,
too, sank into the plush chair.

"My, my, you got some dandy long legs on you, don't you?" Sister
Sis approved. "That means you'll walk long sturdy miles for Jesus."

Brother Bud turned profoundly serious. "Son, that's the name of
our campaign, Write a Love Letter to Jesus. We'd like you to join that
crusade—"

"—and get all those good folks roused up like you did tonight. For
Jesus." Sister Sis leaned toward him, as if to focus more closely on him
through the heavy false eyelashes.

"We're willing to make you a damn good offer, cause we're sure of your
mission, your callin' from the Lord, sure you'll draw lots of righteous
souls," Brother Bud said, "the way you had everybody movin' and doin'."

"Cause you sure got a lot of love to convey. " Sister Sis smothered a
giggle and shook an imaginary tambourine. "Lordee, cowboy, did you
strut!"

"Like a real warrior of the Lord!" Brother Bud approved. He asked
gravely: "Cowboy, where do you think you learned the preacher-strut
if not the Lord teachin' you?"

"Preacher-strut?" When he had become aroused? Did Rose know that
was called the preacher-strut?

To exemplify, Brother Bud hop-hopped, three back, two forward; he stumbled on the third.

"I just did what I saw you do. At first." Lyle said.

"It was the Lord guiding your dance, cowboy, urging you to do the preacher-strut for the joy of his congregation," Brother Bud exulted.

"The preacher-strut happens when angels fly over you and put you in the spirit," Sister Sis said. "The only way to get close to them is to hop, hop, hop. That's the preacher-strut." Sister Sis shook the imaginary tambourine.

"It's in Ezekiel, boy, you just read up in the Good Book." Brother Bud was grave again. "You were receiving all kindsa messages from the Lord."

Actually, from Rose—

"Now what do you say to the Lord's offer?"

Lyle got up. He didn't like this man or this woman who had goaded Sylvia into her weird frenzy. "I don't believe I'm interested in your offer, but thank you a lot," he said politely. "Now, please excuse me, Mr. Bud . . . Mrs. Sis." Determined to be courteous, he bowed—and left, speeding away along the hall.

"Cowboy!"

"Sister Matilda!" She had been waiting for him.

Lyle heard hurried footsteps behind them.

Sister Matilda heard them, too.

Lyle looked back to see Sister Sis and Brother Bud, standing like two alerted soldiers watching him and Sister Matilda until she floated away, her crown blinking like gold dust within every wayward sparkle of light.

3

Sister Matilda meets Clarita and delivers a letter
of further warning.

Looking out the window, Clarita saw a stout black woman stop before their house. She was elegant, too, wearing gloves and a hat. Was she admiring the vines that grew lushly, with tiny white buds—now that the spirit of Eulah Love had been plucked out of them?

No, the woman was checking out the address.

Who was she?

Of course, the woman Sylvia had told her about, who had sung with Lyle at that gathering of *protestantes locos* when Lyle's song had forced some sense into her. The gall of her to come here! Clarita pulled the curtains closed, ready to pretend that no one was there ready to—

"There, in the window, I saw you. I have a letter to leave for the young man who lives here," the woman called out.

What eyesight! Clarita was not about to retreat from a challenge. She went to the door, matching dignity with dignity. "Yes?"

"I'm Matilda of the Golden Voice."

Clarita frosted her words, "I'm Clarita of the Smoky Eye."

"Miz Clarita of the Smoky Eye, I have a letter here, an important letter, for that young man who sang with me at the revival meeting. I asked around and got this address. It's essential that he get it."

"If he's exposed to trouble," Clarita measured her words, "I'll protect him, Señora Matilda."

"Please give it to him—after you've read it, since I know you will—"

"I do not read correspondence that is not addressed to me."

"Good." Sister Matilda marched away.

Clarita tore open the envelope and read:

Cowboy, you must speak to me if you are considering the offer made by two people we both know. Come to the Texas Grand Hotel to discuss this. Bring your guitar—I believe you may have some talent, and I just might want to encourage it. Sister Matilda of the Golden Voice.

Clarita was holding the letter when Lyle walked in. "A love letter, Clarita? Is that what you're hidin'? I bet you get a lot of those." Lyle had come home from school, to eat; he often did. Sylvia had stopped joining, claiming her lunch hour had been cut and she didn't have the time to walk the few blocks required. Lyle knew the real reason; they would have detected the scent of the liquor she now drank at work.

"I do get many love letters, but this one happens to be for you." Clarita pushed the letter at him.

Lyle wasn't surprised to see that it had been opened. Clarita opened everything—closed doors, letters, closets, cans of food if she hadn't purchased them herself, sniffing at them to approve or not. He read the note.

"Going?" Clarita demanded, her voice overflowing with a signal of betrayal.

Lyle hugged her, understanding her rivalry. "There's no one else I could ever love the way I love you, Clarita."

She tried not to smile. "You've got the charm of the cowboy."

"That goddamned son of a bitch?" Lyle said, not pleased by the comparison.

"Yes. You have his charm, God save you, may you not inherit his cruelty."

"I won't," Lyle promised.

4

Another warning at the Texas Grand Hotel.

The Texas Grand Hotel was one of those hotels that lingered, refused to leave, wouldn't surrender. They existed in small towns throughout Texas. They shared old Texan-Spanish architecture, usually, and, most often, a courtyard with a dry fountain, and a cactus garden. Its once-thick carpets revealed frayed patches, wounds from a time of grandeur.

Lyle looked about the familiar hotel, so imposing it was as if he was seeing it for the first time.

"Here to see Sister Matilda?" the old man at the desk said.

"Yes, sir," Lyle said.

"Glad you brought your guitar 'cause she said if you didn't, don't let you up. She's waitin'. Those bigwigs from the revival are stayin' here, too," the old man said proudly.

Did he mean Brother Bud and Sister Sis? Lyle walked up the stairs to the second floor. Over the stairway hung a chandelier that would have been dazzling if it had not been coated with years of dust forcing it to struggle to shine. On one wall was a painting of soldiers bearing the flag of Texas. A few years back, Sister Matilda would not have been welcome here, although Lyle was sure she would have pushed her way in if necessary.

"Come in, I heard you," the Golden Voice responded to Lyle's knocking.

She had left the door unlocked for him.

Sister Matilda sat on a high-backed, carefully pillowed chair. She faced Lyle in a room that, like the hotel, seemed out of a distant time, old prints of trains, landscapes, a four-poster bed, even a washbowl on a table, and faded velvet drapes. She wore her gospel robe, carefully arranged to flow to her feet. And her crown. Did she ever take it off?

"Go ahead, sit down there. It's a wooden chair, that's all they got here except for this one I bring with me. I put some pillows on yours for your rump, not that you have to worry—you cowboys got such flat butts on you."

Lyle located his boots carefully under the chair so that if she got up she wouldn't stumble over them. He sat straight, to emphasize his respect.

"Young man, I called you here to warn you that you may be in a heap of trouble, even danger, if you don't watch it." She shifted her body, slightly, carefully, exactly, so that a streak of light from the window transformed her crown into a halo that added authority to her voice. "And to try to teach you how to sing."

CHAPTER NINE

1

*Considerations about what constitutes grace.
When is it amazing? Intimations of
a secret fraught with danger.*

The urgent note in Matilda's letter to Lyle, and, just now, a clear warning of trouble, were either forgotten or to be kept in abeyance, Lyle realized as, leaning back on her throne—Sister Matilda converted whatever she sat on into a throne—she asked him:

"You got black blood in your background? Any Negro blood?"

"I'm of mixed blood," Lyle said. That's what Sylvia had told him, about herself, although she had not clarified what the mixture was. Still, it seemed to be an answer that might please Sister Matilda.

It didn't. "If you don't, how was it you sang those soulful tones? Not all singers can, cowboy."

Absolutely no need to remind her that he wasn't a cowboy. "I'm not a singer."

"Maybe you could be," Sister Matilda rendered her verdict. She raised her hand as if testifying to the fact. "You put soul in your song." Her eyes looked up toward Heaven, as if to verify her finding. "I heard pain, saw it when you looked at . . . that lady with you—"

"Sylvia," Lyle said. "My mamma. . . ."

"Your mamma," Sister Matilda said, remembering the forlorn woman on the stage. "She's got a load of pain, and you were trying to save her from pouring all that hurt out before those two—" She stopped herself, looking at him as if to gauge how much to say now; she substituted words with a harsh sound.

"You understood what I was doing—right away—and you helped me," Lyle said. He was about to thank her, but she raised her hand, rejecting gratitude. "Will you teach me to sing?" he asked her. From her huge smile he could tell she was willing.

But the smile was smothered by a frown. "Can't teach soul!" she snapped. "You got it or you don't. Maybe you got it, cowboy. *Maybe.*" She hummed, deeply, beautifully, darkly. "God granted me a voice people remember." She looked away from him, lowered her regal head, as if in regret. The crown did not slip. "Maybe now and then I've squandered it."

"My mamma heard you once, you sang a song she loves."

"I bet I know what song a hurting lady like her would love."

"What song?" He longed for her to know, because then she might provide a clue to the mystery of Sylvia.

"'Amazing Grace,' of course," Sister Matilda said easily.

"That's it!"

"Know why she loves it?"

"I wish I did."

"Because it offers grace. Listen!"

> *Amazing grace, how sweet the sound,*
> *That saved a wretch like me,*
> *I once was lost, but now I'm found,*
> *Was blind but now I see.*

"What is grace?" Lyle asked her. "Is it a burst of light?" That's what had augured Clarita's miracle in Chihuahua.

"Yes. A great burst of beautiful light, yes," Sister Matilda agreed, "but it's more than that. It happens when the Lord extends grace to give everyone who seeks it, the strength to carry the loads life heaps on us. Now why is that amazing?"

Lyle shook his head; he neither believed nor disbelieved in God; and if He existed, why would he heap heavy loads on anyone in the first place?

"What's amazing is that grace provides hope that the heaviest loads will lighten. Sometimes, cowboy, that's enough to get you through life. Hope."

"Hope. . . ." Lyle wanted to retain the word, to ponder the whole matter later.

"Know who wrote the song?" Sister Matilda had waited for moments for Lyle to search his thoughts.

"A black man," Lyle guessed.

"A white man," Sister Matilda corrected, "name of John Newton; he was a captain, a slave-trafficker. A vile wretch!" Anger spilled out of her voice. "Dealt in tradin' flesh, human flesh." Her words assumed a deep Southern tone not usually there, and she spoke the words as if she was singing them, finding rhythm here, extending it there, accentuating it all with a soft moan. "Brought slaves, black slaves, to sell, split up their families, husband from wife, children from mother—families treated worse'n dogs, and no dog deserves to be treated like that. . . . Give me an amen to that, cowboy."

"Amen," Lyle said.

"Then, one day—"

Lyle closed his eyes and saw it all as Sister Matilda conveyed it, almost singing parts of her account.

Cap'n Newton looked into the eyes of a shackled black man he had brought on his ship to sell with many others in America, and he looked into those black eyes, and the slave's pain pulled him in, farther in, farther, farther, deeper, the black unblinking eyes of the chained man not letting go, not letting him out, pulling him even deeper, deep, deep, deep into his soul, dragging him in there and tossing him around, and there, in the black man's soul, was a pool of hurt and anger and indignation at what was being done to him and the others, and Cap'n Newton sank still deeper into that pool of sorrow, down, down, into the black man's suffering, and he thought he understood it, feeling the hurt as much as he could, and understood at last what it is to stop hoping, and the blackness he was about to drown in burst with a blast that threw him back on the deck of the ship, and still the black slave's eyes were on him, as the blackness exploded again, again, again, exploded into a white radiance that was the Lord's Grace!

"It was only when he understood—and tried, just *tried,* to feel the other's pain, to understand it"—Sister Matilda spoke with her eyes closed, as if to share the darkness that had burst into light—"it was only when he understood that man's pain that Cap'n Newton was able to write the song that lavished grace on both of them." She opened her eyes on Lyle. "Do I hear an amen to that, cowboy?"

"Amen, Sister Matilda," Lyle said. His mind was echoing words: Feeling the hurt as much as he could and understood it.

In a voice that trembled and soared, Sister Matilda sang:

> *Amazing grace, how sweet the sound,*
> *That saved a wretch like me,*
> *I once was lost, but now I'm found,*
> *Was blind but now I see.*
> *'Twas grace that taught my heart to fear,*
> *and grace my fears relieved,*
> *How precious did that grace appear,*
> *The hour I first believed.*
> *Through many dangers, toils, and snares,*
> *I have already come;*
> *'Tis grace has brought me safe thus far*
> *And grace will lead me home.*

"Now, cowboy," she said, "you sing the words with me and give them even more grace with your guitar."

"No." Lyle slung his guitar back over his shoulders, refusing to join her. "You said Cap'n Newton was able to write that song only when he understood the slave's pain. That song means a lot to Sylvia, and I don't understand her, don't understand her pain. So I can't sing it."

Sister Matilda nodded.

2

A necessary dramatic pause before an abrupt interruption.

There was a loud shuffling outside the door, loud, as if somebody wanted to assert a presence, without knocking.

"They know you're here," Sister Matilda said calmly.

Brother Bud and Sister Sis, Lyle understood.

"Gotta watch 'em carefully, remember all you see," Sister Matilda said to Lyle. "You saw that candy jar?"

"I think they tried to hide it from me."

More shuffling at the door, louder still.

"Remember what you saw in it," Sister Matilda said.

"Jelly beans, orange and black?" Lyle was baffled anew.

The unlocked door opened.

"Look who's here, the dandy cowboy!" Sister Sis trilled.

"Lord if he ain't," Brother Bud said.

Both faced Sister Matilda. "Teaching him how best to serve the Write-a-Love-Letter-to-Jesus Campaign?" Brother Bud tried to sound friendly.

"Precisely. Come again, Lyle," Sister Matilda dismissed him, "we'll talk some more. Serious talk."

3

An invitation from the Lord sent through
Brother Bud and Sister Sis.

Outside, Lyle continued toward the stairs, away from Brother Bud and Sister Sis; but they were pursuing him.

"Whatya been doin' with Sister Matilda, cowboy?" Brother Bud said to Lyle.

Lyle stood on the stairs, under the chandelier. To divert himself from them, he raised himself on tiptoes, blowing away the dust on it.

"So whatya been doing with her?" Sister Sis insisted.

"Learnin' to sing."

They detoured about him, blocking his way down the stairs, to face him.

"No denying that Sister Matilda has a golden voice," Brother Bud offered expansively.

"Still, you gotta know that sometimes she babbles, babbles *mean* stuff, too, *untrue* stuff," the voice under the towering blond wig said.

"She been babbling such to you?" the gray evangelist said.

"No. . . . Excuse me." Lyle dodged past them.

They followed him. "We had a clear message from Jesus," Sister Sis said, reverentially draping the heavy lashes over her eyes, "we get them real often, but this one was emphatic, the Lord told us to refresh our proposal to you, because, cowboy, he *wants* you."

"We'll be flying back to the Lord's Headquarters in California in a coupla days," Brother Bud informed him, "and if you join us, remember the Lord lavishes rewards on those he calls."

"Lots and *lots* of rewards," Sister Sis emphasized.

"Thank you, Mr. Bud, Miz Sis. I'll keep that in mind," Lyle said before hurrying away.

Brother Bud shouted out: "You just keep our friendly invitation in mind, ya hear?"

4

*The matter of Maria is resumed; a frightening
possibility is reconsidered.*

Lyle put it all out of his mind, Sister Sis, Brother Bud, the jar of jelly beans, and—

No, he could not banish Sister Matilda. He longed to return to her, to hear more, learn more, but that would expose him to Brother Bud and Sister Sis and expose her to . . . what? She indicated danger involving them and her, and his presence appeared to aggravate it.

Besides, there was the matter of Maria to tend to now.

In his lot, the two sat against the unfinished wall. At a farther edge of the lot, in a small patch, wildflowers had begun to grow, perhaps because often, in his hurry to come here, Lyle would not wait to go to the men's room, but would sprinkle the dry ground there before rushing away to wait to see whether Maria would join him. Though he often studied the tiny flowers even on the weeds, noting their special beauty, today he had focused on the sadness that was gathering around him. The day, which was bright, seemed sadly bright. The grass, which was green, seemed sadly green; the sky, which was blue, looked sadly blue.

And Maria, who was beautiful, looked very sad as she rested on her school satchel, Lyle beside her on an unfinished step.

"If you are my brother, and we—you know—fucked—what now?" Maria said.

"I'm *not* your brother, you're *not* my sister, my mother lied."

"Don't say that, God will punish you, say a prayer, mothers don't lie. If it's not true, then she believes it, that's all there is to that, but mothers don't lie, but what if you are my brother?"

"It isn't true, and I doubt that she believes it."

Maria shook her head, emphatically. "Mothers don't lie, Lyle."

"Look, I don't even resemble you, nor do I resemble your father. I'm tall, and he's—" He didn't want to be mean.

"—short, *very* short," Maria finished. "That's why he's always stretching, to appear taller. I think he'd like to believe that he's your father because that would mean something about him is tall—you. Still, he says an uncle of his was very tall, and that would account for—"

To settle everything, Lyle leaned over and kissed her hotly on the lips, rubbing his mouth all around hers, probing with his tongue.

She allowed it, responding, then she shoved his tongue out with hers. "What if it's true—?"

"Your father lied, and I told you my mother lied."

"And I told you that mothers never lie, and it's a sin to say they do. Besides, if it's true, our children—"

"You don't make children by kissing," Lyle told her.

"I know, I meant what we already did."

"Look, Maria, I love you."

"And I love you, Lyle."

"Then there's no problem, is there?" He resumed his kissing, even hotter.

She responded, even more passionately. Then she shoved his tongue out forcefully. "But what if?"

"Stop it!"

"What if it was true and we had children and then they were puny like the children of incestuous kings and queens?" She covered her face, tears seeping through her fingers. "Oh, life, oh, life, oh! How strange, how very, very strange!"

"God-fuckin'-dammit! You're not my fuckin' sister, will you get that out of your goddamned silly head?"

"Oh! Oh!" Maria stood up. "Oh! You cursed me!" She made a sign of the cross. "But I know you didn't mean it, and so I forgive you." She looked at him forlornly. "But if it's true, oh, Lyle, if it's true then we shall be damned forever!"

"Knock it off, Maria, you're really being stupid, you know?"

"Stupid! No more, no more!" she screamed and ran away a few steps and waited, expecting him to coax her back. When he didn't, she called out, "I shall always love you, just like I promised—whoever you are!" She waited long moments before she ran away sobbing.

Lyle kicked disconsolately at the dusty lot with his boots. He hadn't run after her because he knew she would just start again with "What if," and he didn't want to explain again, didn't want to think about it, didn't want to consider any such thing. Didn't want to remind himself that it was Sylvia who had allowed this terrible situation.

5

A persistent ghost returns, even more powerful.

There are times in life when something horrible seems finally to have been laid to rest, times when a deep wound seems cauterized and new flesh is welcomed to erase the scar entirely. That is how it had seemed to Sylvia Love that evening at the Gathering of Souls, after her assertion that she deserved damnation, that she acknowledged Eulah's curse, thwarted by Lyle's song. She told Clarita as much. The silly curse had no more power, her frenzied drive for "repentance" had been ridiculous; she saw that now. "I made a damn fool of myself." She laughed, remembering the bizarre scene.

Slowly at first—so slowly that she was not aware of it—and then so quickly that there was no pause, it all returned. She was sure that Eulah was back, although her appearance was always hazy. Sylvia would raise up her glass of liquor to the specter, at times as an offering of peace, at times in defiance of her. Once, trying to stare down the ghost, she dozed for a moment. When she woke, she felt Eulah's white sheet being flung over her body, exactly like on the day that had begun her torture.

She stumbled to the mirror. Nothing was clinging to her shoulders. When she turned away, she felt it again, a gauziness.

"Goddamn you, Eulah Love! You let me be!" she shouted out once. Clarita ran in, soothing her, easing away the bottle she clutched in her hand as urgently if it were her salvation, her substitute for salvation at such a young age.

Lyle was aware of all that.

6

A grave decision.

Lyle sat forlornly in his room, his boots beside him, his feet tucked under him as he sat on the floor. He held his guitar, looking at it as if to locate the mystery that allowed it to make notes.

When she ran into him, Maria cried. She no longer joined him in his vacant lot. Sylvia stayed in her room most of the time. When she would come out unsteadily, she would stare at him as if to locate him within a haze. She might place a tender hand on his shoulder, and then pull it away.

What else but to leave when his presence added complications for everyone involved? Leave for Maria's sake, for Sylvia's sake. How to leave, quickly?

7

The true color of Jesus.

"You could join a rodeo," Sister Matilda sat on her throne-chair at the Texas Grand Hotel.

"Dammit, I don't know how to ride a horse," Lyle said. "Listen, Sister Matilda, you don't understand, joining the campaign is the only way I know to get away, and I *got* to get away." Didn't she understand it meant he would go along with her, too? Didn't that please her? Her reaction was annoying him, adding to his depressed mood.

"You have to leave because you have to leave. That makes sense. If you go with those two, you'll be doing a lot of singing, right?"

"Right." Singing with *you,* he wanted to say. But she seemed not to want to acknowledge that.

She closed her eyes. "All right then, learn, I'll teach you." Her voice trembled as she sang:

> *Were you there when they crucified my Lord?*
> *Were you there when they nailed him to the cross?*

"What the hell!" Lyle blurted. Was she daffy? Her mind did hop around. He lowered his voice respectfully: "Sister Matilda, that's beautiful, but I don't feel like practicing," he said.

Sister Matilda was indignant. "You gonna pretend to sing gospel and you don't want to hear how? Shame, boy, shame. Now listen, and then you join me:

> *And were you there when they nailed him to the tree?*

"To the *cross,*" Lyle corrected irritably what everybody knew.

"Were *you* there?" Sister Matilda aimed at Lyle.

"Were *you* there?" he fired back at her. He was feeling low, very sad to leave his sister—she was *not* his sister!—and Clarita. And Sylvia. Yet here was Sister Matilda singing and sulking as if she didn't understand he'd be going with *her.*

"Yes, *I* was there!" Sister Matilda snapped. "*I* was there when they nailed *my* daddy to the tree!" Her eyes searched beyond the window. "He was nailed to a tree when he was lynched, and I saw him, crucified."

Lyle winced with pain at the sudden image, a little girl watching while . . . He wanted to touch the ample woman, comfort the terrible memory. But even in her sorrow she was so regal touching her seemed forbidden.

"I'm gonna tell you something you never heard and most folks don't want to hear." Her form slumped on her chair. "Jesus was black, that's why they lynched him, too!"

Lyle accepted that, her truth, all that mattered now.

Sister Matilda shook away tortured memories. "You got a darn good voice on you, Lyle," she called him by his name for the first time. "You don't play the guitar all that well, but you got one good voice, and Lord knows you can move around. Use all you have to lift spirits, but never," she said darkly, "to deceive good souls." She leaned toward him, whispering as if she might be overheard: "If you decide to go with them—and I believe you have decided—be alert, cowboy, watch out for wickedness. You might be called upon to remember."

Lyle didn't ask more because he didn't want to hear anything that would shut out the one possibility of leaving right away. "We'd be together, Sister Matilda!" he blurted, to shake that knowledge into her.

Had she even heard him? She was singing, her voice swelling with reverence:

Were you there when they nailed him to a tree?

Lyle pushed away his guitar. Why learn gospel songs when he didn't intend to sing them, ever?

8

A firmed position. A betrayal announced.

"Why should I join you?" Lyle asked Brother Bud and Sister Sis in their gilded office. Goddammit, he *still* wasn't sure, just *considering.*

"To obtain a choice place in the Lord's fold—" Brother Bud said.

"—and a plush job, cowboy, a singing job. Good pay," Sister Sis encouraged.

"—*real* good," Brother Bud agreed, "and good hours, and—"

"—lots of ad-u-la-shun to make you forget all your woes," Sister Sis winked, "and, cowboy, you look like you need some forgettin'."

"Forget?" Lyle grasped at the word he wanted to hear.

Brother Bud cleared his throat: "We're leavin' tomorrow. Come with us."

"*If* I go, I want to leave with Sister Matilda," Lyle was firm.

Sister Sis wiped away instant tears. Brother Bud shook his head.

"Sister Matilda is—" Sister Sis started.

"—a very disturbed woman," Brother Bud said. "Now hold your horses, young man—" He backed away from Lyle's clenched fist.

"She's my friend," Lyle warned about any insult.

"I don't doubt that, in the depths of her black soul," Sister Sis said. With a mean giggle, she added, "Didn't mean that, just meant—"

"She meant," Brother Bud amended, "that at times Sister Matilda babbles like her mind's on its way out, sometimes even seems to be on the side of the demon. . . . Now you keep that fist away from me and listen."

Sister Sis turned her face away in pain. Mascara tears melted on her cheeks. "Sister Matilda's gone, cowboy, fled without a word."

Not possible. They were lying. He'd prove it, he'd go to the Texas Grand Hotel, and she'd be there. He started for the door.

Sister Sis said mournfully. "We haven't told you why she had to run away, be—"

"—'cause," Brother Bud took over, "she absconded with some funds that belonged to us—to the Lord."

Lyle's fist pushed out and landed on Brother Bud's shoulder because he had been prepared to dodge.

"My, my," said Sister Sis in an especially high, girlish voice, "you are strong, young man. You are *very* strong." She turned to Brother Bud and said sternly, "Now you straighten up and bear it like the Lord Jesus bore his cross."

"I'm sorry—" Lyle started, realizing what his fist had done.

Brother Bud rubbed his shoulder, "Nothin' to fret about, cowboy— it's all gonna be in the family now. Ain't it?"

Lyle ran all the way to the Texas Grand Hotel and learned that Sister Matilda had left the night before without a word or a note for anyone.

9

The unsettling mystery of Sister Matilda.

To all his woes, Lyle added this: Sister Matilda had left, abandoned him. Had she really absconded with money? He couldn't believe that, didn't want to believe it, and yet why else would she flee like that? There was also this. If she was capable of fleeing from him without a word, wasn't it possible that the dark tales she had hinted at, about Brother Bud and Sister Sis were false?

10

Some thoughts about farewells.

At times, it seems, life becomes a long good-bye, ending with the saddest farewell. For Lyle, the saddest farewell of his young life contained a series of good-byes he might have to say.

"Clarita, I may be going away."

"What!"

"I may be leaving Rio Escondido." He was sure now, no, he wasn't, yes, no——

Her body crumbled. She adjusted herself. She must give him courage to face his future, a future that, she prayed—*please don't let me shed tears, Holy Mother*—would cast away, at least from him, the curse under which Sylvia still lived. No, she would not cry, especially since she must tell Lyle certain essential things she had not been able to teach him along with his history lessons; must talk firmly, without tears.

"Lyle," she said, and she broke into sobs.

"Clarita! Please stop! You'll make me cry." He hugged her tightly.

"Enough!" she said, rubbing away her tears. "Of course I knew it. You have to, the way everything has turned upside down. Now I must tell you some very important things."

About Sylvia!

"You must rely on the Holy Virgin Guadalupe, the patron of Mexico; she is the source of miracles. You must pray, and let her know that I recommended you to her."

"I will, I promise," Lyle said earnestly.

"I won't worry, ever, about your future, because you have so many gifts, you're smart—even if you haven't graduated from school, like me—I have a diploma, you know—and the Holy Mother will guide you because I'll be asking her to. One more thing—" She knew she'd better rush because she was breathing deeply. "Always remember that your mother was the object of great cruelty—"

"From that goddamned son of a bitch, my father," Lyle upheld.

Much more than that, Clarita added silently. "—and so you must never extend cruelty, so much of it in the world." Could she go on?

"I promise, Clarita," Lyle said, wondering why it was necessary to vow never to be cruel.

Consumed by sobs, Clarita managed only to give him her most powerful silent benediction.

11

The saddest farewell.

"You're considering leaving?" Sylvia Love Clemens heard words she had repeated in her mind for years, over and over, words she had not been able to speak when she had first needed to speak them, not able to because the last time she had seen the cowboy she hadn't known it would be the last time; and so her mind often echoed—throughout the years after she faced that he was not returning to marry her, to love her—often echoed what she would have said to him, adding words, at first pleading words when she cried alone, but, soon, especially when she drank more and more, she added words of unspoken rage: You goddamned son of a bitch, where the hell do ya think you're goin'?

Clarita, of course, was watching from the doorway, clenching her rosary and praying to the Holy Mother to shower her beneficence upon mother and son, intercede in the name of the holy martyrs—"and don't let them scream at each other," or rather, she quickly amended lest the Holy Mother unleash something she had not intended, "Don't let Sylvia start screaming."

"Yes, Sylvia, I believe I am leaving, maybe join the people you took me to, remember?" But, oh, God, would he? Would he?

Sylvia heard only the first words spoken. She turned her back on them, hoping it would not be noticed that she had to grasp for the stairway railing to keep her posture erect, dignified, proud, as she was determined to be.

Her frightening composure! What was it hiding? Clarita prepared to enter the room.

"I have to leave," Lyle explained to her silence, "because everything is very complicated now, for all of us. I don't even know who I really am anymore, and I'm trying to understand—"

"Understand?" Sylvia's mind grasped only that one word. She laughed, a dry, terrible laughter. She leaned against the wall, seeking strength to stand. She heard—again, again, again—the haunting echo of laughter, louder than an echo should be. She covered her ears.

"Don't, Sylvia," Lyle said. "You have to hear me."

Sylvia Love pushed herself from the wall, empowered by rage. She screamed, "Go ahead and leave me, you fuckin' bastard, get the fuck out of my life, never come back!"

The look of horror on Lyle's face made Clarita rush in to stand next to Lyle.

"Good-bye, Sylvia," Lyle said. He walked out with the suitcase he had packed, uncertain until now, and his guitar—left hidden under the stairway until he decided. The decision was made.

Sylvia whirled around. "Lyle?"

"Yes, your son," Clarita said.

"My son? Lyle? He's gone?"

Clarita held her, close. "It's for the best, *muchachita linda,*" she said. "Things couldn't continue like this. It's for the best, beautiful little girl."

12

A litany of farewells.

"Good-bye," Lyle said aloud to the City of Rio Escondido as he stood, for what might be the last time, on his vacant lot. "Good-bye," he said again, and this farewell included several sad farewells, to Maria and Clarita, yes, even Armando, and to Raul, and the kids who had followed him around like the king of the geeks, and—

"Good-bye, Sylvia. Good-bye, Mother"—he could say the word, alone. He shook his head, strummed a few notes on his guitar. He walked slowly—shuffled—with his suitcase and his guitar to the Pentecostal Hall.

Good-bye, good-bye, good-bye!

BOOK

II

·

Hollywood

THE LORD'S HEADQUARTERS IN ANAHEIM,
AND AN UNEXPECTED DETOUR

·

*In which disparate lives wait to entangle Lyle's
as he lands in the City of Angels.*

CHAPTER TEN

1

On the perfection of coincidences, here involving Mr. and Mrs. Renquist
and Tarah Worth. Considerations about Valley of the Dolls.

hen the lives of strangers intersect another's, the
wayward pattern of those lives seems to have
always been leading in a straight line to one
point of intersection. Accidents and coincidences
assume retrospective inevitability. Then it seems
that those distant strangers have been living their lives in preparation
to coincide with another's. Before that happens, those lives proceed on
their own course until every coincidence falls into place to create inter-
locked fate.

At this point, it would seem impossible to Lyle that at the moment
he prepared to depart from Rio Escondido, miles away in Hollywood

(or more exactly one block away from Hollywood) a woman who would become an essential player in his life would be shouting out:

"A remake! Of the greatest movie of all time! Based on the greatest novel of all time! By the greatest writer of all! Jacqueline Susann! A remake of *Valley of the Dolls*!" And she, Tarah Worth, was up for a leading role in it, according to confirmation in Liz Smith's recent column—never mind that a note at the bottom indicated that that particular column had been written by an assistant. When Liz Smith carried an item in her column, Liz Smith made *sure* it would turn out to be correct, even if she had to *make* it be so.

Tarah Worth, sitting before a silvery mirror in her small but elegant home—it had a pool—repeated those words aloud, words she had been saying, cherishing each syllable, since she had read the thrilling news in the daily column by her favorite living writer, whom she consulted religiously, the way others say morning prayers. Reading Liz Smith first gave her strength to face her horoscope, which had been drawn by a hostile astrologer who made sure each day contained a fearful warning. Why? Jealousy. Of course, the astrologer might have suspected she'd given her a wrong year of birth. The astrological sign was right; so what difference did it make? She was born under the proud sign of Scorpio.

In her bedroom decorated in black and white—only black and white—Tarah wore the kind of glamorous robe that only yesterday's most glamorous stars were worthy enough to wear—Garbo! Dietrich! Crawford!—lustrous satin, pearl-white. Any moment now, her manager would be calling her back to inform her about which role she was up for in the remake of the classic novel. When it was originally filmed in the '60s, when she was a mere child, the searing novel couldn't be made correctly. Now it would be done the way the immortal Jacqueline Susann would have wanted it.

Tarah bowed her head in reverence to greatness when she glanced at—reflected in the mirror and arranged to achieve that reflection—the shelf behind her bed. There was only one book there, and that book was *Valley of the Dolls* on an altar of its own. Stunned anew by the existence of such a work, she looked away from the mirror, out of her glistening window at—

Hollywood!

Actually she didn't live in Hollywood; she lived exactly one block away from where she could legitimately claim she did. She had been deceived by the rental manager, who had told her otherwise—and had added that, in the house she would lease, Greta Garbo had lived with John Gilbert. It was Garbo's *lighting man* who had lived here, briefly.

Behind her, the television was spewing words she wasn't listening to. She left it on so she could hear voices, not feel so alone, a self-imposed loneliness that had to do with the fact that she hadn't had a role in almost a year, except for a mortifying stint on that horror called *Hollywood Squares,* where only one player directed a question at her, which she answered wrong. Who would have dreamt that, after her auspicious debut in *Where's Susan?*—in which she played a home-wrecker, a juicy role that had earned her a Golden Globe nomination for Best Up-and-Comer—and after a few starring roles—including two horror films in both of which she was axed—and after several seasons in a featured role as a reformed nymphomaniac in *Summer Comes Once a Year,* a soap opera that had unwisely been canceled—who would have thought that she would *ever* be idle? Especially after having almost, almost, *almost* been cast in the role that made Sharon Stone famous— of all things, by crossing and uncrossing her legs in that reprehensible way. Well, Tarah Worth's bad times were over—and how!

What role, what role? Should she consult her thrilling psychic, Riva? Maybe have her channel Jacqueline Susann for some encouragement, some profound insight into the deep emotional depths the author had explored in her characters? Not yet. She must wait for the call first, so as not to disturb the great author's spirit with indefinite questions.

Would she be up for the role of Anne Wells?—Anne, the undaunted New Englander who leaps from a job as a secretary to being the most famous model in the world . . . Aristocratic, seemingly aloof—but passionate underneath—and wronged, betrayed, but brave. She, too— Tarah Worth!—at the young age of thirty-five—but looking at least ten years younger, everyone said—had been wronged and betrayed, by three husbands—no alimony from any of them and one had the gall to ask alimony from her; two lovers—men who had become interchangeable in her memories; and all of Hollywood—yes, *all* of Hollywood— had betrayed her; she was always up for great roles that actresses who looked like her ended up getting. Was she bitter about all that? Damn right she was! But she, like Anne Wells, was brave. She would bring all that to the role.

She'd be just as good as Jennifer North, the great beauty who plunges into the squalor of erotic films, and utters, while propping up her breasts—Tarah did that now—one of the great lines of all time:

"Oh, let them droop!"

Hers didn't. That line would have to be changed for her. "Let them rise!" Rise? "Let them emerge!" Emerge? "Let them protrude!"

Did she dare dream that she would be offered the role of—

Neely O'Hara!

The most challenging role of all time! A celebrated singer, once on top, now sinking, swallowing "dolls."

"Dolls?" Tarah said aloud.

That had always puzzled her. She'd never heard pills called "dolls." Where had the great author gotten that word? Never mind! Who was she to question Jacqueline Susann?

The greatest of great dramatic scenes! Neely, sinking lower and lower, finds herself in a dump in San Francisco, picks up a grubby drifter, who robs her—and then she staggers out into an alley—an *alley*!—drunk, pilled-up—

"Dolled up?" Tarah tested that word again. It still sounded wrong.

Seized by the power of the role of Neely O'Hara, she pretended her puffy white carpet was a grimy alley, and she screamed out the immortal lines:

"The whole world loves me! I am Neeeeleeeee O'HARRRR-ah!"

Please God, get me the role of Neely O'Hara—

She jumped. The phone had rung. She grabbed the television remote control, punching it randomly to change the TV channel to something that would sound classy over the telephone, but she kept landing on noisy morning cartoons; so she turned the sound off and let the answering machine pick up—not good to convey she was edgy about a call from her manager.

"This is Tarah Worth," her recorded voice said, "Please leave a message. A *kind* one."

"Tarah, pick up the goddamn phone! I know you're waiting to hear from me, and I got news—"

Tarah picked up. "Sorry. I was in the shower, I heard a voice. Who is it please?"

"Stop that bullshit, you were pretending to be unconcerned. It's official, you're in the running for the role of—"

Tarah Worth held her breath to receive one of the magic names. Anne Wells. Jennifer North. Neely O'Hara! Please God, please, please . . . "*What?*"

"You heard me. Helen Lawson."

Helen Lawson! The gargoyle actress, gobbling up young talent, hardly able to pull it off any more, clawing her way to stay at the top, and balding—yes, *balding!* Tarah closed her eyes to prepare for her death in a moment. "Helen . . . Lawson?" Even the name staggered.

"The old bitch, yeah, her," said the coarse, crass voice of her manager, extending the years of battering Tarah had already endured. "Tarah? Tarah? Are you there?"

"I'm here. I don't want that role, I'm too young for it."

"You're forty, and you look it, and it's a meaty role, sweets—kosher meaty, of course, or *I* won't bite! Ha, ha! You got a good chance because they decided to go with someone not well known."

How had she coped with this creature for all these years? Because it was difficult to get another manager, her reason ambushed her before she could block it.

"You wanna comeback or not?"

"Comeback!" Norma Desmond had said it for all time in *Sunset Boulevard.* It's *not* a comeback, it's a return. But hers wasn't even a return. She was *remembered.* Her fan club—

"Now we gotta plan to get you some wild publicity. Gotta show 'em your boobs are still way out there."

"I wish you wouldn't use that word, boo—"

"What's wrong with boobs, babe?—especially big ones, the kind I like to bounce—bob, bob, yum, yum."

Those sounds!

"I heard they've dyked up the part."

"Dyked up?"

"Yeah, butched it up," the horrifying voice turned the words into a bark.

"I am not a dyke."

"Oh, honeybunch, I know that, but so what? Might help you if you were. I heard that Alexandra Easton over at Fox said you're still cute—"

"Cute! I am not cute. I am gorgeous. And, please, please, *please*—" She held her breath for moments, to sustain the courage that would allow her to speak words she had longed to speak, had shouted in her mind throughout the years. "Lenora! Stop trying to sound like a man, you're not. Stop trying to sound like a lesbian, you're not. Stop trying to sound Jewish, you're not." There! She'd spoken it all at last out of the recesses of her tortured artist's heart.

"Whatever, sweet stuff . . . Hey, did you hear that out in the San Fernando Valley there's a drag queen who does a real good imitation of you—but nobody knows whom she's doing? Ha-ha, just a joke!"

Tarah clutched her heart, to keep it from breaking.

"Babe," Lenora said, "I gotta go. Decide what you know you're gonna decide, and then come see me, we'll plot. Ciao, babe."

What a frightening woman, her manager was—and she smoked cigars, and it was true she wasn't Jewish or a lesbian—she was known to screw all those pretty young actors eager for representation, and how they managed to perform would deserve at least a Golden Globe nomination. Her last name probably wasn't even Stern, just wanted one that might be Jewish. It all had to do with power, although Tarah had not yet deciphered how she thought her pretenses would help her. Probably born under the sign of Taurus, the bull, although she'd never asked her, fearing that if she guessed Taurus, the creature would take off with suggestions about being a bull dyke.

"The role of Helen Lawson! Never!" Tarah gasped aloud as she returned to the mirror. That would reassure her. Should she have a facelift, at such an early age? Younger actresses—and actors—did. "I'm gorgeous!" she said, whipping her head about so that her red hair—almost its natural color—swirled, giving her that Rita Hayworth look.

"I'll wait for the remake of *Gilda*," she swore, "before I play that old bag, Helen Lawson."

2

Another impossible connection develops in Encino, California.

"Fluffer! Fluffer!" the director called.

"Oh, shit, not again," said a frumpy middle-aged woman who looked like a trailer wife. She rose from her chair, where she had been enjoying a quiet cigarette.

"You're all coked out, dude," Cecil B., the director, explained the obvious to a man lying naked and unaroused on an opulent bed next to a naked woman almost as opulent; she leaned, bored, on one elbow.

"Huh?" the naked man rousted himself.

"Why don't ya take another snort and maybe that'll get your cock up again?" Cecil B. said. "This is costing me money, you know." The bedroom set, in the director's house in Encino, California, would be passed off as a "mansion" in the porn movie in progress.

The naked woman lay back, and closed her eyes as if readying for sleep.

"Huh?"

"Jesuschrist, Hunk! Is that all you can say?" Cecil B. aimed harshly at the naked man. His booming voice called out again, "Fluffer! Where the hell are you? What the hell d'ya think I pay you for?"

Sandra May O'Connell, the housewifey woman, blowing smoke from the cigarette she had pasted to her lips, made her way past assistants, some camera cables—and, ignoring them, a heavy middle-aged man in a gaudy expensive suit and a smartly dressed woman—both seated comfortably on a plush sofa. Both drank—the woman sipped—champagne from flute glasses. The woman, Mrs. Renquist, occasionally held out the crystal glass so that it captured a splinter of light, which she inspected for a moment or two before returning her full attention to the set. Beside her, Mr. Renquist leaned over to peer into the sparkle in her glass. Mrs. Renquist pulled it away from his inspection.

"Okay, Hunk, stand up—" the frumpy Sandra May ordered the naked man.

"Huh?"

"That's it, that's a good boy." Sandra May spat out the cigarette, snuffing it out with her foot and, kneeling, replaced it with the naked man's soft cock, swallowing it expertly.

Hunk Williams, king of porn—though his throne was wavering as he approached—passed—the threshold of forty—stood dutifully before the squatting fluffer blowing him to give him an erection, the famous erection that had been molded in plaster; autographed replicas of his fabled foot-long cock were sold to fans and collectors all over the world.

Blaze, the naked woman, yawned sleepily. "You might as well give up, Sandra May," she said to the squatting woman. "I tried it myself. It's dead."

"No, it isn't," Cecil B. said. "Don't even think it, I've got money invested on this."

"Indeed so have we," Mrs. Renquist reminded. She wore only Chanel designs, and perfumed herself with No. 5.

"That's right, we've invested good money in this fucking film," Mr. Renquist echoed, laughing at his own reference.

"*Must* you!" the woman said irritably to him. "Must you use that word? *Must* you always be vulgar?" She did not look at him.

"Film?" That word, echoing for seconds before he was able to perceive it, brought Hunk Williams out of his haze for a moment only. "Huh?"

"He woke up!" Blaze said. "Quick," she said to the fluffer, "quick, try to put it in me so we can end this shoot."

"Huh?"

"Oh, shit, he's not worth all this," Cecil B. despaired.

"Even unprepared," Mrs. Renquist reminded, "his property is more prominent than anyone else's in the erotic industry; it mustn't be disdained so easily."

"Yeah, his hard-on's the biggest in the fuck biz," Mr. Renquist said.

"Why must you always echo what I say, and turn it crude?" Mrs. Renquist confronted him, one hand sheltering her cheek from his words.

Blaze yawned, "It may be big, but I don't suppose anyone's ever seen it really hard, maybe half-mast."

"What do you mean?" the flustered director said to her. "When he was younger, he couldn't keep it soft."

"I've never seen it hard," Blaze said, pushing up her breasts, holding them in that position as if to assure they would stay like that. "His dick's so fuckin' long it just plops down."

"*We've* seen it hard," Investor/Producer Mr. Renquist attested. He nudged the woman.

Mrs. Renquist's look stabbed him. "Don't ever do that to me, and don't speak about 'we.' Don't you have a voice of your own? I'll speak for myself." She crossed her hands over her Chanel bag, for added strength.

Sandra May O'Connell was intrepidly performing her duty, to little effect. She'd stop now and then to take a puff from a new cigarette she removed from a package lodged in her bosom, and then she would resume on Hunk.

"Try his testicles," Mrs. Renquist said. "They are known to be organs of extreme sensitivity."

"That's right, he likes his balls licked," Mr. Renquist said.

"I explicitly asked you to refrain—" Mrs. Renquist abandoned the rest of her frosty words. "Mrs. O'Connell," she called out, "I believe your dentures may be chafing too much. Might you—?"

Sandra May stood up, straight, very straight. "I want you to know that I don't have dentures. Capped teeth, yes. Dentures, no! Hey! Why don't you two fuckers get on your knees and blow 'im?"

"We have," the man said. He answered his wife's glare, "She'll speak for herself." He slapped his thighs gleefully.

Mrs. Renquist eyed him with distaste, the lid of one of her eyes trembling. She pronounced her words with care, as if to obviate mispronouncing or misusing any: "You distress me when you insist on being unpleasant." She sipped from the glass of champagne.

"Oh, Christ, it's not working," Cecil B. announced, as Sandra May O'Connell replaced Hunk's limp cock with a cigarette.

Mr. Renquist drank from his champagne. "Good stuff, eh?"

The chic woman snapped at her husband, "Why must you always be interested in what I'm interested in—?" She corrected herself, "—in that which interests me?—and *must* you use that obnoxious interjection?"

"Eh?—that one?" The man shrugged. "Maybe I follow your interests cause you got such fuckin' good taste, ya think?"

"Mr. Cecil B.," Mrs. Renquist called out, "is it possible that Mr. Williams is simply not responding to Ms. Blaze's assets?"

Dressed, Blaze accosted Mrs. Renquist. "Babe, why don't you fuck yourself?"

"I don't respond to such remarks," the chic woman said to the performer, and sheltered her from her sight by holding a hand, lightly, to her own forehead.

"Right, bitch," Blaze said. She called out to Director Cecil B.: "I want my full pay, I sure worked for it. With this guy, a girl deserves an Academy Award."

"Good job that doctor did on her titties, huh?" Mr. Renquist stopped himself from jabbing Mrs. Renquist.

She winced as if he had.

"I want full pay, too," Sandra May called out. "I got a damn hard job," she directed at Mr. and Mrs. Renquist.

"A fucking *hard* job!" Mr. Renquist let out a guffaw that made Mrs. Renquist touch both her temples as if to soothe a sudden blistering headache.

"It's a *difficult* job." Sandra May O'Connell rubbed her jaw.

Mrs. Renquist looked away from her with clear dislike.

"Listen, sweetie," Sandra May O'Connell said, "I earn every buck I make. So don't you turn away from me."

Mrs. Renquist closed her eyes, smoothing her forehead. "Mr. Cecil B.," Mrs. Renquist called the director over. "Perhaps we should begin exploring a more current form of the art, branching out. The Internet? With something spectacular, something fresh."

"Huh?" Hunk Williams said.

3

A decisive meeting with Lenora Stern, Rusty Blake,
and Tarah Worth. The great Liz Smith invoked.

"Know what I'm smoking, babe? A Cuban cigar. Fifty bucks! Smuggled. The guy coulda got killed getting it into the country, and it would've been worth it."

In a two-room office—all solid brown tones—in a two-story building off Sunset Boulevard along the glamorous Sunset Strip in West Hollywood, Tarah Worth sat before her manager, turning her head away to avoid the vile fumes from the creature's cigar.

"So?" Lenora's square brown suit emphasized her blocky appearance. Her hair was pushed back severely. She wore giant glasses that, Tarah suspected, she might not even need. She resembled a giant owl.

"I'll take the part. But they'll have a difficult time making me up to look older. Of course, they do wonders with makeup these days, they—"

"Sweetheart, sweetheart, sweetheart, of course you'll take the part, and you look it."

Tarah froze. That was the creature's tactic, making her clients vulnerable so she could get them to do whatever the hell she pleased.

"Remember, babe, you haven't got the role yet. I hear they're sounding out Liz Taylor. She can play a grand old dame with the best of them. Tough cookie. We gotta come up with a terrific publicity gimmick for you."

"A gimmick?"

"You know. Like Babette. What a gimmick she's got."

Tarah knew who Babette was. She appeared on posters and billboards all over town, parted glossy lips, eyes seductive under mascara-coated lashes, her long, wavy black hair cascading onto soft shoulders, hips agog under a slinky black bikini that revealed breasts like watermelons. Assumed to be a performer of sorts—no one knew what she had ever appeared in—now and then she might be spotted driving a silver Cadillac. She had gained added notoriety recently when a rivalry had developed between her and an equally busty blonde, who drove a pink Corvette, as to who had used posters first to project her sexy image. "*She* did," Babette had surrendered in one of several statements she issued periodically by mail to the press, "because she's been around so many years more than I have. Besides, she uses drawings, *I* use photographs."

"You're not suggesting I jump into their rivalry with posters of my own?" Tarah asked tentatively. The creature was not beyond any suggestion.

"Naw, something new. That's *her* gimmick. I got an idea for you, though. Hey! You know who'll be here in a few minutes? Soon-to-be-heartthrob Rusty Blake, who says he's a great fan of yours."

God, she had a raspy voice, and the way she kept plastering her dark hair over her ears! Rusty Blake? She knew about him vaguely, had seen pictures of him, maybe even in a television appearance; hadn't he been on *Melrose Place*?

"Tarah Worth!" Rusty Blake was there, with aviator sunglasses, an open shirt, baggy khakis—and good looks spilling over his face that remained surly even when he smiled, like now. He was five-foot-seven, officially six feet tall. "Tarah Worth!" He slapped his forehead, slumped into a chair under the weight of the recognition. "My *God,* is it *the* Tarah Worth?"

"It is," Tarah smiled, pleased that this "up-and-coming" young actor had responded so enthusiastically to her. She must determine his sign.

"Hey, I've seen all your movies, I think they're underrated, you know? But I'll bet they'll all be, like, rediscovered. Hey, wow, it's Tarah Worth!" He shook his head in awe, his ashy brown hair tousled as if he had just gotten out of bed and plastered it that way.

"Blake!" Lenora shouted. "Stop bullshitting. I called you in to tell you I've got something real hot brewin' for ya, and it involves Tarah."

"Yeah?" He sprawled on the chair, his hand courting his groin, his blue eyes gleaming with expectation.

"You've heard about the remake of—"

"*Valley of the Dolls,*" Tarah supplied, so that Lenora wouldn't pronounce the title of the great novel in her ugly voice.

"Yeah, man, read about it in the trades. The remake. Hey, hot ticket. You think, like, there's a role for me?"

"Yeah—and Tarah's up for the role of Helen Lawson—"

"The hag, right?"

"Right, and you're up for the role of the fag."

"What!" Rusty Blake reared, almost off the chair. "Hey, listen, Lenora." He deepened his voice. "I'm not, like, a fag, and you know it, man. No one would believe I was a fag, no matter how good an actor I am." He glared at Tarah as if she had been responsible for this situation. His hand came down on his lap with an assuring grope.

"Of course everyone knows you're not a fag, sweets," Lenora's voice turned as sweet as she was able to make it. "You inform everyone often enough. Besides, they're going to macho up the role."

Blake frowned, quickly wiping the crease he had momentarily allowed on his forehead.

"Ted Casablanca," Tarah interjected, asserting her loyalty and knowledgeability about the great novel and film, "wasn't, really, a . . . homosexual. Just accused of that. When Neely O'Hara catches him with the other woman in the swimming pool, he says the woman made him feel nine feet tall—"

Lenora said to Rusty Blake in a lecherous whisper: "Hear that, honeybunch? Nine. Betcha he was referring to his inches."

Blake's crooked smile widened so that it seemed to be about to slip off his face. "Yeah, man, yeah, I like that, man."

Tarah searched her mind for a subtle way to approach this crucial question: "Oh, by the way, Rusty, what is your sign, your astrological sign?"

His grin cut across his square jaw. "The sexy one, man," he winked. "Actually I'm, like, a Scientologist."

Of course. "But your sign——" Tarah started.

"Tarah! Blake!" Lenora ended the banter. "Enough bullshitting. "I've arranged for you two to be seen at Spago's for dinner, together."

Rusty Blake slouched over to Tarah, massaging her back. "Yeah, hey!"

"I'm not aching, thank you!" Tarah pulled away.

"There's a scene in the script that takes place there between Helen Lawson and Ted Casablanca. I can assure an item about how right you look for the roles, how uncannily right." She puffed on her cigar, blew out a noxious cloud, eyed what was left of the cigar as if she was considering devouring it. She barked at Tarah: "Guess who'll be there that night to see about how right you are for the role?"

Tarah could hardly breathe the name. "Liz Smith."

CHAPTER ELEVEN

1

*The flight to the City of Angels, or more accurately
to the Lord's Headquarters.*

And so Lyle flew with Sister Sis and Brother Bud in the first-class section of the plane. Brother Bud explained the expensive means of transportation as Lyle looked around at well-dressed men and women. "The needy souls we minister to don't want us to set a bad example, we gotta exemplify what is possible under the Lord's guidance, and what is possible is travelin' first class. Until we get our own jet. Soon."

"A daiquiri mix," Sister Sis ordered from the steward, who couldn't keep his eyes off Lyle.

"A whiskey sour—with two olives," Brother Bud ordered.

That startled the steward into attention. "An *olive*? In a *whiskey sour*?"

"I said *two,*" Brother Bud asserted.

"And *him?*" the attendant gasped, pointing at Lyle. "What will the stud—uh—what will the—uh—cowboy have?" He touched his blond hair, to exhibit its newly acquired highlights.

"Tea, iced tea," Lyle said, "with a wedge of lemon."

The attendant did not move.

"Now you run along and do your duties!" Sister Sis said irritably. "Keep in mind what the Lord did to Sodom."

"What did he do?" Lyle asked.

"Destroyed it," Brother Bud said, glaring at the attendant.

2

Someone secret knows Lyle's whereabouts.

Lyle landed in Los Angeles and was whisked away by limousine, Sister Sis and Brother Bud sitting close to him as if they suspected he might run away from them before they reached the Lord's Headquarters in Anaheim.

The limousine let them out at a motel that looked as if a giant artificial flower had burst and scattered its waxy pedals over everything. There was a swimming pool with pockets of azure lights. Lyle noticed a beautiful woman emerging from the water. She spread her towel on a pool chair and lay on it. Lyle continued to stare back until they entered the lobby, all chrome and plastic. The three were led by a smart bellboy to—

"Your room, cowboy!" Brother Bud announced proudly.

It had been selected, and probably decorated, by them, Lyle knew, because dominating the room—pleated drapes, shiny tables, flashy lamps, a velvet sofa, a polished sliding window that faced the pool— the gorgeous woman was still there—was a large crucifix over a huge bed; the crucifix glowed in a slab of light within which it had been strategically located.

Lyle's first instinct was to run out of the room—and perhaps run into the gorgeous woman outside—but Brother Bud and Sister Sis were holding on to each of his arms.

"Kinda overwhelms you, doesn't it, cowboy?" Sister Sis asked.

"Yes, ma'am," Lyle said. Her hand—long red fingernails—tightening on his arm had squeezed out his answer.

"Now you stop calling me ma'am," Sister Sis instructed, touching her eyelashes as if to make sure they were still there.

"Yes, Ms. Sis."

Brother Bud was fussing around puffing up pillows.

A knock at the door. Lyle opened it.

"A present for Mr. Lyle Clemens," the motel bellboy said.

"Who else did you tell you're here?" Sister Sis demanded.

Lyle took the small, wrapped box.

"Let me see!" Brother Bud snatched it from him.

Lyle snatched it back and opened it. The box contained a jar of jelly beans, all colors.

"What the hell?" Sister Sis greeted. She grabbed a card attached to the jar. "'Stay put'—that's all it says." She frowned at Lyle.

Sister Matilda? Lyle's heart gave a joyful leap. He looked around the room, as if she would be there, somewhere, with her golden crown, waiting to explain her absence.

"Now what do you think that means?" Sister Sis's frown cracked her forehead.

"Hmmmm," Brother Bud pondered. "You fond of jelly beans, cowboy?"

Lyle knew he had to invent an answer to dissuade any suspicion about Sister Matilda—if the present did involve her. "Yes, Mr. Bud, real fond of jelly beans." He dipped in the jar, stopped, extended it to Sister Sis, who took one, a pink one, then to Brother Bud, who refused. Lyle chewed several.

"Who sent them to you"—Sister Sis's voice was not her girlish one—"and who wants you to stay put, and why?"

"Uh—I guess, you know—that man on the airplane—that steward, remember?" That's all Lyle could come up with.

"The sodomite!" Brother Bud was harsh. "How'd he know?"

"When I went to the restroom," Lyle said, "he offered me some and I told him that was my favorite candy."

"Makes sense," Brother Bud pronounced, "and he wants to see you again. We'll make sure that don't happen."

Lyle strained to look out at the woman by the pool.

Sister Sis chose another pink jelly bean. "Does taste good, doesn't it? Oh, the Lord's little pleasures!"

"Now, then, you relax, cowboy, cause we're gonna rehearse ya tomorrow," Brother Bud adopted his friendliest tone.

Sister Sis said, "We'll send a driver to pick you up. We're already announcing your participation on our stations to inaugurate the Write-a-Love-Letter-to-Jesus Campaign, got some days for practicin', but not too many. Gotta keep that spontaneity in your talent."

When they left, Lyle ate more jelly beans. Stay put! If the jelly beans came from Sister Matilda, they were a reminder, of course; she had asked him to remember what he'd seen in a candy jar back in the Pentecostal Hall, and what he'd seen was jelly beans. The exhortation would mean for him to stick it out with Brother Bud and Sister Sis until—

What? Damned if he knew. In the meantime—

He hurried to the window. The beautiful woman by the pool was still there. He wished he had brought trunks, and then he would join her without seeming obvious. Talking to that woman would keep him from feeling so goddamned low about leaving everyone he loved—and if more happened, well, that would keep his mind even more occupied, away from Maria for now.

3

"Return to the Valley of the Dolls"

The new title is *Return to the Valley of the Dolls*—not a remake any more; it's a sequel. Remakes are flops.

A sequel! Tarah Worth had wanted to tear Lenora's memo apart when she first read that at her home in—near—Hollywood. If it was to be a sequel, then Helen Lawson would have aged into a mummy!

Now, as she lounged by the gaudy pool of this tacky motel in Anaheim—and tried, just tried, to relax before, in a few days, she and Rusty Blake would make their crucial appearance at Spago's with the great Liz Smith in watchful attendance—she read the memo more intently, more assured.

Unfortunately, we're stuck with the word "dolls" in the title. Susann invented it.

Isn't that what great writers do, invent? Tarah defended. She skipped on to read cast possibilities:

Madonna or Courtney Love as Anne Wells, the classy blue-blood from Vermont; Sylvester Stallone or Arnold Schwarzenegger as the English literary giant who betrays her; Jennifer Lopez as Neely O'Hara—

Were they crazy? Tarah forced herself to continue:

Michael Douglas as the plastic surgeon (a new character).

Perfect casting, with his perfect chin!

—for the role of Ted Casablanca, Tom Cruise—or Rusty Blake, if we can't get Cruise.

Wait till Blake reads that Cruise is up for the role! Tarah read on:

Ted Casablanca is still pursued by gossip that he's gay, although he's constantly chasing women; reputedly into (soft) S & M (bondage, hand-cuffs, etc.). In the meantime, beautiful Jennifer North's mother has sworn to terrorize everyone associated with her daughter's death as a result of being in the "flesh flicks" which exploited her beauty and led to her suicide. Everyone in the present cast was involved in one way or another with Jennifer's demise, and so everyone is on the Stalker Mom's list, the first target being the French pimp (George Hamilton) who introduced Jennifer to flesh flicks.

George Hamilton! Perfect!

The Stalker Mom is a frumpy housewife type, not your ordinary stalker. (Bette Midler?) First on her stalk list is Ted Casablanca, vulnerable when he's being bound in sex play with Neely O'Hara. The Stalker Mom's next target is Helen Lawson. (Liz Taylor? Tara Worth?) . . .

On the margin the creature had underlined the misspelling of her name and had written: "This will be you if you try hard enough and Liz doesn't want the part."

Lawson once pushed Jennifer out of a legitimate role, which made her take another step into porn. Lawson, having consulted a spiritual guru, is no longer a gargoyle—she's had a facelift.

Thank God, thank God, thank God, not a gargoyle—and the facelift would erase the years in between the original and the sequel, Tarah had exulted when she read that reprieve earlier. "Thank God," she said aloud, reverentially. She touched her face. Should she? She had been at Neiman-Marcus recently, and all the women had the same noses. Thank God she had been blessed with a perfect nose, needing no surgery, none whatever, none, except for that insignificant bump she had had removed.

The Stalker Mom has announced she will pounce on Lawson on a certain day (the Fourth of July, for added fireworks?). Lawson flees Hollywood, incognito, to a tacky city called Anaheim. There, in a gaudy motel, by the pool, she engages in conversation with a good-looking young man she does not readily recognize. Who is he? The Stalker Mom's accomplice? Or—?

That was why Tarah Worth was here, by the pool of a gaudy motel in Anaheim, to research that scene, already written in revised draft, and right now in her hands. She would capture every nuance of the great role—in the exact setting, all in further preparation for the role of a lifetime. When she appeared at Spago's with Rusty Blake, she *would* be Helen Lawson, and the great Liz Smith would confirm it.

4

A poolside encounter.

The woman wasn't as young as Lyle imagined, but that didn't matter. What mattered was that she was very sexy—and, damn, he sure needed to keep his mind away from Maria and that nonsense about her being his sister.

Under a sheltering umbrella, the woman lowered the straps of her bathing top, and peered at him from under sunglasses.

He spoke aloud what he was thinking: "Wow"—although the thought of Maria tugged at the edges of his mind, no, at the edges of his heart.

The woman took off her sunglasses and sat up. "You recognized me, didn't you?" she asked. "From my movies?" she added when Lyle seemed puzzled. Wait a second! This couldn't be a coincidence. Lenora! The creature was the only one who knew she was here and why, and she was not beyond having secretly hired an actor to challenge her into the scene.

"You're a movie star?" Lyle said. He would write Clarita about it. Not Sylvia, always competing.

"Yes." Tarah said. "Now do you mind moving a little? You're blocking my sun."

He wasn't. The only move he could make put him closer to her—or else he would plunge into the pool; he moved closer.

"Do you work here?" she asked him. Maybe he wasn't a hired actor, just a horny bellboy? With those boots? No.

"No. I'm going to sing for the Write-a-Love-Letter-to-Jesus Campaign." Is that what he was really going to do?

"Hmm." What to make of that? The last thing she needed was one of those shrill born-agains telling her to prepare because the Apocalypse was at hand, bad enough that Rusty Blake was a Scientologist. Removing her sunglasses, she studied the young man before her. Very handsome, very sexy. Definitely an actor hired by Lenora. Had he read the scene, or was he improvising, forcing her to rise to the test, seizing the direction? *Very* sexy. Perhaps she should consider extending the rehearsal beyond the written scene, into the motel room and—

Looking at the sultry body lying before him, a coat of sunblock turning into sequins, Lyle reminded himself that he missed his sister a lot. Dammit! Maria was not his sister!—and damn right—whoever the hell she was!—he missed her. Still—

"Listen, cowboy—" Tarah improvised. Had someone creative in Hollywood decided to make the mysterious stranger a cowboy? A good touch!

"I'm not a cowboy, I've never been on a horse."

An actor, then, of course. She pushed the scene along. "I'm a lone woman getting away from something awful,"—this was a memorized line from the written scene—"and I'm lonely." Susann would be proud of those lines—so blunt, so exact! "So"—she made her voice husky like Helen Lawson's and finished the scripted line that would send chills through the audience—"you wanna fuck?"

"Sure!" That lifted the sadness, a lot.

"But—" Damn, what was the next line? The scene had all those great twists and turns; and this was the crucial point at which Helen Lawson realizes—What?

"I sure would want to!" Lyle reminded enthusiastically.

What was it, the elusive, crucial line! There had been several X'd out, insertions substituted, also X'd out. She had read each aloud, thrilling. Which had remained? "Yes, I want to, but" . . . "I don't have time because—" What?—oh, yes—because I'm dying? Dying? No, that was crossed out. "Yes, I want to, but I mustn't—" she repeated, hoping the rest of the line would hop on. Then she remembered it, the shattering line, and spoke it with all the power that would make the audience gasp: "Yes, I want to, but I never could, I could never have sex with a man I only now recognize as . . . my brother."

Lyle ran back to his motel room.

5

The Lord's Cowboy is born.

"Let's rehearse you for the Lord!" Brother Bud greeted Lyle on the stage of the Lord's Headquarters in Anaheim, California. A chauffeur had picked him up at the motel.

"Praise the Lord and the young cowboy," Sister Sis batted her eyelashes at heaven and spoke loudly for the workers on the set to hear. Technicians, many in sloppy shorts, went about arranging props, electrical equipment, recording instruments.

"I'm not a cowboy," Lyle announced loudly to everyone. "I've never been on a horse."

"Shush," Brother Bud cautioned. "You *are* a cowboy now." He consulted several sheets of paper, notes, neatly typed. "This is how you came to Jesus on your way to becoming the Lord's Cowboy."

"The Lord's Cowboy?" Lyle restrained laughter because Brother Bud was so serious.

"It was a thundering day," Sister Sis said, closing her eyes to evoke it, "gray clouds warred in the heavens, like they did when the first rebellion occurred in heaven—"

"—and mean ole Satan set angel against angel, and they wrestled over doomed souls"—Brother Bud took over—"including *yours!*" he shot at Lyle.

A prop man carrying a huge painting of a happy Jesus stumbled over a coil of wires and bounced against Lyle. "Sorry, Lord's Cowboy," he said.

"Look," Lyle said to Brother Bud and Sister Sis, "none of that happened to me. Those are lies. I can't—"

"Lies!" Brother Bud shook his head sadly, Sister Sis lowered hers as far as the giant wig would allow without toppling over. "The Lord doesn't lie, cowboy," Brother Bud said. "He directed your mission, from the moment you sang peace into all those souls back in Ree-oh Es-con-dee-toe. Now he has sent us visions of your life that not even you may remember."

"—and there you were in the middle of the storm on your horse named—named—" Sister Sis continued fashioning Lyle's new life.

"—named Rigger," Brother Bud furnished.

"You mean Trigger," Sister Sis corrected

"No, that belongs to Roy Roger and his wife Dale, decent Christians committed to the Lord, and may they rest in peace—"

"Brother Bud, Dale's not dead. We had her as a guest."

"May the Lord allow her to thrive. You sure she isn't dead? I do think she has gone to her reward. Is Gene—?"

"Dead," Sister Sis said, "Gene Autry is dead for sure."

"A fine upstanding Christian, too, Gene raffled his hat, once, for the Lord. Now, cowboy, you named your horse Rigger after the famous Trigger, because you'd been inspired by Dale and Roy, may they rest— Sure she isn't dead?" Brother Bud insisted.

Lyle listened. If he did become someone else, at least for a while, wouldn't the pain of leaving lessen, wouldn't sad memories pester him less?

"On that thundery day on the plains, the sky opened, and lightnin'—"

"—almost struck you—"

"It *did* strike you, knocked you off Rigger, but—"

"—you survived, young cowboy, you survived, and knew the Lord had sent you a message—"

"—so you knelt, right there on the plains, and saw, in the sky, writ large in the hand of the Lord, the letters L.H."

"L.H.?" Lyle asked.

"It baffled you then, too," said Sister Sis.

"On their way back from the roundup," Brother Bud continued, "your partners saw you kneeling and staring in amazement, and they derided you, knowing of your wicked past—"

"Wicked past?" Lyle couldn't help it, he thought of Maria, *But she was not his sister!*

"—derided you like they did our Lord in olden times," Sister Sis interjected into Lyle's biography, "laughed and rode on—"

"—except for one roustabout who'd been touched in the spirit, and he carried you home, that humble Christian, and when you opened your eyes, you saw—"

"—on his TV screen you saw the name of our ministry, the Lord's Headquarters!

"L.H.," Lyle said.

"You got it then and you got it now," Brother Bud congratulated.

Should he flee now? Where? Stay put! the message in his room urged.

"Hallelujah! There and then you knew the Lord was ordering you on a mission that led to—"

"Us!" they both announced.

Brother Bud cleared his throat. "Your father was a Christian soul who died early but he loved you so much that—"

"My father was a goddamned son of a bitch," Lyle said, "and I'm a bastard!"

Sister Sis reached for her dormant tambourine and smacked it, hard, in disapproval.

"You're no such thing, and he was no such thing," Brother Bud dismissed.

"Now listen!" Sister Sis's nongirlish voice moved things on, "when you go out there to coax Love Letters to Jesus, you gotta pour your own love into every word you sing, every move you make." An appreciative smile crept from under the makeup, threatening to crack it.

"Get the holy juices flowin'," Brother Bud joined.

He preacher-hopped around Lyle to the rhythm of Sister's Sis's trembling tambourine. She joined him in his jumpy dance, striking her tambourine above her head.

"—juices flowin' and bustin' out for the Lord!"

"—bustin' out and gushin' for the Lord!"

Did they know about Rose?

"That's who you are now," Brother Bud said soberly.

"The Lord's Cowboy," Sister Sis bowed her head in reverence.

"That isn't me," Lyle protested.

Sister Sis snapped: "You think *this* is me?" She touched her wig. She pulled crazily at her eyelashes.

Brother Bud edged her away and brought an envelope out from his coat pocket. "Now, Lord's Cowboy, if you got any doubts about servin' the Lord through our inspired ministry, just listen to what your devoted mamma wrote us."

CHAPTER TWELVE

1

*A troubling letter is received, and love letters
to Jesus are solicited.*

Brother Bud handed the letter to Lyle. "Your mamma's
a servant of Jesus, all right," Brother Bud said, "however low she may have fallen—" When he saw Lyle's
fist clench and rise, he dodged, and quickly added,
"—and been redeemed."

The few words of the letter slid off the page as if
Sylvia had composed them in a daze. Lyle read:

Dear Brother Bud and Sister Sis—Keep Lyle Clemens in your fold.
Forgive my accursed flesh. In repentance—Sylvia Love.

Accursed flesh? Repentance? A surge of sorrow swept through Lyle.
What drove her? Whatever it was, whatever she meant, she wanted him
to stay away.

So Lyle agreed to become the Lord's Cowboy. But he would be *only*
a performer, *never* a convert, he swore to himself.

During the rehearsal that preceded his appearance on the day that
would launch the Write-a-Love-Letter-to-Jesus Campaign, and while
Brother Bud and Sister Sis gyrated about him, encouraging him, Lyle
decided how he would become inspired to perform on the appointed
day. By relying on Rose's expert instructions.

2

The Lord's Cowboy performs.

The Write-a-Love-Letter-to-Jesus campaign opened to a spill-out house
of howling, screaming, hurting congregants gathered at the Lord's
Headquarters in Anaheim on a hot, sweaty night.

On the same set that Lyle had seen at the Pentecostal Hall, a motel-
rectory, two dozen of God's Angels swayed and hummed to each word
of proclaimed revelation.

Wiping massive tears from her streaked cheeks, Sister Sis and Brother
Bud, shaking his head in admiration of God's wondrous ways, took turns
presenting evidence of miraculous intercessions, accompanied by donations from everywhere:

"From a little girl, crippled, skipping merrily along now, a manifes-
tation of gratitude, a few pennies, only that, but her faith will draw
millions—"

"From a man blind for ten years, able to see the light now, a donation of all he has kept hidden—"

"From a sinner drowning in alcohol—"

"From a fornicator lost in lust—"

"From a man deaf in both ears—"

"From a woman crippled when—"

"From—"

"From—"

"From—"

"From—"

"Write *your* Love Letter to Jesus, enclose your heavenly donations, and we'll deliver to Him by prayer's fastest post," Sister Sis begged.

"Give as much as you love him," Brother Bud pleaded.

Lyle heard the litany of names and amounts of donations, of cures and donations, of prayers and donations—an avalanche of pain and contributions.

"To rouse the living spirit, here is—!"

A swell of hallelujahs from the chorus shoved away the sweet trilling of God's Little Angels aflutter in feathery tissue wings and proclaimed the entrance of—

"The Looooooord's Coooooooowboyyyyyy!"

Decked in new jeans fitted by the Lord's seamstress, a Western shirt—an extra button hurriedly opened by Sister Sis—a cowboy hat, which was intended to fall off ("If the Lord inspires you to," Sister had suggested, "send it spinnin' out at the folks to grab and cherish)"—and wearing his own cherished Tony Lama boots, Lyle walked to the center of the set.

Now what?

He strummed a few uncertain, quivery notes on his guitar. How to start? Oh, wait. Would they be watching, somehow? Maria? And Clarita—and Sylvia?

He sang to Maria:

I will love you always and I'm not your brother—

God's Little Angels warbled: "Yea, Lord, I'm your brotherrr, I'm your sisterrrr . . ."

Lyle changed the song quickly. He formed a hurried message to Sylvia:

With all my heart and soul, Sylvia, I pray that you're okay—

"Yea, hope is the heart's soul, Savior!" the chorus chimed.

Lyle was stumped. What to rhyme with Clarita?

"Arouse them in the spirit, send them surging to Heaven!" Sister Sis pled anxiously, over jiggles of her tambourine.

"Do your damn preacher dance!" Brother Bud exhorted.

Go at it, cowboy! Rose encouraged.

Sure! All right!

Now!

He strummed his guitar and sang improvised words, and then abandoned the words and strummed and strummed and did the preacher-strut—and hopped back, forward, forward, back, forward, forward, forward, and he thought of sweet Rose and then thought of Maria, naked that afternoon . . . her legs . . . white flesh interrupted only by the small stark triangle sheltering the pink opening . . . her breasts . . . eager nipples . . . Rose! . . . lush flesh . . . scarlet lips . . . gasps . . . thought of . . . that woman in the pool lobby . . . one leg crooked over the other, tiny sequiny hairs peeking out, tempting . . . glistening—and his body responded just as it had with Maria—(*Don't leave me out, cowboy!*)—and Rose, and like the first time he sang in Rio Escondido, and when his excitement became too prominent he hopped, hopped, hopped, plucking his guitar, disguising his arousal, wiggling sideways—forcing it down but not too much—to gales of approbation, howls of approbation, and the congregation screamed with joy, and some of the afflicted hopped in the aisles, and the panting congregation swayed to the rhythm of the Lord's Cowboy, who was sweating, so hot, oh, Lord—so hot that his shirt clung to his chest with perspiration, where Maria had kissed him and he had kissed her breasts and kissed Rose's and Maria's, but not the red-haired woman's—what was her name? . . . naked breasts, spread white thighs, parted lips—(*Oh, lordee, yes, cowboy, now thrust, and riiiiiiide on!*)—and his erection threatened to bust through, and the congregation went wild and hollered, "Yea, Lord, come to me, come to us, come, O Lord, come, come!"—and their bodies strained toward him, their hands grasping high, as he bumped, ground, pumped—and a woman in the audience screamed, "Oh, Lord!" and fainted in the aisle, knocked dead in the spirit, while a swelling chorus of hallelujahs paused only to allow God's Little Angels, feathers quivering, to be heard trilling sweetly.

"The spirit has grabbed the Lord's Cowboy!"

3

The ascent of the Lord's Cowboy.

On the second day of the Write-a-Love-Letter-to-Jesus Campaign, Brother Bud confided to the congregants, to explain Lyle's odd words: "Sometimes the Lord's Cowboy lapses into tongues, words God dictates to him right on the spot, words you may not understand but God does, words that cause Him to send down His brightest light upon you."

Clasping her hands soulfully, Sister Sis explained, "He sings songs only he hears, songs angels sing to him, and that he imparts to you through God's bounty."

"Gaahhd's Bouuuuuunteeee!" The chorus swelled in adulation as Lyle entered, his guitar over his shoulder to be whipped forward in one moment with a thrust forward of his hips.

The Lord's Cowboy had the spirit, for sure, everyone said—hallelujah, yea, Lord—and, yea, look at him, willya?—the Lord's Cowboy strutting to rouse the dead and the living, doin' the preacher-strut like God and the angels intended—back, back, hop, hop, back, hop, hop, whip around, whip around, arch, toss, bump and grind and toss and hop and whip around—and don't you know that the holy spirit surged through the Lord's Cowboy like electricity oozing out into the congregation.

Beyond the Lord's Headquarters, the devoted audience watching on television gathered dimes and quarters and bills and life's savings and sat down to write Love Letters to Jesus, and marked them "Personal."

4

The Lord's message reinterpreted.

"Leave it there!" Mrs. Renquist ordered Mr. Renquist, who had been randomly aiming his remote at the giant television screen on which they were preparing to watch a video of Bette Davis in *Beyond the Forest.*

"You got religion suddenly, eh?" Mr. Renquist was bold enough to chide. "That's that crazy evangelical station—" He double-blinked at the screen. "Wow, what a fuckin' hunk."

Mrs. Renquist flinched, but her eyes remained on the screen, where, against a backdrop meant to look like the interior of a rectory, a young cowboy was warbling and prancing and hopping on the television screen.

"I bet he could shove a mean fuck!" Mr. Renquist said.

Mrs. Renquist recoiled as if shot. "Why must you reduce everything? Clearly, that young man has a prominent presence; why can't you say that?"

"That kid ain't dancin' for the Lord," Mr. Renquist continued intrepidly. "He's dancing like he's fucking, eh?"

Mrs. Renquist pressed both her hands before her mouth as if to smother two screams, at the coarseness of his words and at the despised interjection. All she could utter was, *"Why——?"*

"Young, fresh, sexy, a real hunk, and unless he's stuffed in the balls, he's sure got a big dong. Christ, has he got a hard-on under those tight pants? Look! Hey, that's why he's hopping up and down cause he wants to shake the hard-on down! Take a gander at his balls, eh? If it isn't stuffed, then he's hung like a fuckin' horse."

"Something new on the Internet," Mrs. Renquist thought aloud.

"With him? No way you could get him away from those born-again fucks; you'd have to fuckin' trick him into something——"

"Yes! Trick him!" Mrs. Renquist agreed, before Mr. Renquist's blatant vulgarity struck at her temples like two thieves in the night, causing her to utter tiny protesting sobs.

5

A column poised to assure a triumph.

Liz Smith

The Return of a Star

Los Angeles.—On my visit to the other Coast, I spotted Rusty Blake and gorgeous Tarah Worth at Beverly Hills' celebrity-studded restaurant, Spago's. Astonishing as it may seem, Tarah looks even younger than Blake, who is—he claims—not yet 30. During a tableside chat, Tarah, as charming as she is beautiful, assured me that her "skin is still virgin skin, unviolated by the surgeon's knife." Hollywood makeup experts will have a hard time aging her for the role of Helen Lawson, although I learned it's being adjusted just for her. "I don't mind playing an older woman of 39," Tarah confided, "because it is a fabulous role, and I am an actress." Spoken like a trouper! I cannot imagine who else would play the choicest role in the sequel to the great classic *Valley of the Dolls* by my good, departed friend, the immortal Jacqueline Susann. Hollywood, take notice! I predict that this role will bring Tarah Worth the Academy Award she deserves. Not only is she abundantly talented, she is also one of the most beautiful women in the world, with exquisite skin, eyes that tilt. She is at once an All-American beauty and an exotic, mysterious woman.

Her body is unbelievable, and it would be at any age. But for a woman of 37 . . . 36 . . . 35 . . . 33 . . . 30, she is miraculous. And that red hair! Really, she is breathtaking!

"Exactly like that!" Tarah said aloud. She sat in her living room penning the column she was sure Liz Smith would write—of course Liz would write it in her own inimitable way, imagination could not match that—about her evening out—tonight—at Spago's with Rusty Blake!

What was all that shrieking? Oh, yes, those crazy evangelists on the television screen. She had landed on one absently when she had begun to pen the imaginary column.

Was that him? The young man by the motel pool. She put on the glasses she never wore in public. It was him—and he was not an actor—yes, it was that sexy cowboy who had run away so strangely after standing there with a hard-on. What to make of the fact that he had now appeared in her life twice? How was he connected to *Return to the Valley of the Dolls?* Call Riva, her psychic advisor? Things had to happen in threes, to achieve powerful significance; Riva had taught her that.

Tarah stood up, gathering about her the filmy negligee that erased any blemish—not that there was any—on her body. It was noontime but she liked to remain in her "bedclothes," luxuriating glamorously. Now! Now she must decide what to wear for this staggeringly important night! Should she consult her horoscope? No, it was always malicious, always warning. Still . . .

She took her chart out of the drawer. Today: "A tall, handsome man is headed your way and may change your life—for good or ill."

A tall, handsome man . . . the cowboy! Again! Still: ". . . for good or ill." Irritated by the astrologer's nasty addition, Tarah took a pen and blotted out the last two words of that entry in her chart.

6

A matter of morality considered.

Lyle felt ashamed, couldn't stand himself, thought every day of fleeing, tossed and turned in the motel bed—occasionally looking out at the pool to see if maybe the woman he had seen there might be out there, even if it was night. He felt even more ashamed when he fell asleep and dreamt that an angry Clarita was teaching him a lesson that he couldn't hear, and then Sister Matilda came in on it scolding him for making sounds in the Lords Headquarter's—"just sounds, don't mean anything." But none of that was anything like the shame he felt when, later that day, Brother Bud and Sister Sis presented him with a big check, more money than he had ever imagined—"just the beginning, Lord's Cowboy, to show how much the Lord appreciates you, boy."

He felt so ashamed that he thought—again—of fleeing—and then wondered whether he should await some further indication of why Sister Matilda wanted him to Stay put.

Too, there was this. He sure could use all that money.

7

At the Lord's Bank.

He walked into the bank named on the check and waited for the prettiest girl teller, who had spotted him when he walked in.

"Can't cash that much," she said, in a winky voice. "You'd want to open an account with it, wouldn't you, cowboy?"

Lyle shook his head. No use explaining he wasn't a cowboy. "I guess," Lyle said.

The pretty girl said wistfully, "I'll have to call one of the managers so you won't have to wait, and he'll open the account for you. Mr. Clarence!" she called out.

A staid serious man responded to her call. He led Lyle to his desk in a small cubicle. "Thomas Clarence here," he introduced himself. "This is a lot of money, young man. Of course, I know the source. Good Christian folk, Brother Bud and Sister Sis, upright folk, decent folk, honest folk, beacons of light within all the darkness of sin and evil, God praise them in these times of liberal upheaval. We have the honor of having them bank with us. That makes me think of this establishment as the Lord's Bank. I'll need to have a driver's license."

"I don't drive," Lyle said.

"Ride a horse?" the man broke his staid demeanor with a tiny chuckle, then became serious again. "I need some kind of identification." He looked at the paper Lyle had handed him. "A birth certificate?"

"It's mine," Lyle said.

The man put on glasses, scrutinized it. "Father—"

"Unknown," Lyle said without hesitation. "He was a goddamned son of a bitch who left my mother when I was about to be born, and so she just as soon not have his name on that paper; but it's me."

Even so, Thomas Clarence—frowning at the young man's language—said he'd have to verify the check with the "righteous Bud and Sis," whom he called "on their private line, always in touch in case of urgency." Obviously on familiar terms with them, he chuckled and said, "God bless you" several times, and added, off the telephone, to Lyle: "I like working for good folks, honorable folks, following their righteous instructions, never question." He spoke into the telephone again: "Ummm, yes, of course, everything's being handled right and according to your wise instructions."

His smile told Lyle they had stood by the check. "They tell me you're a follower of the Word, and their word is good enough for me," said Mr. Thomas Clarence. "I don't question the righteous," he asserted. He proposed a bank account, in the Ministry's name, of course, but for him to draw on. "That way—"

Too complicated. "I'll take the cash," Lyle said.

"Lots of money to carry around with you," Mr. Clarence cautioned.

Lyle opted for the cash.

Thomas Clarence looked at him with steely eyes. "I would strongly suggest that you—"

With a wide smile, Lyle asked for the cash, please.

"Maybe now you'll buy yourself a horse!" Mr. Clarence snapped.

As he walked out of the bank with a lot of cash and two money orders—for Sylvia and Clarita—Lyle told himself that when he found Sister Matilda—and he would, he would—he would explain why he took the tainted money. But what if what Brother Bud and Sister Sis had said about *her* absconding with funds was true?

Dodging behind a building and looking around to make sure nobody saw, he stuffed the bills into his Tony Lama boots.

8

The predicament of the Lord's Cowboy.

Lyle was through, wondering, as always, whether he should bow.

No need to wonder about anything further because—

Brother Dan pounced onto the stage and landed with a loud thud!

He was a ferocious evangelist who had traveled all the way from Georgia for tonight's healings, a star evangelist who had performed more cures and exorcisms than even he, himself, in his humility, remembered. A fierce man whose hair seemed to have been shaken about by a fierce wind, his stocky body agile, he screamed out his message in a flood of words:

"The Lord's aimin' massive wrath right now at evil souls wanderin' the earth, but he's givin' members of this congregation a last chance to placate His ire, be granted a passport to Heaven! Give your hearts, give your bounty. Give!"

Out came new donations and letters carried in boxes by God's Little Angels, cardboard wire crowns sprinkled with tinsel.

"These come from folks cravin' salvation, freedom from pain, and they send all they have, and in return what do they get? A bushel of miracles!" Brother Dan thrust his hands up and shook his head at the wonder of God's wrath and bounty.

Cries came up, echoing, "Grant us miracles."

Brother Dan lowered his voice, seemed about to kneel, sprang up. "Pour out of your heart, pour out of your pockets. Be a soldier of the Lord, wage his war, donate your ammunition to fight the Old Devil. Give, give, give!"

"Praise God!" . . . "Lord protect us!" . . . "Grant us miracles and a passport to Heaven."

They squirmed, they trembled, they grasped at the air, they cried, they laughed, they sprang into the aisles, they quivered and fainted and babbled in tongues, they danced, they howled, they reached for heaven, they sank crouching on the floor.

Brother Dan spread his hands, inviting. "Come forth to be purified of demons, to cast away ole Satan. That will be done not by my humble hands—I am but a lowly servant of the Lord—it will be done by Jesus, through these hands." He scattered the invisible bounty in his hands. . . . "Come forth now and cleanse yourselves, be slain in the spirit of the

Lord." He stretched beneficent hands to those already making their way toward him.

Lyle watched the parade of the pained. What to think about God? How did He allow this suffering—and, then, allow it to be used, abused, this procession of the trembling, crawling, hobbling, screaming to be cured, to be struck on the forehead and healed—for how long? It was sad, it was frightening. He would leave this fraudulent circus he had performed in, right now!

"Just received this!" Sister Sis ran breathlessly sobbing to Brother Dan. "Special delivery!" She was carrying a jar. "Sent to us by saintly woman."

Brother Bud put a reassuring hand on her quivering shoulders, took the fat glass from her, and ceremoniously handed it to Brother Dan.

"Doctors said it couldn't be removed," Sister Sis wept, "told the poor woman she would die in a month, and she—" She stopped, racked with sobs.

"It was during your pleadings with Jesus, Brother Dan," Brother Bud managed to continue, "that the poor soul was able to shed it, just tore it out of her bosom. And here it is: The deadly tumor!"

Brother Bud held the jar up—up high like a trophy—before the congregation.

Gasps! Oohs! Ahs! "A miracle!" Wild applause!

Sister Sis squeezed out words, "She sent this to us in a humble jar as proof of God's mercy, and she sent all her funds to help bring His miracles to others."

Brother Dan inhaled, exhaled—loudly. He roared: "Praise God!" Screams! Delirium!

An attendant took the jar from Brother Dan, who bowed in reverence. As the attendant passed Lyle, Lyle saw the dark mass inside it, bloody streaks of red creeping through a dark mass. The jelly beans he'd seen that first day when Brother Bud and Sister Sis had shushed the man and woman carrying them? Jelly beans squashed and put into a gluey liquid? Yes!—and the jar sent to him in the motel room as a reminder confirmed that.

His legs and feet were returning him to the stage, to expose, to— He stopped when he heard Brother Dan's next words.

"—a ho-mo-sex-u-al"—Brother Dan masticated each syllable— "driven by lust for his own sex, cast into the pit of perdition, and staggering to find his way here, to be driven of his sins, his base desires, his unnatural longings."

"Make me clean!" A young man, slender, knelt before the ferocious preacher.

"He has traveled for miles to be saved," Sister Sis emphasized for the congregation that waited, spellbound now, enthralled by something more, something else, something strange and thrilling.

Brother Dan glared down at the kneeling boy. "—a child who has strayed into Satan's perversions!" he screamed.

The boy held his hands pressed together under his chin, his face raised, his eyes closed, his lips slightly parted. "Cleanse me!"

Lyle recognized the boy. Raul from Rio Escondido.

CHAPTER THIRTEEN

1

Crisis at Spago, and everyone is there.

W here the hell is she?"

"Who?"

Only when Rusty Blake asked her, Who? did Tarah Worth realize she had spoken her apprehension aloud. The rented limousine had minutes ago deposited them at the portals of Spago in Beverly Hills to replicate the scene in *Return to the Valley of the Dolls,* a replication that would challenge fiction and assure her the greatest role of all time. The pretty young woman behind the reservations booth had consulted her seating chart and had asked them to follow her, ushering them past the lush garden (oh, oh—Tarah's pulse quickened with anxiety), until she remembered Lenora's last-minute call: "Changed tactic—it's too damn cold tonight for the garden, and those damn heaters heat up only a part of your ass. Tonight it's inside, or else those doors will clang shut on you like a guillotine blade when the inside people announce they're getting a chill from the garden!—and keep this in mind, babe: Ya wanna show off your boobs; so you can't afford a chill."

The hostess was leading them too far—toward the hidden back rooms ("Doomsville," said Lenora), and so Tarah prepared to speak rehearsed words: "This table will not do," but she was glad she didn't speak them, because she and Rusty were led to a kind table in the main dining room. That's when Tarah, thrust into new waves of anxiety, asked, "Where the hell is she?"

"Who?"

"Liz Smith."

"Uh, yeah, like she's supposed to see how, like, great we look together, right?—just like in the 'doll' movie when we'd be, like, paired up." He ran his fingers through his mane, giving his hair a more disheveled look.

"Hey! There's Barbra and, like, What's His Name," Rusty drawled, careful not to lose his laid-back attitude—but he did, when he slid sideways and recovered with a jerk and even dreamier eyes.

Was he drunk? Coked up? Both! It had been difficult to tell in the car because he always babbled like that. Tarah had a feeling of desolation. If Barbra was here, then wouldn't Liz be catering to her?

But it wasn't Barbra.

It was Sharon.

Tarah considered snatching one of those gleaming knives and killing herself—no, Sharon. Of course, Liz Smith would want to talk to Sharon. . . .

It wasn't Sharon!

Tarah lowered the top of her Versace dress—last year's; would anyone notice that?

Glenn Close!

No, no! Please not Julia! No!

As the sommelier appeared to make his suggestions as arranged by Lenora, there was a buzz at the entrance, unusual at Spago's. That kind of excitement would be aroused by only two people in the universe, Tarah knew, and one, Jacqueline Susann, was dead. So it had to be—

Liz Smith!

Catch her attention quick!

Rusty Blake beat her to it. As the imposing woman in an impeccable gray suit neared, he stood up and said, "Uh, hey, Liz, I didn't, like, recognize you at first, you look, like, different—kinda like it isn't you, ya know?—but, hey, wow—whatever!—you look, like, great—I think!" He sat down, seeming to float away somewhere.

There was a terrifying buzz about the famous restaurant, muffled laughter—and a sob, hers, Tarah Worth's—oh, the embarrassment of it, to have this stupid bit actor talk that way to the great Liz, who stood frozen glaring at him, and then—oh, God, please no—shifting the accusing glare to her. Tarah rose, thought she said, "Excuse me, please," and made her dignified way to the exit. To hell with dignified—she ran.

"Isn't that—?" Mrs. Renquist, sitting in the chilly garden asked as Tarah Worth fled past them. She asked that to herself, not to Mr. Renquist.

Mr. Renquist nevertheless answered. "It is, yeah, that fuckin' bitch—"

"Hmmmm," pondered Mrs. Renquist, soothing her brow.

2

Reverberations out of the horror at Spago.

Liz Smith

Los Angeles.—A horrifying incident occurred last night at celebrity-studded Spago's. Fading "star" Tarah Worth and her rowdy drunk companion created a commotion that involved this columnist. Upon seeing me, Rusty Blake blabbed incoherently at me, causing Tarah to leave him to attendants to usher him out into the street as he asserted loudly that he was not a "fag." Hmmm. I had not known till now that Tarah Worth was what is known vulgarly as a fag hag.

In her bedroom, Tarah woke up with a scream. She had dreamt that Liz had written a column about last night's debacle at Spago. Thank God she hadn't stayed to experience the hideous aftermath that must have occurred. She'd stay in bed, not be tempted to read what Liz had actually written in her column. She would—

The phone rang aggressively, and so it must be Lenora enraged, gloat-
ing, laughing (only she could do all that at the same time) at the debacle. Tarah answered in a weak voice, as if she was ill, very ill—and,
of course, she was.

"Did you read—?"

"No—ummm—not feeling well—uh—what time—?"

"Someone at Spago last night pretended to be Liz Smith and almost
got away with it until Rusty spotted the woman as a fake and blew her
cover. Sweetheart, and your exit! Wow! Terrific loyalty to the real Liz,
and that's what we're calling it in a P.R. release. Great publicity!"

Saved!—and in Liz's favor. Tarah would have wept with joy and gratitude except that now Lenora was barking:

"They're trying to create a new meaning for 'dolls,' and what the
writers have come up with is that that's how they refer to aging stars
like Helen Lawson—'old dolls.' *Ciao,* sweetie. Congrats on your performance at Spago. Think up another gimmick, okay?—a *real* smasher!
Remember: Something that's in the script. I think they're working on
a kidnap angle."

Tarah's mind had snagged on the creature's reference to aging actresses
as "old dolls." She was caught in crosscurrents, one moment saved, the
other damned. She would accept this other challenge—hadn't she survived last night's? She'd come up with a terrific reference to "dolls,"
and it wouldn't be about aging actresses. . . . Now what had Lenora said
about a kidnapping?

3

In which the Lord works His mysterious ways.

A stern judge, Brother Dan stood rigid before Raul. The preacher's eyes
were closed in preparation to stare down the enormity of evil. He raised
his right hand over the head of the kneeling boy. Silence in the giant
hall. Brother Dan jumped, high. Landing with a loud thud that shook
the floor, he shouted, "Do you renounce Satan and all his evil?"

"Yes!"

"Do you beg the Lord to purge you of your vile perversions?" He
stomped about the boy.

"Yes!"

"Will you never again yearn for the forbidden, the unnatural, the sick, the depraved?" He tap-danced about the stage.

"Yes, yes!"

"What?"

"I mean, no, no! Never again!"

"Rise!" Brother Dan spread his hands out, palms up. "Rise, I exhort you, be lifted by the power of the Lamb."

Raul rose, his eyes darting away, seeking something, someone.

Two burly attendants stood behind him, to catch his spirit-slain body.

Brother Dan made slashing motions. "In the name of the Lord Jesus, I cast you out of this body, Satan! In the name of the Lord, I order you back into your infernal hell. Begone, Satan!" His hand, flattened, smacked against the boy's forehead. Guards prepared to catch the limp body. "You are now slain in the spirit of—What the hell do *you* want?" Brother Dan stared at Lyle, who had marched right up to him.

"Lyle!" Raul said exultantly.

Lyle bent toward the boy's face, held it in his hands, and kissed him on the lips.

4

God's mysterious ways extend.

Lyle straightened up—he had had to bend to kiss the shorter boy.

Raul remained standing on tiptoes, with his eyes closed, expecting another kiss. Lyle nudged him out of his revery. Raul opened his eyes and blinked. "You're real."

As the congregation buzzed with baffled consternation, Sister Sis and Brother Bud flung themselves before the television camera that insisted on remaining on the tall young man and the shorter one even after the long kiss. Desperate, Sister Sis held up her tambourine to block a camera, only to realize that another camera was recording the scene. Brother Dan stood paralyzed in the middle of the stage, hair like flames under the hot light. He glowered in bafflement, then leafed urgently through his Bible, stabbing at it with a finger as if to find the passage that would guide him as to what to do next.

Brother Bud shoved a band of God's Little Angels onto the stage to divert the cameras and the congregation. "Go out and sing loud, angels!" he demanded.

Lyle rushed Raul away, to a corner way off the stage.

"Now what the hell are you doing here?"

"I ran away. I'd heard you were on this show with these creeps—"

"You came looking for me?" Lyle was pleased that the boy would trek so far to see him, but he was also baffled—had the kid contrived all this? "You were acting when you were out there?"

"I'm not sure," Raul said. "Maybe, maybe not. We'll just have to figure it out, huh? . . . Wow, Lyle, you sure can dance and sing! Wow!" He became defiant. "Even if I was acting, so what? They're *all* acting. So are you."

What could he say? That was true. "Now what do you intend to do?"

"Call my aunt first and tell her I'm here."

"She doesn't know?"

"Naw, I didn't tell her. I just took the bus, yesterday. I guess I should go back, huh?—before she gets all pissed and calls the cops to arrest me."

Lyle could see it all, the cops grabbing his friend, taking him to a home, calling the mean aunt. He took off one of his boots. "Look— here's enough money to get you back." He brought out the hidden bills.

"Weird place to keep your money, Lyle," Raul said, then added: "I can't take your money, no way."

"I'd take it," one of the little angel girls who had rushed off stage to peer at them said, "and I'd promise whatever he wants you to promise."

"So would I," a boy angel agreed. "Then I'd do whatever I wanted with it."

"Shush!" Lyle said to them. "Okay?" he coaxed Raul.

"Okay, if that's what you think I should do."

"Yes. Promise?"

"I promise. . . . Lyle, since I know you can't be what I'd like you to be, I wish—weird—I wish you were much older than me, and then, you know, you could be my father." Then he ran away. When he was sure he was out of sight, he moistened his lips where Lyle had kissed him.

"Listen, Lord's Cowboy, why the hell did you do that out there?" Fierce, her wig askew, Sister Sis had found Lyle; Brother Bud was rushing to catch up.

"Didn't we pay you enough?" Brother Bud said.

"Too much," Lyle said guiltily.

"Why the hell'dya cause all that pandemonium out there? Why?" Brother Bud moved in.

"Because the Demon that Brother Dan pulled out of that kid hopped into me!" Lyle cried out. He quivered his body, head shaking.

"What?" Sister Sis adjusted her wig. "You mean—?"

"Yes!" Brother Bud seemed resurrected. "Of course, the demon's ways are wily—but no match for Brother Dan! Damn! This is going to be terrific!

"A televised Armageddon," Sister Sis predicted.

Sister Sis and Brother Bud marched Lyle back onto the stage.

When Brother Dan saw Lyle advancing, he pulled back, out of his daze. He sprang to life when Sister Sis and Brother Bud announced:

"The Devil hopped out of that little pervert—uh, child—who was freed right before our eyes, and—"

"—that old demon hopped right on over and seized the Lord's Cowboy," Sister Sis finished.

Gasps! "The Lord's Cowboy has been seized by Satan!" . . . "The Devil has landed on the Lord's Cowboy!"

"—and now Brother Dan will purge the demon in the fiercest struggle witnessed in this holy tabernacle!" cried Brother Bud.

Resurrected by the call to arms against the entrenched demon, Brother Bud hopped higher than ever, high, then landed with a shout, his Bible cocked at Lyle. "Have you been possessed by the Demon that I—through the intercession of the Lord—purged from that perv— that innocent child?"

"Yes!" Lyle made a deep, growling sound.

Brother Dan hopped back.

The angel children hummed delicately over the lower moans of the chorus. The auditorium swayed in terror and ecstasy in anticipation of the approaching exorcism.

"Save the Lord's Cowboy!"

"Drive out the Wretched Demon!"

"Purge the Lord's Cowboy!"

"Yea, yea, the spirit of God lives in Brother Dan!"

"Pull Old Satan out of the Lord's Cowboy!"

Lyle breathed harshly, loudly, eyes rolling.

Burly guards took their station behind him, readied to grasp the cleansed body.

"I cast you back into hell, Evil One, who has seized this servant of the Lord, our own Lord's Cowboy!" Brother Dan swung his Bible around like a saber.

Sister Sis's tambourine trembled. "The Evil One will flee under the power of the Lord and Brother Dan!"

Brother Dan broke into tongues: *"Brolt-yum-christa-welk-arribayare!"*

"Save the Lord's Cowboy!" prayed the congregation.

"Set the cowboy on the straight and narrow!" an old man gasped before he broke into raspy coughs.

Lyle remained upright, his guitar dormant over one shoulder.

"The power of the Lord commands you, Evil Spirit, to exit from the Lord's Cowboy!" Brother Dan shouted—and pushed at Lyle's forehead with one hand. "You are *gone,* Demon!"

Lyle did not move.

"You! Are! *Purged!*" Brother Dan punched at Lyle, hard, with each word. "Now fall! You are slain in the spirit! *Fall!*"

Lyle did not move.

Brother Dan shoved harder, harder, several punches.

"Ole Devil still holds me," Lyle groaned, "Ole Devil won't let go, I feel him——" He clutched his groin. "I feel him groping me now. Grrrr-grrrr, quiverin' with lust, grrrr. Ole Devil givin' me a hard-on, Ole Devil coaxing me to jerk off. Hmmmm, grrrr!" He began to open the fly of his jeans.

"What did the Lord's Cowboy say?" a woman in the front fringe of the stage asked, cocking her ear. "What is he doing?"

"I think he said—I think he's—"

Brother Dan stood before Lyle, arms out wide, blocking him from the sight of the cameras and the congregation. "I said, you are saved and slain in the spirit! Didn't you hear me?" He grabbed Lyle by the shoulders and shoved him back forcefully.

"Stop shoving at me, you damn fake!" Lyle shouted, and shoved him back. "You're the one who's got a demon up your ass!"

The burly guards lunged at him.

"Don't let 'em push you around, Lord's Cowboy," shouted one of the angel children.

"Shove 'em back!" another coaxed.

"Punch the suckers," someone in the front row of the congregation said.

The burly guards grabbed Lyle by the shoulders. He wrested himself free. "Fuckin' fakes!" he shouted at Brother Bud and Sister Sis. "Fuckin' fakes! You're the goddamned perverts—and that wasn't a tumor in that jar, it was squashed jelly beans!"

Sister Sis's tambourine blasted, blasted, blasted. Brother Dan stomped on the floor. Brother Bud joined them, and they all broke into harsh tongues:

"Namligdrahcir!"

"Senrabevilc!"

"Retsehcdrefla!"

"Nedlohnehpets!"

"Drofslairbnerak!"

The choir sang loud praises to the Lord, drowning out the Angel Children's pristine voices.

Queries floated about the congregation: "Is the Lord's Cowboy saved?" . . . "Is he going to sing and dance again?"

Lyle marched off the stage. Sister Sis and Brother Bud and the two guards ran after him. One of the guards spun Lyle around and held him, the other punched him hard in the face.

"Ouch!" Lyle said. Before his fists could punch back—

"You're under arrest!" a controlled firm male voice said.

Two serious-faced men in shiny suits appeared and faced Brother Bud and Sister Sis. "You're under arrest for grand larceny."

Lyle shook his head, dazed at the events and by the pain in his cheek.

"Fuck, why fight it?" Brother Bud extended his hands to be handcuffed.

Sister Sis attempted to run, but was caught by one of the two men in shiny suits. She glared at Lyle.

"—absconding with foundation funds, fraud, tax evasion—" the second staid man was saying.

Sister Matilda! Lyle thought. Sister Matilda had uncovered them, had tried to warn him to stay away, but when he wouldn't, she encouraged him to Stay put and watch them, reminded him with the jelly beans. She hadn't taken any funds; she had fled in order to bring all this about.

"—a part of it all."

One of the two harsh men faced Lyle, who only now registered the words that Brother Bud had just said, or maybe Sister Sis had, both of them, that he, Lyle, had been a part of it all.

"Did you know what they were up to? Were you an accomplice?" one of the men in shiny suits asked Lyle.

He must have known—something—must have from the beginning, and he'd taken the money they'd given him, become a performer in their nasty circus, and he knew about the jelly beans, even if just a while ago. He said guiltily, "I guess I did know."

"I guess you did," one of the staid men said. "We saw you at the bank with their shield, that flunky Thomas Clarence."

5

Lyle in jail with Mr. Magwitch.

Brother Bud and Sister Sis were booked and jailed, along with their accomplice at the bank, Mr. Thomas Clarence, who had "kept their accounts."

Lyle was put in a jail cell, waiting to be interrogated. His wrists hurt from the tight handcuffs, and, God, it was awful to be in a cell. Iron bars! They made you feel captured—and afraid, very afraid—like his life had been taken away from him—and he felt alone, very alone, even if he wasn't alone.

"Name's Magwitch. What they got you for, fellow?" his cell mate asked him. He looked like a big-rig truck driver, hefty, with a flowery tattoo on his thick biceps.

"Lyle Clemens, glad to meet you Mr. Mag—"

"—Magwitch. So whatya do?"

"I don't really know what they got me for," Lyle said. "I think for helping someone with grand larceny," That's what he had retained from a desk sergeant writing on a form. Or were they holding him for exposing himself?

"Whew!" Magwitch was impressed.

Should he ask his mate why he was here? He didn't have to.

"Guess why I'm here?"

"Ah—" What to say that would please him? "Ah—"

"Bank robbery. Needed to get some money for an ungrateful adopted son. But I didn't get away with nothing, shit. Just set off all those alarms, and then those fuckin' bank clerks busted out singing gospel songs louder'n the goddamned alarms!"

"You tried to rob the Lord's Bank?"

"Yeah! That's what they call it. How'd you know?"

6

Mr. Cowboy is born on the road.

Hours later, Lyle was interrogated. No, he had not opened an account at the Lord's Bank—but he didn't tell them he had cashed the check. He told everything else truthfully, that he had been warned—but, just in case, he didn't use Sister Matilda's name. He had, though, opened one button of his pants and . . .

An exasperated detective threw his hands up. "Aw, lettim go, the Lord's Cowboy hasn't done anything to hold 'im."

Where would he go? Where was Sister Matilda? Anaheim was desolate. In the news every day, there were stories about the two evangelists who had been embezzling, lying, cheating in every way. As he was packing his things to move out of the motel, the television on, he heard a newscaster:

"And yet, letters keep coming in for them, with donations," Anchorwoman Mandy Lange-Jones said with a slight smile, "despite the fact that a purported tumor turned out to be squashed jelly beans, mixed with darkened mucilage." She restrained a chuckle. The coanchor, Tommy Bassich, shook his head, restraining a chuckle. "Unbelievable!"

Mandy Lange-Jones continued, "New allegations are surfacing against the founders of the Lord's Headquarters—secret funds, laundered money, back taxes, an account in Switzerland, all handled by bank official Thomas Clarence."

On the screen appeared Brother Bud and Sister Sis, heads lowered reverentially—Sister Sis's hand securing her wig—as they were being led to be booked. Noticing the camera, Sister Sis entreated heaven. "The Lord shall see that we overcome."

He would journey to the nearest city that seemed to promise him shelter from these events: Los Angeles.

Following directions two of the angel children in the choir gave him to the outskirts of Anaheim where he would catch a ride "easy," Lyle stood by his suitcase at the edge of the highway, his guitar over his shoulder, his thumb stuck out.

Cars whizzed by. People turned to look. One car paused—and moved on. Lyle sat on his suitcase without putting out his finger. A car braked.

The driver was a plump, jolly man, about fifty, smiling widely. He wore a plaid cap, slacks that matched. He had a full mustache, which drooped at the edges. Lyle thought he looked like one of the characters in the old mystery movies that Sylvia and Clarita sometimes watched on television. "Hop in!"

Lyle did. The car was full of papers that looked like maps, or graphs.

"Your horse died on the nation's highway?" the man chuckled, a hearty laugh.

"I never had a horse, never even rode one. Maybe I never even saw one except in the movies."

"Naw?" the man seemed incredulous. "Settle down. I got a feeling about ya, boy. You're a lucky sign, I just betcha. He extended his hand to Lyle. "Mr. Fielding," he identified himself.

Lyle introduced himself to Mr. Fielding as Mr. Clemens.

"Glad to meetya, Mr. Cowboy," Mr. Fielding said. "Where ya headed?"

"Los—" An airplane roared loudly across the darkening sky. "—Angeles."

"Hot damn! I told you you're my good luck. That's where I'm headed!—and then back, back to my beautiful bride-to-be. Bet you got one yourself, right? Maybe several?"

"One," Lyle said dreamily. Beautiful Maria. He was tired and sleepy—he hadn't been able to sleep in the jail bunk while he waited to be interrogated—and so he dozed now, a long time, woke now and then to hear Mr. Fielding ask him if he was real tired and saying that he'd better rest up, rest up for "luck-bringin'." Lyle even dreamt—scattered dreams that included Sylvia Love and Maria facing each other, angrily, or as friends, and then dancing off together up a hill, where each tried to shove the other down.

When he woke, they were still driving—he didn't remember that Los Angeles had been that far when they had flown in and been taken by limousine to Anaheim. "How much longer we got?" Lyle asked. It had turned dark outside.

"We're almost there!" the man exulted. "Las Vegas, hut-dam!"

"Las Vegas? I thought you said you were going to Los Angeles?"

"Damn! I thought you said you were going to Las Vegas. You must've got wrong directions because you were headed the wrong way."

What the hell, Lyle thought. He leaned back to fall asleep again.

"Listen, cowboy. I'm playin' my lucky hunch—I always do. You're my good luck, I felt it when I saw you out there on your suitcase. I'm a gamblin' man, rode through life on lucky instinct. We'll be a pair. You tell me how to bet, and I'll—"

"I've never gambled, Mr. Fielding," Lyle said.

"Great! I knew it. My instinct said, That's your lucky man. Take him with you. Trust your luck. Know what I mean?"

"Sorry, Mr. Fielding."

"I'll explain, Mr. Cowboy. We're going to my lucky casino at the Bellagio Hotel, and I'm gonna rely on you telling me what to play—cards, machines, horses—"

"Horses?" Lyle was still half-dozing and wondered whether the man was suggesting he ride on a horse. "I don't—"

"On television—races on television, great big televisions. We bet there, right there, wherever races are running," Mr. Fielding explained happily. "I'll bet your lucky hunch. As my partner, Mr. Cowboy, you'll share in the winnings, half and half." He accelerated. "Lucky day comin', Mr. Cowboy!"

CHAPTER FOURTEEN

1

An unexpected detour. The vagaries of chance.

Ahead, Las Vegas gleamed, shone, sparkled, burst into lights, gushed water, exploded in electric colors!

When they arrived, Lyle squinted awake. They had driven to a section of the city that looked like a lit rainbow, if a rainbow would shine at night. A purple hotel loomed, green neon blazed, splotches of electric red shaded the sky. A medieval castle, a Roman coliseum, a palace, a massive pyramid, a sprawling chateau, a pirate ship among palm trees lit yellow, green, blue, red—the London Bridge, smaller though—and everywhere on the streets, which rose, then leveled, then twisted around—were tourists and taxis and billboards with pictures of women dressed only in feathers, pictures of magicians, lions, singers, tigers—

Was it all really there? An erupting volcano was spewing colored fire. Nearby, a lake rippled like silver foil!

"It's something, isn't it, Mr. Cowboy?—and wait until you see the babes that hang around everywhere!" Mr. Fielding said ebulliently as he drove along a lit driveway, around the lake out of which, suddenly, water spouted in a swaying dance.

At the hotel, bellboys jumped to greet them, take their bags—Mr. Fielding had a small one, Lyle had only one and his guitar. They entered the lobby, golden arches, paintings on the ceilings, a row of pretty women and young men waiting to attend.

"No time for nonsense, we're here to win," Mr. Fielding said, marching under the arches into a giant room that contained many more. Lyle saw: card tables, domino tables, dice tables, people hovering over them, attendants in green meting out cards—and then, everywhere, clanging, banging, tinkling slot machines, lights popping like electric eyes, more machines alive with winking colors, wheels spinning. More people hunched over them, shoving coins—clanging, clinking, issuing money, devouring money, machines with names, all lit up: FILTHY RICH, DOUBLE GOLD, NEPTUNE'S TREASURE, HOUND, HOW WILD, DOUBLE GOLD, WILD CHERRY PIE. FISHIN' FOR CASH, PERFECT TEN. WHEEL OF FORTUNE. HIT THE TOP!

Along the aisles of lights and clanging slot machines, the pretty girls in tiny red skirts and low-cut blouses carried drinks to those humped over the machines.

Lyle's eyes couldn't take it all in.

"Choose, Mr. Cowboy! What are we going to gamble on?"

Lyle read more names on tables: Blackjack, 21, Baccarat, Craps— and there were hundreds of people under what looked like tents, people brimming with exuberance or agitation, groaning, moaning, howling, hooting, clapping, cursing, blessing, weeping, laughing, yowling, hooting—hands waving.

"You fall asleep again, Mr. Cowboy?"

Trying to focus on something definite in this sea of shifting images of racing horses, Lyle's eyes had followed one of the young women carrying drinks sassily on a tray, a dark-haired young woman; her tiny red skirt flared out from her small waist. His eyes followed her as she moved into yet another enclave. He would play his hunches, Lyle decided, like his partner, Mr. Fielding.

"Over there!" Lyle had pointed to where the pretty woman had disappeared.

"The horse races on television!" Mr. Fielding agreed. "Naturally, a cowboy would choose the horses. Good instinct." He was almost panting with excitement. "Let's go play the horses and win, Mr. Cowboy," he said confidently.

They entered the room where the girl had disappeared. There she was milling about the men—all men—who sat intently before individual television screens, horses racing across them. By the side of each screen was a computer keyboard, receiving bets. A huge screen ahead multiplied the images of the horses. Other screens exhibited rows of names, strange names, pretty names to bet on. Attendants moved around, paying or not.

"Choose a name Mr. Cowboy, let's go!"

Clarita had exhorted him to rely on the Holy Virgin Guadalupe. He said a prayer to her and chose: "Cute Gal."

Mr. Fielding bet.

They lost.

Lyle concentrated on more names on the board. He chose: "Texas Belle." "Mexican Lady." He rejected: "Sister Mary." He chose: "Latin Spitfire," "American Beauty," "Great Lady." He rejected: "Jelly Queen." He chose—

And chose.

And chose.

And chose.

And lost, and lost, and lost, and, after hours, lost again.

He was so mortified he hadn't noticed that the pretty young woman had left the room long ago. "I'm sorry I'm not as lucky as you thought, Mr. Fielding," he apologized.

"Happens, Mr. Cowboy! I trust my instincts. You'll bring me luck—eventually."

How could he be so happy if he'd just lost all that money?

"Gamblers pay their debts," Mr. Fielding was saying. "So here—" He plastered Lyle's hand with bills.

"No—"

"Oops! Bad luck if you don't take 'em," Mr. Fielding warned. "Now I'm off to my beautiful woman—eventually." A busty blonde woman swished by. Mr. Fielding winked. "Nice, but I like my babes dark and sassy. Good-bye, Mr. Cowboy."

He was gone! "Good-bye, Mr. Fielding," Lyle said to the man who had disappeared, as if uttering his name would certify that he had existed, that all this had happened.

"Didn't know the rodeo was in town, cowboy," a woman said. "The looks department's improving, if you're an indication. Most of those old cowboys got big asses. Good luck at the buckeroo."

Lyle looked down at the money Mr. Fielding had shoved into his hand. Three hundred dollars: some tens, twenties, a hundred. He wandered among the blinking slot machines.

There was a place like a cage, people lined up before it.

REDEMPTION HERE, the sign read.

Lyle turned away quickly before he realized that those people waiting before the cage-like structure were getting change to feed the blinking machines and for redeeming the coins they won.

A man behind a wired window gave him coins and a container like a popcorn holder. "For your coins," the man explained to Lyle's baffled look. "Good luck, cowboy."

Lyle spotted her, the pretty girl he'd seen earlier, no, another one—they sure looked alike; and she had spotted him, smiling as she carried drinks to the congregants here.

"Hi, cowboy," she said.

"Hi, miss," he said.

"Want something to drink?"

"Oh, uh, yeah, iced tea."

"Iced tea?"

"Okay, make it a Coke."

"Got it." She wiggled away.

Without really looking at it—his eyes following the flouncy red skirt—Lyle inserted coins in the slot machine he was standing nearest.

Clang, clang, clang! *Clang!*

That meant someone nearby had won. He looked around. A machine had lit up madly, but why were people staring at him? Why were they gathering about him, gasping? Had he broken the machine? The pretty girl bringing the Coke almost dropped her tray. What was the excitement about?

"Goddamn!"
"Look at that!"
"Jesuschrist!"
"Oh, honey, oh, cowboy!"
"You hit the jackpot, cowboy!"

2

In which is encountered a reflection of Lyle's
goddamned son-of-a-bitch father.

That night, still weary from the long ride, Lyle collected $4,000, signed a form for income tax, bought travelers checks as was suggested, keeping some cash, and knew that from here on out he would pray to the Virgin Guadalupe, even if she was slow in responding.

He looked around for Mr. Fielding, to share the winnings. But he was nowhere.

Jesuschrist! What would Clarita think of *this?*

In the hotel where he had grandly taken a room suddenly vacated— without knowing that it would cost him $200 for the night, and thank God he had it, and much more than that, considering the salary from Brother Bud and Sister Sis, Mr. Fielding's "tip," and the jackpot just now—Lyle saw a giant poster for THE LAS VEGAS FOLLIES. A row of almost-naked women rimmed the poster.

Clarita didn't need to know that he was wandering over to a place that said: TICKETS.

"Lucky you," said the sturdy woman there, "just got a cancellation. Sold out."

"Am I close up?"

"Any closer and you'll be sitting on their laps," the woman winked suggestively.

"Wouldn't mind," Lyle said.

"Shouldn't have much trouble," the woman smiled. "Hey, I didn't know the rodeo was in town."

"I'm not—" Oh, what the hell. "Yes, ma'am, it is—and there'll be a lot more of us here real soon."

"Not like you, honey," the woman said. "Give us a kiss."

She wasn't exactly what he longed for—of course, first of all was Maria—but there she was, her lips puckered. He pecked her lips.

"That was some kiss," she laughed, "the kind you'd give your sister."

My sister! Lyle moved away as fast as he could past the crush of people.

The show he had bought tickets for was at another hotel, and wouldn't start for another hour. Lyle ate in a restaurant that didn't require reservations: The Buffet. "Rodeo rider!" the female keeping the folks waiting in a long line said when she saw him. "Rodeo rider coming through! Rodeo rider coming through!" Everyone parted, and he went ahead.

Still more time. He wandered off outside onto a veranda—a small rotunda—that faced the large artificial lake. There were a few tables and chairs there. A telescope pointed toward the sky. He focused it. The lighted city almost obliterated the stars. But he was able to see one, then another. He heard a spurting sound. The lake had erupted into its dance, music swelling.

He sat down at a small table.

At another table next to him were two women.

Very pretty, made up—but not like Sister Sis. No one like Sister Sis. Lyle smiled grandly at them. They smiled back, but looked quickly away. One of the two women was older than the other—maybe ten years older—more heavily made up. Soon, two older men appeared, in suits, no ties. They introduced themselves to the women. So the women had been expecting them, but why didn't they seem to have met them until now? The man who sat next to the older woman stared at her—and looked away. The older woman talked hurriedly, laughed, drank from her glass, tilted it empty. The two men concentrated on the younger woman.

A third man appeared, older than the others, in a suit, tie, with glittering rings. He must have known the younger of the two women, who got up to hug and kiss him. He responded to a quick motion from one of the other men. He bent to listen. The third man nodded and whispered something to the younger woman. She got up, motioning the older woman to join her and the older man a few feet away. The man took out his wallet, peeled several bills, gave them to the older woman, who took the money. The younger woman said something to her and touched her face, gently. The older woman squared her shoulders and walked away.

Lyle followed her back into the hotel. "Excuse me," he said.

She turned. "I'm not working tonight!" she said angrily.

"All I wanted to say was that you're just about the most beautiful woman I've ever seen. That's all."

She raised her head, held her breath, controlling tears. "Thank you," she said. "Thank you very much." She hurried away.

Lyle thought of Sylvia Love when his goddamned father had walked out on her and tried to pay her off for rejecting her.

3

Some considerations about magic and illusion,
and intrusive reality.

He was in a huge showplace of colors within the hotel, a theater, where a squadron of ushers was roaming about the audience in search of "volunteers" for the magic show, preparatory, Lyle assumed, to the parade of women the poster had promised.

"You, cowboy," one of the ushers signaled to Lyle, whose seat was close to the aisle.

"Go ahead, bashful!" a woman next to him chided.

Lyle was not bashful. He had jumped up at the occasion to be on the stage with those beautiful women.

The usher, a jaunty young man, took him by the arm and surrendered him to the stage as other ushers rustled up the requisite five more "volunteers."

Lyle sat with the others in an arc on the stage. There was a woman who looked like one of his teachers, the plainest one; next to her was a burly man like one of the truck drivers who didn't stop at Rio Escondido. There was a rotund, stern-faced woman, her chin trembling even when she didn't move, and, with her, a small man—certainly her husband—who seemed to be about to fall asleep. There was a young man who looked like a smart student.

"Well," said the stout woman, "I don't know why I was yanked out of my seat to be on this show. Well, you know I'm a skeptic about these exhibitions. Well, if this so-called magician thinks he's going to hypnotize *me,* well, he's got another think coming. . . . Well, wake up!" she barked at her husband, who woke with a start.

They weren't there to be hypnotized. The magician, a flashy man in black, with a swirling cape and inky-black hair, appeared, in a flash of flames, from the darkened back of the stage. With him was a woman in mesh tights; she seemed to Lyle to have jumped out of the enticing poster that had lured him here. "Damn!" he approved aloud. The stolid woman nearby said, "Well, I never heard such a vulgar sound."

With a flurry of his hands and his purple-lined cape, the magician explained that he was going to do the unprecedented. He was going to allow the "witnesses" on stage to watch his magic tricks—"Close up!" He said, "You've all seen a beautiful woman sawed in half, right? But has anyone seen it done before the watchful eyes of audience members?" He cocked his ears, waiting for the inevitable chorus of "No's."

An oblong box like a coffin was brought out by two young men. The pretty woman stood apart, one leg slightly looped over the other, legs in mesh stockings, a pink and black leotard dipping at her breasts and up both thighs, blond hair cascading over milky shoulders.

The magician opened the box. The woman sauntered up to it, her hands tossed out gracefully, breasts proud in their full glory, hips challenging her breasts' pride.

Two male assistants propped the box upright. The woman moved into it, her hands encouraging applause. The magician closed the lid, like a door. The two male assistants moved away.

Lyle winced when he saw the magician produce an ominous electric saw. He wanted to shut his ears when he heard it buzzing.

"Well, it's all just tricks anyhow," said the heavy-set woman.

Lyle looked at her, closely, curious. There was something sinister about the plain, plump features, the trembling chins, the set of the mouth, a half sneer, half nasty-smile, eyes that shifted as if she wanted to take in everything, to judge it all. With a shudder, Lyle turned away from her.

"I'm afraid," said the schoolteacher as the magician poised himself to slice the propped box with the buzzing saw.

"I won't look." The college student took off his glasses and leaned forward closer.

"Shoot," said the truck driver.

With an agitated grating sound, the saw sliced at the box, deeper, deeper.

The horrified voice of the woman inside screamed: "Help me, help me! He's *really* sawing me, help me please, someone!"

The saw carved in deeper.

The voice pleaded: "*Please,* this is for real, he's—Oh, *oh!*"

Those seated about the box looked at each other, disturbed. People in the audience stood up, some moved into the aisles, closer to the stage.

"Well, I certainly will not be taken in," said the stout woman. But she leaned forward with anticipation of something gory.

"*Please!*" screamed the voice from inside as the saw sliced on. "This isn't an act! He threatened me earlier! We had a fight!" Something red, liquidy began to ooze out of the box. "Oh, please believe me! Please— oh, no, oh, oh—*pleeeeease!*"

Lyle's boots pushed him up, his hands became fists, his legs bounded toward the magician. His fist crashed on the man's face. "You son of a bitch!"

The magician staggered back, the saw, still buzzing, hobbled noisily along the floor. Everyone was standing.

The magician fell to the floor, his cloak draping him. He struggled to get up, managed to grasp the saw. Lyle's fist pounded him again.

The door to the box pushed open. There stood the woman, her arms outspread, legs curved enticingly. "You saved me, cowboy!" she shouted.

"Well, I knew all along he's part of the act," the stout woman declared, elbowing the silent man beside her.

The audience burst into applause.

Lyle looked around, baffled.

The magician stood, rubbing his jaw as he struggled to stretch his lips into a smile. "You son of a bitch," he hissed at Lyle. "Didn't you get it? It's all part of the act, and you fuckin' ruined it, you fuckin' idiot." He tried to recover, sweeping his cape in a swirl about his body. "You better pretend you're part of the fuckin' act or I'll saw *you* in half, and *that*'ll be for real, motherfucker!"

The applause grew.

"Bow, you son of a bitch. They're clapping for you! *Bow!*" the magician ordered Lyle, as he himself bowed deeply, his cape sweeping the floor in a swirl of black. The woman beside them dipped in a sexy curtsy.

God *damn!* Was this happening! The applause increased, insistent. Lyle bowed. The applause mounted.

"Bow again, you son of a bitch!—and then get the fuck away from me!"

Lyle bowed again to even more applause. The magician gave him a harsh push.

"Stick around after the show, cowboy," the woman whispered to him.

Had she really said that? Had someone on the panel said that to someone else? On the off-chance that she had spoken that, he asked, "Where?"

"Outside. Right exit." She dashed away.

Lyle walked off the stage to renewed applause. Sure he wanted to see
the rest of the show. But if he stayed and the woman he had attempted
to save assumed that he had not accepted her gracious offer and was
waiting for him in her pink and black leotard, how would he be ahead?

As he proceeded out, a freckled girl with braces said. "You were terrific, cowboy, but you didn't fool me—I knew you were part of the act."

"It was obvious," a man near her said.

Lyle walked outside, around the back of the theater.

"Meeting someone?" a security guard asked him.

"I hope so," said Lyle.

"Go ahead and wait," the guard said with a suggestive slurp, "she'll
show up."

How the hell did he know? Lyle wondered. Now would it be proper
to say a prayer to the Holy Virgin Guadalupe to ask that the beautiful
woman turn up, and that they would get together? Why not? So he
asked the Holy Lady to help him out.

He waited.

Waited and waited. Had he heard right?

"Hi, cowboy, who ya waiting for?" Lyle turned to see a man, slender,
in his thirties.

"Yeah," Lyle answered, smiling. Then it struck him: "You're not *her,*
are you?"

The man laughed. "No, I'm not a her, wouldn't want to be. Mind if
I join you while you wait for whoever?"

"No." He would welcome company while he waited.

"Do you recognize me?" the man asked hopefully.

"Uh, yeah, you look familiar," Lyle tried to be kind.

"I was in the chorus line—you know, with the women; ten of us come
out tapping, remember?—in tight pants and little vests? We danced
around the girls."

"I remember," Lyle made up. That would have been the part he
had missed. "You were good, a really terrific dancer, I saw you, sure I
remember."

The man leaned back, wearily. "Chorus boy," he said, "not much of
a future in being a chorus boy."

"I've never been a chorus boy," Lyle explained.

The man chuckled. "I can't believe you, cowboy. You're—"

Please, not strange, Lyle thought.

"—different. In a good way," the chorus boy added quickly.

"Thank you."

"The man sighed. "You break your heart out, tapping, knowing that, really, most of the people aren't even looking at you, they're looking at the women's boobs, and there you are tapping your heart away."

"I bet some people are looking at you," Lyle said, not wanting to be obvious about the fact that he was searching ahead for the magician's assistant.

"Yeah, now and then, an old breed of sugar daddies."

"Sugar—?"

"Older guys, you know, who wine and dine us. Not much future in that either," he said wistfully. "They're always after younger ones, and younger ones keep coming."

The lights of the bright city cast smoky pastel reflections even in this darker section where they stood. Lights blinked off and on constantly, from somewhere. The sound of voices floated into the warm air, music wafting.

"It's a beautiful night," said the chorus boy. "Nights like this make me feel lonelier than usual. Too bad you're waiting for someone already, or I'd ask you to have a drink with me."

"I would if I wasn't waiting," Lyle assured him.

"You would, you really would?" the chorus boy said enthusiastically.

"Why not?"

"How old do you think I am?" the chorus boy asked abruptly.

"Uh—" He looked to be about thirty-five; older? "Twenty-five?" Lyle said.

A smile pushed away the saddened look. "You hit it on the nail. . . . Cowboy, do you mind if I put my head on your shoulders just for a minute and look up at the sky?"

Lyle thought of Raul. "Sure, go ahead."

The man was shorter than Lyle by several inches. Lyle dipped down. The chorus boy rested his head on Lyle's shoulder and looked up at the sky, toward invisible stars. He straightened up. "Thank you," he said. "That's all I wanted."

There she was, the magician's assistant.

"So long, cowboy," the chorus boy surrendered. "Lord love you for being so nice."

"Lord love *you,*" Lyle responded.

The woman approached him. He was disappointed that she wasn't wearing her costume. She was wearing a black dress. She was still gorgeous, though.

"Hi, cowboy."

"Hi, ma'am."

"Oh, honey," she said, "you're as precious as I thought you would be when I saw you walking in and asked the usher to bring you onstage. I'm crazy for cowboys, you know. You with the rodeo?"

"Yes!" No purpose in telling her otherwise.

She threw her arms about him. "Oh, honey! Oh! I'm Amber," she breathed her name. "You staying in the hotel?"

"Yes."

"Invite me?"

"Yes!"

"Toldya she'd show up," the security guard said to Lyle.

4

A question of love.

Was it a dream? Was he in an expensive hotel room with this beautiful stranger? Was he in bed with her and listening again to Rose's masterful instructions? Were they having sex? Terrific sex?

Fuck, yes, they were!

"Do you love me?" Amber asked, her eyes misty, after he had come three times—or so it seemed—and she had seemed to come at least ten.

"I loved what we did," he said enthusiastically. "Let's do it again!'

She lowered her eyelashes. "That's not what I asked. Do you love me?"

I love Maria, he thought. "No," he answered truthfully. His voice seemed to speak on its own, the way his fists acted. "I love Maria."

She sat up. "What! You brought me to your hotel room and you love another woman?"

"Yes, I love Maria, in Rio Escondido." But she might be my sister, his mind pursued.

"How could you make love to me? *How?*"

"Easy—you're sexy, you're gorgeous."

"You betrayed your beloved!" she said, standing up, pulling on her clothes. "You are an unfaithful bastard!"

"Uh-uh," Lyle denied. "I may be a bastard because of my lying son-of-a bitch father, but I wasn't unfaithful to Maria, no way." He spoke aloud Rose's lesson, "People aren't unfaithful *here*," he touched his groin, still aroused. "Only *here*," he pointed to his heart, "and *that's* where Maria is."

Amber stood up, trembling. "And *this* is where it hurts!" She slapped his growing hard-on.

"Ouch!" he winced.

She headed for the door.

"Wait, I'll walk you back."

"Go to hell," she said, and slammed the door.

5

Back to the glorious City of Angels.

This time, at the edge of Las Vegas, he didn't bother to stick out his finger for a ride. That hadn't worked before, but this had: He sat on his suitcase and asked the Holy Virgin Guadalupe to send someone to give him a ride soon.

Not too soon, but soon after, a car stopped. "Where you headed?"

"Los Angeles!"

"Hop on!"

Lyle hurried to the car, got in. "Mr. Fielding!"

"Mr. Cowboy! Why didn't you tell me you were headed for Los Angeles, I'da saved you some shoe-wea—boot-wear," he corrected himself with a jovial chuckle that shook his belly. "What happened to your horse?"

"I told you, I—"

Mr. Fielding had gone on, "Mr. Cowboy, I believe in fate, circumstances, all that stuff—and I keep running into ya. My gambler's instinct tells me—"

"—that I'm bad luck," Lyle said dourly, "but it turned to good luck when I prayed to—" He was about to tell him about the money he'd won, share it, partner to partner.

"Shush now!" Mr. Fielding said sternly. "Can't mention prayers when you're gambling. Bad luck. Take back whatever you were going to say—"

"But I won—"

"I said, take back whatever you were going to say!" Mr. Fielding insisted, cross.

"Okay," Lyle shrugged, "I take it back." What else to say?

Mr. Fielding had been so intent on the promise that he didn't realize he had veered across the highway, almost running into a Greyhound bus. "See, we didn't hit it, we became lucky when you took that back," he said.

They drove on, along miles of desert, past craggy mountains like giant faces—until, after dozing off and on—Lyle woke up to see tall buildings sparkling like splintered diamonds.

"Here we are, Mr. Cowboy," Mr. Fielding said when he had swept off the freeway and they were riding along a wide, palm-lined street that said "Wilshire Boulevard." "My instinct tells me to let you off here. See ya around, cowboy." He opened the door for Lyle to get out.

On the street, Lyle started, "Mr. Fielding—" to thank him, but he drove off. Lyle rubbed his eyes to make sure that the man was real this second time.

BOOK

III

·

Los Angeles

·

*In which Lyle Clemens finds himself
in the City of Angels*

CHAPTER FIFTEEN

1

*Lyle relies on his instincts and
Clarita's prayer, and encounters
B A B E T T E .*

On a day full of sun and jacaranda blossoms, Lyle stood on a street lined with trees whose branches were shedding flowers, scattering petals like lavender snow on the ground. He saw a bus. Its destination said: HOLLYWOOD. A name everyone knew! He boarded the bus, its passengers mostly Hispanics and blacks on their way to work.

"Huccome you're riding a bus, cowboy? *Dónde está su caballo?*" an old man asked Lyle, arousing friendly laughter.

"I'm not a—" Lyle started, and stopped. What the hell. "My horse died on his way here, sir, got hit by lightning. His name was Rigger," he said, with profound earnestness.

"Trigger," a black woman corrected.

"That was Gene Autry's horse," a man said.

"Belonged to Rogers," an Anglo woman corrected.

Lyle sat down and looked out the window. The City was on display for him—buildings like slabs of mirrors, palm trees lording it over everything, flowers climbing up light posts, and along every block, billboards with pictures of . . . everything.

He didn't know where he was going, with his suitcase, his guitar, and his boots full of money. Now why was he here? he pondered that, and then gave himself the answer: To find out *everything* about life. Everything! For now, he'd rely on instinct, like Mr. Fielding, get off the bus when his hunch told him to.

The bus crawled along heavy traffic, past—

My God! Who was *that*? On a huge poster—the bus had stopped for a red light—that picture of a woman, standing, arms up, exultant, black hair tumbling over white, velvety shoulders, scarlet lips, moist, parted, enormous blue eyes inviting from under extravagant eyelashes, a face like a seductive pouting angel's, an angel with huge breasts, a tiny waist, a body given almost total display by a black bikini, mere swaths of black cloth.

"Wow!"

Lyle read the name under the picture on the poster:

BABETTE

"Babette," he said her name aloud, straining to look back back until the picture had entirely disappeared form his sight. Never in his imagination had he seen anyone like her.

He got off on Franklin Avenue, a strip of apartment buildings draped with flowery vines. The stretch was a mixture of grand old homes that retained a weathered splendor, lesser new ones, and apartment buildings with names like "Spanish Arms," "California Manor," "Palm Mansion." Several had courtyards and fountains and trees like leafy umbrellas.

Farther along the block, young men and women lounged drinking frothy coffee in small outdoor cafés. Nudging each other, several turned to look at the tall young man wearing a cowboy hat and boots and lugging a guitar and a suitcase. Lyle heard a woman's voice say, "hot," fol-

lowed by her boyfriend's nervous laughter. Along that block pretty shops
housed fresh flowers, artificial flowers, psychics, palm-readers, vintage
clothing.

Again in the spirit of Mr. Fielding's reliance on chance—it wouldn't
hurt to back that up with a prayer to the Virgin Guadalupe to help
him choose right, reminding her of course, about Clarita's introduction—he walked on, then stopped and closed his eyes. When he opened
them, whatever came into his mind would decide his next destination. BABETTE. No, that wouldn't do for now. He closed his eyes
again, opened them, and saw:

A Spanish-style building that reminded him of the Texas Grand
Hotel. There was a For Rent sign—and a fountain in a leafy courtyard,
warm sun splashing it with pools of light. There was even a cactus in
the garden. The Fountain Apartments.

A reedy older woman came to the door marked MANAGER. "Yes?"

"I want to rent the apartment."

"You ain't seen it, cowboy."

"I'm not a—" Oh, hell. "I like the place." He looked around, liking
it more when he saw a dark young woman who reminded him of his
beloved, Maria.

"We got high-class renters, lots of movie stars," the woman informed.
"You know who Vampira is?"

Lyle shook his head. She sounded sinister.

"Real famous hostess of late-night movies—used to live here. You
know who Babette is?"

Babette! The gorgeous woman on the poster! "She lives *here?*" Lyle
gasped. He sure believed in instinct now and in the efficacy of Clarita's
prayer.

"No, but she drives by now and then in her silver Cadillac. I seen
her parked across the street once, admirin' the building like she might
want to live here."

"I'd like to move in," Lyle said, doubly encouraged.

"Whoa, cowboy. Listen to more. Greta Garbo lived here."

"Wow," he said. He knew to be impressed.

"If you wanna join those legends, you gotta expect to be respectful."

Lyle took off his hat, tipped it, and bowed.

"Okay, cowboy, the apartment to let is over there, Number seven.
It's furnished real nice." The woman pointed to a unit that faced the

fountain. "I'm Mrs. Allworthy, and here's the key, go look at the apartment, then we'll discuss deposit and rent."

Lyle didn't need to discuss that, he'd already decided, and, besides, he had lots of money in his boots. "I'll take it, ma'am."

"Go look at it, will ya?" the woman insisted.

It was a one-bedroom apartment with a small kitchen and barely enough furniture to qualify as "furnished." It had high ceilings and tall, arched windows. Lyle sat down on a chair before a small table that doubled as a desk. There was an abandoned pen, some paper, envelopes; on one sheet was written, "I can't believe that you—" That was all, as if whoever had lived here had rushed away from what was about to be said.

Lyle's instinct took this as a signal that he should write Maria and Clarita and Sylvia now that he was in Los Angeles. To Maria: "I love you, and I hope you've gotten that silly idea out of your beautiful head. Please?" He rewrote it and left out "silly." He wrote Clarita: "I miss you; thank you for telling me about the Holy Lady"—and dug several bills out of one boot to enclose for her. What to write to Sylvia? "Dear Mo—" He started again: "Dear Sylvia. I miss you a whole lot. Love, Lyle." Later, he would get a telephone, and call her—and Clarita and Maria. He reconsidered. No, he preferred to write, and he would write often. Talking by telephone to those he was so far away from would only add to his missing them.

A knock at the door. There stood Mrs. Allworthy.

"Gonna be looking for a job, huh?"

"Yes." He might as well, rich as he was.

She let herself in, sat on the bed, and appraised him. "You look to me like you could get into a lot of trouble in this city."

"Not going to," Lyle assured her.

"They hire good-looking young people at Disneyland, but they specialize in hideously cute ones; you'd be too sexy." She winked, caught herself, pretended to have an eye twitch.

Lyle sat up, to obviate whatever sexiness he was indicating.

"I got a notice of a job you'd be ideal for, though. Need young guys to tend to people at a big rich—*very* rich—party, parking cars."

"Don't know how to drive," Lyle confessed.

She looked startled. "Really? Oh, sure, you rode a horse."

"No, I just like to walk and run," he informed her, but she had moved on.

"You can be one of the attendants at the party. *Big* party," she said mysteriously, wanting to be asked whose.

"Whose?" he asked obligingly.

She whispered, about to divulge delicate information. "It's Huey's," she said, with the air of someone who has managed to give information without breaking a confidence.

"Huey's? Wow!" Whoever he was.

"*I* call him Huey. He came by a few times, one of his girls lived here before she moved into the Mansion. The agency Huey uses—the most trustworthy of course—calls me when he needs guys like you to usher famous people around for his parties. This one's in honor of . . ." She paused in awe. "Ms. Universal!"

"Sounds good," Lyle said.

"Pay's good, tips are better, Huey's a big tipper. I won't be there myself because my duties keep me here. Don't think I haven't been invited," she said gruffly.

"Thank you, Mrs. Allworthy. I'll apply."

Again she was struck with a flirtatious eye twitch. When Lyle didn't say anything, she sighed, "Oh, well," and she was the assertive manager again, taking the rent, a deposit, giving him a receipt—after he returned from the bathroom, where he had drawn money from his boots.

The next day, he walked long, long blocks to an office building on a side street off the Sunset Strip, where Mrs. Allworthy had instructed him to go to be interviewed. Before locating the address, he stood astonished by what he saw. Towering murals, huge billboards that whirled about, and winked and blinked, outdoor cafés under circus awnings, shop windows with indifferent mannequins, more billboards that changed colors, turned upside down, lit up, grew.

About to feel woozy, he entered a building that looked like an expensive house. In a waiting room were several other young applicants. They all addressed each other as "dude" or "man," had tans and highlighted haircuts that made them look as if they had just gotten out of bed. All kept a hand over or near their groins.

It was Lyle's turn. He walked into another office, glassy, glitzy, chromy where a jolly man and a big woman sat behind a small, shiny antique desk. When he saw Lyle, the jolly man put his hand to his lips and said, "My, *my*"—and then proceeded to write down an answer to everything the woman asked Lyle, whether he responded or not.

He was hired. The jolly man escorted him to yet another room. "I answered every question correctly for you so you'd get the job," he confided to Lyle.

A woman measured Lyle in order to make adjustments on the clothes he would wear as attendant—black pants, white shirt, black bow tie. The jolly man remained there smiling until the woman motioned him to leave.

"You can wear your own shoes, as long as they're black," the woman told him.

He returned to the office with the big woman and the jolly man, who again said, "My, *my.*" The woman instructed, "On the day of the party, you turn up here with the others, and you'll be driven up to the Mansion."

2

Lyle discovers Hollywood Boulevard. His excursions
about the city; its sights, excitement,
and grave dangers.

As Lyle awaited the day when he would usher the rich, the beautiful, and the famous about the grounds of Huey's Mansion, he encountered a world far away from Rio Escondido.

And what a wonderful, beautiful, sexy city this was! Flowers managed to push out of cracks in the sidewalks and to shove out of thick shrubs. Bougainvillea draped walls and balconies, like a bunch of Clarita's ruby-colored rosaries. Too damned arrogant, those palm trees; and all over the city, drawings of feathery angels appeared daily on billboards and posters, winged sculptures in the city's plazas.

Hollywood Boulevard! The Wax Museum—somber, smiling statues of movie stars that looked dead and stuffed. Across the street, a dinosaur pounded on the top of the Believe It Or Not Museum. At the Chinese Theater, he gazed down at footprints and handprints embedded in the courtyard.

"I bet you'd fit *these.*" A giggly girl pointed down.

He straddled the prints. He fit them. He read the name: Gary Cooper.

He gazed at huge portraits on one side of the Chinese Theater—Charlie Chaplin, Shirley Temple, Marilyn Monroe. At the end of the row, on a rented billboard, there she was again!

BABETTE!

Lyle's heart pounded, his cock twitched. He tore himself away, reassuring himself that he could return to gaze at the luscious woman whenever he wanted. He wandered the blocks of army surplus stores, movie-poster shops. Before the Stella Adler Theater, a pretty girl with glasses sat cross-legged on the sidewalk, earnestly reading.

"Whatcha reading?" he asked her.

"Chekhov!" she said.

Had she told him to jack off? He'd better be careful about being too friendly too soon. He lingered before the windows of Frederick's of Hollywood, imagining Maria in one of those undies with a cutout heart right *there*—and Rose, in a red see-through—what was it? He passed young men and women—about his age, several younger—with spiked hair streaked red, green, yellow; earrings piercing their noses, belly buttons, nipples, eyebrows, tongues; tattoos crawling over their pale bodies.

When he discovered that the guided tour he took by bus was a tour of cemeteries, he stayed on not to be disrespectful of the others, older men and women. With them, he trooped like a pilgrim through Forest Lawn, rolling green hills, blocked tombstones—he removed his hat out of respect—white naked statues, oblivious of sorrow, and a huge replica of David rising like a triumphant giant over the realm of death.

At dusk, the tour ended at the Hollywood Forever Cemetery. As if attending the funeral of a dear friend, the group traipsed somberly along the rows of ornate stones, mausoleums large enough to live in. Lyle held his hat over his heart as members of the tour sighed, gasped, wept. "Valentino!" . . . "Tyrone Power!" . . . "Clara Bow!" . . . "Cecil B. DeMille!"

Later that night, he saw yet another world as he walked back to his apartment. Within the freeway underpass he had to cross were piles of trash. One stirred, then another. Bodies slept under the debris. Bands of shabby boys and girls scurried into the further coves under the freeway.

How difficult to find amazing grace even in the City of Angels.

In the following days, anticipating his job at Huey's Mansion, which grew grander and larger every day in Mrs. Allworthy's constant descriptions of it, he took the bus and the subway everywhere, smiling at the question about the whereabouts of his horse. He went to a concert under the stars, although fog obscured the stars. He roamed the La Brea tar pits, awed by real-looking saber-toothed tigers. At the silent movie theater, he wondered how Charlie Chaplin was able to make you laugh and cry at the same time. He studied the *Portrait of a Woman* at an art museum, admired its colors, but where was the woman?

After a long bus ride on the freeway—and, damn, can you believe the freeways?—he discovered the Central Library in Downtown Los Angeles.

He has never seen anything like this—rooms and rooms full of books and magazines, and eager young and old people pecking out information on computers. He paused to watch a young man gliding excitedly through image after image. Of nude women! He stopped to look, but the young man immediately punched at the keyboard and the nude women were wiped away by tall pine trees. All these books! Would every book get read sometime?

"May I help you?"

Lyle turned to see who had spoken to him. He didn't find anyone until he looked down and discovered a midget looking up at him, a neat, pretty, trim woman with glasses. A tag indicated she was a librarian.

"Yes, ma'am; will you help me?" he said because she seemed to want very much to help him. "It's my first time here."

She stood next to him. "See how short I am, especially next to you?" She measured herself against his hip.

"You sure are," Lyle said. He squatted down to face her. He read her name tag: "Mrs. Small."

"That's really my name," she laughed. "Your first time here? Then follow me." The tall cowboy and Mrs. Small entered a grand room with arches that soared over everything.

Mrs. Small said she wanted to introduce Lyle "to the thrills of reading." He didn't tell her that he had gone through required reading in school, all taught dully, and that, now and then, there was more than enough to "thrill" to—like Tom Sawyer's trip downriver, and—

He focused all his attention on her because she was going about the matter of introducing him to thrills with remarkable diligence, pulling out, considering, putting back, or removing books on lower-level shelves that she could easily reach, except for one that she asked Lyle to get. From the dozen or so chosen, she picked three—"to begin the thrills." She left him with a merry chuckle, passing her hand over her head and onto the place she reached on his hips. "I'm very small," she said happily.

"*Very* small," Lyle complimented.

He spent the rest of the day trying to read everything he could, replacing one book with another, wishing he'd done more of this in Rio Escondido. With his new library card, he checked out the three books Mrs. Small had chosen: *Huckleberry Finn, Oliver Twist,* and *Wuthering Heights.* ("The third one because it's my favorite—do you mind?" "Oh, no, I bet it'll be one of my favorites, too.")

"You sure don't look like a bookworm to me," a testy young man with thick glasses said to Lyle. "Where's your damn horse?"

"I don't—" To hell with him.

Glaring back at him, the testy young man stumbled on Mrs. Small, who had emerged to say good-bye, "for now," to Lyle. "Watch where you're going, shorty!" the testy young man barked at the natty midget.

"Hey, you!" Lyle called out, ready to defend Mrs. Small.

But the young man ran out.

"Forget him," said Mrs. Small. "He's just insecure because he's neither very tall nor very short."

On the bus back on the freeway, Lyle read from each of the books he had checked out, shifting from one to the other. He got off before his stop so he could read as he walked, very slowly, to his apartment, two books under one arm, another in his hand before him. Damn! How sad that no one could ever read *everything*!—and, wow, Catherine Earnshaw sure had spunky spirit, like Maria.

During the following days, he roamed along the chic shops of Melrose Boulevard, choosing presents to buy later for Sylvia, for Clarita, for Maria. He moved on to Santa Monica Boulevard, wondering why so many guys with terrific muscles looked at him instead of at each other. He traveled to the Watts Towers, a monumental sculpture of millions of fragments of colored glass—shards of bottles, cups, saucers embedded into concrete, forming a dazzling ship that had, through the years, assumed an aged, ghostly gauziness like an apparition; an Italian immigrant, Lyle read in a pamphlet, had dedicated his life to constructing it.

As he walked to the bus stop nearby, he was aware of angry, resentful stares, mostly from younger black men, whom he nevertheless greeted, eliciting some grudgy, some friendly greetings back—but, mostly, even more hostile glares. Sister Matilda had seen her father lynched, and the black slave had to challenge Cap'n Newton to feel pain. So it was easy to recognize that the men and women on these streets *had* to suspect everyone. They had no way of knowing that he felt em-pa-thy for the down-trotten, because there wasn't all that much in the goddamned world, was there?—and if they—

"Look at the cowboy! Whatcha doin' wanderin' around here, man?"

A wiry young black man with a cap slouched back had swaggered up to him with two others, circling him.

"Just lookin' around," Lyle said.

"He just lookin' around," said another of the three, a short, heavy boy, no more than fifteen years old.

"Whatcha lookin' around for?" the third one, tall—with muscles that seemed to strain for action—faced Lyle, his nose inches from Lyle's. "Trouble?"

"I got no problem with you," Lyle said. He asked the Virgin Guadalupe to help him find the right words to get out of what looked serious, very serious. "I want you to know I feel lots of em-pa-thy for you."

The three looked at each other in exaggerated disbelief. "Did ya hear that? Fuckin' white cowboy says he got a lot of em-path-y for us," the wiry young man announced.

"What the fuck's em-path-y?" the short, heavy one asked the tall one.

"Ask the cowboy, man. He's the one that's got it."

"Feelin' for another," Lyle said seriously.

The three broke into laughter, slapping at each other. The muscular one pushed Lyle, hard, on the chest. "You feel that? You feel em-pa-thy?"

"No," Lyle said, "it just hurt."

"Maybe this'll make you feel *more* em-pa-thy." The short, heavy one shoved him to one side. The wiry one shoved him back. They bounced him back and forth, gathering closer to him, a tightening triangle, fists ready, feet dance-kicking. Lyle's fists prepared to move, but he cautioned them—they had to learn when to wait. He was in real danger. The bus was approaching. He tried to back away from the three—but they closed in, anger on their faces spilling into rage.

"Look. I got no problem with you," Lyle repeated. He was afraid, very afraid.

"Maybe we got lotsa problems with you, motherfucker!" said the tall one.

What was the boy reaching for? What was he holding? Something that gleamed in a flash—a knife, a gun? It was all a blur now for Lyle as sweat blistered his eyes and the three figures pressed in about him, jostling him roughly back and forth, blocking him from sight.

"Y'all get away from him, ya hear?" A black older woman with a pretty hat, a band of tiny flowers around it, had rushed to the scene from her house on Grape Street. "He came to see the Towers, that's all, I saw him walking there." She stood before Lyle, facing down the three men.

"Get away, old bitch," the tall one said, "we don't want no shit from you."

She didn't budge before Lyle. The bus halted, the door swooshed open. "Jump in quick, white boy!" the woman ordered, "and don't come 'round any more where you don't fit."

Lyle hopped into the bus. The doors closed. Rushing to a window, he called out to the woman, who was already sauntering away, "Thank you, ma'am, thank you"—and then to the others who had followed menacingly, striking at the sides of the bus as it drove away: "I swear I got no problem with you." He was trembling, sweating, terrified. He had to figure this all out. If only he could ask Sister Matilda what to think, what to feel.

3

An essential decision about life and living.

But you couldn't go on being afraid all the time, could you?

So, the next day, Lyle resumed his treks about the city that contained lots of dangers, yes, but also lots of fabulous excitement—and exceptional people like that black lady with the flowers on her hat. Very soon, he'd be going to Huey's mansion, the party for Ms. Universal! In the meantime—

Along Sunset Boulevard at night, scantily clad girls and leather-garbed young men posed outside nightclubs with sinister names, "The Viper Room," "The Vortex," "The Pit." He wasn't old enough to go in, wouldn't really want to—so many people pleading to be let in by hulking, sulking attendants at the doors. Often, young men and women standing outside or coming out of the darkened nightclubs—or sitting in one of several outdoor coffee houses sipping foamy drinks—responded to him. "Cool" . . . "hot." How could you be both? he wondered.

Along the streets, and in the coffee shops where he ate, people were often friendly—a family once asked him to dinner at their home Sunday—and he'd talk, listen. At times he was invited to parties going on somewhere. Once he smoked from a joint someone at an outdoor table handed to him. He became so dizzy and disoriented he had to sit down with them until the weird sensation passed.

He was so excited by everything he saw, everything he experienced— trying to figure it all out, including the hostility he had generated on the black streets—that he preferred to roam alone, to absorb it all fully. Sometimes he took his guitar with him, slung over his shoulder so that, if he felt like it, he might sit down somewhere—anywhere—just as he had in his lot in Rio Escondido—and he would begin a song in his mind. When he left his guitar behind, he might return at night to test some notes and jot down words that might become a song. *Black eyes deep with anger*—" He'd work on his songs until the man who lived in the apartment next to him would bang on the wall and ask him if he was crazy.

He took a bus to Venice West, and walked about the small quaint city—canals, buildings with arches, carved columns; in the distance, neat rows of stacked condominiums, and, nearby, oil plucking at the earth like dinosaurs.

He loitered about the boardwalk by the beach. Girls in bikinis and athletic young men in trunks skated by. He stopped to watch men with huge, oiled muscles work out in an outdoor pit. The most muscular man put down his weights and walked over to wink at him. Kids performed tricks on skateboards, bikers glided off toward the ocean, gangy boys slouched in baggy clothes. Stay away from them!

Tourists strolled, dancers danced, musicians played, drummers beat on drums—and men and women passed out leaflets offering solutions for everything.

"See the face of God?" a bearded old man sitting on the ground and wearing a loincloth called out. Because nobody else was stopping, Lyle paused. The man drew tangles of lines on a piece of paper, a harsh black X across it. He handed it to Lyle. "Twenty bucks." Lyle thanked him and hurried on.

Gypsies telling fortunes, clowns cavorting, a butterfly lady fluttering along with gauzy wings, gymnasts soaring into the air, jugglers,
ragged bands, fake jewels, sticks of wafting incense, artists sculpting
sand, tattoo shops with drawings of maddened butterflies, coiled pan-
thers. Everywhere, dazed men and women, young, old, like zombies,
begging for money, shivering under the warm sun.

He had left the ocean for the last, looking away from it even though
he couldn't avoid glimpsing it as he walked along. The day waned,
crowds thinned.

He walked barefoot toward the endless expanse of water. The tide was
advancing. Slow waves gathered into larger ones, splashing the beach,
retreating, gaining force, climbing. Nearby, two lithe men and two
women in black tights performed a slow dance of graceful motions as
they faced the setting sun—now a fading blaze of umber—as if greeting
the coming night. Flocks of birds perched on the sand, facing the ocean.

He stood as close to the water as possible. It was as if everything, including the setting sun, was waiting for the sky to fuse with the ocean
into darkness. Was there anything else this amazing? Was grace? Beyond
that expanse of water and sky, what? Mysterious, beautiful, secret. Like
so much of what he was encountering in this city of astonishment, mysterious, beautiful, secret.

Like Sylvia.

4

Has Lyle met BABETTE during the savage attack
of the peacock at Huey's Mansion?

Inside the gates of Huey's Mansion, but not yet inside its lush grounds,
Lyle stood in a row with ten other young men his age, all handsome.
Before them, a black woman in shiny black leather instructed them
about this evening's affair celebrating Ms. Universal.

"My name is Honor!" she announced. "Now, everyone listen up! We
don't take crap from anyone. We got guards all around, serious guards
with guns. Lesser guests gather in a parking lot at UCLA and will be
bussed only after they show picture identification. VIPs are allowed up
to this area in their cars, mostly limos. People will try to break through,
to catch a glimpse of Huey, maybe Ms. Universal. But they'll get in

over my dead body." She reiterated their "duties"—roam around answering questions about where this or that is, guide guests there, summon waiters for hors d'oeuvres and wine if anyone was missed. "Show the guests where the towels and the robes are if they want to take a shower or use the sauna."

Take a shower?

Lyle's eyes scanned the large arena they would rove, an area tented as if for a circus. Inside the tent were tables and mountains of flowers, and several bars tended by young men, a rainbow of bottles behind them. Beyond the canvas structure, on a vast lawn that rolled on to the edge of a forest of trees, monkeys swung about and birds chirped merrily in plant-filled cages. On slopes that disappeared into the horizon, a deer—another one!—more!—idled about. Peacocks tended by a woman in safari khakis sauntered haughtily along. Far away, remote, high, ascending upon level upon level of flowers—birds of paradise, exotic lilies, roses—and, somewhere a waterfall was murmuring—there, up high, higher, was The Mansion, resplendent in early evening brightness as if the very earth had begged it to emerge.

A helicopter lurked watchfully over everything.

Like a drill sergeant in leather, Honor moved aside for a thin man to inspect the attire of the attendants.

"Boots!" snarled the man.

"Tony Lama," Lyle announced. "Black ones."

"Cool, dude." the young man next to him said, and loosened his tie.

"What's going on, what's going on?" Honor was there.

"He's wearing cowboy boots!"

Honor looked around, as if considering whether to call someone to find a pair of shoes for him, escort him away, or shoot him.

Bubbles of laughter floated over them. The first fleet of guests was sailing out of limousines—and there, as if materializing out of the extravagant setting, and across an impervious pool of diamond-gleaming water, on which white lilies relaxed—there, ready to greet the first guests, stood—

Huey and Ms. Universal.

Huey was a short man in a wine-colored velvet robe. Next to him—and from this distance—Ms. Universal seemed to have been airbrushed

against the verdant background; she was all silvery-blonde, wearing a
sheath of a dress that made hot love to her voluptuous body.

"Too late to do anything about the damn boots!" Honor scowled at
Lyle. In substitute anger, she tightened the loosened tie of the young
man next to him and didn't stop until he protested, "Ouch!"

"All of you!" Honor commanded. *"Move out!"*

Lyle thought Ms. Universal was the most dazzling woman he had
ever seen, next, of course, to Maria.

And Babette. . . .

Wait! Was Ms. Universal Babette—now a blonde?

Several other young women, all pretty, all sexy, dressed in tiny skirts
and low tops were idling about looking like bunnies. Oh, God, they
were wearing rabbit ears—and cotton tails!

"I'd sure like to fuck Ms. Universal," the young man next to Lyle
said earnestly as they began to break up to their stations.

"Me, too," Lyle said just as earnestly. If he could get closer to her,
he'd determine whether she was Babette!

The young man who had loosened his tie sidled up to Lyle. "Name's
Shandy—well, that's my stage name. Hey, you're, like, a handsome
dude, man. You think I'm, like, good-lookin'?"

Lyle nodded his head, yes.

"Yeah? Hey, do you ever, like, go with guys?"

Lyle thought of Raul and the lonesome chorus boy in Las Vegas. "I
like guys," he said.

"Great. I'm not a fag—I bet you're, like, not either, dude—but at
these parties there's, like, always some bitches or some guys who, like,
wanna get something going with us good-looking studs. Wanna, like,
pull a sex gig with me after? Pays good, y'know?"

Male prostitutes? He knew of course that there were female prostitutes. But males?—getting paid for something as terrific as sex? "Oh,
uh, maybe another time, dude Shandy," Lyle said, because he did not
want to offend the man.

Shandy cocked the thumb and index finger of each hand in imitation of a double-barrel gun. "Gotcha, dude!" he fired.

Lyle had maneuvered closer to Ms. Universal! Those breasts! Those
lips! Those hips! Those legs! That smile that stayed and stayed! Definitely Babette. No two women could look like *that*. Who was she

smiling at? No one. Just smiling. He stared until he saw her blink, having made sure she wasn't a cutout of the poster.

The blonde apparition and the man in the velvet robe disappeared along the paths, to mingle away from lesser guests spilling out of buses.

As Lyle milled about answering questions—"Where is—?" "Where is—?" he saw a peacock that had wandered away from the attendant in safari khakis.

The peacock had caught sight of him. Otherwise, why did he point his beak, sharply, at him and spread his tail as if to be noticed? The monkeys had already spotted the peacock and were making sounds . . . egging him on?

Lyle stared back at the peacock. The bird did not budge.

Guests sauntered in and out of the tent, flitting toward one or another of several bars. Everyone was dressed in black or gray, except the bunny-girls, in pink and black, and Ms. Universal in sheer white, who, as if she had been placed there just now by invisible forces, appeared just inside the tent.

Uh-oh. What was the peacock up to? The bird had managed to stray away from the attendant in khakis while she was placating the other peacocks who had become flustered when the monkeys had thrown pebbles at them.

Dammit if he was wrong, but the loose peacock now was focusing his attention on Ms. Universal. His comb stiffened—goddamn if it didn't; Lyle was as sure of that as he was that Ms. Universal was the woman on the posters, the glorious Babette! The caretaker in khakis looked around and became aware of the missing peacock advancing into the tented area, where guests were circulating. Leaving behind the other birds to deal with the pebbles raining on them from the monkeys, she advanced cautiously to capture the stray peacock. That would not be difficult if everything remained as it was now, the peacock transfixed—no doubt about it—by the spectacle of the blond, smiling Ms. Universal.

What he wouldn't give to cup those perfect breasts!—which on the billboards were about to push out of her black bikini—and here, in the flesh, even closer to doing that. She was as irresistible to him, Lyle knew, as she was to the peacock—who dashed into the tent area, dodging expertly away from the caretaker at the exact moment that she had reached out for him but instead fell facedown—and the peacock gal-

loped straight at Ms. Universal, while the fallen woman in safari khakis shouted at everyone:

"Take cover, take cover! That fuckin' peacock bites mean!"

Everyone scattered, including Huey—but not Ms. Universal. She
remained standing where she had been, smiling, as the peacock charged
toward her.

Lyle ran toward the peacock rushing at Ms. Universal. At the point
that the peacock would have—done what? Bitten Ms. Universal? Kissed
her? At that point, Lyle grabbed the peacock, lifted him, held him under
one arm as if all his life he had been tending to rampaging peacocks,
and he let his free hand clasp Ms. Universal's breast, and he sighed:

"Oh, Babette!"

At the same moment that the peacock bit him meanly, on the hand,
flashbulbs popped. Ms. Universal smiled even more radiantly. Lyle,
startled, looked in the direction of the increasing flashes, one intrepid
hand still on Ms. Universal's breast, moving on to the other. Done!

Over the squawking of the bird, he heard a purring voice that said,
as he retained his clutch on the luscious breast and held the enraged
peacock with his other hand:

"That was nice. Thank you," Ms. Universal breathed.

"You're welcome. Thank *you*. You're more beautiful than your posters," he managed to say as more flashbulbs popped in his eyes and he
dropped the screaming bird and knew he had to run like hell to get
away because Honor was charging at him like a mad bull and guards
were converging from every damn direction.

CHAPTER SIXTEEN

1

Maria's inviolate decision.

L yle is not my brother, he is not, is not, not, not, *not!*"
Maria screamed at her placid mother and her irate
father.

"I know he's not *my* son," said Helen, Maria's mother,
Armando's wife. A pleasant-faced woman who remained so even when
she glowered in accusation at her husband, Helen had come from St.
Louis with her parents and met Armando in Fort Worth, Texas, where
he had tried to establish his practice as a legal consultant before moving on to Dallas and, now, for at least as long as he and Helen got along,
commuting to Rio Escondido periodically.

"Not yours, but *mine*," Armando was steadfast.

"He doesn't look like you." Maria made that a severe indictment of
her father. "He's *tall*, and you're *short*."

Armando stretched, to adjust to the sting. "He's handsome, like me."

"He's handsome all right, but not like you."

"What do you mean by that? That I'm not—" Armando, although he often had to remind himself to hold in his stomach, had become even more pleased with his good looks than he had been when he had shown his chiseled abdominals to Sylvia in the Catholic church.

"*You* know what I mean," Maria emphasized, "and what I mean beyond all that is that I'm going to Los Angeles to be with him. The only man I shall ever love, ever, ever, *ever!*" She formed two crosses with the thumb and index fingers of each hand and kissed them, sealing her vow.

Helen sighed. "That's not a city for a green girl."

"*Green girl!* Listen, Ma"—she knew Helen hated that rednecky word, preferring Mother—"Lyle and I—" She was about to say, "had sex," but that sounded dirty; so she said, "Lyle and I fucked, remember?"

Armando slapped himself twice.

Having heard and been thrilled by hearing her own words, Maria—eyes bright with determination and remembered lust—said, "And fuck you if you try to keep me from going to the man I love." She let her eyes fall for a second, conveying the enormity of her desperate love, allowing tears she had gathered to stream down her cheeks.

"Yeah? Yeah?" Armando sputtered. "I'll tell you something right here and now. You're going to stay put and you're not going to marry anyone I don't approve of."

"You'd like me to marry one of those creeps you keep bringing around—like that fat creep who keeps calling me 'babe.'"

"Creep? A powerful man, rich enough to give you everything you want, everything—clothes, cars, jewels!"

Maria seemed to ponder for a moment.

"Powerful *and* rich," Armando emphasized, "very, *very* rich."

"Well—" Maria paused. Then she stamped her foot. "No, no, no, no! You can't force me to marry who you want! We're not in the Dark Ages, you know."

"You run away and I'll follow you and bring you back!" Armando swore.

"If you can find me!" Maria decided, for now, to hide in her room. In the future, she might have to hide at—at—at the very end of the earth if need be, that is how powerful her love was for Lyle Clemens was!—despite her suitor's fabulous enticements.

2

A film sequel to a great novel changes yet again.

The wind rushing through her gorgeous red mane added to her exultation as Tarah drove in her snazzy Mercedes—all windows open—along Hollywood Boulevard, her favorite street, on her way home from a drive along the Malibu coastline, to think, think, think. The street had turned tacky, but it still evoked the yesterdays of Hollywood, which would return, were returning with the new building for the Academy Awards, huge murals of great stars on the walls of the Chinese Theater. She, Tarah Worth, was poised to help lead it back to its past grandeur in the role of glamorous Helen Lawson in *Return to the Valley of the Dolls.* She felt exhilarated; today even her nasty horoscope had implied some encouragement: "You will think through to a resolution; make sure it's the right one."

Obviously that referred to the problem of the strange reference to "dolls" in the title. How to give it a meaning favorable to her? What if she began calling everyone in Hollywood "doll"? It would take over!—and add an even more contemporary touch to the script. She should read the great novel again, find more inspiration. But she didn't want to tamper with her memory of it. That was too sublime. Besides, she hadn't really read the novel, just some parts of it—but she had seen the great movie too many times to count. "Dolls" . . . She decided: She would start calling men and women that, and the word would spread—

The buzzing of her car phone startled her.

"Better start practicing your huskiest voice, honey," Lenora said, "'cause they've definitely turned Helen Lawson into a sister—a dyke."

Oh, Lord, Lord, would there ever be an end to this torture?

"Another lesbian said—"

"Lenora! You're not a lesbian! Dozens of young actors claim yours is the most used casting couch in Hollywood." Would she finally succeed in insulting the indomitable creature?

"Yeah? What if they're just bragging?—and what if next time I saw you, I lick your—"

Vulgar creature! Tarah held the telephone away from her ear, did not want to listen to this coarse onslaught. When she listened again, she said, "Of course, I'll adjust . . . doll"—why not start now?—"and I'll turn her into a beautiful fem lesbian."

"What did you call me?"

"Doll." The word fell with a thud. That she had used it first on Lenora—what psychic effect would that have?

"Are you comin' on to me, sweetie?" Lenora laughed into the telephone. "But, hey, I'm taken! . . . More stuff for you, doll. It's definite. There'll be a killer kidnap scene involving Helen Lawson. They can't decide if she'll be kidnapped or she'll do the kidnapping. Ciao, doll. Keep working on your big gimmick."

A kidnapping. A kidnapping.

3

Lyle's flight from Huey's Mansion and
an unexpected angel of mercy appears.

Bulbs popping after him! People surrounding him! Panicking at all the commotion he had created (why, why?—because he had touched Ms. Universal's breasts—the glorious Babette's breasts?), Lyle ran past wide-mouthed guests, a gaping Huey, past Honor, who tried to block his path but stumbled over a painted rock, past iron gates and guards (about to draw their guns?—why?)—and out of the Mansion, shoving himself into a thicket of trees and shrubs to take off his boots and stuff his money securely way into their toes with his socks so that he could run—dodging and running and twisting and running down, down, down, running and stopping on a fancy stretch of Sunset Boulevard where he tried to hitchhike and no one even paused until . . .

A motorcycle roared to a stop.

"Put your boots on and hop on, cowboy; and don't try anything because I'm a dyke."

"Great, I like dykes!" Lyle said, without knowing what a dyke was.

"The pigs after you, dude?" the biker asked him.

Pigs? Had pigs been chasing the peacock? "Uh, no," he said.

"Jump on anyhow," the biker said.

Lyle jumped on the back of the motorcycle that this angel of mercy was driving and he held on tightly while she dodged in and out of traffic.

4

The search is on for the Mystery Cowboy.

"Lyle! They're looking for you!" Mrs. Allworthy, having waited at the window of her unit at the Fountain Apartments since she had heard the early evening news, dashed out and shoutes those words at Lyle, and added: "You're on all the news! They're calling you the Mystery Cowboy."

This must be it: Brother Bud and Sister Sis had probably convinced everyone that he was part of their illegal schemes, and now they were after him. He would give himself up, but not before escaping to Rio Escondido to say so long to his sister—dammit, he sure was rattled—Maria was *not* his sister!—and to Clarita—he'd give her some money to buy herself a VCR of her own, so she might watch her old Mexican movies—and to Sylvia, he'd give—

"They're calling you the Mystery Cowboy because nobody knows who you are," Mrs. Allworthy raised her voice to alert the others in the building of the new celebrity among them.

"I have to get away quick!" Lyle said, "before I give myself up."

"What are you talking about?" Mrs. Allworthy became impatient. She gasped for the others gathering to hear: "You! . . . saved! . . . Ms. Universal! . . . From the! . . . rampaging peacock!"

Lyle wasn't sure whether he was entirely relieved. Was that the only reason they had seemed about to surround him? Was there something else they weren't saying? Had he harmed the peacock? Had he knocked down Honor when he was rushing out? Was Huey furious?

Other tenants were coming out of the unit to join in the commotion.

"Nobody knows who you are except us," said one enthusiastic neighbor, "and we won't tell how you got that bite on your hand, does it hurt?"

Lyle hid his hand, still smarting from the mean bird's bite.

"Of course, we won't tell. We can keep a secret, can't we?" said a prim old lady.

"Everyone describes you as wearing boots. To a formal party! Did you wear your hat, too?" asked a girl with jet-black dyed hair, streaked red.

"We'll hide you, dude," proposed her male partner, who had several earrings on his nose, tattoos eating each other up on his arms. "I don't dig the pigs myself, ya know?"

"It's not the pigs, man," his girl said. "It's—what?" she asked Mrs. Allworthy.

"Yeah, what?" Lyle wanted to know. The pigs again. He remembered monkeys, yes, and birds—but *pigs*?

Mrs. Allworthy threw her arms up in dismay. "They didn't say why they're looking for you. Maybe to give you a reward? Maybe a movie contract? Oh, and Lyle, one paper said you were an obsessed fan of Babette's, that you were heard gasping her name when you—uh—Did you touch Ms. Universal's breasts?"

She wasn't Babette? Lyle was disappointed and relieved, disappointed because he had not been with her, relieved because that meant she'd still be roaming around in her silver Cadillac for him to find.

A middle-aged lady who dressed very youthfully joined the group: "You looked very handsome, Mystery Cowboy, real swoony, real dreamy, real groovy."

Lyle looked around, as if expecting that photographers would be there at any moment to trap him again.

"You'll keep it all secret, about me, right?" he pleaded with them.

"Yeah, sure, man." said a tough Chicana.

"Just be cool, man," said her boyfriend, his head shaved, "and they won't ever catch you. Stay cool, okay?"

"We'll take you into our hearts, Mystery Cowboy, that's my senti-ment," said an older man, who taught piano to children—very noisily, because he was hard of hearing.

"Thank you," Lyle said, sincerely. He certainly did *not* welcome people going around trying to find him, although he still hadn't the slimmest idea of why they would.

5

Reverberations.

Tarah Worth opened the newspaper. As others say a morning prayer, she read Liz Smith's column. There was always food for thought, and today Liz had—

That photograph at the top of the page! Was it—? She squinted. Yes, it was that cowboy who'd talked to her by the motel pool in Anaheim. Definitely a mystic sign for her, the way he kept recurring in her life. Four times now! Now there he was holding a peacock—was a peacock significant psychically? Should she call Riva and ask? Tarah read the caption. "Mystery Cowboy saves Ms. Universal from rampaging peacock and disappears—"

He would certainly bring anyone a lot of attention after this, wouldn't he? she thought. BEAUTIFUL ACTRESS TARAH WORTH IS RUMORED TO BE THE ONLY PERSON IN TOUCH WITH THE MYSTERY COWBOY. Hmmmm. She resumed reading her favorite column.

No, please God, no! It couldn't be true that Joan Collins had expressed interest in the role of Helen Lawson.

She needed the gimmick Lenora kept reminding her of, to secure the role. The Academy Awards were approaching. Photographers from all over the world would be here. . . . That great kidnap scene in the new story line of *Return to the Valley of the Dolls* kept bobbing up in her mind, and her eyes kept returning to the picture of the Mystery Cowboy with the peacock.

6

Still more reverberations.

"Must you? Must you! Must you be so vulgar, always? Always?" Mrs. Renquist pushed at her temples, to contain an exploding headache as she sat by the pool in her Encino home. She was sheltered from the damaging sun by a hat, gloves, heavy sunblock applied by her Salvadoran maid—who'd done an erotic film for the Renquists and then had aged—and a huge umbrella that cradled her in shadow; she had been looking through the newspaper and lamenting, again, that Chanel did not design swimwear, when she had seen the photograph and had called out to Mr. Renquist, who had been floating in the pool like an ugly brown whale.

"What the fuck, honey, the way you called, I thought you were fucking drowning," he had responded. Now he stood looking at the newspaper photograph she had wordlessly handed to him, his bikini entirely concealed by folds of hairy flesh, mauve-tanned skin oiled heavily so that, out of the pool, he shone like a lubricated balloon.

He roared with laughter. "Jesus. What's that guy doing with the peacock? Hey, wait, isn't he feeling up the blonde bitch? Wait, goddammit, honey, isn't he the guy in——?"

"——the religious program, yes," Mrs. Renquist had recognized him instantly; she restrained her anger at Mr. Renquist's sticky designation, for now. "Apparently he thought the woman was that notorious Babette."

"The broad with the giant boobs, right. Must be real hot for her, eh?"

This time, Mrs. Renquist only brushed aside his vulgarity, even the interjection she loathed. Recently she had read that someone had impersonated Liz Smith at Spago—she had been there but detected only the commotion—and had almost gotten away with it. That gave her an idea. An impersonator. Hmmmm. If they could . . . encourage . . . the Mystery Cowboy into an Internet "performance"—that was where everything new was occurring—their erotic enterprises would surely take an upward swing. The pressure inside Mrs. Renquist's head lessened at the thought.

7

Unwanted fame.

Lyle's photograph with the peacock and Ms. Universal—could everybody tell he was groping her breast?—appeared in a newspaper that asked: "Where is the Mystery Cowboy? Who is he? Why has he run away? Why is he hiding?" First a gossip column, then another, soon the "trades," showbiz journals, more newspapers—all extended the buzz. Entertainment-news television segments conjectured: The Mystery Cowboy was the "son of a wealthy recluse" . . . "an ordinary would-be actor who carried out a gimmick" . . . "a stuntman out of a job" . . . "Huey's secret son, who invaded the famous mansion." . . . A Hollywood producer announced plans for a movie. A tabloid demanded to know: "Is he stalking Babette?"

Lyle couldn't understand how if everybody was looking for him they couldn't find him, since he continued to roam Hollywood, and here he was looking up at the huge blowup of Babette on the wall of a new building. No, he was not stalking her. No, he wasn't in love with her. He loved only Maria, remember? But, goddamn, will you *look* at her?

"Hey, you're the Mystery Cowboy on television," a teenage boy said.

"Look, here's the guy that saved the woman from the mad peacock. Huccome you're hiding?"

"You see me hiding?" Lyle demanded.

The kid shrugged. "TV says so, dude."

"There's, like, the peacock guy!" said one of a group of young men with pitched-back baseball caps.

"Don't, like, call him that, he's, like, the Mystery Cowboy."

"Can I have your autograph?"

A teenage girl was poking him with an autograph book.

"No!"

"Cummon, Mystery Cowboy." The girl poked harder. "I already got what's-his-name on the *Millionaire Show.*"

Lyle signed her book: "Lyle Clemens."

The girl looked down at the entry, up at him in disappointment. "Who the hell is he?"

"I don't know," Lyle said. "I really don't." Finding out everything about life sure could be difficult.

As long as nobody could find him, he would continue his life just as before. He traveled by bus and subway, discovering intricate routes, studied maps, rode everywhere in this wondrous city. He was a hit on morning buses. Many workers would respond to him with pleasure, "*Hola,* Mystery Cowboy, how ya doin', guy?" Mexican women, on their way to work, giggled, and flirted with him, and often called him "*el charro misterioso.*"

8

Em-path-y for down-trotten lost angels.

Regular runaways on the Boulevard recognized him now. "Hey, Mystery Cowboy dude." He felt for these young people about his age who hovered in shadowy corners with their spiky hair and pierced bodies; they looked sad even when they laughed. They seemed to be waiting for nothing, anything. Raul might have been one of them if he hadn't gone back home. Stubby, mean-faced boys with shaved heads and scowly looks, boom-boxes ranting out curses, taunted the young gypsies, who always looked hungry.

Seeing five or six of the stray young people counting out meager change and coming up short in front of an open food stand, he bought them hot dogs and Cokes, and sat on the sidewalk eating with them, while people paused to stare.

"Why don't you give yourself up and end the search, Mystery Cowboy," an old man stopped to demand. "I gave myself up once, threw myself at the mercy of the court, and they went easy on me."

"I'll do that, sir, thank you."

"Naw, Mystery Cowboy, man," said one of the runaways, a tough girl, "don't do that; ain't no mercy in those fuckin' juv. courts."

A group was boarding a tour bus of Hollywood, and he joined, waving back at the tattooed children.

"Can't just hop on, cowboy," the driver said, not crossly. "Gotta buy a ticket."

"Oh, let him on," said a young couple. "Don't you recognize the Mystery Cowboy?"

"Okay, saddle up," said the driver/guide.

Lyle hopped on the bus.

"Well, don't think I didn't see you with those trashy runaways on the sidewalks. Well, they're all on the road to perdition if you ask me!"

Lyle turned to look at a woman and a man who seemed vaguely familiar. She was heavy, huffed even when she wasn't speaking. Her chins jiggled. The man with her remained silent. Not possible! It was the nasty woman who had sat onstage with him at the magician's act.

"No one asked you, ma'am," Lyle said.

"Well, aren't you the rude one!" the woman snapped. "Well, you know, we come to this Babylon once a year," she announced loudly to everybody. "Well, every time we leave, something terrible happens— a slaughter on the freeway, a big earthquake and, well, we always miss it. Well, don't you suppose God just loves us?"

"Wouldn't think so, Mrs. Well," Lyle said.

"Well, how on earth do you know my name?" the woman reacted. "Well, even if—"

"Ma'am," Lyle said, "would it be rude to ask you to please shut up so we can hear the driver point out the sites?—and, maybe"—he added this for himself and Clarita—"you might try to feel a little em-path-y for the down-trotten."

Several on the bus applauded.

"Well!" huffed the odd woman.

"To your left," the tour guide directed, "is the Hollywood Hotel, the site of the first Academy Awards. They say ghosts of great movie stars roam its lobby . . . "The Ambassador Hotel, where Joe diMaggio proposed to Marilyn Monroe . . . The Biltmore Hotel, where Robert Kennedy was murdered . . . The Brown Derby, where Lana Turner— . . . There are many ghosts in the City of Angels, and there are many living lost angels."

CHAPTER SEVENTEEN

1

A windy day in Rio Escondido.

It was a windy summer day in Rio Escondido. Usually, the winds in Texas fade in mid-spring, having exhausted themselves by then. The violent thrusts of dust and tumbleweeds, gathered along miles of desert, diminish, the howls of windstorms become an angry whisper, then die. For the past few days, however, wind had intensified, not lessened, along with the heat of premature summer. The wind panted with desert heat.

The wind, the heat—all that had put Sylvia into a terrible mood, Clarita knew; but today it was more than that, much more than the liquor. She sat in her living room, her hand holding the television remote idly, trying to work up enough energy to point it at the blank screen.

Beside her, Clarita waited for a picture. Though she now had her cherished VCR, bought with what Lyle had sent her, she had found the thrill of it lessening; she missed the quarrels with Sylvia about what to watch—missed her asking her to translate every line of a Mexican soap opera they would sometimes watch together.

Sylvia sighed.

That was the seventh sigh of the evening; Clarita had begun counting them only after she had noticed that Sylvia was sighing more than usual.

Sylvia looked at her. "When is Lyle coming back?"

"You got a letter from him yesterday," Clarita reminded her, and quickly seized the opportunity to bring it to her from the small table in the hallway.

That's where Sylvia placed Lyle's letters, keeping each for a time when she felt especially sad, and then it might lift her spirits. She had begun several letters to him, all unfinished. There was too much to say that she could never tell him.

She took Lyle's letter from Clarita. She opened it. Several bills fluttered out. With a terrible cry, she let the money and the letter fall to the floor.

Clarita gathered the bills and the letter, knowing the painful memory Lyle's gift had stirred.

"He'll be back," Sylvia said softly.

"Of course he will," Clarita encouraged. "He left to find himself, and he will, he's a smart boy, and—"

"Boy?" Sylvia frowned.

She hadn't meant Lyle, she'd meant the cowboy! It was time to speak out, bluntly: "The cowboy is never, never coming back!"

Sylvia remained impassive. She sipped her bourbon, and smiled as if at something only she knew. "Lyle the First is coming back very soon, wait and see," she said.

2

In which an invitation assures the site of the gimmick.

"I can assure it—you and Rusty will be invited to the Academy Awards, doll," Lenora barked over the telephone and into Tarah's ear—even to give good news she barked, and the ringer had growled.

Doll! Tarah gave a tiny gasp of pleasure. Her tactic had worked. "Doll" would spread through Hollywood, and people would remember it was she who had reintroduced the word into its current use. Finally the title of the great masterpiece would make sense, in *Return to the Valley of the Dolls*.

"What you do to get attention is up to you," Lenora had rumbled on. "I'm sure you're working on something terrific. You're wily, doll."

"Yes, I am," Tarah said, fascinated by the coldness in her own voice.

"Great!" Click.

Everything was falling into place. All she needed was to find—and quick!—the Mystery Cowboy everyone was talking about, the one who'd been so hot for her that day at the motel pool in Anaheim, the one who would double the publicity she needed.

A kidnapping at the Academy Awards!

3

Some observations about hiding.

Now it seems impossible that questions about the identity and whereabouts of the Mystery Cowboy continued and extended all the time that he wandered in full view along the streets of the city. How could anyone miss him? A tall, slender young man wearing cowboy boots and—though he did take it off now and then—a cowboy hat was a startling sight. What was occurring was that no one expected him to be so visible, and so everyone was looking for him where he was not, where he should be hiding, out of easy sight. What better way not to be found than not to be in the places suspected, but be where no one would think he would hide.

Certainly he would not be hiding on Hollywood Boulevard on this beautiful warm evening—not yet dusk—when everyone was out, a Michael Jackson lookalike was signing autographs, tourist buses were pausing before everything, pale young Scientologists fished for customers, men sauntered in and out of porno shops, and cops in shorts biked along the blocks.

"Hey!"

"Me?"

"Yes, cowboy, you! You want a ride?"

My God, my God, my God, my God, my God, oh, Jesuschrist, yes! Thank you, Holy Virgin Guadalupe! Babette was asking if he wanted a ride! The luscious woman in the posters sat in her slinky silver Cadillac. She had stopped at the corner—in a no-parking red zone!—as he was about to cross. He was speechless.

"Well?"

He still couldn't talk, but he could hop on and he did. Would he ever become used to this? Beautiful women approaching him—not that he wouldn't have approached them; they just beat him to it.

She was even more stunning than her poster, definitely a sexy angel. (No competition for Maria, of course, who belonged in his heart).

Those eyes!—Lyle had lifted his eyes from the woman's spectacular breasts—eyes with a ready-to-jump-into-bed look, but not for sleeping. Her flesh was so white—he was getting used to tanned flesh everywhere—it was as if she had never allowed the sun to touch her even though the sun would certainly want to. Her silky blouse barely covered the tips of her luminous breasts, her skirt hardly covered her legs, which he was now staring at. As she pushed the clutch to shift the car into drive, her tiny skirt inched up.

"You like sex, cowboy?"

"You bet, ma'am!" (I love you, Maria, he sent her a message across the miles, with all my heart—but remember, you keep saying you're my sister.)

"Smell me." She held out her palm to him.

He smelled her perfume, a wisp of sweetness that tickled his nose wonderfully. My God, my God, my *God*! He was actually with her! "You are—aren't you—?" Lyle was sure who she was, but he wanted to hear it, to enhance the wonder of it all.

"Of course I'm who you think I am," she purred every word. "You call everybody ma'am?"

"No, just ladies."

She laughed, golden giggles, bubbles. "You are sooooo cute! . . . But stop calling me ma'am, all right, sweetheart?" she pouted. "You make me feel old, and I doubt that I'm any older than you."

She was about thirty-five, Lyle assumed; so what? What mattered was that she was the sexiest woman he had ever seen—next to Maria, of course, and Rose.

They drove past a giant auditorium, the Hollywood Bowl, up, curving, up, along narrowing streets, green, greener, greener yet, up a lush hill where flowers peeked out of trees and bushes.

"—later than I thought . . . Yes . . . Yes."

She was speaking—no, mewing like a cat—into her car phone, clearly changing earlier plans in order to be with him. Great! He sure didn't want to rush. Who would? Goddamn, goddamn, goddamn! Los Angeles was one wonderful place, wasn't it? Goddamn, yes!

She parked in a garage that belonged to a house that looked like a glass bird about to soar above the spectacular canyon they had driven to. Night was coming fast.

"Come on, cowboy." With bubbles of giggles she swept out of the Cadillac, and led him inside the house, past glassy rooms, leading him by the hand because all the lights were out and it was dark, leading him straight to the bedroom!

A stairway—intersected by shadows—led to a loft, a knot of deep darkness.

She turned on the light—one light, a cone of light that sprawled on the large bed spread with pink, shimmering sheets.

"I'm hot for you, cowboy, so let's fuck!" she said.

"God*damn*," was all that would come out of his mouth, because she had already slipped out of her blouse—nothing under it except that ravishing flesh—and her skirt—nothing under it either, except that white skin, gleaming within the isolated light.

He had his clothes off just as quickly, his cock eagerly at attention.

"My, my, will you just look *that*! she squealed. "Put your boots back on, cowboy," she begged.

Well . . . okay.

"—and your hat."

"Uh . . . sure." But he hoped it wouldn't stay on too long.

In the center of the bed, and fully illumined by the cone of light, she stretched, staring above into the higher darkness as if for mysterious inspiration.

What Lyle was staring at was the delectable woman, resplendently naked. He closed his eyes and pinched himself, hard. She was still there!

"Come on, it's all yours," the sumptuous creation said.

Rose's voice began to instruct, *Now, cowboy, at first*—but Lyle didn't need guidance any more, and so the voice of Rose faded into a soft sigh . . . like a blessing.

Lyle parted the velvety legs with his knees. The cowboy hat tumbled onto her breasts. He removed it from them quickly. He arched over her.

Rhythmically and steadily he entered her—and stayed there, barely inching in and out. Then he was riding her. Then she was riding him. Then he was behind her, holding her breasts. Then they were connected sideways, one of his booted legs curled over hers. (Odd—but she kept trying to put his hat back on and it kept falling off.)

He pulled out, almost entirely, and then he pulled in, and she—

"Scream out my name, go ahead!" she demanded.

"Babette, *Babette!*"

"Yes, yes, Mystery Cowboy! Yes!" she said loudly, too loudly. "Yes, Mystery Cowboy!"

Mystery Cowboy? She knew who he was? Time enough to wonder about that later. There was this to attend to now. He—

Another woman's voice came out of the darkness in the loft, muffled, but, in its anger, loud beyond its control:

"Must you always be obscene? *Must* you?"

"What the hell!" Lyle stood, clutching his pants to cover his groin— unsuccessfully. "Who's up there?"

"Nobody's up there, come on back, I'm waiting," said the gorgeous woman.

"Who the hell is up there?" Lyle raised his voice.

4

An untimely introduction.

"Hi, cowboy, I'm Max Renquist," a voice called down from the darkness, "and with me is my wife, Mrs. Renquist."

"I have a name of my own," came the brittle voice of the woman. "Must you, always?"

Lyle peered into the loft, sheltering his eyes from the light so that he could see more clearly—and he did; he saw the outline of a bulky body leaning over the railing, another shadow beside him.

"Why don't you just go on and fuck the brains out of that hot bitch and don't mind us?" said the man's voice. "She's just using our place, phoned ahead to ask if she could when she found you—uh, met you— but her twat was so fuckin' hot she didn't give us a chance to leave before you started jamming her—so we just hid, that's all. You just go on ahead and pump the fuck out of her, okay?"

"Oh, oh, *oh!*" the woman's voice resounded from the loft, "I cannot abide the coarseness one more moment!"

Lyle tried to adjust to all this. He weighed his choices: Demand to know more about whoever was up there, or—?

"Ah, cummon, Mystery Cowboy, whatcha waiting for?" the woman on the bed whispered. "Cummon, my cunt's hot for your hot cock, Mystery Cowboy, whatcha wasting time for? Put it back in, cummon, I'm hot, I'm wet, ya wanna see how wet I am, huh? Yeah, Mystery Cowboy! Sweet cunt's asking for Mystery Cowboy's big cock, cummon, Mystery Cowboy!"

What should he do?

To hell with whoever was up there. He returned to the woman in bed.

5

Information is supplied, but matters remain unexplained.

After the woman claimed she was entirely exhausted—how many times had they done it?—Lyle decided he didn't care about the weird woman and man who had been watching them; so what? They had probably sneaked away. He fell comfortably asleep. When he woke groggily, he saw a dark wig on a stand next to the bed. It gleamed in a splash of dawn. My God! Had he slept with Sister Sis in a new wig? That horrifying thought woke him entirely. Thank God, no, it wasn't Sister Sis he'd slept with. Lying next to him was a blond woman, pretty, yes, and curvy, but she was not—*not*—Babette—again! Remembering the shadows in the loft, Lyle stared up. The man and woman who had been up there were gone.

The woman next to him stirred. She looked like someone else now. So it would be like making it with another woman.

It was.

"You're a great fuck, cowboy," the woman said. "Now I gotta go to work or you'll kill me. I'll drive you wherever you need to go."

The Cadillac was gone from the garage. He didn't ask why she had pretended to be Babette; he assumed it was some kind of fantasy, and that had been all right with him—and, too, it still left his yearning for the real Babette intact.

The woman drove him down in a station wagon, the radio on loud, canceling any possibility of questions. She dropped him off in front of the Chinese Theater. "Good luck, Mystery Cowboy," she said. "I hope you won't think too badly about me." She whizzed away in her station wagon.

6

The revelation of duplicity.

MYSTERY COWBOY, PREVIOUSLY THE LORD'S COWBOY, FUCKS FANTASY POSTER WOMAN!

For a price, subscribers would be offered the film on the Internet, the film Max Renquist had taken last night. Later, when excitement spread on the Net, a tape version would be put out for expensive sale. An event! Cutting edge! An Internet sensation—and consistent with Mrs. Renquist's dedication to broadening the scope of that most denigrated of the art forms, intercourse films.

In her spacious Encino home—often called a mansion—Mrs. Renquist waited in her plush living room, sipping a cool fumé blanc. With Detective Seagrim (drinking—what else?—a beer)—a bother that he was there, but what could she do?—she was waiting for Mr. Renquist to emerge from his home office with what would make them a tidy fortune and put them back in the galaxy of erotic art. They had involved no outsiders—except for this barbarously hairy detective waiting to be paid the last installment for his services, and that would occur as soon as Mr. Renquist emerged with the treasure. Soon, a loyal contact at *Variety,* who owed her money, would carry the item she was already fashioning in her mind.

Those still looking for the Mystery Cowboy, (formerly known as The Lord's Cowboy in evangelical circles) may stop searching. He has been found by enterprising erotic film producers Mr. and Mrs. Renquist of R&R Productions. Now everyone may see the legendary cowboy—with his boots and his cowboy hat!—at www.mysterycowboy.com—when he "performs" with—

All professionally elegant, Mrs. Renquist assured herself—not like those murky, coarse Rob Lowe tapes, nor those even worse things with Pamela Lee and whatever-was-his-name, with all those vile tattoos. Trash, yes, but estimates were that they had made over a million dollars. What a brilliant idea, too, Mrs. Renquist congratulated herself on her enduring cleverness, to hire that actress to enact the poster woman all the trades and television segments claimed the Mystery Cowboy was obsessed with; she herself had chosen the expert detective—never mind that he sat there now studying her as if her face would yield something scandalous he might use against her. Let him stare; there was nothing he could find.

Mrs. Renquist sipped her wine, delighting in its dryness, studying its delicate shadings, fumé shadings—and ignoring the squalid presence waiting with her.

"Gone. Nothing."

Mrs. Renquist looked up to see Mr. Renquist in his most hideous yellow-striped shirt. "Gone? Nothing? What? Must you always speak in riddles, must you?"

"The motherfuckin' camera. Fuckin' shit thing fucked up."

"You mean—?"

"It didn't record a fuckin' thing," Mr. Renquist said.

"You idiot!" Mrs. Renquist rose from her chair, toppling the glass of chilled wine she had been about to celebrate her accomplishment with. "You've bungled! Again! Just like with the Dorothy Hotchkins film!"

"Dorothy Hotchkins," Detective Seagrim repeated.

"Pay this man," Mrs. Renquist ordered. "Pay him so he'll get out of my sight! You idiot!" she said to Mr. Renquist and rushed up to her bedroom, her temples pounding, pounding, hammering, beating, pulsing, throbbing, pummeling, trouncing, grinding—

7

Thoughtful moments, a twinge of sadness, and a familiar voice.

When he returned his apartment, Lyle lay in bed, pensive. He'd have to admit he was a little exhausted. Was this what his life was destined to turn into?—a series of sexual encounters with beautiful women? Was this all there was—?

On second thought, that wouldn't be exactly bad.

Still, there had to be more, much more to life, including matters he needed to resolve. There was his love for Maria, to whom he had never been unfaithful where it mattered, in his heart—Rose certainly had convinced him that was where it mattered, only there.

He longed for Maria, the sweetness of their kisses—longed for her with all his heart. He would, of course, marry her, the sooner the better, and she would be the only one then. He also longed for the tart wisdom of Clarita, who wrote him frequently, in the careful, correct English she was so proud of having learned so well. Her letters were full of love and concern: "Are you learning about life, which can be as baffling and complicated as a beehive?" she seemed to read his thoughts. Well, he was sure as hell trying to, and it damn sure was complicated. She always went on to assert that Sylvia loved his letters, would soon answer them all. Soon. Soon. But no letter came from Sylvia; she was a mystery that deepened. Often—like now—he tried to replay the scene of accusations that had finally flared between them, to see whether in his memory of it he might find a missed clue. "You can never understand."

Tired, tired. He closed his eyes, only to be jolted awake by an urgent voice at the door calling, "Lyle, Lyle, help me!"

CHAPTER EIGHTEEN

1

A sordid development to be resolved.
Mr. Scala in pursuit.

aul!" At the door, Lyle reacted with pleasure at the sight of the kid he had whisked away from Brother Dan's "exorcism" that time at the Lord's Headquarters. Immediately he was angry, "What the hell are you doing still here? You were supposed to go back to Texas, I gave you bus fare."

"I'll tell you all about that later." He kept looking around, wanting to hide. "Let me in quick!" Already he'd pushed past Lyle into the apartment. "Wow, this is cool!"

"How the hell did you find me?"

"Hanging out on the Boulevard, I saw you and followed you, but I didn't have the nerve to talk to you then. Hey, Lyle, what were you doing with that peacock?"

Damn, had everyone seen that picture? "Now who the hell are you hiding from?"

"Scala, the guy me and my friend work for, the guy who drives us out to street corners to sell these—" He showed Lyle a sheaf of folded printed papers.

"Maps to the Stars' Homes," Lyle read aloud.

"Fuckin' shit kept cheating us, and so me and my friend went to another corner to sell the maps and pay ourselves, ya know?"

The kid had put on some weight, grown a couple of inches; he didn't look scrawny any more; and damn if he wasn't wearing an earring— only one—and his hair was sort of spiky, with blondish tips. Lyle wasn't sure whether he looked terrific or terrible. Terrific, he told himself. He intended to sound stern: "Did you steal from that guy?"

"Me? No way. He stole from us. My friend Buzzy's the one who got the idea to go into business for ourselves at another corner. Holy shit!" he said when they heard another voice outside:

"Let me in, Raul!"

At the door Lyle saw a skinny boy, Raul's age, with bursts of freckles and strawy cropped hair that curved inward toward his cheeks so that occasionally he reached out with his tongue to touch the tip of one side or another. As long as everybody was coming here, why not him? Lyle let him in.

"That fuckin' Scala caught up with me, but I ditched him again," the new visitor blurted.

"I told you!" Raul said to Lyle. "The mean fucker's after us, he'll kill us." Formally, he introduced: "This is my friend I told you about. Her name's Buzzy."

Buzzy was a girl? "Buzzy?" Lyle said.

"That's what I call myself," said the freckled girl. She squatted on the floor, as if daring to be moved.

Lyle wanted to believe they were getting cheated and so went into business for themselves. Look how scared they were—well, Raul looked scared, not Buzzy. Sure, he'd hide them, and if—

A loud rap at the door! Buzzy tried to squeeze under the bed, but didn't fit, thin as she was. She followed Raul into a closet.

Lyle faced a red-faced man—his shirt was open to reveal a tangle of bristly black hairs matted with urgent sweat. He pushed inside the suddenly crowded apartment. "Who the hell are you?" Lyle asked him.

"Tony Scala! That's who, and I guess you'll be answering who *you* are when they question you about harboring a coupla criminals. I saw them running in here when I was circling the block in my car. Damned parking is a fuckin' killer!" He marched to the closet door, opened it.

Raul and Buzzy rushed out.

The flustered man swatted at them with hairy hands.

They screamed shrilly.

Lyle heard doors opening along the courtyard.

The man flailed at Raul and the girl with his fists and feet. Every time he connected, they screamed louder.

"Whoa," Lyle stood before the angry man. "Hey, Mister, you watch who you try to hit. They're kids, ya know. And they're my guests," he added.

"Keep out of this!" The man chased Raul, who would pause, let Scala advance, and then would dash away. When the man cornered Buzzy, her skinny body slithered away. Standing securely next to Lyle, Raul held his ground: "You didn't pay us, you crook. We'll turn you in to the cops—"

"Yeah, and who the fuck do ya think the cops'll believe? Me, Tony Scala, a fuckin' reputable citizen and businessman—or a fuckin' faggot spic and a ratty little dyke?" the man shouted.

That word again—dyke. He'd heard it before. Lyle said earnestly to the blustery man, "Sir, what is a dyke?"

"You want me to spell it out? A dyke is a girl-faggot—and over there with her is a boy-faggot-spic."

"Sir"—Lyle put one hand almost gently on the man's shoulder—"I hate to be disrespectful, but—" He held out a hand to shake courteously in introduction, but the other hand closed into a fist and punched the man.

"Hit the fucker again for all the times he's cheated us, Mystery Cowboy!" Buzzy encouraged, offering her own tiny fists.

"And for selling fake maps—" Raul caught himself, adding in a quick whisper to Lyle: "We didn't know they were fakes when we went into business for ourselves, honest."

"Son of a bitch, that hurt!" Scala rubbed his jaw. "But this'll hurt more." He rushed at Lyle, jabbing at him.

Both of Lyle's fists shot out, and punched. The man reeled back. Lyle steadied him before he could fall to the floor. "You okay, sir?"

"No, you son of a bitch! I'm not! What are you? Some kind of faggot yourself, harboring two thieving queers. I bet you've never even ridden a horse."

"How'd you know that?" Lyle asked, genuinely pleased not be asked where his horse was.

Taking advantage of Lyle's surprise, Scala attempted to strike out at him again, but he stumbled on Raul's outstretched foot and connected only with Lyle's shoulder.

"Sir," Lyle said politely, though his fists remained readied. "Maybe you'd better get out—"

"—and never come back!" Raul yelled.

"—and if you try callin' the cops, you'd better remember that we're underage!" Buzzy warned

Were they? Raul was only about a year younger than him, Lyle figured; but Buzzy looked like a kid. Screw it, both looked like they might be underage.

"Fuckin' faggot queers!" the man grumbled as he tried to leave without encountering Buzzy's fists striking at his butt.

When the man was gone, "Now what?" Lyle asked Raul.

Buzzy was adjusting her hair, which had whipped out every which way during the ruckus. "I guess we'll just have to stay here with you, brave Mystery Cowboy," she said.

2

A timely meaning of the word "dolls." Tarah Worth
recognizes another person, herself.

"—High Holy Days—"

"What?" Tarah had begun to think that nothing Lenora did or said would surprise her, but what she had just said did.

"I said that I didn't call you back because we were celebrating High Holy Days."

"*You're not Jewish!*" Tarah shouted at her. The creature had waited two days to answer the urgent question on a recording machine that growled like her.

"You lower your voice, doll."

That much was good. The new meaning of "dolls" was settling in.

Tarah was talking on the telephone in her living room, where the reflection from the pool at this time cast a soft, comforting light on her
face. "I'm glad to hear you using the term 'doll' that I reintroduced to
Hollywood."

"*You* reintroduced? Hell, *doll,* I've been using that word for years."
Oh, the creature!

"About your question concerning the script update. They're thinking of having Helen Lawson die during the kidnapping, and that'll take
place very early in the movie, before the credits."

"They can't kill her!" Tarah screamed. She *wanted* to kill, someone,
anyone. Preferably Lenora, this hideous creature who stalked the earth
and brought terrible news, which her malicious astrological chart—
she hadn't been able to resist it, merely glanced at it—had suggested:
"Difficult endings bring big challenge you may not overcome."

"When I know more about the scene—who's involved and how—
I'll let you know, and when you hatch your big gimmick, let me in on
it and I'll throw in my million bucks' worth. You gotta do it, doll, gotta
make them know you're still out there, ready for a *big* role, not ready to
be killed in the first seconds."

"I don't intend to do other than *make* them know I'm ready for my
big role, Lenora," Tarah said. She heard a steeliness in her voice. She
tested the voice again: "I'll get that role, whatever I have to do." It was
there, the steeliness. She would let it stay. She was in the Valley of the
Vultures, after all, and she had meant it, the harsh affirmation that,
whatever she needed to do, she would get the attention she needed. And
deserved, godammit!

Even Lenora detected the powerful, steely resolve, Tarah knew, when
the crusty creature merely signed off, sounding—impossible!—not
entirely cruel:

"Ciao, Tarah, ciao."

3

The new Tarah Worth moves forward with her plan;
an emergency call to her psychic.

"Riva!"
"Tarah!"

Riva wasn't one of those frauds on late-night television. She was an *inspired* psychic, a specialist in problems connected with Hollywood. The entire cast of *The Young and the Restless* had consulted her in one mass reading. Riva was exclusive, she didn't give readings to just anyone; she interviewed prospective clients—"consultees"—before she accepted them, by certified mail. She read the tarots, looked at palms—outlining invisible signs with a blue pen; she made copious entries that she kept in locked files. In emergencies only, she was available by telephone, following a strict procedure: her name spoken by the consultee on the telephone, then the consultee's name spoken back by her. That asserted a strong, uncluttered connection, and that was occurring now.

"Riva!"

"Tarah!"

This was the next step: Tarah waited long, intense moments, concentrating—eyes closed, breathing deep, deep, assuming a smooth rhythm—so that Riva would immediately begin receiving psychic "beeps."

In preparation for her psychic session, Tarah had run carefully through her plan after Lenora had called back with more specific details about the crucial scene. She had prepared her questions, questions she was now asking Riva, mute questions, barring nothing. Now she waited, allowing psychic energy to carry those questions on invisible currents to Riva's arboretum, where she received her most profound illuminations. ("Plants are the earth's children," she had thrilled Tarah by informing her, "and their flowers are their grandchildren.") Tarah signaled that the requisite steps were over:

"Riva!"

"Tarah!" More moments of silence. "Do it, just do it, doll!" Riva said.

The woman was absolutely amazing! She had delivered the answer she sought *and* the assertion that "doll" had a new meaning, which *she* had donated. Simply amazing—wasn't it?—how she recognized consultees instantly by the way they spoke her name, just one word—although once she had called her "Sarah" but explained that a departed consultee named Sarah had come in on her, Tarah's, psychic waves, eager to contribute her own input, that's how close she felt to her.

Emboldened by Riva's superb advice, Tarah called Rusty Blake. "Come over now," she said in her new voice, which still fascinated her.

"Uh, like, why?" started Blake. "I was, like, purging my horizon, ya know? L. Ron says——"

"I said come over now if you want that role in *The Return*."

She hung up, and waited, making herself up to look like the beautiful version she would be of Helen Lawson in the decisive scene.

Blake arrived a few minutes earlier than Tarah had anticipated. She greeted him in her living room. She didn't offer him a drink. Look at him, slouching on her favorite couch—assuming that everyone wanted to make love to him—and he was facing the pool where she had sat, in the best reflected light. "I have a plan that will guarantee us the roles we both want. All the signs are in place."

"Ya know, Tarah," Rusty mused, "I don't, like, get you with all that, like, psychic stuff, man. L. Ron says that——"

No time for his silly nonsense. "Just listen, Rust!" Tarah chopped his name.

"Uh, like, what is it, man?" He soothed his frown.

"You're going to the Academy Awards with me."

"Cool." He brightened up.

"Yes, and at the Academy Awards there'll be a kidnapping."

He sat up. "Am I, like, in danger? What L. Ron advises is to stay away from danger."

"You're not in danger. A kidnapping attempt will be made, exactly like in the script."

"Uh, by who? Like on who?"

Tarah reached for the newspaper picture she had kept. Blake leaned over to look at the photograph.

Tarah pointed to the Mystery Cowboy everyone was looking for.

4

A declaration.

"Lyle, I'm going to go back home to Rio Escondido."

Raul sat up from the pile of blankets he'd slept on last night and said that. Next to him, on her own pile, Buzzy woke with a start, her red hair pointing up in strands like sparks of fire.

On his bed—he'd considered letting Raul and Buzzy sleep in it while he slept on the floor but then that had seemed too uncomfortable for him—Lyle shook his head, orienting himself to the words spoken. When he did, he nodded, Yes, approving.

"But only until I straighten things out that went all wrong there, when I was hiding and stuff like that—and get my aunt off my back," he muttered, "and then I'm going to come back and be a movie star, come out publicly, and let everyone know who I am."

"Shit," said Buzzy, "big fuckin' deal, coming out. Shit, dude, I came out when I came out of my mamma's womb." She clamped her hands on her hair, which, when she removed them, sprang up again.

"Congratulations, Raul," Lyle said, trying to match Raul's seriousness.

Buzzy peered out the window, the first thing she did on waking— to make sure no one had found her.

"I owe it to other people like myself," Raul was going on, standing bravely in his shorts. "There's a lot of actors who stay in the closet, hurting themselves and others and becoming Scientologists, and I won't be one of them," he extended his proud declaration.

"Christ, dude," Buzzy offered, "what kind of bullshit you layin' on?"

"Makes a lot of sense to me," Lyle said, to assert how earnestly he was taking Raul's declaration.

"Before I go, Lyle—and Buzzy, you can come with me if you want—"

"To that hick town in Texas, man? Fuck, just hearing you tell about it bores the fuck outta me."

Raul continued as if there had been no interruption: "Before I go, Lyle, I want to tell you that I love you, like I always did, at school." He rushed the next words: "But don't worry, I don't expect you to love me back," he said bravely.

"Hey! Now we're gettin' somewhere," Buzzy sat back down on her pile of blankets, leaned on one elbow, and watched as if she was at the movies.

"I do love you," Lyle said, truthfully. He did, he loved this kid who had followed him around, who had then faced those weird evangelists, and who had bravely made his way out of Texas and was, equally bravely, now going back, and who longed to do something wonderful.

"I believe you, but I know you don't love me the way I do you." But he looked at Lyle with pleading eyes.

Buzzy turned and looked up and said to Lyle, "The dude means he'd like to fuck and he knows you won't."

"All right, Buzzy, you shut the fuck up, I mean it," Raul said to the girl. "This is between me and Lyle."

"Fuck you, then," Buzzy said, and lay back as if asleep or dead.

Lyle had understood Raul, of course. It didn't matter, that they loved each other in different ways.

Raul gathered his belongings about the room.

"I guess that means I gotta go, too," Buzzy said. She rose, searching for her measly belongings scattered about everywhere.

"You can stay, Buzzy," Lyle offered.

"Shit no, cowboy." She smiled a jagged smile. "There'd be a lot of gossip about the two of us."

"You got enough money to get back?" Lyle asked.

"We got plenty of money," Buzzy said. "We stole a lot from that Scala son of a bitch before he caught us at it."

"Buzzy!" Raul tried to shut her up, too late.

Lyle laughed, no way he would recriminate them for taking money from that mean shit who'd busted in. If they'd asked him, he would have helped them get it.

In a moment Buzzy was packed and waiting. "So?" she asked Raul.

"So let's go." Raul let Buzzy go ahead of him. "Good-bye, Lyle."

"Good luck, Raul." That seemed so inadequate. "And—uh—say hello to everyone for me!"

5

An expected unexpected.

In Rio Escondido, Sylvia Love Clemens did not even rub her eyes to check whether what she saw was imagined. Only Clarita did—at her frequent post at the window—and she rubbed her eyes again to banish any reality there might be to what she saw—

Lyle Clemens the First was at the door.

Coolly, Sylvia, who had had only two "tiding-over" drinks that early afternoon, turned to Clarita and said, "I told you he would come back soon."

"*Dios mío!*—he has," Clarita surrendered to the fact that Sylvia Love had gone to the door, opened it, turned back to announce the astonishing fact—and had now let Lyle the First in.

6

A critical quandary.

Clarita could not believe how in control Sylvia Love Clemens remained
when she faced Lyle the First, who had walked out on her years ago, who
had never seen his son, never even known that he was born. She watched
in fascination, aching for her and praying for mercy on them all.

"Hello, hon," the cowboy drawled, and he handed Sylvia a bouquet
of flowers. White roses!

"Lyle, you're back," Sylvia said, as if he had just gone out earlier and
had now returned for dinner. She sniffed the flowers delicately and laid
them carefully on the small table in the hallway, next to Lyle the Second's
latest letter.

"Yeah, darlin', I am—" He swept his wide hat gallantly before her
as he bowed.

God would forgive her, Clarita prayed, for being amazed at how
handsome the son of a bitch still was. You'd think he'd have let himself go, drunk himself awful, developed a stomach. No, he was almost
as trim as he had been, mounted on those damned boots. His hair was
brushed with gray, true, and there were lines on his face, which was
still tanned, but his smile was just as wide, and—yes, God forgive her
for noticing this—he was as "sexy"—that was Sylvia's word, not hers—
as ever.

Whether Sylvia was noting this or not, Clarita was not sure, because
she just smiled, her most charming smile.

"Goddammit if you're not more beautiful than ever," Lyle said.

Oh, but that wasn't true, Clarita thought sadly. The liquor and the
pain had drained Sylvia's face, made it drawn, but—oh, wait! Look! A
sudden miracle!—the Holy Mother had extended mercy to Sylvia in
these moments, because—it might have been the twilight, or the smile
that had returned—Sylvia Love, looked radiant, mysteriously so, as if
Lyle the First had restored her; *Dios mío,* if *she* didn't look, in those
moments, like the young woman he had promised to marry.

"May I?" Lyle the First asked, indicating the couch on which Sylvia
was now seated, calmly.

"Of course," Sylvia said. "How rude of me. I simply assumed, well,
Lyle, that you're back and don't have to ask."

"Hon," his voice gained in confidence, "Ah swear to Jeezus that it is great bein' back, seein' ya so goddam pretty—not changed a bit."

"Thank you for your compliments, Lyle," Sylvia said. She thought: He's as handsome as ever. She looked at his hands, the hands she had longed to be held by, night after night after he had left, looked at the body that had thrust into her, and with each thrust, pushed more love into her, she had thought, love, all love—and so she had responded to this man who had sworn to adore her, forever, to love her. He was here again, next to her, and she felt—She felt for him just as she had before he had left.

He held her hand. "My sweetheart, always my sweetheart," he said, and glanced up at Clarita.

Smiling at me, trying to enlist me, too. Clarita shook her head and glowered her blackest. She wasn't about to budge; she would stay until the flames of hell were extinguished, because she wanted to make sure that son of a bitch didn't bewitch her Sylvia again. She remained out of their sights, but assuring that she could watch, under the hall stairway.

"A drink?" Sylvia asked.

"Why, yes, a little bourbon."

"That was always your drink," Sylvia said. "Now it's mine." She didn't have to travel to get it, because there it was beside her. She poured herself another and poured him one.

"I take it back, you're not as pretty as you used to be—"

What was the *cabrón* up to? Of course, she guessed it before he finished:

"—you're more beautiful than ever." He touched her face, lightly.

"Lyle—"

Clarita heard what Sylvia had put into that name, all the love she had felt, the love she had told herself had turned into anger. Now it was there again, stripped of everything except what had remained, no matter how ragged, all along—her love for him.

"I never changed, toward you," Lyle the First said.

Now the lies. Clarita didn't want to listen, didn't—

"I know you didn't, Lyle," Sylvia said. He was so close to her, so close, so very close. In a moment he would reach for her, embrace her, kiss her, the way she had dreamt would happen, again, had counted on, until hope almost ran out, but never entirely, never, the expectation that he would come back always there.

He touched her hair, letting his fingers run down her neck, and then—

Toward her breasts, the breasts he loved to make love to, talk to, even—once—sing to. I'll let him, and he'll come back, and he'll love me for all the lost years, yes, and—

His hand slid down. "My darlin' sweet, my darlin' sweet—"

Clarita almost screamed at Sylvia, Have you forgotten what he did? Have you forgotten the pain? That he doesn't even know he has a son. She didn't scream that out. She watched in horror as she saw Sylvia lean toward the cowboy, toward Lyle the First.

Sylvia sighed. She longed for him to embrace her, assure her, beg her to take him back, just ask her to take him back, even just say that he was back and would stay—and he would, and she would—*"Take your filthy hands off me, you fucking son-of-a-bitch!"* She slapped his hand away with all her force, and stood up.

He jumped up, startled.

Clarita's heart burst with love and pain, and triumph. She no longer needed to hide. She stood there, with her hands crossed over her bosom.

"You think you can come and sweet-talk me and think that everything will be like it was? You bastard, bastard!" She pounded on his chest.

He did not stop her. "Say whatever the hell you want to me, do whatever the hell you want," he said, "but don't tell me to go away, 'cause I'm here to see my child."

Sylvia inhaled. "Your child! You paid me to get rid of it, remember?"

"I knew you wouldn't, I always knew. I know he was born." For once, he seemed sincere: "I've grown lonely, older, want to see him, want to—"

"You'll never see him, be with him. Nothing!" Sylvia said.

"You can't keep me from seeing him," Lyle the First challenged.

"Your son is dead, Lyle," Sylvia said.

Ay, Dios mío, why, this now? But Clarita understood, it was her revenge.

"You're lying."

"Am I?" Sylvia taunted.

"Did he look like me?"

Does he believe her? Clarita marveled. He was now standing solemnly before her, quiet. Jesus and the Holy Mother would forgive her for thinking this, but if anyone deserved torturing, it was the cowboy for what he had done to Sylvia.

Sylvia struck, "No, he didn't look like you. He was dark, not tall, very handsome. Like his *real* father."

That's where she was going. Clarita had exhausted the names of the saints she was invoking to see them all out of this, safely. *Please God, what would Lyle the Second want? Jesus, you who knew about mothers*—did he?—*help me out.*

The cowboy had reeled. "What the hell do ya mean, his real father?"

"I only tried to make you believe I was pregnant by you. I wasn't. I had already known that I was pregnant, by—"

Reaching for something—a broom, anything—Clarita prepared to advance on the cowboy, who stood menacingly before Sylvia. If he attempted to strike her Sylvia, she would pounce on him, make him regret he'd been born. She would—But she needn't have worried.

The cowboy retreated. He said quietly, "When I see him I'll know right away—"

He would—Lyle was the image of him, despite the difference in the color of their hair, the eyes, Clarita saw. But Lyle the Second was kind, the kindest. Still, hadn't Sylvia told her that the cowboy, too, had been kind, loving? Men were a mystery, weren't they? That's why young girls had to flee to the hills when—Again? Where was she? Oh, yes, not back in Chihuahua, but back within this critical situation that involved her beloved Sylvia and Lyle the First.

"But you won't see him, ever!" Sylvia shouted at Lyle the First.

He whispered, as if only to remind himself, "I did see him once with you Sylvia, years ago. I drove by when you were both walking along the street, caught just a glimpse. I even thought you saw me, but that you weren't sure it was me. I didn't have the courage to stop then, talk to you."

What surprises life contained! Clarita felt a spark of compassion—a spark, no more—for the son of a bitch.

Lyle the First turned to Clarita: "Clarita, tell me. Where is he? I know he's alive."

Clarita prayed to God that she would do what was right, what Lyle would want: *Please, let me know what to say! What to do!*

7

A crucial decision.

Clarita let her eyes wander—making sure that Lyle the First would follow her gaze when it landed—onto the table where Sylvia had placed the roses, where she placed Lyle's letters.

When she saw him move toward it, Sylvia rushed there, about to grab the letter, but the cowboy grasped it away first. With one hand keeping Sylvia away from tearing it from him, he looked down at the address on it.

"Son of a bitch!" Sylvia shouted.

Lyle the First sighed. "I know you'll never believe me, Sylvia, but I truly came back hoping I could make it all up to you. And him."

Sylvia shook her head. "You'd never be able to make up what you've done to me!"

Clarita prayed, Don't let her start crying or the son of a bitch will embrace her and kiss her when she's most vulnerable and she'll let him come back and I'll have to kill him.

"May I try to make it up to you?" Lyle the First reached out to hold Sylvia.

Sylvia pulled back. "I would kill you before I let you come back into my life," she said.

He bowed and swept his hat before him, but this time it was as if the gesture itself had grown tired, weighted down by the years, whatever they had been like for him.

He's growing old, too, Clarita thought. She saw it now that the impression of him from the past was fading. She saw him stoop, slightly.

He stood at the door—oh, he seemed truly sad, very sad—and he said:

"Just believe me, my Sylvia, that I never stopped lovin' you, no one ever took your place—"

"—and I'm sure there've been many!" Sylvia thrust at him.

"Maybe so, but I've loved only you, always will, my beautiful Sylvia. Please believe me."

Dios mío, why have you given us all these strange mysteries? Clarita marveled, because, oh, Lord, he seemed sincere and even she believed him, at that moment, but, immediately after, she didn't know what she felt, her emotions jumbled, fighting each other when, after the cowboy had left again, after the sound of his boots had faded—and Sylvia seemed to lean toward the diminishing sound—Sylvia slumped into her chair and she answered his parting words aloud:

"Yes, I do believe you."

CHAPTER NINETEEN

1

The pending matter of Maria's broken heart.

"Lyle, Lyle, I knew I'd find you! I knew I would, even if I had to go to the end of the earth."

"Maria!" Lyle's heart opened as he stood by the fountain, the way he usually paused, on his way into his apartment or on his way to his travels about the city from morning to night, when the world of daylight changed.

Lyle scooped her up in his arms, spun her around. Her dark hair swirled about her face as she laughed joyously. He kissed her over and over at every turn. She kissed him back, or tried to, her kisses landing all over his face and head because he was spinning her around so gleefully. He put her down, eased her away so he could look at her, and stared in wonder, and felt terrific that he had been entirely true to her, in his heart, where it mattered.

"I begged Clarita to tell me where you are, although at first she swore she wouldn't, but I pleaded—"

"Maria, I wrote you, you have my address."

"Oh, that's right," she seemed disappointed that it had been so easy to find him. Undissuaded, she extended her difficulties in reaching him. "You must never tell your mother, ever, that Clarita gave me your address because she'll crucify her, I just know it; and, oh, Lyle, Lyle, Lyle, I ran away from my father. I don't care that he'll be furious—is that strange for a father to feel that way?—of course, he must have already discovered it—and, well, Lyle, here I am—isn't it strange?—and I want to make love to you right away, this moment, because my heart has been breaking from being away from you."

"Right away!" Lyle said, and put his arms around her, the finger of one hand already tugging at his belt. Walking backwards so that he could continue to see her, gaze at her in awe of her beauty and to assure himself that she was here, with him, he led her back to his apartment, pushing away a disturbing thought that gnawed at his mind.

In his apartment—"What a wonderful place you have, my beloved, although it's somewhat small, that means we'll have to be even closer!"— Maria pulled off her blouse, revealing her breasts, even fuller now, even more beautiful than he remembered. "I want you to make love to my body the way you did that first time, remember? And I want to make love to your body, the way I did that first time, remember?"

He remembered all right. And remembered—oh, no, not *that*! Not now! Maybe later he'd allow the thought that was nibbling at his mind.

They made love on the bed, both gloriously naked. He mounted her. (*Whoa, cowboy,* Rose refused to shut up and Lyle didn't mind, *you ram in like that and she won't feel everything she should. Give her a chance to be on top, so you can see her breasts flaring out, and her legs—*) He lay back and she got on top of him, hopping up and down, her fingers weaving through her hair. He eased her just slightly back (*so both of you can see it all, that adds to what you're feeling*). Then they were head to toe, and he licked her glorious flesh, and she licked his—(*isn't this terrific?—wonder who discovered it*)—their mouths and tongues exploring, darting— and then they returned, over and over, to kiss again. (*Kissing can be the most intimate—and don't shove your tongue in, let it slip in, and then coax hers.*) Lips pressed against each other's, Lyle straddled her, entered her. When she gasped and he knew she was coming—(*nothing is better than doing it at the same time, cowboy, hold it, hold it, ah, ah, ah, now, cowboy, you too, ahhhh!*)—he exploded in her. They both fell back—all three fell back? Lyle wondered—laughing with joy.

When she quickly fell asleep, the thought Lyle had managed to keep away, ambushed him: What if she is my sister! Of course, she wasn't. No way was it possible, no way.

He managed to fall asleep, a fretful sleep.

He woke with a start. Twilight glistened in the room.

Maria opened her eyes and sat up. She was so beautiful he wanted to love her again, and reached for her.

"No," she said. "Once is all I needed."

"Needed?"

She sat up, adjusting her clothes, while he lay back in bed and looked at her, frowning, knowing that something very awful was about to be said.

"To remember you forever, Lyle, to remember the perfect lovemaking— to remember and cherish every bit of it—is that strange?—until I die, because I shall love you, forever, even after death." She spoke the words with profound passion and conviction. "Remember that!"

"Remember?" he repeated. He must grasp this slowly, word for word, was already grasping, without knowing exactly what, something he heard in her voice as if for the first time—no, he was hearing only now what had always been there, from the time she had blurted out in Rio Escondido that she loved him.

He tried to laugh, tried to make it all be this: "You're not going to tell me that we can't be together because we might still be brother and sister?"

"Oh, that," she shrugged. "Even if it's true, it can't be a sin if we're not really sure. God would understand."

Perfect logic.

"What I mean is that—" She paused, touching her eyes, where more tears had appeared. She allowed one to fall slowly, allowed another, another, traced the course of yet another, before she dabbed at them all. "See?" She held out her moistened fingers to Lyle. "Aren't tears strange?" She adjusted the straps of her brassiere, straightened the edge of her panties. She arranged her hair so that it fell on her shoulders. She faced him, mournfully.

Preparing for what's coming next, Lyle thought. What?

"If it should turn out that we are brother and sister, I won't regret anything," she said. "It would all seem, you know, even more tragic and strange. Didn't it create more passion between us because God forbids it? Just now, when we were making love, I"—she giggled— "told myself that we *are* brother and sister and that our love was so great we would surmount even that, and it made everything even more exciting." She added tears to her cheeks, then to her fingers. She touched Lyle's cheeks with them. She frowned, disappointed not to find his own tears there. "Oh, Lyle," she sighed, "have you been unfaithful to me?" She pouted.

He touched his heart. "No, never, not here."

"Oh, but I bet you've slept with hundreds of women, haven't you?"

"No," he answered her truthfully.

She giggled, then became serious. "I forgive you, though." She ran her fingers through her hair, allowing full waves. "Because throughout it all, you grew to love me even more, didn't you? Didn't you?"

"Yes."

"Isn't it thrilling to forgive?"

"I guess—" Still, Lyle's heart did not breathe. What was she preparing to tell him?

"I've proven my love for you, Lyle, in infinite ways, and now by having traveled miles to see you, risking my father's wrath." She looked around, as if detecting grave danger. "He might be here at any moment—he threatened to follow me. Don't you think it's unnatural for a father to pursue his daughter that way? Isn't it wonderfully strange to love like this?"

"Maria!" He put his hands on her shoulders and shook her, not hard. "What the hell are you babbling about?"

She twisted her head as if he had hurt her. She rubbed her shoulders as if he had bruised her. "Lyle, Lyle," she cried, "don't hurt me."

"What?" Of course he wasn't going to hurt her, he hadn't hurt her.

"I have to marry him," she said.

"Who?" He accepted it immediately, there was no doubt, this is what she had come to tell him, amid the most spectacular drama which she could conjure.

"He's been in business with my father. He's rich, has a political position, but—oh, Lyle, Lyle—he's not handsome and he's always so damn happy, oh, and he's rich, very rich—and he may be running for senator, imagine. I'll be a senator's wife! But, oh, Lyle, when he calls me 'babe,' I want to kill him."

"You're going to marry someone else, and you came to make love to me?" Anger was threatening to push away the pain he was feeling. He had counted on marrying her, being only with her then, only her.

"It makes sense once I explain it." She was fully dressed now, sitting down. He stood clumsily, naked, before her, trying to assess it all. "Oh, Lyle, put some clothes on or I won't be able to tell you. You're very distracting, you know, you're the sexiest man, I guess, in the world." She sounded genuinely wistful, "I wish he was just this bit as sexy as you." She measured with two fingers, almost touching. Her voice was serious. "I wish he was sexy, period."

Lyle wanted to tell her that she made no sense, that he did not accept what she was telling him. But it was much too outrageous not to be true, and he did grasp it. Finally, he understood her.

"That's why I have to remember what it was like, with you. I'll carry that memory with me, always, and every time he touches me, I'll close my eyes and try to pretend it's you, try to hear your passionate voice telling me what you're doing . . . Oh, Lyle, I've changed my mind, let's do it one more time, and then I'll remember even better!"

He put on his clothes. He looked away from her.

"Lyle, you're not mad, are you?" she asked. "You can't be—because I'm so honest. Don't you think I'm honest, terribly honest?"

He remained with his back to her.

She sighed, an enormous sigh, another one. She produced a loud sob, another. She said, "I'll always love you. Only you!" she gasped. "But I have to marry that despicable man—"

"Because he's rich and you'll be a senator's wife?"

"Oh, oh, my beloved, how can you be so cruel to me? How! No, no, not that reason but—"

"Maria!" This time he did shake her. "Tell me the truth!"

She brushed his hands away from her shoulders, rearranged her hair. "Well, it helps that he's rich, since he's not handsome, like you. Everybody's got to have something, you know," she said, composed. "Lyle, please look at me."

He didn't. "Good-bye, Maria."

Her sobs resurged.

"I said, *Good-bye, Maria!*"

He did not turn until he heard her footsteps, echoing away with her sobs, the echo of her footsteps becoming louder in his mind.

2

More speculation about the Mystery Cowboy.

The Hollywood Reporter

What's the Buzz?

The Mystery Cowboy has still not been located, unseen since he saved Ms. Universal from a savage peacock at the Huey Mansion while assorted guests watched in amazement. Speculation continues. A man purporting to be his cousin called this desk to say that the Mystery Cowboy is actually the famous pilot who disappeared into the Atlantic Ocean during—

Pushing away memories of Maria—the old Maria making it difficult for him to forget the new Maria—Lyle stood at the newsstand on the corner of Franklin and Beachwood and read about his total disappearance:

The Los Angeles Times

Here and There

Another sighting of the Mystery Cowboy was reported by teenage surfers at Zuma Beach. "He strutted across the sand saying nothing," one said, "and then he walked right into the ocean." "On it," said another.

Now Times Weekly

About LA

A maid who worked for one of the founding families in Los Angeles and who was fired recently reported that the august family is hiding the Mystery Cowboy for reasons known only to them. She reports having heard strange bootsteps pacing about the Hancock Park house late at night.

LA Weekly

Who Says What from the Left?

Indications increase that the Mystery Cowboy is waiting to reveal himself at the proper time of fullest attention in order to clear the name of his grandfather, one of the Hollywood Ten.

Variety

Show Biz Down & Close

Producer Andy Kowansky is reported to be bartering with agents to film the Mystery Cowboy's life—"when—if—he's found." Tom Selleck and Tom Hanks have expressed interest in playing his father, and Jennifer Lopez is being mentioned for a role not yet designated. Actors vying for the part of the Mystery Cowboy include newcomer—

Hollywood Insider

See All, Tell All

The mystery surrounding the identity of the so-called Mystery Cowboy has been compounded by the fact that regulars along Hollywood Boulevard report that an imposter is roaming the streets, claiming to be the Mystery Cowboy himself. "The fake's easy to spot, though," said one knowledgeable denizen, "because he doesn't attempt to hide."

"Hey, dude, I bet you're that Mysterious Cowboy!" a young man with a baseball cap backwards, lowered almost to his nose, sidled right up to Lyle and said.

"Mystery Cowboy," Lyle corrected.

"He's the fake," said a reedy girl to the young man with the backwards baseball cap.

"You the fake?" the young man asked Lyle indignantly.

"Yeah," Lyle said, walking away.

The two followed. The girl said to Lyle, "Know how I know you're the fake?—cause the real Mystery Cowboy would say he's the real one so they'd think he's the fake."

"Cool," said the young man to her.

Now exactly who am I supposed to be? Lyle wondered.

3

A matter of good luck kept pending.

"Where the hell is she? I had a detective follow her, he followed her here. Where the hell is—? Oh, my God, it's Mr. Cowboy!"

Everyone was converging in his apartment, and here was—

"Mr. Fielding!" Lyle recognized the man who had given him a ride to Las Vegas, and then to Los Angeles.

"Good to see you again, Mr. Cowboy. I knew I would—" Mr. Fielding held his hand out to Lyle.

Lyle took it.

Mr. Fielding's other hand smacked him. "—but not with the woman I'm gonna marry," he finished.

Lyle accepted the blow, even pretended it hurt by rubbing his cheek. More difficult to accept—but here he was in person again—was that his gambling partner was the man Maria intended to marry.

Mr. Fielding, apparently accepting it all as easily as he accepted everything else, just shook his head. "That goddamned woman!"

"Don't you say anything bad about Maria."

Mr. Fielding laughed. "She's something, isn't she?"

"I love her," Lyle said, but he wasn't sure, not at all. He just felt he had to defend her.

"I thought I did, too. . . . Hell, I guess I'll go ahead and marry her," Mr. Fielding said. "I'm a gambler, so why not?—and, Mr. Cowboy, remember I told you I knew you'd bring me luck?"

"I remember, Mr. Fielding."

"I was right, cause you gave me that beautiful little woman. Didn't you? You do promise not to see her again, even if she returns, right?"

"Yes. Right," Lyle promised, knowing his heart would never be hers, ever again.

Mr. Fielding brought out his wallet. "Here, Mr. Cowboy, I always reward those who bring me luck. . . . Now I'm off to meet her; she came ahead of me, and now I know why."

He left several impressive bills for Lyle. As he walked out whistling, Lyle said:

"Good luck, Mr. Fielding." He thought: I'm not so sure I brought you luck.

4

A violent interlude.

"Motherfucking trash!"

"Shit motherfucker!"

In front of the Chinese Theater, two gnarled-faced young men with shaved heads pummeled a crouching figure, whose arms, decorated with one glittering bracelet, flailed vainly to thwart the blows. Tourists milled, watched, some looked away and walked on hurriedly.

Lyle's body moved to where the beating was occurring. The figure on the sidewalk looked up, a young woman in a lacy blue dress, ripped in the altercation. Lyle saw that only in a flash because his fists were already striking out at the attackers, swiftly. One jumped on him, hopping up because he was short. The other aimed at Lyle's groin. Lyle dodged, thrusting the man off his back; his fist punched so hard his fingers throbbed. The crowd began to root for him. Two other young men emerged to help him. The two attackers sprawled on the concrete among movie star prints.

"Why the hell did you wanna hit on that lady?" Lyle asked the two attackers, softly although his fists were on their way toward them again.

"He ain't no fuckin' lady, he's a fuckin' queer, man!" one of the two shouted at Lyle.

"A fuckin' faggot, motherfucker!" the second one shouted.

As they struggled to get up, they were shoved away along the street by the two who had joined Lyle.

Standing up, the man in drag wiped blood off his face. Lyle offered his handkerchief and helped him brush dirt from his dress.

"I'll walk you to your car, ma'am," Lyle said, with a tilt of his hat.

Holding his hand to his swollen cheek, the man in drag looked around in triumph. "There are still some brave men in the world," he called back to the crowd. "Still some decency to be found." He bent down, trying to disguise the rips in his dress.

"That's a pretty blue dress," Lyle consoled.

"Thank you, it's della Robbia blue, my favorite," the man said softly. He linked the arm Lyle extended. They made their way along the Boulevard.

"I'll be fine now, thank you," the man in drag said when they had reached a residential side street and were approaching his parked car.

They unlinked arms.

"Has anyone ever told you that you look like a prince?"

"No, ma'am, no one, ever."

"Well, you do," the man said. "But whoever you are"—he kissed his own fingertips and extended the kiss gently to Lyle's lips—"I have always relied on the kindness of strangers." He walked to his car with dignity, paused, turned. "My name is Blanche."

5

Lyle sees more of the world.

He was returning to the Boulevard when a car screeched next to him. Two of the earlier attackers joined now by two more rushed out of the car. "We're back, motherfucker!"

They wrestled him to the ground. A heavy man held him while the other three struck him with their fists, kicked him, laughing.

"Take his boots! Take his boots!"

One of them yanked at his boots, tossing one into the street, pulling at the other.

"Hey, man, look!" one of them had found the bills Lyle had stashed in one boot.

Police sirens screamed nearby!

The attackers jumped into their car, racing away.

Lyle lay on the sidewalk. He tried to stretch his legs, he could, but they hurt. He raised his arms, they ached. He touched his eyes—one was pulsing, maybe bleeding. He felt throbbing pain all over. He stood up. Okay, just a little wobbly, he told himself as his legs threatened to buckle. He stood, until he had steadied himself.

Barefoot, he began to walk to his apartment. Wait. The other boot, across the street. He couldn't bear to leave it there. He hobbled across and retrieved it.

Stumbling along and holding on to his remaining boot, he thought, Damn, the world sure can be mean.

6

Back on the Boulevard—

Three days after the violence—days during which he mostly slept and
Mrs. Allworthy tended to him, soon bringing him food and eventually, as he recovered, filling him in on the latest gossip about the stars
as if she had learned it by herself—Lyle was ready to go out again—
still slightly sore, sure, maybe hurting in some places if he moved
too fast—wearing another pair of boots. This time, he stuffed some
of the travelers checks he'd kept in the apartment into his jeans' front
pocket.

He was back on Hollywood Boulevard. "Fell off your horse?" a fat
tourist asked him, nudging his wife, who giggled.

Damn—and he'd thought all the bruising was gone.

He heard a deep, soulful voice humming, breaking into words: "—
crucified—lynched—cause he was black!"

There she was, on Hollywood Boulevard—Sister Matilda of the Golden
Voice, standing there with her Bible in her hand and a crowd—

Lyle's joy dropped. There was no crowd, nobody had gathered to listen to her, everyone just walked on by, glancing and clucking at the
woman in a flowing dress, wearing a crown.

"Another crazy," sniffed a snotty woman walking by.

"No, she isn't, ma'am." Lyle followed the woman to tell her that.

"You get away from me or I'll scream that you're molesting me, I'll
sue you! Say aren't you—? Oh, my God, it is the Mystery Cowboy, and
he's a stalker!" The woman ran away.

Lyle returned his attention to Sister Matilda. She looked different,
everything the same but frayed, except her crown, which sparkled
golden. No, it didn't. He'd just wished it had sparkled. It was tarnished,
yellowing with age.

He stood before her. She squinted, rubbed her eyes, shook her head.
She continued her preaching: "Jesus was black, y'all hear me?—and he
was lynched because of that." She hummed, sang:

Were you there when they nailed him to a tree? . . .

Lyle joined her, aloud but very softly:

Were you there when they laid him down to rest? . . .

"Is it you, Lyle?" She squinted, hard.

"Yes!"

She moved toward him with difficulty, grasping her Bible.

"Sister Matilda!" He embraced her, tight.

She allowed the embrace, returned it. "There now, cowboy, don't you go upsetting my crown," she tried to disguise her delight.

Some people lingered to see the handsome cowboy and the black woman with the crown.

"Why are you staring at my crown?" she asked Lyle.

"Because it's so beautiful," he said.

"Hmmm. I thought maybe you were thinking it's odd on the street. But you remember this, cowboy, Negro ladies never go out formal without wearing a hat."

"I know," Lyle said, and linked his arm through hers, noticing that she walked unfirmly now and that her hair was speckled with gray.

7

A bittersweet reunion at Musso & Frank's.

Lyle took Sister Matilda to Musso & Frank's Grill on Hollywood Boulevard. The grand old restaurant attracted every ilk of people, those who, back on the Boulevard, were asked for autographs, and others who were just a part of the awesome old area. He had eaten there himself, and the waiters now greeted him like a friend, even gave him a booth when the place wasn't too crowded, although he preferred the counter, where there would always be somebody interesting eating right next to him, once an ex-countess.

The attendant, a dapper gentleman, gave them a booth, to accommodate Sister Matilda's girth.

Used to seeing exceptional people, those in the restaurant merely glanced at the extraordinary couple, the cowboy and the elegantly frayed black woman.

Quietly, she and Lyle studied the extensive menu, prepared by a "chef from Paris, France," Juan Galán, his favorite waiter, informed Sister Matilda.

"Hmmm," Sister Matilda clucked. "They've got chicken pie. Huh! My mamma baked the only chicken pie worth eating, but I'll give it a try."

"I'll have the chicken pie, too," Lyle told the waiter. He wanted to feel close to Sister Matilda. Of course, her girth made that possible; he didn't have to move much to be close. Why was she so silent? Why was she looking at him so defiantly? Did she want to be asked what he hesitated to ask? "What happened, Sister Matilda?"

She said sternly, "Because I'm on the street preaching the word of God instead of singing and trembling before television cameras and fakes?"

That wasn't what he had meant; he had meant to ask why she had left without saying anything to him. But he didn't have a chance to clarify.

"Doin' penance for being a part of that corruption," she said. It was as if everything she spoke turned into a possible song, the deep sad, joyful sounds, the inflection on certain words so that they came out as a rhythm: "Doin' PEN-ance for *being* a part of the cor-rup-SHUN."

"But you broke away, and you warned me, and I didn't listen," Lyle defended her from herself. He didn't add, You ran away without telling me, and I expected you to show up all along, and I stayed because you said "Stay put." . . . No, that wasn't the only reason I stayed, he knew. There was the money that Brother Bud and Sister Sis had offered him.

"When I saw they wanted to corrupt you—and figured, yes, the Lord knows I did—that they just might, you being so green and stuff—that's when the Lord gave me a jolt, and I felt real harsh about my own contribution to them. All those years—yea, Lord, you saw it all—Amen to all the Lord sees!" she ordered.

"Amen," Lyle smiled.

"Amen," echoed a small man alone in the booth next to them, as he cut into his grilled pork chops.

"—all those years I stayed playing queen, being praised, getting paid," Sister Matilda had continued. "I even left, for a short spell, and then came back." She shook her head in dismay. "I sold them my golden voice. I did, and the Lord knew it."

"You were never corrupted, you extended, really extended." Lyle thought of how much her voice meant to Sylvia. "People heard you and you stirred their hearts, Sister Matilda. You were never corrupted."

"Never, never corrupted!" the small man in the booth said to himself.

"Don't you tell me what I was and wasn't!" Sister Matilda aimed her words at the man. Then she resumed with Lyle: "I knew years ago that those two were deceiving poor folks. Things like fake tumors, envelopes full of pennies they put there themselves to draw hundreds of dollars."

"I saw all that, too," Lyle said. He wanted to share in her guilt, to contribute his, lessen hers. "I thought you'd get in touch with me, to support what you said about them." He couldn't withhold that any more and quickly wished he had.

She sighed deeply. "Some of it went wrong. I signaled you with that note—and the jelly beans," she chuckled. "I was going to get in touch with you right after they were arrested, but you had to go and volunteer that you were guilty of something or other and they took you to jail. Went there to get you out, but you were already out, thank God, and you'd left. I helped the Lord's judgment on them, couldn't wait for their penalty that was sure to come afterwards. I sat in that court chair and told how they robbed and stole and cheated the poor."

"Still goes on," the small next to them opined, "and that sure doesn't deserve an Amen."

This time Sister Matilda just waved her hand toward him, either dismissing him or extending him her blessing. "I had to do penance for my part in it all those years," she said.

Penance. The word had a harsh sound, like a curse, Lyle thought.

The chicken pie arrived, an ample portion. Sister Matilda eyed it with suspicion. "It's large enough." She buried the fork into the crust. "Let's see how many chicken chunks it has." She speared a portion on her fork. "Now we'll tell—"

Lyle waited for her verdict. She just ate, took another piece. To him, as he ate, it tasted great. "What were you doing with that peacock?"

What? Everyone had seen that picture! Lyle felt too happy to be embarrassed, and she apparently was willing to withdraw her question.

"Hmmm." She tasted more pot pie, holding it in her mouth, testing it. "Yes, penance!" she resumed. "That's why I'm out there on that corner—travel around to different places. As long as I can get around, I'll say what I should have said then but didn't on the television, about cruelty and meanness—"

"And about Jesus being black," Lyle offered to her.

"Jesus wasn't black," the small man said. "He was Jewish."

"He was black and Jewish," Lyle told the man, quietly so Sister Matilda wouldn't feel contradicted.

The man nodded.

"Somebody's got to say the truth about the Lord." She pondered another forkful of chicken pie. "Sometimes, cowboy," she said, looking deeply into his eyes, "a life begins before it begins. The past has a lot of power. It's there before you're even born—and then without knowing it you're doing penance for what happened to someone else. Like a curse passed on that you didn't bring on."

The odd, tangled words resounded in Lyle's mind. Was she talking about him now? About Sylvia? But how? What kind of curse? . . . Doing penance for what happened to someone else, like a curse passed on? Was she just saying words? "Were you talking about me, Sister Matilda?" he ventured.

"Cowboy, I was talking about *myself!* Doing penance now for not bearing witness to what I saw done to my daddy, lynched, nailed to a tree." Her mind drifted away to the horror of that time. She opened her mouth, a silent scream. She bowed her head. 'Amazing grace'?—is that what you asked me?"

A long time ago, yes, and she had answered, but not too clearly, something about "hope" and "understanding another's pain," and about em-pa-thy—no, no, that was Clarita. It was as if, now, some memories spoke to her and she answered them aloud. "Yes," he said, "I did."

But Sister Matilda's mind had moved into the present. "This chicken pie is *good,* eat up, eat up, cowboy, it is *really* good!"

When they were finished and Lyle had paid—and the small man paused at their booth and nodded, or bowed, before Sister Matilda, who smiled graciously—Lyle tried to give her money, but she refused it, placing the bills gently back into his hand, enclosing his fingers over them, holding her hand over his for long moments. She arranged her girth, preparing to leave. She stood, adjusting her crown. She looked up, up, her eyes fixed up, way up. She turned her gaze back on him and smiled.

"Oh, yes," she said. "You asked about grace? Can't understand grace, Lyle, you *feel* it."

She moved out of the restaurant, like an exiled but undefeated queen.

CHAPTER TWENTY

1

Yet another unexpected turn.

aul!" There he was—*again!*—at Lyle's apartment door. This time Lyle's first reaction was anger. "You little bastard!" Ummm, he was a bastard himself. "You little fucker!" That was off too. "You little shit!" He let it go at that, except that Raul wasn't little any more. He had grown even more, a young man, with budding muscles, and, now, an earring in each ear, and a tattoo—very small, though—on one of his biceps. "You promised to go back—"

"Don't get mad at me, Lyle. I won't want to stay here, I got a place of my own. But I'm—"

"—hiding out again?" Lyle tried to sound harsh. He looked around, expecting Buzzy. "Where's—?"

"Buzzy's hiding, too, probably heard what happened."

Lyle crossed his hands over his chest. Once—okay. Twice—well—

Lyle stood aside to let him in. "I'm going to have a hard time believing you, Raul," he warned.

"I know." Raul sat down facing Lyle, who sat on the bed with his arms crossed before his chest. "Lyle, I swear on my mother's name—well, I don't have one—I swear on my aunt's name—she can't stand me—I just *swear* that I'm not lying." He made two crosses, thumbs over index fingers, kissed both, and swore. "I'm gonna tell you everything, not leaving anything out, just listen, and don't think I'm dirty because of what I'm gonna tell you—"

2

A move back in time to learn what Raul told Lyle,
involving more of life's impossible coincidences.

Fiction rejects coincidences, but life abounds in them, and, for Raul, they just kept piling up, and that's what he asked Lyle, please, please, to believe.

After he had bought his ticket back to Rio Escondido, he returned with Buzzy to the Boulevard, to say good-bye to other runaways. Buzzy was still trying to decide whether she'd join Raul and help him "clear the mess up in Rio Escondido." On the Boulevard, Spike, a kid who dressed in black vinyl and had spiky hair, was telling everyone he'd got a real easy job "as a model"—and he was going to make "cool contacts" from it. Contacts! That meant talent scouts, producers, directors, agents. Spike showed them the advertisement he'd found in a throwaway newspaper:

MODELS. Young (18–24), good-looking, with good bodies. Excellent working conditions, excellent pay. If you think you're right, call for appointment.

It made sense. Make a good contact before going back to Rio Escondido—that was Buzzy's idea. She called on behalf of Raul, preparing to become his manager.

Both went to the building on Highland, a slick building occupied by offices with impressive names listed on the lobby directory: agencies, production companies, just as he had expected. The office they were looking for took up half a whole floor. Buzzy wished Raul good luck, promised to meet him—"for my manager's fee"—and left.

Raul walked into a reception room, where the attendant, a huffy man who seemed to peer—not see—sat at a desk. He asked if Raul had an appointment, and then buzzed him into a classy office. There was a spectacular view from a window—Los Angeles sprawling toward the ocean. Behind a desk with nothing but a telephone on it sat a heavy man, well dressed in a flashy way. "Hey, dude!" he said. "Fuckin' good to see ya." Talking like that.

"Thank you, sir," Raul said politely.

"Must you? *Must* you?" That's what a woman sitting on a taller chair said to the man. When he had said "fuckin'" she winced and with manicured fingers applied pressure to her temples. She was very well dressed, she even wore gloves. She said to Raul: "How do you do, young man? Please do sit down." She spoke very formally, pronouncing every syllable exactly. "As good-looking as you are—I am quite certain of this, but correct me if I'm wrong—you are hoping—aren't you?—to become"—she sniffed—"a movie star."

Raul beamed. "It looks like it? That clear to see?"

"Yes," the woman said with a smile that didn't smile.

"Are you tal—?"

"Talent scouts, right, and producers, young man," the woman said.

"Sure, and we have lots of fuckin' contacts," the man told him. "The kind that can help a smart kid like you climb as high as ya fuckin' wanna in Hollywood."

"Must you always—?" the woman directed at the man, brushing her hand over her hair, but, more, as if to thrust away an echo of the man's words. "All you require is to be discovered; am I right?" she asked Raul.

Imagine! All those days on corners selling star maps for fuckin' Scala and hoping a limousine would stop and it would be a movie scout—but nothing. Now here he was being discovered—so easy, too—by these two great people! Who wouldn't take this great opportunity?

"We're going to ask Ms. LaGrande, our most prominent director, to join us for an interview." The woman called out to into a farther office: "Ms. LaGrande!"

Out tottered a huge drag queen, heavy, made taller by the fact that she—that's how they referred to him—wore spike heels and a monstrous, frizzly blond wig. She inspected Raul, circling him, tripping once on her own heels, almost toppling. *"Mais oui; je suis enchanteeze,"* she approved in what seemed to be French. *"Mais—"* she seemed to search her vocabulary, gave up: "Your type is *toujours* quite *po-poo-lar, trésor.* Of course, we'll have to see more of you," she tittered.

This is what they explained to him: The Internet was the place to be discovered. That's where he would be seen—if he had proof that he was of "legal age"—and he did, like everyone else on the streets, whatever their real ages. When he appeared "on computer screens all over the world," big studio people would spot him and the offers would pour in like rain in Seattle.

"Wanna be star, *trésor?"* Za-Za LaGrande asked Raul with such an assertive wink that a false eyelash fell out.

"Can't wait!" Raul said.

Raul followed Za-Za LaGrande and the man and woman to another large room. Against one corner, like a set in a small theater was a bed, an ordinary bed, a lit lamp, and a droopy artificial tree. On the rumpled bed were two young men, naked, doing—

His eyes widening to take in what he saw, Raul still couldn't tell. Two young men were entangled so that it was difficult to see what anyone was doing. Naturally he was puzzled, wondering what the hell was going on. Still he was curious, right?

The woman smiled at the scene, as if she was seeing something very pretty. "Sweet," she said.

"Tray dulce," Za-Za translated.

"Fucking hot, eh?" the man said to Raul.

Yes, it was hot, especially since one of the two young men, a slim one, had smiled at him as he glanced over, or from under, one limb or another. Raul was attracted, and, well, hot. After all, he'd never been with a guy, but, oh, he wanted to be, God, did he!

With small cameras, two men, clothed, danced around the couple on the bed, filming the activity. Another man, with a cap on backwards, was calling out instructions, like a coach. "Shift . . . Go up . . . Go down—" Next to him, smoking heavily so that it was impossible to see her face behind a cloud of smoke, was a stocky woman.

"So now let's see what you got in your repertoire," Za-Za LaGrande said to Raul in a distinctly male voice.

"That means get buck-ass naked!" the man said.

The chic woman cringed.

"*Au naturelle,*" Za-Za said, giving her stuffed breasts a hefty heave up.

Raul stalled. He wasn't about to get naked in front of all these people.

"What's the matter? How do you think all those fuckin' big stars got their breaks, dude?" The man caught Raul staring at the slim performer on the bed. "How'd ya like to pair up with him?"

Would he! He didn't tell them that, but he wouldn't lie about the fact that, yes, he would want to. Still—

"So easy, young man," the elegant woman said, "and you'll be prompted by Mr. Cecil B., and his assistant, Ms. Sandra May O'Connell, who have been in our employ forever." She sniffed her wrist, a sweet scent.

"What're you fuckin' stallin' for? It's your big fuckin' break, kid, take it for chrissakes, take your fuckin' clothes off. Now!" the man said.

"Must you?" the woman despaired.

"How much?" Raul said. What he really cared about, right then was to make it with that guy who'd smiled at him. Of course, he was looking for his big break, too—and the money wouldn't hurt, either, especially since, by then, he'd missed the bus to Rio Escondido and didn't think they'd offer a refund, and he felt a responsibility to Buzzy because her rent was overdue, and she had, in effect, become his manager.

"One hundred dollars," the woman said, "and then more. Much more."

Wow! Raul thought. His first time having sex with a guy—while being coached—*and* the first step into big-time movies—*and* he'd also make a hundred bucks, even more. Still, he was nervous. Za-Za La Grande held two small cellophane packets. She tore one open, and sniffed from the white powder it contained. "Here, *trésor,* have a sniff, it'll make it all feel even better, loosen you up, *n'est-pas?*"

Raul barely sniffed, knowing what it was, from being around the Boulevard and seeing other guys sniffing.

The other packet contained a rubber. "For *quelques-choses,*" Za-Za stumbled, "whatever occurs," she clarified with a naughty gurgle, which bounced against her deep man's voice. "Sandra May over there will help you put it on, if you need help. *Vous le*—uh-*vous*—?"

Sandra May O'Connell ambled over. "Christ, what a life—from fluffer to stuffer."

Raul performed with the slim kid—and don't for a moment think he wasn't shy and embarrassed to have people watching—discovering his desires, acting out his yearnings—even before Cecil B. the coach gave instructions, which he and the other kid didn't follow—and he and the other kid kissed and kissed and kissed—and it was great, that was the best!—and fuck it if those guys were hovering around them. He didn't care. It was his first time, a forbidden dream realized at last, and it was beautiful and great and not wrong!

When it was over—terrifically, messily over—the slim guy whispered hurriedly to Raul, "Don't believe 'em, dude, about directors calling, like nobody's called me for a movie. Ask them for the money now, or they'll, like, cheat you. See ya later?"

"Yeah!" Raul agreed eagerly. . . . "The money," he said to the man and woman. Difficult to believe, sure, but it was dawning on him only now that he'd been lied to from the beginning.

The man gave him a twenty-dollar bill.

"The rest!" Raul said, feeling queasy about what was coming. "You'll have to do some more fucking and shit to get full pay," the man said.

The woman shielded her ears, delicately. "These were auditions, young man," she explained to Raul.

"The money," Raul said, his bad feelings increasing.

"Very little work, really," the woman sniffed, "and, truly, not unpleasant, was it?" she asked Raul.

It had been great because he'd been making it with that guy, a first time. But this was something else, a business, and there was Buzzy to pay. "The hundred," he raised his voice. "Give me what you said!"

"Ah, screw 'im," Za-Za La Grande suggested to the man. "He wasn't that fuckin' good." She added: "The *ingrat!* I can find a hundred like him on the Boulevard on a slow day, they're all hungry and eager and easy, and fuck him." She tried to snap her fingers, but they merely slid against each other. "Give the fucker the boot!" She kicked one foot up, and one of her shoes slipped off.

"The money, the money, the money!" Raul raised his voice.

"Give him the money!" the woman said to the man. "My head is about to burst!"

"Here, little shit—" The man fished for his wallet.

"Must you use that hideous word?" the woman flinched.

As Raul reached for his money, a burly, hairy gross guy he hadn't seen before grabbed him roughly by the shoulders, and dragged him out of the room, along the hallways, and then tossed him out into an alley like trash.

3

Back in Lyle's apartment—

"See?" Raul displayed heavy bruises on his arms.

Whether Raul had told everything exactly as it had happened or not, he had real bruises. "You remember where you went?" Lyle asked.

"Sure."

Why did he feel so damn protective toward him? the question nagged Lyle. Perhaps because he was a bastard, like him. Except that Raul was a *double*-bastard—no father, no mother. Or maybe it was only that he, Lyle, was so much taller than him.

4

The past invades the present.

Detective Seagrim looked like a pirate in a movie, with an angular face and an eye patch as he waited for Tarah Worth to answer his ringing.

He didn't wait long because Tarah had seen him through a window and had rushed to the door, eager to get the report from the detective Lenora claimed was "the best in the industry, everyone uses him."

"You found him?"

"It wasn't easy, Miss," he lied. The *real* mystery about the Mystery Cowboy was that everybody was looking for him and couldn't find him and he was everywhere.

Tarah took the paper with the information that would enable her to execute the scene that would get her worldwide attention.

"I discovered something else," Detective Seagrim said. "About you."

"Oh?"

"Yeah, before you were even a starlet," Detective Seagrim said with a squinty look perfected to indicate threat.

That could mean only one thing, gauging from that man's mean look: That scoundrel in her past was pushing his way into her present—at the worst time possible!

She paid the man and retreated to her bedroom. She closed her eyes. She saw before her, as clearly as if it was there:

Liz Smith

Scandal!

Los Angeles.—Super-beauty Tarah Worth, on the eve of what would have been a smashing return to the screen as the lead in the eagerly awaited sequel to great author Jacqueline Susann's classic bestseller *Valley of the Dolls* has been forced into retreat after sources learned that in her early years—

Tarah's eyes shot open, banishing the imaginary column. Goddammit, would she have to kill for the role?

5

A confrontation.

"Look who's back, the Mystery Cowboy, also known as the Lord's Cowboy and hung like a fuckin' horse in heat—"

"I will *not*—" Mrs. Renquist measured her words but not her rage at Mr. Renquist as they sat in their office facing Raul and Lyle, who had barged past the protesting receptionist.

"I figured you'd come back to us, Mystery Cowboy," the man said. "Wanna be paired next with this kid, eh?"

Lyle tried to remember them. The man and woman in the loft? To hell with it—he was here to speak up for Raul.

He had rehearsed what he would say. Raul had coached him, revising some phrases, adding words, helping him memorize the exact delivery. Standing perfectly straight in order to assert his declamation, Lyle began: "Sir, ma'am, I don't want to make trouble for you, because you've made enough for yourselves picking up homeless boys and probably girls and enticing them with lies"—although he wasn't entirely sure that Raul had been quite as unaware about what was really going on as he claimed to have been. "Now I want you to understand—"

"Get quick to the part where you call the guy a low-life motherfucker," Raul coaxed.

Lyle continued with the part Raul had said was very important to make clear, dictating it word for word: "—want you to understand that neither I nor Raul, here with me, care a damn about what people do as long as there's no force, and no children or cruelty, and no one's exploited—"

"—and as long we get *paid* the way we were *promised*!" Raul thrust at the man and the woman.

Baffled by the strange scene, Mr. and Mrs. Renquist watched and heard.

"But you've lied to them about how they're going to become movie stars," Lyle went on.

"Get to the part where you tell the bitch she's no better than the motherfucker even if she is wearing gloves," Raul encouraged.

"Oh!" One of Mrs. Renquist's eyes twitched and she covered her mouth in shock.

"So—" Lyle waited because this was the point where Raul had determined that he would take over. "So—"

"So pay up, you thieving shits!" Raul addressed Mr. and Mrs. Renquist.

"Give them the money, please, I have a beastly headache, pounded by all this rampant vulgarity," Mrs. Renquist pleaded.

"Maybe I *would* pay him now if the little punk hadn't lifted my fuckin' wallet," Mr. Renquist accused.

Lyle glanced at Raul, who shrugged.

Mrs. Renquist dug into her Chanel purse and plucked out bills, which she flung out. "Here, here, here! Take them, take them! Only *please*—" She clamped her hands over her ears.

As Raul gathered the bills gleefully, the door opened, and there he was, the young man he had performed with.

"Lank!" Raul welcomed him.

"Raul!" Lank welcomed back. Then he addressed Mr. and Mrs. Renquist: "I'm here to collect *my* money, you cheating fucks."

Mrs. Renquist flung more bills out.

Lank gathered them.

"Nasty faggot shits!" Mr. Renquist shouted at them. "You're not so damn innocent, you little fuckers. You knew the score."

"Then why didn't you pay us?" Lank demanded.

"Because you're dumb shits!" Mr. Renquist said.

"Must you? Must you call these children such vile names?" Mrs. Renquist cradled her head.

"Now we're leaving, ma'am, sir," Lyle declaimed, and added for himself: "And don't think I approve of all that's going on here, either, with these street kids."

"Kids! Those little shit whores? Now, listen, you creep cowboy, get the fuck out of here with those two queer bastards."

Lyle's fists decided fast. They clenched and one socked Mr. Renquist.

"That's for being a low-life bullshitter!" Raul added.

"Ouch, shit-motherfucker!" Mr. Renquist surrendered comfortably to the thick-rugged floor.

"Oh, must you? *Must* you be so crude even in pain?"

"Bullshitters!" Lank aimed at Mr. and Mrs. Renquist.

"Shit lying fuckers!" Raul shouted at them. "Both of you—but especially *you,*" he aimed at Mrs. Renquist.

"Oh, please, oh, please stop! Please stop raising your voices, children!" Mrs. Renquist said, "my headache is assaulting me with every foul word. *Please!*"

6

A discovery.

When Lyle, Raul, and Lank were outside and standing awkwardly wondering what to say to each other, and Lyle was thinking, what a strange, complicated world this is—how difficult to know what is always right and what is always wrong—Raul looked at Lank, the first time he'd seen him fully dressed, and saw that he was wearing boots and a cowboy hat. Then he looked at Lyle's boots and cowboy hat. He looked at Lank, then at Lyle, Lyle, then Lank, back and forth.

"Hi, cowboy," Lyle said to the lanky young man.

"I'm not a cowboy," Lank said. "I never even been on a horse."

7

A promise, this one to be kept.

Lyle, Raul, and Lank took a bus back to Lyle's apartment—all flush with money.

"So now where are you going?" Lyle asked Raul, who sat facing him, Lank beside him.

"I guess——?" Raul's look entreated Lank's.

"Find a place together?" Lank offered.

"And take Buzzy in?" Raul pled.

"Sure," Lank said.

Raul looked at him with delight. He transferred his wide smile onto Lyle. "I guess we'd better go now."

"Guess so," Lyle said, glad and sad, glad to see Raul happy with Lank, sad to see yet another person go out of his life—if, that is, this time Raul was really going to stay away.

"Bye, cowboy," Lank said to Lyle.

"Bye, cowboy," Lyle said back.

Raul lingered after Lank had walked out. "I'll always love you, you know that," he said to Lyle. "I guess next best was to find someone who looks like you—a little bit—because, really, there's no one else like you."

"Nor you," Lyle said.

Raul hugged Lyle, tightly.

Lyle held his face and this time, not to save him from Brother Dan's accusations and curses but because he wanted to—he kissed him on the lips, sealing their special love.

"What're you going to do now, really?" Lyle asked.

Raul smiled his widest smile. "Become a movie star, what else?"

"Cummon, Raul, cummon!" Lank called from outside.

"I'm coming," Raul said to Lank, and left, not looking back.

Lyle prayed to the Virgin of Guadalupe: Let him be okay, please. Clarita told me to turn to you. Don't let him end up on the Boulevard like those other kids. Please, beautiful lady Guadalupe, don't let him be one of those sad lost kids.

CHAPTER TWENTY-ONE

1

The persistence of the past.

The new Tarah Worth evaluated her situation harshly.
The detective she had hired to find the Mystery Cowboy would now attempt to blackmail her with information she had thought dead in the past. She did not even wonder how he had uncovered it; the fact of it drew her total concentration. She was on the brink of getting the role of a lifetime. She was forty years old. All right—she was forty-two. Goddammit, forty-five! Screw it, screw it, screw it!—she was fifty. Almost fifty. Nearing fifty. Some people still thought of her as a starlet. All this called for adjustments, and she would make them, one at a time.

She called a cab.

When the driver stopped to let her off before the designated address, she waited for him to ask for an autograph. He didn't. Of course, Tarah tried to dismiss, he didn't speak English, or perhaps he had been so struck by her beauty, or maybe the giant Versace sunglasses she was wearing had disguised her too entirely. Fuck it, she was facing it all. The cab driver didn't have any idea about who she was.

She took the elevator, a clear cylinder that allowed passengers to gaze at the breadth of the city. As she made her way along the corridor to the office she had called ahead, she made sure her high heels tapped on the floor to announce her assertive arrival.

She brushed past the little creep at the receptionist desk. She said: "Tarah Worth!" and swept into the main office.

"Max!" she greeted the man seated in the expansive room.

"Dorothy Hotchkins? Is that you?" the gaudy man asked.

For a moment she hadn't recognized her real name, but she did recognize the man who was again intertwined with her life—and her future.

Tarah looked around. Was that hated creature, his frigid wife, lurking here, despite her demand on the telephone that Max send her away, whatever it might require?

He understood her trepidation. "No, Wilma isn't here. She's having her hair colored."

"That dreadful black without a hint of highlights," Tarah remembered.

Max moved a chair next to hers. He held her hand. "It's good to see you, doll—"

Doll! She had succeeded in giving a relevant meaning to the word "doll." "You've changed very little, Max," she lied. He was even grosser than she remembered, his suit shinier.

"Except for a few pounds, less hair—and some fresh bruises on my face, donated by a dissatisfied . . . performer," he tried to laugh off the last. "We all change, Tarah Worth."

"Ummmm. . . . I'm not here to renew our . . . relationship, Max," Tarah got that out of the way, though she'd never been sure what had really existed between them.

"The time when we did that movie?" Max said. "That time is gone, Dorothy. I make videos now, for the Internet. Big porn movies died with poor Hunk Williams; remember him?"

"Is he dead?"

"Worse than that, he stopped being able to get it up!" Max laughed. "Now he rummages wistfully through the dildoes fashioned from his famous organ. I use him now and then; he's a trusted chauffeur."

"I'm here because of that movie, Max."

"The short blue movie you made for us? . . . Blue movie. That sounds odd now, in the time of live sex on the Internet. Performers are a dime a dozen, on every corner in Hollywood. When they're through after their brief span, there're dozens more—and there's something for everyone!— and me and Wilma are at the crest of it," he said proudly. "We've survived well."

"Wilma," Tarah tossed the name away with disgust. "The prude, the porn empress who can't stand foul language. Do you still drive her insane with your foulest vocabulary, Max?"

Max threw himself back so far with laughter that his suit—which would certainly shine in the dark—made a threatening sound. "Yes! One day she really will die from those headaches she claims my coarse language gives her. You always knew—didn't you?—that I speak that way only because it drives her crazy."

"Everyone knew but her." Tarah touched her lips, to make sure her gloss had not been smirched. "Max! I believe you may be getting a call from a smarmy detective I had occasion to hire; he will be asking about that movie—"

"Nasty Desires?"

She winced.

"Nasty Desires," Max repeated. "Sounds sweet now."

"It *wasn't* sweet," Tarah asserted, "it was ugly." Like you, she wanted to add, like you and your hideous wife—even more coarse now, bragging about your sordid recruiting; I needed the few dollars you paid me, very few. But she couldn't say any of that; she needed him as an ally. "Now the tabloids and God knows who else will be trying to get a copy of it if that detective carries out his not-too-subtly hinted threat to expose me to—"

"Dorothy—Tarah," Max interrupted her, "I doubt that a copy even exists."

"What?"

"An eight–millimeter film, all grainy and worn?"

"Gone? Destroyed!" Tarah was surprised to hear herself gasp.

"Maybe someone from the past treasures it, keeps an obsolete projector on which he can view it once more before he dies."

Tarah refused to face that this complicated matter had turned so easy, so banal—so, *really* filthy. "If—when!—that dirty film surfaces, I will overcome the scandal."

"No one would care today," Max interrupted her.

She ignored his words. "Monroe survived those photos, and so will I! I don't care what I have to do to get the role of Helen Lawson! Whatever it takes!"

Max said with a crooked smile, "Whatever it takes?" He applauded, slowly, one hand on the other, then again. "So you've become like the rest of us. Welcome to the valley of vultures, Dorothy—Tarah Worth! You'll do whatever it takes to get what *you* want, and damn anyone else. Right?"

"Yes!"

She stood up, turned to leave—and recovered quickly when she stumbled on a box that turned over, spilling dildoes.

2

A type of meanness exemplified.

There is a kind of cruelty that exists purely for its own sake, with no purpose other than making the wounded squirm, like ants captive under a child's sun-magnifying glass. Max Renquist leaned back in his chair and smiled, pleased, very pleased, that he had produced a similar effect on Tarah Worth.

"What did that woman want? I ran into her in the elevator," Wilma Renquist, her hair freshly darkened, walked into her husband's office.

"That pretentious bitch, that . . . that . . . 'Tarah Worth,'"—he gave the name a nasty sound. "So fuckin' high and mighty now. I lowered her a few pegs, quite a fucking few. I didn't tell her that the fuck flick she made years ago never even got developed."

"The one you bungled," Mrs. Renquist remembered, sniffing her perfumed handkerchief to disguise the stench of crassness.

"That one. I let her believe it was just obsolete. Like her."

"Good," Mrs. Renquist approved.

"*Fuckin'* good, eh?" Mr. Renquist revised.

Mrs. Renquist crushed the scented handkerchief in her anguished hands. "Always? Always? *Must* you—?"

3

A plan is put into motion.

Outside, Tarah fished in her purse for the address the detective had given her, where the Mystery Cowboy lived. She would use his notoriety for her ends. So what? *She'd* been used, abused. She'd *learned*! No, she had been taught by masters.

In the cab, she was still trembling with indignation, not the indignation she had brought with her into Max's office. She was shaking with a greater indignation, Max's intimation that *any* performance of hers would be forgotten.

4

The next step.

VARIETY

Show Biz Down & Close

A knowledgeable source alerted this column that actress Tarah Worth is profoundly concerned about a possible stalker who has made menacing overtures toward her. Police officers cannot move against anyone until an actual crime has been committed, or is clearly about to be committed. The actress is a strong contender for the role of Helen Lawson in *Return to the Valley of the Dolls,* the sequel to the late Jacqueline Susann's *Valley of the Dolls.*

They had used it! Tarah stopped on her way from Max's office to pick up the new issue of *Variety.* Her long-time friend had printed the item she had given him.

Now she would cast the horny Mystery Cowboy in her real-life drama.

5

The state of Lyle's troubled heart.

In the very center of his heart, Lyle was sad, deeply, deeply sad. Life was full of problems and complications! That was his thought as he wandered along Hollywood Boulevard, which at night turned into a shattered electric kaleidoscope, shards of blazing colors. He walked past newly arrived squads of people, a new invasion preparing for the ritual of the Academy Awards.

Just as in Rio Escondido he had gone to think and ponder matters in the vacant lot, he now went to the foyer of the grand Egyptian Theater to sort things out. Its outdoor court—with its gurgling fountain and glazed mosaics of sunbursts and Egyptian monarchs—was flanked by palm trees, eight on each side, lit invisibly from their base and enclosed by oval concrete benches. At times the palm trees seemed to hover over him with understanding. At other times, when a breeze created a flurry along the Boulevard, they turned away, ignoring him. A few people usually milled about the court and moved on when there was no event in the theater. Today, the palm trees were as pensive as he was.

"I wish—" he said aloud. There was so much to wish for. That Sylvia would be happy, that . . . "I wish—" He investigated wishing. How odd that the heart—or, Sister Matilda might say, the soul—could yearn for anything, anything in the world, the most impossible things—like being able to fly, say—but the world wasn't made to grant those wishes. Was that where hope filled in—being able to hope? He hummed and strummed on his guitar:

> *Why is the heart allowed to hope*
> *for what the goddamned world*
> *cannot—cannot—give?*

6

The matter of fate.

Tarah stared into the mirror because her new look fascinated her. Determination? Yes! Finally. Cruelty?—life was cruel, wasn't it?—cruelty? Yes!

"Sit down," she commanded when Rusty Blake arrived in response to her latest summons.

"Y'know, Tarah, I don't like the way you, like, just call up and, like, demand that I be here."

She ignored him. She was going to secure for him the chance of his lifetime. "We have to rehearse it all, very carefully," she said.

"Uh, like what—?"

"The kidnapping."

"Hey, I, like, thought you were, like, making that up. I still don't get it. . . . Listen, I'm not putting myself in danger. No way, man. L. Ron says stay away from danger—"

"The only danger you're in, if you don't cooperate, is of losing the role of a lifetime." That thrilling coldness in her voice! "I've enlisted others, a detective, a chauffeur. All you have to do is save me."

"I think I get it, man. Like in the script, right? . . . Uh, like save you from who, what?"

The new Tarah ignored him. "Do you believe in fate?"

"Sure, who doesn't?—like when—in *Rebel Without a Cause* Dean— Like what?"

She hadn't even heard him. She said: "You have to push fate along in the direction you want it to go. When it reaches a certain point, you shove it! *Then* it becomes fate!"

"Uh, yeah, like—"

7

Back in Rio Escondido—

Clarita kept a close eye on Sylvia that whole day, following her when she seemed to be heading for the liquor cabinet, even standing outside her bathroom door where she kept a pharmacy of pills, stood there, glaring, until Sylvia would retreat from the bathroom or stop pouring "just another nip." So she was sober—well, as sober as she ever was now—when the time came to leave for the wedding of Maria to the politician and gambler Enrique Fielding. (The *cabrón* called himself a politician although he had never been elected to anything—and "Enrique" wasn't his real name; he had chosen it in order to appeal to "Hispanic constituents," whoever they were.)

Clarita was always amazed by how well Sylvia could hold several drinks, and then, on the next one, would collapse. Today she was determined to keep her from that one fatal drink. She also marveled at how beautiful Sylvia could still become—when she cared—beautiful.

Today, she was beautiful, and she herself—Clarita admitted—didn't look half bad, in a dress she had recently bought at a discount that Sylvia managed for her, a very chic dress, she knew—and she was wearing a hat, the way one should for a wedding. Alas, she had forgotten to buy gloves!

"You look like a movie star," Clarita told Sylvia.

"I do? Not Miss America?"

"Even prettier."

Maria was marrying Mr. Fielding in the Catholic church where Armando had bared his oblique muscles to Sylvia in a rivalry with Jesus Christ's buffed body. There was no question in either Sylvia's mind nor in Clarita's that Maria was marrying the man because he was powerful and very rich. But so what? thought Sylvia; that was a much better reason than falling in love with a no-good son of a bitch.

Sylvia had become very happy when she learned of the impending wedding. That girl Maria was impetuous. She had disappeared in search of Lyle—and returned with Mr. Fielding. That was *that* between her and Lyle.

In the ornate Catholic church—arches, stained-glass windows, glittering gold and silver everywhere—Sylvia sat and Clarita knelt in a pew reserved "for close friends of the family"; Clarita intended to kneel throughout the whole ceremony. "That will show you, God, my devotion to you, even though I haven't been to Mass in a year. You'll take this into consideration, especially because of my bad knees," she explained, begging Jesus to nurture Lyle the Second's heart if he still loved the fickle girl. But her knees hurt too much and she sat as comfortably as church pews allow.

Sylvia looked around at the glamorous saints. Once, they had reassured her that she would win the title she longed for, change her terrible life. Now they seemed indifferent. She thought, They always were, I just didn't see that then.

The church was crowded, of course—"with as many Anglos as there are Mexicans," Clarita tartly observed, "and many are *protestantes,*" she sniffed.

"He's homely," Sylvia said as Mr. Fielding appeared at the railing of the altar, to await the bride. He was flanked by the best man and three ushers, his Anglo friends from wherever they came, staid, pale, uncomfortable men who had arrived accompanied by staid, pale, uncomfortable wives. "I'm glad he's homely," Sylvia whispered to Clarita. "She deserves a homely man."

That might be so, but he certainly must have deserved a beautiful wife, because Maria looked gorgeous, in white, the veil not quite able to disguise the dark lush hair. She was accompanied by her father, Armando in a tuxedo, looking entirely middle-aged and prosperous. Difficult to remember that he had actually once been "the sexy Chicano." Sylvia winced to remember that at a desperate time she had even allowed him to think that he had fathered Lyle. She never really regretted it; who knows what would have happened between Lyle and this unstable girl, given the direction they were moving at the time?

Now *there* was something to approve of, Clarita interrupted her prayers to observe—the bridesmaids, in pale blue chiffon, lovely girls, probably Maria's friends, if she had any. They looked like budding flowers. "To the hills!" Clarita blurted uncontrollably, in the clasp of past memories. She quickly hushed herself, her hand over her mouth.

There was the swell of organ music. A wedding was always so lovely, wasn't it? Clarita was about to observe aloud when she remembered that Sylvia hadn't had one.

The slow procession of flowery bridesmaids and the white apparition in satin and veils made its way toward the altar. The groom and ushers waited, looking stuffed.

As she passed with Armando, arms linked, Maria stopped next to Sylvia.

Actually paused as if about to speak to her! Please, God, no! Clarita begged. If she had been able to, she would have pressed her hands against Sylvia's *and* Maria's lips because no telling what might be exchanged.

Maria glided past like a pretty sailboat.

That moment. What did it augur? Clarita fretted. Something. Some unresolved animosity lingering from those earlier times, surely. Sylvia was capable of anything, and that Maria had spirit, too.

In a pew ahead, Maria's mother looked stern even as she smiled, the smile becoming icier when Armando passed by like a stuffed penguin.

The priest in bright garb. Vows exchanged. Tears shed.

The ceremony was over.

Music surged, the procession out of the church began.

Flowery girls fluttered about, like a floating tide of colored water lilies. The stiff men beside them shuffled awkwardly. Mr. Fielding, smiling and nodding, became even more rotund and satisfied in his expensive tuxedo.

"A moment, please!"

What? Everyone froze, including the priest and the altar boys.

It was Maria, at the exact center of the altar, who had halted the procession. She tossed off her veil, which floated to her feet, creating a cloud on which she stood in a glorious prism of light that filtered through a color-paned window and cast on her face an angelic glow.

It was coming, whatever had passed between her and Sylvia, it was coming! Clarita held Sylvia's hand, preparing to restrain her from whatever would happen now.

"Although—" Maria held the word there for moments. "Although I have made my nuptial vows and will in the eyes of Heaven honor them—"

Buzz, buzz, buzz, buzz. Oh! *Ay!*

Clarita's hand locked on Sylvia's arm.

"Still, I must be true myself, and so"—she paused—"I declare that I shall always love Lyle Clemens!"

Ah! Oh! *Ay!* What? What? *Qué?*

Was Sylvia about to get up? Confront her? She had thrust Clarita's hand away and was standing up, facing the girl at the altar.

Silence. Deep, deep stunned silence as the two women stood, just stood facing each other, one at the altar, the other in the pews.

Then Sylvia Love laughed aloud, a throaty, sustained laughter.

Stunned murmurs rippled through the church.

Then laughter erupted from the altar—Maria's laughter. Sylvia's laughter rose even louder and Maria's matched it.

Ay, Dios, Clarita prayed, her apprehension having not conceived of *this*. Please make them stop laughing. "Hail Mary, full of grace—" she whispered holy words.

For the first time—or had there been another moment, when she had first met her?—Sylvia was fond of Maria, for her daring, her spirit, the mutual defiance that had been acknowledged between them just now; the joined current of laughter asserted that, as if they were involved in a rampant opera. But more than anything else, Sylvia Love was laughing at the absurdity of romance, of trust, of love.

Clarita's voice pierced the laughter: "—the Lord is with thee, blessed art thou among women. . . . " Please make them stop this laughing, please. "Blessed is—"

Now a man's laughter rose, louder, still louder, raucous. It was Mr. Fielding, adding his own howls of laughter, a trio now, convulsed—he, Maria, and Sylvia Love.

"—the fruit of thy womb, Jesus." Please, Jesus, stop this horror in your church. "Holy Mary, Mother of God—"

The priest at the altar turned away from the congregation, facing the crucified figure. His body quivered, as he burst into chuckles, then laughter, now joined in by titters skittering among the congregation. More gasps, more outbursts of laughter here and there, and, soon, the whole church rocked with wild laughter.

"—pray for us sinners," Clarita persevered, "pray—pray—pray . . . Ah-harrr! Harrr! Harrrr!" All her restraint broke, and her own laughter soared even above the growing tide.

A prim altar boy pushed his way to the railing of the altar.

"Stop it! Stop it! Stop it! This is the Lord's House!" he protested. "Stop—" But his next words were drowned by his own gales of laughter.

Then Clarita noticed this: Sylvia's laughter had turned into sobs. And her own laughter stopped.

8

An ill-timed development?

Los Angeles Times

Liz Smith is on vacation.

When Tarah Worth read that—a mere item for so cataclysmic an event!—she fell into a depression of speculation. She figured quickly on her fingers and asserted that the great columnist would be back on the job by the time of the Academy Awards. But how strange to take a vacation as it all heated up toward the monumental night.

What if she was really dead?—they often maneuvered to withhold big news about big people, until adjustments could be made. She was relying on her to break the news of her triumph at the Academy Awards, Lenora ready to relay the story the moment it began to unfold, thus handing her a great exclusive.

In her home, staring at the cloudy pool which would soon be filled with clear water—or would it also turn murky, like the prospect of the day?—Tarah realized the one thing she hadn't counted on was Liz Smith's mysterious absence.

9

Growing concern about the truth of
the fabulous columnist's absence.

Two weeks had elapsed. No one took more than two weeks for a vacation. Tarah Worth tossed aside the irrelevant pages of the *Los Angeles Times,* in search of Liz Smith's column. There it was again!

Liz Smith is on vacation.

It hadn't been two weeks, of course not. Only a couple of days—maybe even yesterday. It had *seemed* like two weeks. Still, her readers would be thirsting for her by now.

Was it possible that the malicious astrological chart might yield some encouragement today, just today? She opened the drawer casually, shifting papers, and peeking. Today's entry: "Severe loss of a potential ally—" She shoved the drawer shut.

Vile! Vile! Was it possible to sue an astrologer? In the meantime, she'd turn to someone much more reliable. She dialed.

"Riva!"

"Tarah!"

She waited the required long psychic moments that would send the question undulating to her superb psychic in her arboretum.

"Riva!"

"Tarah!" Another moment of psychic affirmation. "Yes!" the voice of Riva answered the unstated question.

Reassured by the terse, unflinching answer to her question, Tarah opened the drawer where the vicious astrological chart lay, and she began to tear it. Wait! Would that upset the planets? She put the chart back in the drawer and swore never again to consult it. Why should she?— when the radiant Riva had just assured her that—yes!—her plan that involved the Mystery Cowboy would bring her attention throughout the world.

CHAPTER TWENTY-TWO

1

A new kind of love comes to Sylvia.

Sylvia could write him! There were ways of finding Lyle the First. Clarita had changed her mind entirely because of the growing desolation in Sylvia Love's life. She cherished the memory of her laughter at the wedding, but she wondered whether it had been only pained laughter, even before it had turned into sobs. Would that be the last time she would hear her beloved Sylvia laugh? As she tried to recreate the fateful day when Lyle the First returned to beg Sylvia to take him back— he *had* begged, hadn't he?—Clarita heard sincerity in his voice, probably missed earlier because of the startling events.

If Sylvia relented—wrote him—took him back, there would be happiness. Lyle would return. He and she and Sylvia and Lyle the First would live together. Lyle would marry an honest-to-God Mexican-American girl whom she, Clarita, would shelter from the raids of Villa and—There she went again, slipping into somebody else's past. . . . Lyle and his wife would live with them, of course, she continued her reverie; they'd get a larger house when Lyle had children. Lyle the Third! Clarita was so deep into her thoughts of happiness that she was jarred by Sylvia's presence, a presence who moved soundlessly through the house.

"What are you jabbering about?"

She'd been talking aloud, not just thinking? Let her hear it. "I was thinking that perhaps our lives would be happier if you wrote the cowboy that you would take him back."

"I am happy without him."

She said that without emotion, without hesitation. She meant it. The saddest development had occurred. Sylvia was in love with her loss.

As Sylvia missed whole days at work, hardly sober any more, reading Lyle the Second's letters over and over—and never writing back—she drifted about the house as if she were preparing to join the prowling ghost of her mother. Passing Sylvia in the hallway once—she was a gaunt, pale form now—Clarita felt a chill that the windy, dark Texas night had not brought. For the first time in her life, she prayed that her terrible premonition of that moment would be incorrect.

2

A comeback.

"Lyle!"

"Maria!" Here she was again, looking even more beautiful. He wanted to put his hands about her waist and whirl her around as he'd done the first time she'd sought him out in Los Angeles and had found him here in this apartment.

She poised her lips for a kiss, closed her eyes, and stood on tiptoes to receive it. When he did not kiss her, her eyes shot open. "Lyle, don't you understand? I ran away again, from my father *and* my husband—yes, I'm married and very, very unhappy, and, Lyle, the worst thing was that when I laughed aloud after I declared—in *church,* Lyle, I declared it aloud in *church!*—after I declared that I'd always love you—and your mother laughed, too, Lyle, your wonderful, doomed mother who knows the depths of despair—and I don't even care now that I never made you sing me her song—your poor, doomed mother laughed with me, approving!—and so did that dear humble soul, Clarita—and, when that all happened, Lyle, my *husband* joined in the laughter. Do you understand, my beloved? Isn't that tragically strange?"

"I guess—" Lyle was trying to catch up, figure out what part was tragic, what part funny, sort out what he felt—and what the hell she was really saying. He took it one by one in order of greatest importance. "First of all, you never could have made me sing that song, and, second, my mother is not doomed."

"Let's not waste time. Kiss me!"

He yearned to. "No."

"Don't you understand the horrible danger I've put myself into? I'll have my marriage annulled, because I'm a devout Catholic, and with my settlement money we can pay the Pope to do it. Will you kiss me and fight for me when he comes after me?"

"No."

"Really?" She seemed honestly startled.

"Really."

"You really, really mean it?"

"Yes."

"All right, then, I'll kill myself."

"You won't."

"What if I did, you'd be sorry."

"Of course, but you won't."

"Yes! I shall. I shall throw myself in the river, the Rio Escondido."

"It's dry, Maria."

"Then I'm going to become a nun."

"You won't."

She sighed in exasperation. "Lyle, I don't understand you, you're so strange."

"Maria, I don't understand *you*," Lyle said, "and I don't blame Mr. Fielding for laughing, because you're very funny; that's not to say you're not beautiful—and you're *really* strange, because you're not strange and want to be."

"Lyle!" She whipped her head to one side as if she had been physically struck. When he did not move to assuage her, she said, "Then it's really, really good-bye?"

"Yes."

"Can't we have wonderful sex?"

"No."

"All right then." Copious tears flowed. "Good bye. Forever!"

"Good-bye," Lyle said, as Maria left again, carrying her overnight bag and sobbing loudly.

3

Anxiety about Liz Smith's absence.

Without even glancing around to see whether anyone in the neighborhood—she would soon move to Beverly Hills—would see her without makeup, Tarah reached for the paper that had been flung halfway down her walkway by the insolent Guatemalan paper-man. Sometimes he'd throw it at the very edge of the pool, as if in warning—all because she hadn't given him a Christmas present.

Inside her house, she opened the paper to the entertainment section. There it was again, like a terrible curse:

"Liz Smith is on vacation."

4

The monumental Hollywood event nears.

The day of the Academy Awards was approaching! Even palm trees seemed mesmerized in awe of the sacred Hollywood event. Preparations were made for fabulous parties at Spago! At Morton's! Everywhere! Huge replicas of "Oscar," the statue of a golden, impassive, naked man, already flanked the prepared entrance, the sweep of stairs up to the grand site. A white Los Angeles sun glinted on the gold men, and their bodies sprinkled the air with gold dust, star dust. A red velvet carpet was ready to be spread for the stars to make their entrances—as panting fans mounted on backless bleachers set up in advance but not occupied until the magical day—some fans camped overnight—screamed in ecstasy when they glimpsed their favorites.

Sad because Maria was gone—but good riddance. Sad because the world could turn so ugly in a moment. Sad, always sad because Sylvia, a deepening mystery, would not write him—sad, just plain sad, Lyle sat on one of the oval concrete benches at his favorite thinking place, the foyer of the Egyptian Theater, with its dejected palm trees, as dejected as he was.

Too dejected!—so he walked on along the Boulevard to refresh his spirit.

He was even sadder now!

The picture of Babette, reclining in her black bikini, was no longer on the side of the new building. Was she real? Was it possible that she existed only on posters?

All that sadness piling up on him, more and more and more, made him horny, very horny. Horny as hell!

5

The crucial step in Tarah's plot is taken.

"At last I've found you, Mystery Cowboy! I've been looking for you since that afternoon—at that motel, by the pool."

Lyle had been talking to Mrs. Allworthy in the courtyard of the Fountain Apartments, hearing "the latest celebrity news" she had learned "firsthand" ("Elton's having an affair with that M&M fellow!") gleaned from her favorite tabloids—when the glamorous woman who had emerged from a taxi had gasped her pleasure at "finding" Lyle.

"It's Tarah Worth!" Mrs. Allworthy recognized the actress. Jeezuschrist! It's the woman I talked to at that motel in Anaheim, Lyle recognized. Both the memory of her sprawled body that day and the spectacle of her here was enough to add to the chafing itch in his pants, because—remember—he was lonely, shaken by the events of the past few days, and all of that had funneled into a yearning for—

This woman!

"Please join us, Miss Worth, we'll all have a cup of tea," Mrs. Allworthy was beside herself to have such a living celebrity on her premises. She spoke loudly, to assure that others in the Fountain Court would hear her, see who had come calling.

"How kind of you," Tarah Worth said. Damn this intrusive woman. She hadn't counted on her. "I would love to—"

"Fine, then, let's go." Mrs. Allworthy linked arms with Lyle and Tarah Worth, leading them toward her apartment.

Tarah eased her arm away carefully. "I'd love to, but I have some very urgent business to discuss with this gentleman, and"—she consulted her watch—"I have a rehearsal in—oh—very shortly."

Mrs. Allworthy was displeased. In order to linger, she pretended to be fishing pigeon feathers out of the fountain, which had stopped working, a stream of water bubbling at the top and cascading around only for a moment, and then becoming a trickle down the sides.

"Do please, *please* forgive me for depriving myself of the pleasure of having tea with you," Tarah smiled, putting a reassuring hand on Mrs. Allworthy's bony arm. She must make a hurried adjustment to incorporate her into her plan. How? She had it! When the time came, this nosey woman would assert *her,* Tarah's, version of events, if planted carefully.

Mrs. Allworthy was still miffed. "You're not the only movie star— uh, celebrity—uh, well known person—who's come here. Garbo was a regular visitor, and Vampira was frequently here."

She had taken a wrong step, alienating the woman, Tarah knew. She had to win her back.

"Mrs. Allworthy, I know why Miss Worth is here"—he had no idea— "and it is private, but I'm sure she'll come back to have tea with you, won't you?" Lyle placated Mrs. Allworthy, eager to be alone with this woman. Whatever business she had with him, this is what he was certain of: When Maria had invited more lovemaking and he had had to turn her down, he had been ready, and it seemed that his hard-on was surviving. Yes, and he wanted to hear Rose's voice again.

Mrs. Allworthy smiled. "I understand, Mr. Clemens!" she acquiesced. "We'll do it another time, and I'll prepare some scones."

He certainly had a way with her, Tarah saw. Better still, he was charming, and caring. Her distress at having to deal with Mrs. Allworthy— when subsequent events were set into motion—disappeared. She would definitely be able to use this woman. She knew her kind, a pushover, the kind who would eagerly go on television—her hair stiff as a plastic helmet—to say how surprised she was at the actions of a criminal she had unknowingly harbored. It would make it all even more delicious in Liz Smith's column, which she imagined just then:

Hollywood.—The handsome Mystery Cowboy who became so infatuated with great beauty Tarah Worth is remembered by his apartment manager as a quiet sort who—

Please, God, let the great columnist end her vacation soon! . . . To assure what her revised plans now welcomed—Mrs. Allworthy as an ally—Tarah Worth reached out to her, as if the parting, though necessary, was painful. "Mrs. Allgood—"

"Allworthy," Lyle supplied.

Fuck! "Dear Mrs. Allworthy, what an honor to touch the hand that touched Garbo's and—"

"Vampira's," Mrs. Allworthy reminded, proudly offering her hand as if for kissing.

Tarah did this—inspired!—she leaned over to Mrs. Allworthy and whispered—so what if Lyle heard?—"I will confide in you because I see honesty in your dear face. I'm in terror because a stalker—"

Mrs. Allworthy's face lit up.

"—is threatening me. I am, at this very moment taking extreme, dangerous measures, gambling that they work."

Mrs. Allworthy was beside herself. "And Lyle—?"

"Shhhh," Tarah cautioned. "Please!" She looked about her in abject fear. She turned to Lyle, surrendering her hands.

He took them and led her to his apartment.

They left Mrs. Allworthy in a state of excitement by the fountain, which suddenly started working, spattering water all over her.

6

The scheme is hatched.

"I need your help, Lyle. Ever since I saw you that day in the motel in— I forget the name of the town—I've thought that only you can help me. When I saw your picture in the paper, when you saved that Miss Whatever from that vicious attacker—"

"A peacock," Lyle said, sitting on his bed, ready to have her join him.

"Yes, and they're deadly," Tarah wanted to move on. "Ever since then, I knew you were the only one I could turn to for my special needs, for protection!"

"Oh, sure," Lyle welcomed. "Sure."

She sat on his one chair, locating it exactly before him. Then she began crossing and uncrossing her long legs. My God! She wasn't wearing any—Lyle wasn't sure. She had snapped her legs shut too quickly, but he was on alert. Again! She shifted her legs. Too quickly. He relocated himself on the edge of the bed so that he could look more closely. Damn! She *wasn't* wearing underpants. Whoosh, and she closed her legs again, shutting off the magnificent spectacle.

"What?" He had been so entranced that he hadn't realized she had continued to talk.

"—a stalker, I said, a dangerous man who's been following me around, a crazed fan, who writes me letters, who terrifies me and who threatens to make himself known to me in the most horrifying way. At the Academy Awards! And why? So that the whole world will know of his obsessive love."

Lyle tried to catch up, but he couldn't without asking her to repeat what she'd said, and he wasn't sure he wanted to hear it again, because once again, in a flash, she had uncrossed her legs, and there it was, in all its glory, winking at him—and then, *whoosh*, it was hiding again.

"Help me, *please,* Lyle. Escort me to the Awards. Please protect me!"

"Well, I—I'm not sure—" If what she was saying was all she'd come for and he said Yes, maybe she'd just get up and leave. Better to barter some more. "Not sure." That increased his anticipation, too. He heard Rose's voice remind: *When a woman's no longer a virgin—and you'll be able to tell—that's another kind of challenge, cowboy, because you'll have to overcome all the others she's been with, and, often, there'll have been plenty before you.*

"You don't happen to be a virgin, do you?" he asked the woman, sounding entirely casual; he wanted to verify that before he determined which of Rose's strategies would be more apt if she stayed, and please, Holy Virgin Guadalupe, let her.

"What?" It was her turn to be baffled. Never mind. Just as she had intended, she had enticed him, of that she was sure—just look at him! She'd hypnotized him, and if he hadn't yet promised to protect her from the stalker, he would, even if she'd have to sacrifice herself to him, to assure his promise, and it was obvious that's what he wanted—and, really, it wasn't that much of a sacrifice, she admitted. In fact, she could hardly wait. What a stud! So fresh!

"Maybe I'm a little bit of a virgin," she said coyly. Her whisper became a growl: "Are *you?*"

"Uh—" What could he say and not lie? "Well, I'm embarrassed to admit that I—" He didn't lie; he just didn't finish.

"You *are*!" She growled again. Just right—for both of her needs, her immediate one—she hadn't had sex in Lord knows how long because all that occupied her was the role in the sequel—and he would also fulfill her longer-term need when he'd promise to escort her. She would tend to her immediate need.

"Lyle, Lyle, I've wanted you since that afternoon. Let's do it. Now!"

They did. She was great—even Rose remained quiet, impressed—and he matched her, checking himself now and then to assert his violated virginity—and finally abandoning the pretense when it became intrusive, then resuming it when it became tempting. It would be difficult to know who was doing what, because their flesh shifted, melded, fused.

"Oh, God," she said, "oh, God."

"Oh, Lord," he said, "oh, Lord!"

She had insisted he keep on his boots, and she kept her stockings, and wow—naked flesh, stockings and boots, sighs and moans, and, yes, yes, yes, yes!—and, oh, yeah! and shove it in again, and give it to me, babe, yes, yes, yes, yeah, yeah—in, out, in, out, in, in, in, in, in!

"Oh, *God!*"

"Oh, *Jesus Lord*!"

"What was *that*?" Lyle asked. The room itself was shaking. The bed tilted, everything in it rattled noisily.

"An earthquake, forget it, let's go on." They did. She thrust her hips, up, up, to meet his, pushing down, down, down. They tumbled over each other as the room quaked. He fell off the bed, she fell over him, and they let the vibrating of the room take over, until the trembling rolled them apart, and they adjusted quickly back on the bouncing bed. Up, up, tilt, tilt, down, down, in, tilt, up, down, up, in, in, out, in, tilt, tilt, out, out—god *damn!*—in—*yes, yes!*—in, in, in. *In!*

"*Ah!*"

"*Ahhhhh!*"

When had the room's shaking stopped?

Tarah jumped up from the bed, adjusting her clothes carefully. Would he be so terribly upset with her (after what she had to do) that they wouldn't get together again (after he came out of jail)? She could not explain the matter to him now, of course. It all had to occur spontaneously, like the saving of Ms. Universal from the peacock at Huey's Mansion.

"Do you promise, now?" she asked him, her voice quivering.

He lay there looking at her, getting hard again. "Sure, yeah, whatever you say," he said, still not knowing what it was exactly he was promising to do, but knowing he would keep his word, because it was proper to help a woman who was in danger.

She pouted. "Now remember. You promised, I have to count on you to escort me, that dangerous evening."

He held up his hand to emphasize the sacredness of his vow. What exactly had he promised?

"I'll pick you up at——" she consulted her watch, to approximate today's time. "On——" The magic day, the day of the Academy Awards. She tossed off the next as if it was of the most minor importance: "I'll be in a limousine with Rusty Blake."

Now he was even more baffled. "Who is Rusty Blake?"

She sat down. Again, she crossed her legs, uncrossed them, and again his mind threatened to sneak away, but he had to listen to what he was to do.

"Rusty? He's——uh——you know, gay. The studio just wants him to be seen with me, for his reputation. He's a wimp and wouldn't be able to protect anyone from a——from a——midget." Had that come out right? "He'll just step out of the limousine and drift away—— and that will embolden the stalker to strike. Then you'll come out and be my grand, *brave* protector, and we'll have caught him in the act!"

It all sounded nutty; maybe she was nutty. Anyway, what was there to lose by going with her to that big show? Maybe she wouldn't even pick him up, just part of her pretending. A fantasy, like whatever Amber had going in Las Vegas, and that Babette lookalike; and if it turned out that she really wanted him to protect her, Clarita would be proud of him.

"You may wonder why I don't go to the police or hire guards. That would only scare him away. We need a trap." She produced tears. "Lyle, the terror of being stalked, night and day! He's sworn to kidnap me—— in view of everyone!——and then take me away and spend months with me, having sex, over and over and over——"

"Oh?"

"——and, Lyle, you must wear your best cowboy clothes."

"Oh, ah—" He hesitated on purpose, and goddammit if it didn't work. His visitor had pulled up her skirt and was sitting on his lap, lifting herself up and down.

"Oh, oh, *oh!*"

"*Ah!*"

7

The confirmation of a possible ally.

On her way out, Tarah ensured that Mrs. Allworthy would hear her footsteps. She did and she rushed out with a notebook and pen. "Did you feel it? It was only a four point one rumbler. No damage!"

After granting her an autograph—and ignoring more information about the small earthquake that had threatened to give the hard-of-hearing music teacher in the court a heart attack—Tarah wiped away more tears. "I think—" she gasped. "I think I've talked him into agreeing, convinced him—"

"Of what, of what?"

"To change his course," Tarah said. "I had to sacrifice—"

"Huh?"

"Oh, Mrs. Allworthy, dear Mrs. Allworthy, I'm here because that terrifying stalker has invaded my life and is determined to strike at the Academy Awards!"

"Lyle?"

Tarah rushed away, sobbing softly for Mrs. Allworthy to remember; and what she would remember was that in a futile attempt to keep the now-uncovered stalker from proceeding with his promise to kidnap her at the Academy Awards, Tarah Worth had come—with enormous courage and great risk to herself—to attempt to talk him out of his nefarious act.

8

The triumphant return!

Item: Liz Smith is back from vacation and will resume her column while covering the Academy Awards.

9

And a sad return.

"Who the hell are you and how the hell did you find me?" In his shorts—he'd been in bed resting—Lyle asked the tall man standing outside his apartment door, the tall man he recognized immediately although he had never seen him until now.

"I'm your father," answered the tall man wearing cowboy boots and a cowboy hat.

"If you are, then you're a no-good goddamned son of a bitch," Lyle said.

Lyle the First laughed, a sad laugh. "That's what Sylvia called me." Lyle forced his fists close against his sides, but he wouldn't guarantee that in a moment they wouldn't push out. "What makes you believe you're my goddamned son-of-a-bitch father?"

"First, she gave you my name—"

"It's just a name," Lyle tried to dismiss.

"—and, next, all ya gotta do is look." With his eyes, Lyle the First measured Lyle's full length, lingered on his face, and traveled to the hat tossed on a table, then to the boots readied by the side of the bed—and one odd lone boot nearby. He allowed his eyes to rest on the bountiful crotch under Lyle's white shorts.

Lots of people resemble each other, Lyle readied words to speak; didn't some of those kids on the Boulevard tell him he looked like this guy or that on television or in the movies?—and that didn't mean the person was related to him. What he could not deny was that this man, whoever he was, had prepared for this visit. Everything on him looked fresh, even new. His breath carried the scent of mint freshener. He was a fit, good-looking man, Lyle had to admit; how old? Fifty? How old had he been—if he was who he claimed to be, Lyle still kept that in abeyance—how old would he have been when he invaded Sylvia's life and branded her so harshly with his presence that she could never forget him, no matter how she tried, with liquor?

"Lyle, son, let me come in." The arrogant man was almost shy.

Lyle felt waves of rage. His fists quivered eagerly at his sides. "Don't call me 'son'. Only my mother can." But, he remembered wistfully, she hadn't wanted him to call her that—mother; nor had she ever called him 'son'. "Go ahead, come in," he heard himself say. He stepped aside to let the stranger into his apartment.

The man sat, awkwardly. He looked around. "Nice place ya got here, s——." He stopped the word. "How long you been here? Intend to stay in LA? Got a girlfriend?"

Lyle dressed and sat down on his bed. When he realized that now they were both wearing boots, he removed his and stayed in his socks. He did not answer any of the questions the stranger had asked only to fill these strange moments—two strangers, one claiming intimacy, face to face.

"I went to visit your mamma."

"You son of a bitch!" Lyle said. "I bet you had to push your way in cause she refused to see you, and I bet you conned her out of my address, didn't you? There was no way she'd tell you where I was." Clarita. Of course.

"Your mamma didn't tell me, she didn't want me to find you." Lyle the First bowed his head, held his hat in his large hands, playing nervously with it. "Listen now: It was a terrible thing I did to her," he said, "and I wanted to tell that to your mamma—my beautiful Sylvia—when I saw her again, but she wouldn't believe me, she——"

"Good!" Lyle said. "I would've bet she wouldn't. She hates you, you goddamned son of a bitch."

"So much so that she even tried to make me believe you're not my son," Lyle the First said softly.

"It's true, I'm not your son," Lyle seized the opportunity. "There's a guy named Armando. I got his color, this isn't a tan, you know." He wanted to hurt this man, not for himself, because, strangely, he had grown up without a father, and so he had thought of him only as the goddamned son of a bitch who had left his mother. It was not for himself that anger was bursting out of him. It was for Sylvia and all the lonely years she had waited for this man he was facing.

"She even told me you were dead," Lyle the First whispered.

"As far as you're concerned, I am dead, dead to you, for all you cared to know about me." Why was he talking this way, as if, for all the time when he hadn't even thought about a father, he *had* been. "I would have been dead if my mamma had followed your instructions. Am I worth the money you gave her, you lying son of a bitch!"

Lyle the First winced. His broad shoulders sagged.

One of Lyle's tightened fists rose, up, out—but he ordered it to ease. Instead of becoming a fist, the hand reached out, as if to touch this sad man, but he did not allow the intended goal. Unclenched, his hand fell, open, to his side. "You never even tried to find out if I'd been born."

"I did—once I even came to see you." The words were soft.

"You *saw* me?" The man was a fucking liar.

"That one time, when I paused. Sylvia was with you. I thought she'd seen me. Maybe she did. I wanted to call out, but I got all edgy, and so I fled."

"You fled all right, you never even wondered what would happen to her." Not to me, he insisted to himself; that didn't matter to me, that you didn't wonder if I was all right or not. "You didn't care how she'd get along, didn't—" Had all these accusations always been there?— rushing out so easily?

"I helped her out."

"You never—"

"Your mamma—bless her—your mamma never paid much mind to financial matters. I've made deposits regularly for her, knowing she wouldn't even notice. . . . And I left you a guitar in that vacant lot I knew you went to." His voice became a whisper, as if he were only remembering: "A guitar I bought long ago, used only once, to serenade—"

Lyle saw the guitar now, resting on the chair where he kept it. "Why did you leave Sylvia?"

Lyle the First shook his head. "I was stupid, afraid—and married—"

"Married—and promised to marry her?"

"I didn't tell your mamma, no, didn't tell her I had a daughter. Yes, I lied to her, because—because—" He paused, looking up at Lyle. "—because I loved her, a lot, loved Sylvia like no one before or since, or ever."

The son of a bitch, to say that, to face him with that. Yet he wanted to hear more, learn more, understand more, try to understand more.

"Your mamma was hurt, deep, long before I met her."

"Don't try—"

"No, no, I'm not excusing myself. I added to her pain, that's all I'm saying. In her sleep your mamma used to mumble about how she was cursed."

"Cursed?" Was that what Clarita withheld?

"My beautiful Sylvia—your beautiful mamma—would wake up scared, some nights, and then she'd cover herself. Yes, I even turned away from her pain."

Damned if he would let this son of a bitch see him crying! Lyle swore, even if he was crying inside, for Sylvia, and still trying to understand it all. Fragments were emerging—what Clarita had hinted at, pulled away from—about some terrible event, a terrible curse; had that propelled Sylvia to the revival meeting, coaxed her letter to the evangelists? There was more he had to know now, understand, about a long-ago curse that seemed to hold them all in its clutch. He longed to ask more, much more, but he didn't want to assert any intimacy with this man.

Lyle the First had moved on: "I was trapped, and like a coward I ran, and I'm sorry, sorry, worse, because I do love your mamma, and I love you, and now that I'm divorced—"

Lyle stood up, fiercely. "*I* don't love you, you son of a bitch! Talk all you want, but don't expect me to believe you, because you're fucked, you shit! You expect me to say, Yeah, dad, come on, let's be friends, let's make up for all the years you didn't see me, didn't come back to my mamma who was waiting for you—if you think that, then—" Lyle shook his head, wearily, wondering whether he'd be able to control his anger, or his tears. "I hate you, you goddamned son of a bitch!" he shouted at this intimate stranger.

Lyle the First slumped. "I deserve your hatred, and hers. I *am* a goddamned son of a bitch. But"—he looked up directly at Lyle, who turned away—"all I want now is for you to know that I have always loved your mother, and you, and that I am your father."

Of course he had never really doubted that the cowboy was his father, nor had Sylvia. The man before him must have looked exactly like him once.

When the stranger who was his father walked out, slowly—Lyle stalked to where his guitar was. He took it and raised it, high, bringing it down to smash it. He stopped. He lowered it and held it. Damned if he would cry!

CHAPTER TWENTY-THREE

1

The Academy Awards!
The terrible deception.

This is Claudia Mans with my cohost, Tommy Bassich
. . . Hi, Tommy!" Claudia held the microphone away
from her lips so that the gloss would not smear.

"Hi, Claudia!" said Tommy Bassich in an expensive
rented tuxedo.

"We're here covering the Academy Awards for station—"

"They're arriving, the stars are arriving!" Tommy Bassich interrupted
with forced excitement.

"So they are," said Claudia Mans, dressed in a black drape by Valentino.
"We're going to interview—who is it?"

"It's Julia and Tony! Julia! Julia! Over here!"

Reporters and photographers shoved and jostled to get prime posi-
tions from which to capture the entrants. Cameras collided, wires coiled
into nests of warring snakes.

It was still light, not yet evening. The day was dusted with sun-
shine. Bleachers groaned with eager fans mounted on boards stacked
like unfinished bookshelves, skinny fans, heavy fans, old, young, drab,
mostly drab fans—a few exceptions emerging to the surface of the
dowdy tide.

Lizardy limousines spilled out a new stream of stars and almost-stars,
some in gaudy clothes, some glamorous, some almost naked, the men
coiffed—all looking less beautiful in the daylight and anxious to enter
the area of benign lights inside.

"Leo!" fans screamed. "Jennifer!" "Cameron!" "Rob!" "Ben!"

Shouts, moans, screeching, applause, whistling!

"There's Mona!" . . . "There's Clint!" . . . "There's Emma!" . . . "There's
Fernando!" . . . "There's Amanda!" . . . "There's Michael!" . . . "There's
Pete!" . . . "There's Bill!" . . . "There's Lauren!" . . . "There's—?" . . . "Who
is she?" . . . "I don't know—someone." . . . "There's Brad!" . . . "There's
Sandra!" . . . "There's Kevin!" . . . "There's Ben!" . . . "There's Melissa!"
. . . "There's Emma!" . . . "There's Russell!" . . . "There's Jean!" . . . "Oh,
my God, my God—there's—"

Waving and blowing kisses at the dauntless fans, the stars paraded on
the velvet carpet. They paused, they sauntered, they marched, they
primped, they glided—they waved and blew kisses—they hurried, they
dodged, they paused, they posed, they danced—they waved and blew
kisses—they giggled, they sighed, they cried, they denied—they waved
and blew kisses—they leapt, they wept, they saluted, they exuded, they
cheered, they jeered—they waved and blew kisses—they tripped, they
skipped, they swirled, they whirled, they sidled, they idled, they waltzed,
they pranced, they confessed, they professed, they strutted, they swaggered—and they waved and blew kisses.

More limousines lined up on the street, timed so that the stars they
expelled did not interfere with each other's entrances and breathy in-
terviews. Television reporters, men and women, gushed the same compliments, asking the same questions: Who did your dress? Who is
your date tonight? Is that a diamond? Is it borrowed? You look lovely!
Who did your dress? How does it feel to be nominated? Are those
borrowed jewels? Who did your dress? Who did your dress? Whose

tux are you wearing? Who did your dress? You look gorgeous. Jewels by? Hair by? Clothes by? Jewels by? Who did your dress?

Armani, La Dona, Everett, Karan, Versace, Sybil, Mr. Bracci, Anna Richardson, Bulgari, Cartier, Francesca, Alexandra of Milan, Zegna, Armani, Gucci—

"I made it myself," said soon-to-be-star Zella Riley.

"It's beautiful anyway," gushed Claudia Mans.

"Beautiful!" said Tommy Bassich. "Look, there's Billy! Billy! Over here!" He turned to Claudia: "Grab Jack before that bitch Rivers tackles him! . . . Jack! Over here! . . . Keanu!"

As the white limousine drove up to the entrance, to deposit its occupants at the foot of the red carpet, Lyle, wearing a new pair of jeans, a pearl-button denim Western shirt and jacket—gifts that had arrived that afternoon—his newest Tony Lama boots, and his favorite hat, looked out of the tinted windows and saw the jammed bleachers, heard the screams of fans. He welcomed the frenzied mobs congregating here, welcomed being here, anything that would chase away the memory of the encounter with his father.

Rusty Blake—black leather jacket, tight black pants, black shirt, no tie—stepped out of the limousine. "Rusty!" "Rusty! Rusty!" Waving at the fans, he turned gallantly to help Tarah Worth out.

Grandly she emerged—steel-blue gown by Felix Franquiz, diamond earrings on loan from Harry Winston, hair by Bob Geevar of Transcend. She glanced back to smile at Lyle, looking resplendent in his new cowboy regalia.

Lyle smiled back and prepared to step out from the opposite side of the limousine, ready to escort the actress, as arranged, after Rusty Blake drifted away. So what if she really wasn't in danger and had made a big story—as he suspected? Here he was at this big movie festival that would keep him from remembering—

"There's Sharon Stone!"

Photographers rushed away from Tarah and Rusty Blake.

"Sharon Stone! Over there!"

"Sharrrron!" screamed the fans. "Sharon!" screamed the interviewers. "Sharon!" screamed the photographers.

Let the bitch get attention! thought Tarah Worth. She'll soon be dust.

A female announcer who had been knocked down by those rushing to gather about Sharon caught sight of Rusty Blake.

"And here getting out of their limousine, is—oh, yes—it's Rusty Blake, with— Uh, Rusty is escorting—" She paused to whisper to her male partner, who was bending to help her up, "Who is the old broad?"

"Tarah Worth of yesteryear!" the male announcer remembered. "She's looking greater than ever. Tarah! Over here!"

Lyle stepped out of the back side of the limousine and walked toward Tarah, ready to take her arm and stroll into the auditorium with her, ready to submerge himself in this obliterating pandemonium.

Tarah recoiled from him in horror. *"Help, help!"* she screamed. *"It's the stalker!"*

"He's threatened to kill her in front of everybody!" Rusty shouted in alarm.

Photographers dashed back toward them in a squirming tide.

Lyle looked around. Then it was true that someone was threatening her? But where was he, the dangerous stalker?—and why was she pushing *him* away and why did Rusty Blake seem to be preparing to head-butt him?

Bulbs flashed, television cameras spun and jerked.

"Let me go, let me go!" Tarah shouted at Lyle, who had grabbed her, to protect her from the stalker—who must be somewhere. Where? Why the hell was she fighting *him*?

"It's the Mystery Cowboy! He's attempting to kidnap Tarah Worth!" Rusty Blake screamed. Reporters danced madly about them.

"In a brazen act, the notorious Mystery Cowboy is attempting to seize Tarah Worth!" Claudia Mans shouted into her microphone and over the screams and shouts of the fans.

"Brave Rusty Blake is attempting to—" Tommy Bassich pushed his way in with his mike.

Fans screeched with delighted fear. From the bleachers, a heavy woman with a jiggly chin rose, nudging awake a small man next to her, and she announced victoriously, "Well, I just knew that man was a criminal, that Mystery Cowboy! Well, haven't I been keeping my eye on him?"

Counting on the police rushing over to restrain Lyle, Rusty Blake lunged at him too soon and was greeted by Lyle's fist, flattening him.

"My face!" Rusty Blake pleaded, cringing on the red carpet.

Cops surrounded Lyle, forcing him down on the ground. Terrified, struggling, trying to orient himself, he looked up at Tarah Worth. "Tell them who I am! Tell them I'm protecting you!"

Encircled by every interviewer, every reporter, every photographer, Tarah Worth stood like a triumphant empress over Lyle as cameras recorded every move, every word. "I'm sorry for you, young man, Mystery Cowboy, whoever you are. I tried to talk you out of this. I found you and pleaded with you. I understand your infatuation. But I cannot allow you to destroy my life because of your desire."

"It's just like that scene from the sequel to *Valley of the Dolls,*" a reporter alerted by Lenora Stern said. "*Exactly* like it!"

Two burly cops handcuffed Lyle, who lay on the ground quietly.

A deep voice rose out of the bleachers; and a glamorous figure, assertive, commanding, emerged out of the sea of excited fans. "It's a fake, it's a fake!" The figure struggled through the crowds, shoving to clear a path.

There stood Blanche from Hollywood Boulevard.

"I saw the Mystery Cowboy exit the limousine," she said to reporters and cops. "This is all a hoax. That bitch Worth staged it all, it's a fake!"

2

A true report.

Los Angeles Times

Cara's Hollywood:

As difficult as it is may be for rational people to believe, a scene right out of the script of the movie sequel *Return to the Valley of the Dolls* was played out at the Academy Awards by actress Tarah Worth, 52. But that was no coincidence. It was staged! Even more difficult to believe is that the aging actress should have thought she would get away with such enormous fraudulence, which also included a shady chauffeur, a former porn performer known as Hunk Williams, and up-and-coming (now down-and-going!) actor Rusty Blake. The so-called Mystery Cowboy, the subject of speculation for weeks, was reportedly manipulated into a cruel hoax. He was handcuffed as the supposed stalker but was quickly released when a man who said his name was Blanche and who identified himself as a friend of the Cowboy uncovered the charade. It seems that in her desperation to get the role of Helen Lawson, in the sequel to Jacqueline Susann's famous *Valley of the Dolls,* Worth, with the encouragement of manager Lenora Stern, orchestrated the faked kidnapping scheme. Producer David Wesbourg informed me that Tarah Worth needn't have gone to such extremes because the role of Helen Lawson has already gone to Sharon Stone.

Note: Liz Smith was not at the Academy Awards but will be reporting on the great parties of that night.

3

The saddest event of all.

Betrayals, betrayals, betrayals! Lies and deceit! Meanness, and fraud, betrayals, more lies and deception, and cruelty, goddammit, so much meanness, so much cruelty! Goddammit if life wasn't fuckin' ugly. He'd been deceived, arrested, mugged, robbed, used, lied about, lied to, beaten, handcuffed.

At the sounds of mayhem at the Academy Awards—police sirens, and shouts of "kidnapper!" and "stalker!"—movie stars elbowed each other as they threw themselves on the red carpet, glitter and sequins flying into the air, tight gowns splitting, hairdos crushed. Assured that danger was over, they struggled uneasily to resume their entrances into the auditorium, a few limping, having sprained something, and waving. "Who did your gown?"

Released by the police, Lyle fled with Blanche, who drove him to his apartment.

"Good-bye, beautiful cowboy, I'll see you in my dreams forever," she said.

He kissed her hand.

In addition to all the ugliness, there was kindness, he assured himself. He threw his body on the bed and lay there, tired, weary, tired, tired, despondent, tired. Without bothering to remove his clothes, not even his boots, he fell into a troubled sleep that lasted deep into the next day, when he was wakened by Mrs. Allworthy at the door.

"Lyle! Lyle!"

She was here to comment on last night's events—she'd certainly seen it all on television. He didn't want to hear any of it, needed to forget, try to. He lay silently, hoping she would go away.

"There's a special delivery letter for you!"

From whom? Why? He stood up.

"You're all right, Lyle?" Mrs. Allworthy called in.

"Yes, thank you. I'm in the shower. Please put it under the door."

Quickly, he retrieved the letter from the floor. It was from Clarita. He sat on the side of the bed and read:

My dear, dear Lyle,
My heart breaks to tell you that your beautiful mother, our Sylvia, has been taken by the angels to heaven. She went in her sleep, a heart attack.

Lyle stood up, as if lightning had bolted into his body. *No!* But no news is more quickly understood than the terrifying news of the death of someone loved. Once announced, that fact rushes into comprehension, and everything changes. The world stops to allow that full reversal. In that moment, a new presence is born, an absent presence, the person gone. Memories of that person halt. There will be no new ones, everything about that life becomes final, like the inevitable sum of an exact equation.

Lyle grasped immediately that, however much his mind and heart protested—*No, no!*—Sylvia was dead. If he shouted his pain, that would not be enough.

He read:

Her sorrows are laid to rest. I am released of my vow not to let you know what I now reveal, what you have long wanted to know.

She had enclosed a copy of an old newspaper clipping:

The Alamito Gazette

HOWLER AT MISS ALAMITO BEAUTY PAGEANT!

An enraged woman claiming to be the mother of Sylvia Love, a contestant for the Miss Alamito County Beauty Title, stole the show last night when she rushed onstage brandishing a Bible and then threw a sheet over her daughter during the bathing suit competition. According to others onstage, the contestant's mother shouted a series of curses at her daughter for exposing her body. Miss Love attempted to flee the stage but tripped on the sheet, creating a scene that could have come out of a slapstick comedy and that was greeted with howls of laughter from judges and spectators alike, a hilarious commotion that must have lasted 15 minutes, during which Miss Love continued to struggle with the sheet, stumbling over and over, causing gales of laughter each time, until she managed to leave the stage. According to one judge, Miss Love impressed the panel during the talent competition, when she "sang 'Amazing Grace' very sweetly," and when she said her first wish would be "to banish meanness from the world." According to this judge, right up to the time of the uproarious intrusion, Miss Love was the leading contender for the title that would have taken her to the Miss Texas competition and eventually might have earned her the Miss America title.

Oh, Sylvia—Mother!—Lyle longed to say to her, if I had been there, I would have killed them all! His fists tightened and pounded the bed. *Goddamn* them for laughing at you! Goddamn them all!

And finally from Clarita's letter Lyle Clemens learned about the hope the contest had offered the beautiful girl, hope of escaping the dismal life her mother—"a miserable, heartless woman"—was assuring; about the crushing of that hope by the crazy woman's act, by her curse—repeated at the Pentecostal Hall with her last breath—hope swept away in waves of degrading laughter.

Lyle heard echoes of the song Sylvia had sung sweetly, heard the diminishing hope she had put into it, heard the pain that replaced it— and that lying goddamned son-of-a-bitch father of his had heard that pain, had walked out on it. Where, goddammit, had grace been extended to Sylvia Love?

"Our Sylvia would have won the contest," Clarita wrote.

"She would have!" Lyle said aloud. The figure she had drawn on the school poster—that was her in her moment of near-triumph.

Lyle reached for the piece of paper Clarita had enclosed, written by Sylvia "just days before she died."

"My dearest Lyle—" Sylvia had written, and then crossed those words out with a line. In their place she had written: "My son, know always that I love you. Your Mother."

Lyle gasped, the first time she had called him son, the first time she had called herself his mother.

He did not go on to read the rest of Clarita's letter, about arrangements to be made, did not go on to read her plentiful blessings. Now, within all the memories that were gathering, there returned to him echoes of Sylvia's words that had formed a refrain in his mind, ghostly words now: "Understand? . . . You can never feel what I've felt. You can never understand."

He took his guitar, put on his hat, and walked out.

4

A naked cowboy.

From his apartment he walked to Hollywood Boulevard—unaware of anyone, unaware of anything. He did not answer any smiles, answered no greetings. He walked on, ahead. It was not yet evening. Only a pallid sun lingered behind gray clouds in the distance.

He walked past stores that had become familiar during his excursions on this street, coffee shops he had eaten at, walked past street people who now welcomed him easily, past the many tourists always here, walked across streets until he came to the Egyptian Theater. There, on one of the cement oval benches that enclosed the palm trees in the court, he sat down. He removed his shirt. He pulled off his boots. He took off his pants, stripping down to his briefs. He slipped his boots back on, and adjusted his hat. Heat shot through his body in waves of fever, as if pain had turned into fire. He stood up and waited for a moment, inhaling. He closed his eyes, to transport himself somewhere else, somewhere back in time, to another place, another time.

He plucked at his guitar, scattering a few broken notes. He began to sing, words, a jumble of words, sung, spoken, breaking. His voice quivered, cracked, stumbled on a smothered sob. Desperate sweat drenched his stripped body.

"Look! A naked cowboy!" a kid shouted, doubling over with laughter.

"Everybody, look at the cowboy singing naked!" someone else yelled.

People gathered quickly, encircling him. They laughed hysterically as he began to perform a jagged preacher-strut.

"Cowboy's dancing a jig without any clothes!" a woman's voice gasped out of her laughter.

Tourists ran over from across the street. They joined the chorus of jeers and ridicule, some hopping up to see over those in front.

"Hey, you, naked guy, cowboy, you're fuckin' hilarious!" a young man heckled and faced the crowd for approval, which he got with cheers. Jeers grew, the heckling rose.

Lyle continued the shattered song, the harsh notes, the jerking motions. Heat crawled over his perspiring body, sweat soaked his briefs, rendering him naked.

The derisive circle expanded. A boy and a girl did an imitation of him, quivering motions, voices croaking.

"Check that weirdo cowboy dancin' nekkid!"

A young man with a pinched face walked up to him, laughed in his face, and hopped around him.

Lyle heard the laughter, howls of laughter, howls of derision. Frantic, sweat gleaming like oil, he sang on and danced—a tall, lanky puppet out of control.

More people gathered. They poked each other, hooting. They shouted, giggled at the weird cowboy, his stripped body out of control, jerking about.

Waves of ridiculing laughter drenched him as powerfully as the sweat flowing down his body. He felt feverish, then cold, he shivered, his eyesight blurred from the sting of sweat and tears. A cold, hot darkness began to envelop him, a darkness that closed in, closer, closer, enclosing him in violent swirls that threatened to pull him in. His breathing became ragged, and still he twisted and uttered tattered words, and plucked at the strings of his guitar, and heard the laughter that Sylvia had heard, and felt what she had felt, and understood her at last, her surrender of all hope, her surrender to hopelessness, just as now he would surrender, like her, just like her. His body swayed toward the cement and he began to fall, surrender, fall, and—

The sun broke through gray layers of clouds along the horizon and it swept a dazzling light along the street.

Lyle lifted his fingers from his guitar. His gyrations slowed, stopped. He sighed. His body slackened. He sat on the concrete ledge. He plucked again at the guitar, a note, another. He began to sing softly, tentatively, words rehearsed in his mind for years, notes he had never played, words he had never sung.

"Shhhh," someone calmed the laughter.

"Listen!" someone else said.

Laughter diminished, only vagrant bursts lingering, fading, stopping.

"Shhhh!" someone commanded. "Listen!"

Lyle's voice floated above the muffled silence about him. Into that suddenly intense silence, he sang in a voice that began with hurt, a voice that was sad, sorrowing, pained, and then it moved past sorrow, slowly away, drifting away.

> *Amazing grace, how sweet the sound,*
> *That saved a wretch like me—*

His body was calm, his voice firm. More people gathered about him, responding to the triumphant words he sang in a voice that was entirely his own:

> *I once was lost, but now I'm found,*
> *Was blind, but now I see!*